Rhona Martin's first book, *Gallows Wedding*, a novel of witchcraft in Tudor England, won the Historical Novel Prize in memory of Georgette Heyer in 1979. Her second, *Mango Walk*, a love story set against a background of racial tension, was short-listed with Special Commendation for the Romantic Novel of the Year. *The Unicorn Summer* was a sequel to *Gallows Wedding*. She is currently working on a non-fiction book about the writing of historical novels.

Rhona Martin lives in Kent, and works as a lecturer and tutor to various writers' courses and schools as well as serving as a member of a number of literary and artistic committees. She also paints and exhibits miniatures and is a committee member of the Society of Limners.

Rhona Martin

Goodbye, Sally

CORGI BOOKS

To Walden Garland Greenwell

GOODBYE, SALLY
A CORGI BOOK 0 552 13234 9

Originally published in Great Britain by
The Bodley Head Ltd.

PRINTING HISTORY
The Bodley Head edition published 1987
Corgi edition published 1988

This book is set in Plantin

Corgi Books are published by Transworld Publishers
Ltd., 61–63 Uxbridge Road, Ealing, London W5 5SA, in
Australia by Transworld Publishers (Aust.) Pty. Ltd.,
15–23 Helles Avenue, Moorebank, NSW 2170, and in New
Zealand by Transworld Publishers (N.Z.) Ltd., Cnr.
Moselle and Waipareira Avenues, Henderson, Auckland.

Printed and bound in Great Britain by
Cox & Wyman Ltd., Reading, Berks.

Part I

Fugitives

The great ambition of women is to inspire love.
—Molière

CHAPTER ONE

It always rains at funerals, as if the dead had to be puddled in like plants. At cremations it is different; the sun shines cruelly, drawing scent from the remembrance roses to mingle with that other, insidious odour, inescapable if yours is not the first service of the day.

What are we all doing here, thought Zoë, some twenty or thirty years too soon. Why did you have to die, and so pointlessly – why, *why*! A twinge of panic surged upward through the blanket of Valium, to be quelled by her brother's disapproving eye. She looked away, refusing to meet it, turned her gaze out through the polished windows of the waiting room to the grass outside, green and immaculate in the brightness of the day, nourished by the griefs of half the town. Or were the ashes insulated inside those plastic urns, contained and sterile, disciplined like Charles . . .

He would never show emotion. But then he doesn't care, she thought resentfully. Not really care, not like I do. She was never truly a person to him. Just a pair of hands, a useful provider of meals, someone to fall back on when his marriage broke down. She could hear their voices still. Sally's, all kindness and concern: You could always come home, you know, until you're settled. It would be nice to have your company. And Charles, ungraciously: Suppose I'll have to. And then arriving complete with five-year-old Tiggy and both the dogs, terrorizing the cat and filling the house with noise and mayhem and unwanted furniture, elbowing Sally into a corner of what had been her home . . . She compressed her lips. Even now the memory had power to stir her anger. She held on to it, a bullet to bite on, staving off the tears.

It was not as though he had shown any appreciation, put on even the most perfunctory show of being pleased to be invited. Under a thin veil of polite tolerance had been the obvious truth that he was making do, that he was there only because it was convenient. As of course it was, a ploy to keep custody of Tiggy, which he might have lost had he become homeless after the sale of the house. Not that he had cared much for Tiggy, he just had not wanted Jenny to have him. He had always been like that; when he and Zoë were children he had taken away her dolls, not because he wanted them but just so that she should not have them. Nobody must have what he didn't have. She felt the old childhood antagonism rising in her gorge at the memory . . .

She must not sit here nursing spiteful thoughts. Not here, not now. Sally would have hated it. But she had to grip something hard to keep from breaking down. She looked around her at the others. Avoiding their eyes for fear of a sympathetic glance, limiting her attention to their hands.

Her grandmother's, quietly disposed, primly gloved; her father's large and well manicured, calmly folded on his knee. What did he feel, she wondered, attending the cremation of his first wife, here in the presence of a family long-abandoned? Embarrassment, possibly; but he was self-contained, like Charles. You never knew what he was thinking.

Next to her Mark sat rhythmically clenching and un-clenching his hands, the interlaced knuckles showing white as vertebrae. Her own, nervously gripping the edge of her handbag . . . She loosened them with an effort, pushed her gaze away to the heavily ringed fingers of the stranger among them: the fashion editor of Sally's magazine. Why the fashion editor? Deputed, she supposed: Someone ought to go, you've got your piece ready, haven't you . . . She caught herself wondering if those thickly enamelled nails were natural or false – she jerked her mind back to order, a wayward puppy tugging on its lead.

8

It had been cruel not to let Tiggy come. Tiggy had loved Sally, and children needed to be allowed to mourn. But Charles had forbidden it, and there was no arguing with Charles. His handsome face closed like a trap, and there was an end of it. She noted his hands; restless, fidgeting, whether with boredom or merely the itch for something to do, she could not tell. Beside him Tina, his current lady, sat with thin arms tightly folded across her flat chest, fingers tucked into armpits in an attitude of tension and unease. Zoë could sense her tuning in to Charles, trying to divine his mood . . . perhaps she could not tell either.

Nobody seemed disposed to talk. They all sat still, tense in the grip of silence, like patients in a dentist's waiting room. Someone shifted a foot, a shoe whispering over the spotless floor; they all looked up startled, then immediately withdrew into themselves.

Zoë drew a short, painful sigh; pushed her attention again to the round of hands. Sally had once said that you could read people from their hands. Not their future, but what they were like. Perhaps it was true. Sally had seemed to have the answers to everything. Now they were all going to have to find their own answers, she and Charles and all the others, all those millions of strangers who had drawn on Sally's store of wit and wisdom. Oh, God . . . oh, Sally! How could you, when I need you so . . . How could you be so careless! She swallowed hard, trying to get a grip on her emotions. She was being unfair, she knew it. But she could not help herself . . .

Involuntarily, her spine stiffened. A crunching of tyres on the gravel outside had brought them all to attention as, in the square of the window, the nose of the long black Daimler glided into view.

9

CHAPTER TWO

Charles leaned forward on his chair, preparatory to standing up. Beside him, Tina moved too, her movement only a little behind his. Like his shadow, he thought. Controlling his irritation, he moved back. She did the same. She never seemed to do anything he didn't do first. Women . . . He glanced sharply towards Zoë. She looked unstable, her eyes riveted on the approaching hearse; he hoped she was not going to break down and embarrass him. Well, Father too, perhaps. But mostly himself. He abhorred these emotional occasions, they were all the same, weddings, funerals, whatever – all designed to drag your private feelings into the open, put them on display. It was supposed to be good for you. Cry, they said, you'll feel better. Let it all come out. But you didn't feel better, only shamed and exposed; if you told other people your troubles you couldn't call your soul your own . . .

Zoë was the wrong one for him to have as a sister, let alone a twin. They were so unalike, she was a constant source of embarrassment to him, worse even than their mother. Sally at least had learned to leave him alone, to stop making him hot under the collar with a show of affection he couldn't cope with. By the time he reached his teens she was no longer saying, Shall we go to the pictures? It had finally got through to her that he preferred not to be seen out with her by his friends – even though he had had to put it bluntly into words. For her to look hurt had been uncalled for and it was wrong of Zoë to intervene, to suggest that he didn't mean it. He did mean it; it was surely bad enough to have a mother twice divorced without her writing about it for

10

some women's magazine. One needed one's parents to behave, to stay decently in the background while one was trying to grow up, not to make an exhibition of themselves. Father at least had had the good sense to disappear, not to perform his antics in the centre of the stage . . . Not that it had been entirely a matter of one's age; Charles had always found maternal affection cloying, could not recall a time when he did not prefer to recover from a tumble in private and preserve his self-respect.

That was where he and Zoë differed most. Zoë was weak and clinging, lacking the strength to stand up on her own. He was true to himself and independent, he didn't need the approval of others; he believed in speaking truth or nothing, had no patience with evasions in the name of tact. That was just hypocrisy, dishonest and a waste of time. If people weren't going to like you as you were, there was no point in dissembling. Zoë could never grasp this principle; she would go into convolutions to avoid a clash of opinion, had to be liked at all costs.

Only in one respect were they surprisingly alike. She had a stubborn streak almost as broad as his own; convinced that her way was the right one, she tried unremittingly to convert him. And already she was working on Tiggy. He frowned. She had him doing it now! His son's name was Theodore, not Tiggy – a ridiculous nickname, better suited to a cat, one of those torpid, hair-shredding idlers with which Sally had surrounded herself. That was Zoë's doing, too: teaching the child to call his grandmother Sally. It would make her feel younger, she had insisted, to be spared the label of 'Grannie'; encouraging her in a delusion of youth that could not be sustained. Well, there was no reason for it now . . .

As soon as possible he would make other arrangements for the boy.

It was a blow that he had not been left the house, though perhaps foreseeable. It was for Zoë, of course, he should have known it would be. She had always been the favourite. Getting round their mother even when they were children,

11

forever complaining that this or that wasn't fair, always winning over him with a show of crocodile tears. Zoë, who was 'sensitive' and mustn't be upset, while he was shrugged off as the tough one with no feelings to be considered. Psychiatrists had a name for it: the tyranny of the weak. The truth was that life wasn't fair, and the sooner one learned it the better . . . Well, she had won the house. She was not having Tiggy as well.

Outside, a car door was carefully opened, discreetly closed. He glimpsed the sombre face of a pallbearer and thought: Why should he pretend regret, he didn't even know her. More hypocrisy.

The sound of the outer doors being opened reached them in the waiting room. The others were exchanging glances, uncertain what to do next. He stood up. Tina followed, a split second behind, an ever-present echo. As if she had been watching him for the first sign of movement.

'Tina, for God's sake!' he snapped, and she jumped. He averted his eyes from the sight of her cringing. He did wish that, just once, she would do something on her own, without waiting to see what he was going to do first . . .

The door opened and the minister appeared among them, co-opted from a nearby parish since Sally had not been known to attend a church, wearing a white surplice and a supposedly suitable face. Behind him could be seen a coffin heaped with flowers, supported by strangers trying not to look bored, or as if their burden were heavy. With him was the man with whom the arrangements had been made.

'Good afternoon. Good afternoon . . . may I know who is the closest relative . . . the next of kin . . . there are twins, I understand . . .'

Charles looked sharply at Zoë. 'I am,' he said. Quietly, but firmly. He was, after all, the senior by half an hour. And male.

The man looked confused. 'And with you?' He glanced towards Tina.

'My sister.' He indicated Zoë.

'Then, if you would lead in behind the coffin . . .'

He was aware of Tina, watching for her cue, and avoided her eye, determined not to give it. She was not family, and he did not want her assuming that she was.

Tina followed the others into the chapel, slipping in behind Mark and Zoë; not too close to Charles, because she was all too well aware that he wanted to forget she was there. She felt humiliated, as she always did when he brushed her off in public.

It was a hopeless situation, she knew it was. Knew too that she should not tolerate it, this relationship of the kind that people wrote to Sally about and were told: This man does not love you, he is merely using you to feed his ego. Forget him, you deserve better than this; concentrate on making a good life for yourself and be ready to make a fresh start with someone new . . .

She knew all the advice by heart, had read Sally's column regularly, hoping, always hoping for a spark of encouragement to someone like herself. She had never found it, had tried to console herself with the thought that as none of the cases quoted was actually hers, a reply to her own problem just could have been different. And it was more than pride that precluded her from putting it to the test.

She had known she was fooling herself. Although she had persuaded herself that she could not ask Sally's advice for this reason or that — because personal ethics forbade it, because she would have felt disloyal to Charles — there was something underhand about inviting his mother to criticize him, albeit unknowingly, and when all was said and done, it had been none of Sally's business — she knew it was simpler than that: she already knew the answer, and shrank from hearing it endorsed. She had toyed with the idea in the early days, had tried in her more desperate moments to screw up her courage: it had never been a genuine option. Even in their worst patches when she had lain awake crying in the dark, stifling the sound for fear of waking Charles, she had never felt able to turn to Sally, because fame and self-possession had made her too daunting. Even in writing

13

and shielded by a pseudonym, she would have been scalded by the thought of exposing her inadequacy to Sally's expertise, her high-gloss professionalism. Her advice was so right, so incontrovertible – even predictable: think of what you least wanted to do, and that was likely to be it. It was also just a little too smooth, as if laminated in plastic like the covers of her magazine.

The voice of the minister floated towards her on a wash of muted music: '*Let not your heart be troubled, neither let it be afraid . . .*'

She walked stiffly, head erect, trying not to take notice of pitying glances. They were sorry for her, but they did not respect her. They thought she was a fool, and perhaps she was. Perhaps she should cut her losses and look after her – perhaps. But what was the point of looking for someone else when she only wanted Charles. How could she be sure of finding anyone she could really care about . . . after all, she was twenty-seven and had not felt as deeply before. How could one know, how could anyone know? It all looked so right on paper, sounded so simple. But the folk who dished out the advice weren't the ones who had to go through with it. It was all very well for the Agony Aunts, sheltered and successful and surrounded by admiration – how could they expect to understand the ache of rejection.

'*Blessed are they that mourn, for they shall be comforted . . .*'

Platitudes! she thought angrily. What does he know about it, standing there smugly with folded hands, watching people suffer? I bet he does this every day, churning out platitudes to fill in time while people take their seats and the coffin's put where it belongs . . .

A waft of scent reached her from the flowers preceding them up the aisle, great mounds of roses, carnations, freesias; everyone seemed to have been aware of Sally's passion for freesias. Prominently displayed was a sheaf of orchids, scentless but exotic, bearing witness to the affluence of the

14

mourners, the prestige of the mourned. Sally had never had to scratch about for affection, to go on her knees for love. One could not imagine her suffering in isolation . . .

'*We brought nothing into this world, and it is certain we can carry nothing out . . .*'

That was true enough. She was isolated now. Alone in that immaculate box on the plinth behind the rail. Flowers or no flowers. Would the coffin go forward into the unknown, or sink discreetly out of sight? At her grandmother's cremation it had glided forward through red velvet curtains. Like the mouth of Hell, she remembered thinking . . . if you believed in that sort of thing. Though of course it would be Heaven in Sally's case. Everything properly organized with nothing left to chance.

She hesitated as Charles took his place in the front pew, uncertain whether to follow him. She glanced at him for guidance but he was assiduously looking away, his profile unreadable. She felt a gentle nudge, and realized that she had stopped moving.

'Go on, er . . . Tina, isn't it?' Charles's father, a little behind her; tall, still good-looking, distinguished with his greying temples. Polite. Always polite. Smiling, just the right amount.

'Yes . . .' she responded nervously, and moved forward again, lightly propelled by his hand under her elbow.

She sidled into the narrow pew, uncertain as usual whether to sit, stand or kneel; trying not to look to Charles for her cue, sandwiched between him and his father. They were both looking straight ahead of them now, as though she were not there. Two cold fish, she reflected, surprising herself. She had not realized how alike they were before. Superficially the resemblance was strong enough, you couldn't meet them both and fail to recognize the family connection; yet as you came to know them . . . Charles was so blunt, his father so imperturbably courteous. And the quirky sense of humour that attracted people – herself included – to Charles, seemed to be lacking in his father. Perhaps that came from Sally.

They must have been an ill-assorted pair, Sally so vibrant that it was hard to believe she was dead, Gerald so reserved he barely seemed to be alive. No wonder they had ended in divorce. Sally must have had her problems, she conceded, at one time or another; it was just that one could not think of her in that context. She wondered how much Sally had known or guessed about her relationship with Charles. He would never have discussed it with his mother, of that she was sure; they had never been close enough, from what she had gathered. But once or twice she had caught Sally looking at her in a way that suggested sympathy. Had it been fellow feeling, she wondered now, because of Gerald? Maybe it was merely that she knew her own son, knew about his boredom threshold, guessed that she, Tina, was due for the chop . . . she was not the first, after all; not even the third or the fourth. There had already been a wife, a succession of girlfriends; one at a time, he was quite proud of that, but none the less a succession. How many more, after her . . . best not to think.

The taped church music had come to an end. People had stopped shuffling their feet and switching from side to side of the aisle. Like a wedding, she thought inconsequentially: the bride's side, or the groom's . . .

The vicar had finished his repertoire of consoling thoughts and was beginning the service proper. She stared at the white card in her hands, tried to take in the words, fumbled the response. Charles, beside her, refrained from making one. She glanced at him, furtively, saw his eyebrows draw together. Her ineptness, which had once amused him, allowed him to patronize her, was a source of irritation to him now. Sooner or later she would have to face up to her predicament, change it for better or worse, make the break herself if it had to be. But not yet. It was not the explosion that frightened her, not the anger nor the searing words; they were part of her daily life as it was. No, it was the gulf that she dreaded, the yawning nothingness of life after Charles . . .

Another prayer. Another response. She came in automatically, a fraction behind the others. This time, his patience fraying, he withered her with a frown.

'Sorry . . .' she whispered, her eyelids smarting.

Trying to distract herself she peeped across him to where Zoë and Mark stood side by side. They were another odd couple, she thought. Rumour had it that Mark had fluttered around Sally's candle before he turned to Zoë; she wondered if Zoë had known.

Although they were everywhere together they never seemed to look at one another. There was no eye contact at all − not even what passed for contact between herself and Charles − and surely even lances of anger and resentment were better than nothing at all. Perhaps it was that dreadful business of the baby, although you'd think it would have drawn them closer.

She had often wondered how things were between them.

Mark stole a surreptitious glance around the chapel. George was nowhere to be seen. He would hardly come now, even allowing for his haphazard timekeeping. Although, knowing George, he could well be outside waiting in the car, placidly chewing sweets, his upper set of teeth comfortably gathering fluff in a back pocket. Or maybe swigging away at a hip flask. He was well on the way to alcoholism. What on earth had Sally seen in him! A teddy bear man, she had once said − a teddy bear with a ferocious temper, which had only revealed itself too late. By then they had been married, Sally firmly trapped, and he, Mark, unable to effect more than a gesture at rescue. She could not, she had maintained, break up a second home under her children's feet; and anyway, there was the age gap, and besides . . . and besides . . . and . . . Mark compressed his lips. He was roughly as many years junior to Sally as he was senior to Zoë; and yet no one had seen it was a barrier that way round. He had been younger then, unsure of himself, lacking the confidence to carry off an affair with the wife of his patron; and that, undoubtedly, was what George had been to him

17

at the time. It was only through him that he had met Sally at all. Through George, who had protected him from his father's wrath when he could not concentrate on a career, allowing him to potter about their home instead of studying, appearing not to notice his quietly falling in love with his wife. Until that terrifying, out-of-the-blue accusation. He had blushed, stammered, gone to pieces, taken refuge in bluster; had blurted out the unforgivable, the unforgiven . . . even now, he went hot, remembering. His blunder had got back to her, he was sure of it. Or nearly sure. He had never been able to ask her, because if she hadn't been told it was the last thing he wanted her to hear. But it was then that she had turned her face away, and it couldn't be mere coincidence. It had really been all over from that time.

He had hung on in the shadows at the edge of her life for years, shamefaced, unable to bring himself to explain. How could he in any case justify such a betrayal, such an act of arrant cowardice. In the moment of danger he had panicked and disowned her.

She had never reproached him with it. In fact he had asked himself time and again if she could ever really have known. But of one thing he was sure: if she had, she had not forgiven him. A wall of glass had grown up between them, the polite facade of a gracious hostess too well-mannered to speed the unwelcome guest; never again had he found himself admitted to the smallest intimacy. She avoided his eyes – just as Zoë did now. Zoë, the pale shadow of Sally, to whom he had turned increasingly as she grew up, and as Sally retreated further and further into the distance . . .

The words of the psalm cut across his reverie.

'You cut them short like a dream;
'Like the fresh grass of the morning . . .'

Now, her retreat was absolute. He would never know, never be able to ask. There would never be another chance for him to redeem himself.

> *'Teach us so to number our days:*
> *'That we may apply our hearts to wisdom . . .'*

He sighed. Who was he fooling? Given a thousand chances he would blow them all, just as he always had. She had never really wanted him. If she had, she would have accepted him, Sally who had strength enough for anything. Her marriage to George had foundered anyway. She had soldiered on, laughing in the face of defeat as she always did, until after years in limbo they finally divorced. But by then he, in his loneliness, had already made Zoë pregnant; once again it was all too late . . .

> *'And let their children see your glory . . .'*

Zoë and Charles, as children, had quite liked George, or had seemed to; perhaps 'enjoyed' would be nearer the truth. Uncle George, they had called him, and others – occasionally even Sally – had followed suit. He had opened up their lives, introduced them to bubble gum machines, sweets between meals and fish and chips in the car, and the fun of missing school when his succession of broken-down old bangers failed to get them there. Until, that is, he began to compete as a child, and threw the weight of an adult behind his jealousy.

Zoë had taken refuge in whining; Charles had rebelled, had turned surly and insolent, while he, not yet twenty and helplessly gauche, had been forced to watch Sally torn apart between the three of them, sensing through all the fine tentacles of love the painful conflict beneath her polished surface. She had had a sardonic wit even then and was more than capable of holding her own with George; but she shouldn't have had to, not with the husband who professed to love and protect her. She had been somewhere in her thirties then, George in his late forties and old enough to be Mark's own father. Of the same generation, in fact; tall and confident, with the indelible stain of an expensive education, his booming, cultured, overbearing voice, his smile that implied that he had always had what he wanted and always would.

He, Mark, had been helpless; incapable of conducting his own life, let alone helping Sally with hers. Why then did he still feel the weight of his own disapproval, his inadequacy in the face of her need? There was nothing he could do. Nothing. And that was what he had always done for Sally. Much as he had loved her, he had been as much use as a piece of wet rag. It was fruitless now to castigate himself. It was too late; just as it had always been too late, or too soon, or too risky, or too something . . .

There was nothing anyone could do for Sally now, lying there in that narrow box with light and air shut out, with everything and everyone shut out, the narrow box that was what her world had shrunk to . . . numbly, he watched as it disappeared from view.

Abruptly, the service seemed to be over and he realized he had heard none of it. People were stirring, clearing throats, avoiding each other's eyes, shuffling towards the doors, the dazzle of sunlight outside. Blundering into one another, as he supposed they all would now, treading on who knew what emotional corns without Sally's unobtrusive hand to guide them.

Beside him, Zoë stood still, not speaking. Not looking at him, staring helplessly before her as if not knowing how to move, to pick up the threads of her life and go on with it. He touched her arm.

'Zoë?'

She looked up at him. Bewildered, like a startled animal. Her lips parted, as if she were about to speak. She said nothing.

'Come on, love,' he whispered, inclining his head in the direction of the door. Perhaps, after all, there was something he could do for Sally.

CHAPTER THREE

Mahlia Rhys came to attention as a car drew up outside. Surely not her taxi, she thought with irritation, she had distinctly told the driver to come to the house in time for the train, not here to the crematorium. Her brief had been specific: at least a few minutes to be spent at the reception, enough to get acquainted with the family, to express a proper regret. It could be interesting, she conceded; they were a rum lot, hardly what she would have expected. But then, what had she expected, a typical suburban set-up with kids at university and Dad playing golf on Sundays? Hardly. Sally had been many things, but 'mumsy' was unlikely to be one of them. Or was it? Who could tell what professional women were like at home, away from their desks, the pressures, the need to be always right and on the ball.

The daughter – Chloe, was it? – looked dazed. And pallid. That shade of green was all wrong for her anyway, made her more sallow than she was. There was something to be said for the old tradition for funerals, you could do so much with black . . .

A man had got out of the car, an ancient and rusting Buick; she noted with satisfaction that it was not her driver, then glanced at him again in faint amusement. A very large man in thornproof tweeds that looked as if he had been under the car in them, he strolled over to join the others, inspecting the flowers with an undeniable air of command; a bit, she thought, like a slightly motheaten lion, receiving scant acknowledgement and needing none, secure in the confidence that he would not be challenged. It was curious that no one seemed anxious to greet him although clearly

21

he was well known to some of them. The girl Chloe looked at him and then away. The young man with her wore a curious expression, uneasy was the word she would have used. And the one called Charles looked openly hostile. She could not recall ever before being part of a gathering with so many cross-currents; they sizzled back and forth between one and another like a charge of electricity.

She glanced at her watch. She would not be sorry to get back to the office, to the relative peace and calm of the magazine. Hectic it might be, but it was at the same time superficial. The bolts that flew there could be damaging, but not with the wounding intensity that she sensed beneath the surface among these people.

Reminded of *Gloss* she moved forward, discreetly moved the orchids from their obscure corner to a more prominent position. The large man treated her to an intimidating stare; she ignored it and moved on. When she looked back she saw that he had removed the orchids and replaced them with a showy cushion of roses, presumably his own.

There were a great many flowers; Sally must have been better liked than they had guessed on the magazine. Her death would be a blow to *Gloss*; the name of Sally Braün had become an asset they would not easily replace. She was glad it was not her responsibility to find a successor.

Gloss had done a lot for Sally too, had established her as a nationwide personality. It had proved a good partnership, a successful marriage of talent with the right outlet. Not, of course, that it had been roses all the way. She, Mahlia, had respected her work from a distance carefully maintained; she would not have cared to cross swords with Sally, that acerbic tongue of hers was a blade to think twice about, and her air of being capable of any job on the magazine had made more than one highly competent journalist feel threatened. Not style, of course; that was too specialized for anyone but herself . . .

'You are coming to the house?'

She turned to see the speaker, a tall woman, immaculate and well dressed for her age. The senior – who would dare to call her 'old'? – member of the group, possessed of an elegance almost Edwardian, she was surveying Mahlia with a faintly quizzical expression. 'I am Mrs Hammond, Mrs Geraldine Hammond; excuse my glove. Perhaps you would like to share my taxi? Unless you have transport of your own.'

'No – no, I haven't. Thank you.' Made aware of this oversight in her arrangements, Mahlia felt her normal suavity slipping in the face of the lady's impressive self-assurance. This one must be more than a match for the lion. She took the proffered hand. 'Mahlia Rhys,' she introduced herself.

'Miss or Mrs, or doesn't one ask?' Mischief informed the fading eyes.

One certainly does not, thought Mahlia. 'Ms,' she said firmly.

'And Mahlia?' Mrs Hammond inclined her head slightly, implying that she couldn't have heard correctly, since clearly this was not a real name. 'How is that spelt?'

Obediently, Mahlia spelled it out. Her interrogator's smile was gracious, with only the smallest hint of patronage. 'How unusual, quite charming. Is it Welsh?'

She knows damn well it isn't, thought Mahlia, smiling back to cover her annoyance at having her invention challenged. 'No, no. Indian, I think . . .' The Gwladys with which she had been christened was Welsh; but she wasn't admitting to that.

'You think?' The old lady's eyes sparkled with mischief tinged with malice. 'I see, dear. Well, let's look at the flowers while we wait.'

They turned back to the long grid under the canopy where the flowers were displayed. 'So these' – indicating the orchids – 'are from my daughter-in-law's magazine.'

'From *Gloss*,' corrected Mahlia. 'The magazine we both worked on.' Sally hadn't owned it, for God's sake. She was beginning to dislike this woman. A master of the put-down. Some mother-in-law, she thought. Now, what was she doing? Going through the flowers as if she were making an

inventory. Making notes of the backsliders, no doubt.
Anyone not sending flowers will have their names and
addresses taken . . .

She looked up and met the eye of the large man, who
was lounging with his back against a pillar and rolling a
cigarette from a battered tin. She could have sworn she
caught an answering glimmer of amusement in his regard.

The house was a fair distance from the crematorium. Mahlia
sat in a corner of the long back seat of the limousine,
which was not after all a taxi but chauffeur-driven private
hire, and attempted to parry politely the small-talk of her
inquisitive companion: And does the magazine pay well?
Do they buy you all those expensive clothes? And you are
the Editor? Then do you hope to be, some day . . . What
was she up to, Mahlia wondered, angling for information
she'd been unable to extract from Sally? Perhaps not.
Perhaps the need to know everything merely went with a
domineering personality. She fended off the questions
tongue-in-cheek, thinking of the leonine man who had
evidently guessed what she was in for.

The car drew up at last on the edge of a housing estate.
Parking well away from the house, no doubt, too many cars
to fit into Sally's drive. They alighted, and she found herself
without thought handing out the elderly autocrat on to the
pavement; being graciously thanked, a menial who had done
her duty well. She thought briefly of offering her share of
the hire, but decided against it. A servant, after all, should
know her place. She looked up and down the road for an
indication of which way to go.

'We shall wait here,' said Mrs Hammond as the car drew
away. 'The others are a little late.'

It occurred to Mahlia that they were themselves a little
early, having left before anyone else, and she suppressed
a smile. 'Shouldn't we walk on?'

As Mrs Hammond opened her mouth to reply, two more
cars arrived and discharged their passengers. The girl Chloe
– or was it Zoë? – preceded them up a steep path and

24

inserted a latchkey into the ordinary front door of a very ordinary house. Were they collecting someone, some other mourner unable to make it to the crematorium? She waited until, the others having filed past her, someone said, 'Do come in.' She followed them in through an entrance lobby into a single living room from which a kitchen opened off, trying to disguise her confusion. She had been given to understand that the reception was to be at Sally's house, and this was surely not the setting for the Agony Aunt of *Gloss*, not for the Sally Braun whose designer clothes and upper-crust accent had suggested spacious living, Adam stairways, terraced lawns . . . to say nothing of the income she must have attracted.

It was probably the daughter's house. More convenient for the occasion for whatever reason, if a little cramped. It was certainly not a large room, although pleasant enough in its way, lined with books, the walls covered with pictures – originals, by the look of them – with a baby grand piano taking up more than its fair share of space; expensive hi-fi equipment occupied an alcove, its various speakers, silent now, posted like lookouts at vantage points about the room. The furniture was a hotch-potch of up-market modern and elegant but out-of-place antiques, deep sofas upholstered in cream-coloured hide jostling a delicate envelope table which might have been Sheraton, everything crammed together to produce an effect near claustrophobic. Even the piano, a Steinway, was jammed into a corner where it would have been almost impossible to play it, while every available surface, from coffee table to piano top, was covered with objects: plants in hand-crafted pots, small sculptures, pieces of crystal and porcelain, cheek by jowl with studies of cats and children, tourist souvenirs from everywhere . . . she felt her eyes like refugees running away to the nearest window.

Through it she caught glimpses of a garden, shady in the broiling afternoon, a green sanctuary of moving shadows and whispering leaves. She wished she could slip away and be out there; it looked just the place for an afternoon stolen out of London. In here not only the heat and the crush of people were oppressive; the whole atmosphere was charged with concealed emotions, smothered animosity, anything, it seemed to her, but simple straightforward sorrow. These people looked angry, or furtive, or hostile under cover of the polite murmur of conversation, the occasional muted laughter. Not one of them looked truly unhappy, except perhaps the daughter. And yes, possibly her partner. She tried to recall when she had been to a funeral before, but could not. Perhaps it was etiquette for 'mourners' to keep their feelings under wraps until they got home. Mourners . . . maybe she had not been the only one not to mourn the passing of Sally Braun.

Someone was offering her wine. 'Dry, please.' She took it and returned her attention to the books. Six – no, seven copies of Sally's only volume, *The Divided Heart*; she had always thought that a bad title, more suited to a formula romance than a serious treatise on the children of divorce. Still, it had sold well enough, gone into paperback and foreign editions and formed the basis of a television series. She found herself wondering why the daughter had seven copies . . . and who would get the loot? There must be a fair bit of that, from one source and another. She supposed the son would inherit; a dishy bastard, but a bastard just the same, she could recognize the look. She had been aware of him eyeing her up, regardless of the fact that his obvious lady was equally obviously distressed.

She noted from the tail of her eye that Mrs Hammond was closing in on her. Without looking at her she began to weave her way over to where the daughter stood near the buffet, her eyes slightly glazed. Booze, drugs, grief . . . who could tell. Chloe, was it? No, Zoë, she was almost sure. No one seemed to be talking to her, so she said, 'Very warm, isn't it?' The girl looked at her blankly, as if she hadn't heard. Mahlia repeated, 'Very warm, for September. The weather.'

'Oh . . . oh, yes. I'll try and find the air conditioning. I forgot, I'm sorry . . . not sure where the switch is.' She moved off, calling, 'Mark, can you remember . . .'

26

Not, then, her house after all. The son's . . . no, it lacked the flavour of a man's pad. Ah, well; one of life's little mysteries. Not important anyway, just something to keep boredom at bay while being ignored by her fellow guests. She remembered that she was supposed to be scraping acquaintance with the family, picking up a few names, facts for the obituary. Not that she would be the one to write it, but whoever did produce a few words would need at least a bit of local colour, would want a little more than she had so far gleaned. Such as a glimpse of Sally's own home, since it seemed unlikely that Sally Braun, well-heeled and noted for her taste, would have squandered her money on tarting up this boring, overcrowded place to an acceptable level of comfort and convenience. She would surely have unloaded it and looked for something better.

She took a sip from her glass and prepared to mingle, but everyone seemed to be talking in groups, their backs turned towards her. One thing was clear; if she wanted information from anyone here, she was going to have to suffer Mrs Hammond in order to get it. Resignedly, she turned towards where that lady was holding court. Then, as a cool breeze drew a sigh of appreciation from the guests, the doorbell and the telephone shrilled their alarms together.

She saw Zoë struggling through the crush towards where the telephone was evidently buried at the far end of the room. Before she could reach it, there was a faint crackle and an unmistakable voice announced the number.

'Oh, no!' Zoë's voice fell somewhere between a gasp and a moan, as into the shocked silence the voice continued:

'Sally speaking. I'm sorry I can't come to the telephone at the moment—'

'Switch it off!'

'Where is it?'

'Someone's left the volume turned up—'

'Somebody – please, let me through . . .' That was Zoë. She reached it at last, fumbled with switches, silenced it. Nobody spoke.

The doorbell screamed again, accompanied by frenzied

tapping on the glazing of the door. 'Let me in, let me in!'
A child's voice, pleading.

Someone leaned over, opened the door, and he fell inside:
a boy of about seven, thin, grey-eyed with straight hair and
scabbed knees, clutching tightly a Siamese cat plastered
closely to his shoulder.

'Sally's here, she's not dead! I heard her—' He broke off,
confused by the blank, embarrassed faces.

Zoë fought her way to him, went on her knees to embrace
him and the cat. 'Oh, Tiggy . . . no, darling, I'm so sorry—'

She looked about her as if for help. None was forthcoming. No one knew what to say. 'Look, take Selina
upstairs and put her in the bedroom, I'll be up in a minute.'

The child continued to look bewildered, his eyes searching
one face after another. They lighted on the leonine man, who
said gruffly but not unkindly, 'Run along upstairs, old chap.'

'But Sally – I want to see Sally . . .' Doubt had crept
in; his eyes were filling, and Mahlia noticed that they were
already red-rimmed.

'You can't see Sally, she's dead.' It was the brother who
spoke. 'What you heard was the answering machine.' He
shot a stony look at his sister. 'Your aunt Zoë forgot to
switch it off.'

The boy's face compressed into a mask of pain. A huge
tear dropped on to the sleek beige fur of the cat, one of
whose paws stretched and contracted as if in sympathy.
As the small head drooped, Zoë lifted them both and
carried them away. Mahlia thought she heard a sob as they
disappeared up the open staircase. But instead of the
sympathetic murmur she had half expected from the guests
there was merely a resumption of formal conversation.

She decided there and then that she had had enough. She
had established at least that this improbable abode had been
Sally's after all. Whoever took on the obit, would have to
make do with that. There might well have been more to
Sally than met the eye. But whatever was going on here now,
she wanted no part of it.

CHAPTER FOUR

A momentary silence marked the departure of the taxi. Then hubbub broke out as everyone started talking at once.

'Damned cheek!' rumbled George. 'Sending that woman to a private funeral, no business to be here—'

'It's a mark of respect, dear. From her magazine.' Geraldine Hammond set down her empty glass, picked up her gloves.

'A damned fashion writer, according to Zoë. They might have sent someone more suitable—'

'At least she was on time,' Charles said pointedly. He turned away and added under his breath. 'And sober.'

'What did you say?'

'I said,' repeated Charles with careful emphasis, 'that she was sober.'

'And what's that supposed to mean? That I'm not?' George was too practised a drinker to allow his speech to slur, but the truculent light in his eye was a giveaway. 'Is that what you're saying? Eh?'

Charles raised an eloquent eyebrow. 'If the cap fits . . .'

George's face which had been flushed turned white, his lips compressed and livid, the flesh about them faintly green. 'You'd better come outside, young man, and I'll give you a lesson in manners. Cheeky young pup!' His balance all too obviously impaired, he was struggling to withdraw one arm from his jacket, while Geraldine and Mark on either side of him tried hastily to stuff it back in.

'Now, now,' soothed Geraldine. 'He doesn't mean anything, take no notice, dearie . . . oh!' Abruptly he had freed himself, tearing his jacket out of her hand and Mark's and gone lunging unsteadily in the direction of Charles, the garment trailing inside out behind him. 'Oh, now don't make a scene, dear – Gerald, can't you do something?'

Gerald could not. His method of dealing with scenes was that of imposing his own impressive dignity; it had rarely worked with George in the past and he had no faith in its success rate now. In this instance he was on the other side of the room, which enabled him not to hear.

George lurched in pursuit of Charles, who was making his way towards the stairs. 'Come outside!' he said thickly. 'You've been asking for a hiding for years and by God! you're going to get it—'

'I don't fight old men or drunks, George.' Charles spoke over his shoulder. 'You're making an exhibition of yourself, go away and sober up.'

'Don't call me George!' He renewed the struggle with his jacket. 'I can see it's high time you were taught to respect your parents, I should have done it long ago—'

Charles smiled, a tight-lipped, square-jawed grimace: a danger signal to those who knew him well. 'And since when were you my parent?'

'I married your mother, didn't I, looked after you all when you had nothing? And small thanks I ever had for it—'

George was six foot three inches in his stockinged feet, and George in his raging cups was a force to be reckoned with. Charles turned back and faced him from the vantage point of one stair up. 'You married Mother, yes, for her sins. As to looking after us, you couldn't look after a rabbit – take a look at yourself, for Christ's sake, you can't even keep yourself presentable. You're like a bloody kid, playing on the floor among your toys while the roof falls in!'

George, freeing his arm at last from the out-turned sleeve of his jacket, took a swing at him which had it connected might have laid him out. As it was his aim was impaired by what he had consumed. Charles ducked. George missed, and the impetus of the blow unbalanced him so that he landed on his back against the sideboard, bringing down a shower of canapés in his fall.

Charles regarded him with contempt. 'Right,' he said quietly, 'now go and put your head under the tap. I'll send Zoë down to make your usual black coffee.' He turned at the sound of a door opening above, and started up the stairs. 'Zoë? Will you come down, please. I'm the one to deal with Tig – with Theodore.'

Tiggy lay face downward in the softness of the duvet, his cheek pillowed on Selina's warm body, the rich vibration of her purring spreading through him in deep comforting waves. Aunt Zoë had gone to the bathroom for something to sponge his face with, but he didn't want it. He just wanted to stay here with Selina and think about things.

Everything had gone wrong. He hadn't wanted to go to Nigel's after school, he'd wanted to come and see if Mummy was here. He hadn't seen Mummy since Christmas, and last night when he tried to think about her he couldn't remember her face. That was frightening; it made him wonder if she was forgetting him, too. There was somebody called the Court who said he had to live with Daddy, although most of the time he had been with Sally or Aunt Zoë, and he had never seen the house where Mummy lived. He'd been sure, so sure that she'd be here! Funerals were for grown-ups, Aunt Zoë had explained, and surely that meant Mummy? Even Daddy had said, 'Possibly' in his don't-ask-questions voice. He knew he shouldn't have asked but he couldn't help it, it had just burst out of him.

It wasn't that he didn't love Daddy. Of course he did. Daddy called him 'Theodore' and treated him like a grown-up – he was going to take him sailing when he'd learned to swim – only, he wanted Mummy too. He knew it was wrong of him, because whenever he mentioned it Daddy's face had a special look that told him he had said something he shouldn't. Perhaps it was greedy to want them both. Like asking for all the cakes on the plate.

He tried not to talk about Mummy any more, because it made people look uncomfortable. Except to Sally; he could tell Sally anything, because she never looked shocked or told tales . . . but Sally wasn't here any more. Neither was Mummy, and his grief welled up afresh at the thought . . .

Abruptly, Selina stopped purring, wriggled free and jumped off the bed, where she seated herself on the rug and briskly cleaned his tears from her coat. He watched her feeling utterly abandoned. Nobody cared. Even Aunt Zoë had not come back, and he lay still, wallowing in a consoling flood of self-pity.

Downstairs he could hear raised voices. It sounded like Uncle George. When somebody was shouting it was usually Uncle George. Tiggy was a little nervous of him, you didn't know what to expect of someone who was joking one moment and angry the next. He hardly ever saw him, and didn't want to see him today; the last time he came to see them he had shouted at Sally, Tiggy had been sent to his room and had been glad to go. It was all right not to like Uncle George, because Daddy didn't like him either. It was only Mummy that you mustn't speak about . . . he drew a long shivering sigh.

Selina looked up, made a little 'Mrr' sound without opening her mouth. He blinked at her. She gave her shirt front a last quick polish, and jumped back on to the bed. He sniffed. She settled down nose to nose with him, her paws tucked into her chest, her rough tongue gently grooming his eyebrows. Selina liked doing that, and he liked it too; it tickled his face and made him laugh. Selina loved him. He was beginning to smile when the door opened and Daddy came in.

'Don't let the cat lick your face,' he said. 'It's not healthy. Right, then. Now that we're all here, we can go home.'

Zoë did not go down immediately. Someone else could make coffee for Uncle George; someone always had to. She had never known him to attend a party without disgracing himself, had not forgotten Sally's amusing account of the time he threw up on their hostess's Aubusson and had to be taken home. Had she really found it funny, she wondered now, or had it been her way of coming to terms with a bad situation? You could never be sure with Sally, so much of her was hidden and, even though she had been closer to her than most, the Uncle George set-up was an area greyer than grey. Uncle George, thank God, was no longer any of their responsibility.

She sat on the edge of the bath, still holding the dripping face cloth she had fetched for Tiggy, half hearing the voices in the little room he had occupied so often, and numbly prayed for this endless day to be over. The Valium was wearing off now, the thoughts she had fended off with it crowding in again. Mark had already asked her whether she wanted to move in here: it was her house now, he reminded her. She could not take it in, could not think of it as hers, it was Sally's as it always had been. This was her bathroom, steeped in her personality: the peach-coloured walls, the cream carpet, her soaps and bath oils and talcums all screaming, I am Sally's . . . only they were not Sally's any more. They were nobody's. Like her photographs, and her piano, and her cat . . . even her grandson, lost in the limbo of anger and pain between his parents.

Zoë felt her eyes fill. If only Tiggy had been born to her instead of to Charles and Jenny. Strong, healthy Tiggy, instead of the poor little premature thing that she had not even seen. Only Mark had seen, and had agreed with the nurse: it was better not to look. Anacephalic was the word they had used, and she was still not clear what it meant. If only she had looked, had had the courage, had insisted . . . if only Sally had been there as she promised! Instead of being abroad, instead of coming home too late and saying then, You should have looked. And it was true, she saw that now, for as it was the whole pregnancy, all those months of waiting, had ended in a blank. As if she had been in hospital for an operation, or an accident, or a disease too dreadful to be mentioned; after more than a year she was still trying to convince herself that somewhere in the midst of all that anguish there had been a baby. Not a foetus, not a symptom, but a baby, her only child. There would never be another. And in the shadows of her mind lurked a guilt so unspeakable that she hadn't been able to name it even to herself: that having once wanted to abort him, she had left him to die among strangers, had not even seen his face . . .

She jumped as the bedroom door opened and Charles emerged shepherding a very subdued Tiggy.

'Oh . . . where's Selina?'

The child's eyes flicked from her face to his father's, swiftly back.

'In the bedroom. I'd leave her there until the cars have gone.' Charles spoke evenly, looking at his son. 'Don't want any more casualties, do we?'

'No, Daddy.' The words were barely audible.

'But I thought . . . didn't Sally want Tiggy to have her . . . she always said, if anything happened to her—'

'It's not convenient.' Charles's face was closed and locked. 'Better to keep her here with you. He couldn't take her away to school with him anyway.'

To school . . . Zoë opened her mouth to speak, quickly closed it at the sight of her nephew's face. 'Of course.' She tried to speak lightly, reassuringly, as Sally would have done. 'I'll keep her here for you and look after her, Tiggy. You wouldn't want her to get lost in a strange place, would you?' He shook his head, his eyes squeezed tightly to contain the tears that oozed from the corners despite him. 'And you can come and see her as often as you like . . .' She reached out to sponge his face just as Charles turned him about, marching him away from her and down the stairs.

She stood on the landing, swallowing the bitterness and resentment she could not express. Charles knew she would not argue in front of the child; he was trading on it, as he always had. 'Away to school . . .' The words sparked her anger, lifting her out of her own depression. Dear God, she knew he hated cats, but how could he do this to Tiggy, and just now? Wasn't it enough to lose first his mother and then his grandmother, to be carted off to live in a strange place with that girl he hardly knew. Did he have to be parted from Selina just at this moment? As if not taking her to school had anything to do with it. Unless it was to be . . . oh, surely not boarding school, not just now. She knew the thought had been in Charles's mind, but even so . . . not yet, please not yet! Tiggy was barely seven and a half . . . tears of rage and frustration rose up and choked her. She fled back into the bathroom and rocked distractedly, head in hands, before she could control herself enough to bathe her face, scrub it with a towel, and follow them downstairs.

Uncle George was sprawled on the floor where he had fallen, his back propped against the sideboard, contentedly munching the fallen canapés. 'Mm-mm, yummy! You people don't know what you're missing – here, young Zoë, have you had one of these?' He scooped up another from the carpet and crammed it, fluff and all, into his mouth. 'Here, Tiggy, young fellow me lad, come and sample your aunt's cooking.'

'He's tired, I'm taking him home.' Charles pushed Tiggy ahead of him out through the porch. 'Tina, say goodbye, we're leaving.'

'Goodbye, darling,' Zoë called after them. 'Come and see me soon . . .'

She could not tell whether Tiggy had heard her. The last she saw of him was a small figure tagging behind his father, casting longing glances upward at the bedroom window.

'Poor little fellow,' her grandmother spoke at her elbow. 'It must have upset him, hearing her voice like that.' Reproof was implicit in Geraldine's tone, and Zoë remembered that Charles had blamed her.

'Charles wouldn't let him take the cat,' she said defensively. 'That's what really upset him.'

'Well, of course he couldn't take her, not with the dogs. I wonder you didn't think of that, dearie. You might have prepared him for it.'

I'm always the one in the wrong, thought Zoë, the more furious for knowing it was true. She stared at Geraldine coldly. 'Did you know he's going to send him to boarding school?'

Geraldine's smile was complacent. 'Well, if he does I'm

sure it will be for the best. We must remember that Charles is the boy's father, and it's up to him to decide.'

Tight-lipped, Zoë moved away. It was useless to talk to her grandmother. She would always side with Charles, just as she had always sided with their father. Hers was the generation of women that graciously deferred to the authority of its men while ruthlessly controlling them by guile between the sheets. 'There are ways of getting your own way with a man,' she had confided cosily to Zoë, then fifteen. 'When you're a little older we'll have a nice long chat, and I'll tell you all about it.'

'No, thank you, Gran.' Zoë had declined, knowing even then that she could not love a man she could make a fool of. No doubt it had been a mistake; Geraldine had not warmed to her since then.

People were beginning to leave, and she took up her position by the door to see them off. Mark joined her, his hand on her shoulder in a gesture of supportiveness. She noticed her father glancing at his watch, and wondered whether to invite him to stay and eat with them. Not that she much wanted him to, what she really wanted was for them all to go, to be left alone with her Valium and a mug of strong tea. But he might feel slighted if not asked. Or again, he might be eager to get home himself. It was a sign of their lost relationship, she thought, that she did not know. She leaned towards Mark.

'What should we do about George?'

'We'll have to sober him up, he's not fit to drive,' he murmured. 'God, he doesn't change. Gerald, thank you for coming.' He looked inquiringly at Zoë. 'I'm sure we can find you a meal, would you like to stay?'

'Thank you, no.' His habitual calm, his charm, were unimpaired. One would think, thought Zoë, that he had merely stepped out for a paper. He smiled, courteously. 'Alexis will be expecting me.'

Alexis . . . always Alexis. Even at Sally's funeral. Well, she should have known. She smiled back, matching his politeness, his formality, with her own. 'Of course,' she said, hoping to sound less cynical than she felt. She sensed Mark's eyes on her and said lightly, 'Uncle George is a bit the worse for wear, he'd better stay instead.'

'Er, yes . . . yes. I dare say Mother will help you to cope. She's good at that sort of thing. Goodbye, then. Take care of yourself . . .'

'Take care of yourself,' thought Zoë, watching him go: meaning, 'so that I don't have to.' Like wishing your kids a happy birthday instead of giving them one . . . she was thinking spiteful thoughts again.

She turned to Mark. 'I think I'll put a kettle on. You can see if anyone would like some tea.'

She escaped into the kitchen, found her handbag, and rummaged for the little screwtopped bottle of pseudo-calm.

Uncle George's snoring reached a crescendo. He snorted, stirred momentarily, and settled into a more comfortable position on the sofa. Three hours had passed since the departure of the last guests, neighbours or chance acquaintances who had piously called in the hope of seeing somebody famous and did not know when to leave, and for most of that time the noise of his slumbers had reverberated through the house.

Zoë looked at the clock, then at her grandmother, catching a glimmer of amusement in the old lady's eye. 'My dear, how did your mother ever manage to sleep with him.'

Zoë smiled, remembering. 'Shouldn't think she did, much. He used to keep me awake in the next room.' She leaned forward in her chair to call to Mark in the kitchen. 'Do you think we ought to wake him?'

'He won't wake till he's ready,' came Mark's voice above the sound of the dishwasher. 'He's in no state to drive, anyway.'

'He wasn't when he came,' remarked Geraldine drily. She lit a cigarette, looked thoughtfully at Zoë. 'Whatever did Sally see in him, after your father?'

One of her searching questions, thought Zoë. She spread her hands. 'Who knows? What does anyone see in someone else, it's so personal, isn't it? I remember we liked him as children. He was great fun to be with, very happy-go-lucky, quite different from—' she checked herself just in time – 'most people of his age. Probably still is, when he's sober.'

Geraldine nodded sagely. 'That's the trouble with men who drink, it's always progressive. Thank God, neither your father nor your grandfather ever had that weakness.'

Poor Uncle George, thought Zoë; if he'd been the Archangel Gabriel he couldn't have measured up to Father. To avoid venturing further into a minefield she said, 'I think we ought to try, you know. Waking him, I mean. Otherwise he could be here all night.'

'Might not be a bad idea.' Mark appeared in the doorway. 'He could look after the cat.'

'No—' said Zoë quickly. 'No, I'll do that.'

'It's a long way to come in the morning, just to open a tin. Remember, you won't have the car.'

'I won't need it, I'm staying here.' She saw him about to protest. 'Just for a day or two. It's what I want—'

'Not on your own, love—'

'Yes. On my own. I'll be quite all right, I promise. Only I'd rather he wasn't here. I thought one of you might see him home.'

'No.' Mark was emphatic. 'That's not on, you know what the doctor said. If you really want to stay I'll stay with you. Anyway, what about George's car, he can't just abandon it.'

'Wouldn't be the first time, you know Uncle George. I thought perhaps Gran wouldn't mind dropping him off . . .'

'Oh, no, dearie, I let my taxi go. I quite thought you and Mark would take me home.'

A little matter of fifty miles . . . how typical of Gran. Oh, damn Uncle George and his drinking! Charles was right, up to a point, he was like a child. She appealed to Mark. 'Darling, I'm so sorry . . . could you possibly manage both?'

Mark sighed. 'I suppose so.' He reached for a towel, began drying his hands. 'Better wake him, then. What shall I do, come back for you, or are you coming with us?'

'No, it'll be far too late. I'm desperate for sleep, hardly any last night.'

'All right then, put yourself to bed and I'll come back and join you—'

'No!' She had spoken too sharply. 'No, Mark, I don't want you to.' She floundered. How to explain without wounding him . . . she couldn't. Yet suddenly it was vital, imperative, the only thing that mattered, to be left alone in this house to sort out her thoughts, to get to grips with the nightmare, to see past the blood, the horror, the awful tragedy, to the Sally she had known. To understand, if she could, what had brought it all about . . . to know if it had been her fault. Her mind still drugged, she fumbled with the words. 'I want to be alone here, to try and understand—'

'Maybe later, not tonight. It's much too soon.'

She felt hysteria rising again, sharpening her voice, threatening her fragile self-control. 'I must, can't you see! I've got to stay here – I've got to know why. Oh Mark, please, please . . .' Despite herself her voice cracked into sobs.

Through them she heard her grandmother pouring out platitudes. 'Now, now, dearie, Mark knows best. You go home and have a good night's rest, try not to think about it . . .'

Anger rescued her and she shouted, 'No, he doesn't, he doesn't, and neither do you – for God's sake stop trying to control me!'

There was a silence. She had overstepped the mark, marched through the borders of respect for age, but she could not help it. Nor could she stop crying. Mark tried to comfort her but she pushed him away, desolate and out of control.

'Oh, what is it bleating about now?'

It was an echo from her childhood, the rumbling of Uncle George, planting both big feet in the middle of a family row. It was too much. 'Oh, shut up, Uncle George! Just shut up, and mind your own business, and go home!'

Still drunk, he might blow up in her face, hit her, do

anything. She was past caring. Drunk or sober she could take no more.

She heard him chuckle, felt a large hand ruffle her hair.

'Oh dear, oh dear, oh dear . . . it has got its little feathers ruffled.' He had come out of his sleep benign as a baby, his ill temper evaporated with the alcohol. 'Nice cup of tea, that's what we all want. Anything left to eat?' He hauled himself, yawning, from the sofa and shambled off towards the kitchen.

Jolted back into a measure of calm, Zoë clamped her head in her arms, stunned by the need to humour so many others when she was barely able to manage herself. 'Oh, Gran . . . I'm sorry.'

She heard Geraldine unsnap the clasp of her handbag, felt pressed into her hand a lace-edged handkerchief redolent of cologne and menthol cigarettes.

'You go upstairs and lie down, dear. It's been a very long, hard day for you. Mark and I will take care of Uncle George.'

She pulled herself together, dabbed at her eyes. Never blow on a borrowed hankie, she remembered just in time, and wished she had a piece of kitchen roll. 'Can you get rid of them for me? Everyone . . .' Try to say it nicely. 'I really do need to be alone here.' She looked beseechingly at her grandmother, willing her to comprehend that need.

Geraldine's face composed itself in a faint smile of indulgence. 'Leave it to me, I know how to handle them. Mark can take George home, and I'll ring up for a taxi in the morning. I'll be quiet as a mouse in little Tiggy's room, you won't know I'm there.' Zoë moved her head in a gesture of despair. 'Now, dear, I know it's not what you wanted but Mark is right, you mustn't stay here on your own, not just yet. You've had a terrible shock, and you must give yourself time to recover. Now, up you go, and I'll bring you a nice glass of hot milk.'

Zoë drew a deep breath, made a mighty effort not to scream and run stamping up the stairs.

'Gran . . . forgive me, I know you're trying to help but I don't want hot milk, and I don't want company – any company! What I need is peace, time to think, sort out in my mind what really happened, what could have

40

made her do something so — so incomprehensible.'

'Incomprehensible, dear? I don't see what you mean. A sudden loss is always a shock, of course, it takes us a little time to take it in, but one wouldn't say it was incomprehensible.'

'It is to me. I can't come to terms with it, not until I understand what made it happen.'

'It was an accident, dearie, nothing made it happen. We have to accept that your mother was killed crossing the road. It happens every day, alas.'

'Not like that! Not strolling across a motorway—'

'Zoë?' Mark's voice cut across hers. 'Uncle George has slept off his tiredness.' Mark was more tactful than Charles. 'We're making a pot of tea and then he's off. Have you decided what you're going to do?'

'Yes.' She rose, steadied herself, returned the handkerchief. 'I'm going to let Selina out, I can hear her scratching at the bedroom door.' Before anyone could raise an objection she was halfway up the stairs, calling over her shoulder. 'You'd better take Gran home with you for the night, the spare bed here hasn't been properly aired.' It was only Gran who worried about the airing of beds in these days of central heating, but it was the only thing she could think of likely to clinch the argument.

She released Selina and watched her run downstairs, dark paws twinkling rapidly down the treads while her body maintained a perfect level above them: something that Sally had pointed out to her. Who could have guessed that Selina would outlive her . . .

She went into the bathroom, bathed her face for the second time, then availed herself of Sally's dressing table to repair the ravages. Her powder, a shade too light. Her lipstick, a little on the warm side . . . she felt like a thief.

She waited until the jumble of voices downstairs had quietened, mingled with the clink of teaspoons. Then she went down.

'Zoë, dear,' Geraldine spoke as she appeared. 'I really don't like leaving you here. All this dwelling on the past,

41

it's quite morbid. In my opinion, Mark should insist.'

'Mark knows better than to insist.' She was calm now, in control of the situation. 'And there are papers, things I have to go through. I can make an early start on them tomorrow.'

Geraldine wavered visibly. 'Promise you won't be lonely? I don't like to think of you crying yourself to sleep.'

'No harm in crying, it's people who can't who suffer.' Would Tiggy be allowed to cry, to let the agony out . . . 'If it gets too bad I've got my Valium.'

'You've got four,' said Mark. 'Two for tonight and two for tomorrow morning. I'm taking the rest with me.' He grinned a little sheepishly. 'Call it blackmail.'

Uncle George regarded him keenly. 'I wouldn't call it blackmail. Just an obvious precaution.'

Mark flushed. Zoë caught her breath. It was Geraldine who rose to the bait.

'Precaution, what on earth do you mean?'

In George's bloodshot eye was a look that Zoë recognized: a gleam of satisfaction at having set a cat amongst the pigeons. 'He thinks it might run in the family, don't you? The tendency to suicide.'

'Suicide!' Geraldine was outraged. Suicide to her spelt cowardice, disgrace, a sin against the Church, a blot on the family escutcheon. 'How dare you! It was an accident, we all know that, a moment's carelessness—'

'Sally was never careless in her life!' thundered George. 'God knows, we all knew that, if anything she was too damned well organized to be human. She would never have tossed her life away like that. Unless, of course,' he added maliciously, 'she was driven to it.'

'Driven to it?' Geraldine searched for her handkerchief. 'That's a dreadful thing to say, and in front of poor little Zoë.'

'It's all right, Gran, don't upset yourself. As a matter of fact the thought had crossed my mind. Only,' she shot an angry look at Uncle George, 'I wasn't going to distress everyone by saying so. It's true, Sally wasn't the sort to walk under a lorry unless there was something on her mind. That's what I have to find out, if it means reading every shred of paper in this house. And I'll tell you one thing, Uncle George, you needn't look so smug. If there was any driving her to it, you did more than your share of it.'

The gleam in George's eye was extinguished and he seemed to crumple down into his chair. 'Well . . . it wasn't easy, you know, young Zoë. What with you and Charles always quarrelling. And him.' He looked balefully at Mark, who pretended not to see.

Why, Zoë wondered; what was it that occasionally passed between them, a mysterious undercurrent to which she could not put a name. 'I always thought Mark helped you about the place,' she said.

'Oh yes, he helped me. In all sorts of ways, didn't you, Mark? Perhaps he helped me to drive Sally to suicide, who knows?'

Mark jumped to his feet. 'It was not suicide, I tell you! It couldn't have been, she was perfectly happy that day.'

'And who should know better than you,' drawled George dangerously, then snapped without warning, 'considering you were with her when it happened!'

For a moment they all sat speechless, stunned. Then Geraldine said frostily, 'They were both with her, George, as you very well know. And I think it most unfeeling of you to bring it all back in this way.'

George did not reply. Mark said nothing. Zoë stared hard at her hands. The silence was shattered at last by the slamming of the cat-flap in the kitchen door, and Selina appeared among them with soft sounds of greeting, innocently looking for a lap. Geraldine straightened her already ramrod back and said briskly, 'More tea, anyone? Zoë . . .' and the tension slowly eased.

'Yes, well . . .' said Zoë. 'I'll be here tonight, if anyone wants me. Perhaps longer, I don't know. Until I'm satisfied, I suppose.' She busied herself collecting cups, wondering if she would ever do so again without remembering this night.

43

'I'm off.' George turned at the door. 'You sure you know what you're doing, young Zoë? You don't know what you might uncover.'

She hesitated, assessing his intention; when he called her 'young Zoë' it was usually benign. 'Whatever it is I'll have no peace until I know. And I have to do it alone – no distractions, no advice, no ideas put into my head by anyone else. Besides which, there's a respect for Sally's privacy. If someone has to go through all her private papers, letters and things, it ought to be me. I was closest to her.'

'Were you?' He looked at her enigmatically. 'Walk out to the car with me, I've something to say to you.' They sauntered down the path, his hand on her shoulder in the old easy way of childhood. 'Look, I lost my rag with Mark – well, it's an old story. But whatever you find out, remember one thing.' He hesitated, looked suddenly self-conscious in the half light, awkward as a schoolboy. 'I was fond of your mother,' he mumbled. 'Very fond. Just bear it in mind.' He dabbed a clumsy kiss on her forehead, clambered into his ancient car, and drove away.

'Wonder what that was supposed to mean,' she mused aloud, watching his tail lights disappearing.

'What does he ever mean?' Mark's voice at her elbow. 'Probably still boozed. Sleep tight, love. I do wish you'd let me stay.'

Smiling, she shook her head. 'I'll be all right.'

He took her face between his hands. 'I must admit, you look better than you did this morning.'

She nodded. 'Now that the strain is off. And I know where I'm going, what I have to do.'

'Are you quite sure you know what you're doing?'

That was what George had said. For answer she kissed him gently. 'See you soon. Take care of Gran, I'll ring you in the morning.'

CHAPTER FIVE

Zoë watched them drive away through a warm summer twilight pierced with the lurid yellow of street lamps; strange, she reflected, that Sally who had loved wild places had remained in suburbia long after the need for her to live in towns was past. To her, Zoë, it had been home for so long that selling-up would be difficult and painful if the need arose. Yet neither was she sure that she could live here without Sally. She looked about her at the familiar street. A young moon hung entangled in the dark leaves of the willow across the road. Dew was falling, drawing the scent of bruised grass from a newly cut lawn somewhere. As she turned back into the house where she had spent so much of her life, a kind of peace descended upon her. Now, at last, she could be alone with Sally.

As she entered the living room she was assailed by stuffiness, the stale smell of tobacco smoke. She went from room to room, upstairs and down, throwing wide the windows and doors, letting in the scent of the honeysuckle they had planted together, moving like a ghost through rooms in which she could have found her way blindfold; drawing comfort from the house that folded itself about her like an old familiar garment.

Outside the garden door she paused, leaning her back against the roughness of the bricks, and listened. A few gardens away she could hear children playing late; their laughter came faintly on the evening breeze, faded into protest as they were called into bed. A distant radio was offering Bach, the mathematical precision of the notes falling like drops of water into the stillness. In the hedge

45

a sparrow stirred, fluttered, and was quiet. This garden was a small oasis of seclusion, in a street of gardens either planted with regimental precision in flower beds like barrack squares, or used only for the drying of laundry on grass scarred by bicycle tyres and the feet of footballing children. Sally's garden, like her house, had moulded itself subtly around her; what she had called her pocket handkerchief of lawn was now so thickly set about with shrubs that it was virtually sealed off from its neighbours by the roses, camellias and azaleas she had planted, the flowering cherry in the corner where she had buried her favourite cats.

Under the window, the nicotiana flowers were lifting their pale lamps, their scent beginning to burgeon, and on the tiny lawn a small white table and a garden chair stood beckoning. Zoë picked her way towards them, followed by Selina, her quaint monkey face upturned inquiringly, her dark paws finicking through grass distastefully wet with dew. Zoë sat down, leaned back, closed her eyes. Presently she felt the soft weight of the cat across her knees, and for a long time they sat unmoving: Sally's daughter and Sally's cat, in a silence mysteriously shared.

Zoë woke with a faint shiver to the realization that it was raining, the heavy drops whispering down all around her in the darkness, falling like kisses on the parched earth. The smell of it excited her, and for a moment she turned her face upwards, savouring the curious tingling it made upon her skin. She peered at her watch, wondering how long she had slept, and saw only a blur of raindrops in the gloom. She shivered again. Her thin dress was wet through, her hair as she moved sent a trickle into her eyes. Reluctantly, she rose and went indoors to find a towel.

Selina, with the good sense of her kind, was already in the kitchen, nosing her empty dish across the floor. Zoë opened a can for her, snapped on the gas fire in the living room and knelt before it, towelling her hair. She had slept the edge off her exhaustion, her body no longer crying out for bed. What she wanted now was a bath, and a change into dry clothing. There must be something in the wardrobe upstairs she could 'borrow' – still the thought persisted – a kaftan or a kimono where the difference in size would not matter.

She re-set the programmer, heard the boiler ignite, and made her way upstairs to Sally's bedroom.

As she opened the wardrobe door a handbag fell out.

She picked it up, frowning. It was old and shabby, made of cheap plastic in a long-outmoded colour, the lining of the straps cracked into segments by long use. Surely not Sally's . . . and yet? She stared at it, turning it over in her hands, trying to make out what it was saying to her, to catch a faint recollection in a far corner of her mind . . . she opened it, shaking her head.

Inside were three letters, the edges of the paper softened and furred with age, the stamps relating to a bygone rate of postage. She picked one out to read the envelope. 'Mrs Gerald Hammond . . .' The handwriting was her grandmother's, the address that of an earlier house, the first that she remembered. The corner of a black and white photograph was visible between the pages. She drew it out, a snapshot of a woman and two children on a beach; a much younger Sally, her childhood self and Charles, uneasily posed for the camera under a Japanese umbrella. She remembered that day, the sand so hot it had burned their feet, heard again her own voice whimpering incessantly, '*Why* isn't Daddy coming?', saw her grandmother's smile congealing at the edges, Sally laughing relentlessly as if determined not to cry. Oh yes, she remembered . . .

There were other letters in the bundle, addressed in her father's hand to 'Mrs Sally Hammond'. Making the point, she supposed, that someone else was now 'Mrs Gerald'. Not Alexis, of course. Not then. In that respect Charles and Father were alike: when they became bored, the offender had to go.

She sank down on the edge of the bed, savouring the smell of the inside of the bag, an aroma compounded of old face powder, faded scent, the distinctive odour of black tobacco from two crushed Gauloise in a packet, and was gripped by a wave of nostalgia. She recognized it now, of course, remembered it swinging from Sally's arm, saw it in memory in her shopping bag, or her bicycle basket when she picked them up from school. No car, in those days. No holidays, hardly any clothes, Christmas and birthdays the only occasions for treats. It had been tough, she realized, looking back. Yet they had survived it somehow, and grown strong. At least, she had. Charles had merely grown harder.

Her eye roamed along the wardrobe rail, tightly packed with dresses, coats, suits. A fold of fabric caught her attention, navy cotton with a white spot – surely not, it was not possible. Coincidence, it had to be, something else of similar material . . . she drew it out, looked again at the photograph. It was not coincidence. This was the dress that Sally had worn that day, and had kept for some God-only-known reason ever since; faded, musty and many sizes too small for her, it hung stiff as a corpse on its hanger. Next to it was another of like vintage – and another, they were all here, even a few they had shared in their hard-up days, in the one brief period when they both wore the same size. Mystified, she picked up her grandmother's note which had fluttered to the floor.

'Eh?' Surprise had jerked the word from her aloud. She read it again. She had not been mistaken. There were the words, halfway down the single page: 'Can't you find it in your heart to forgive and take him back, for the sake of those darling babies who need their Daddy. I shall be seeing my Gerald on Sunday, please say I can encourage him to hope.'

Encourage him to hope . . . she'd had no inkling that he had had the smallest wish to return. She marvelled at how totally they must both have concealed the truth. Was it then not a desertion but an eviction that had ripped up their family life . . . it was hard to comprehend, difficult in a moment to reverse the thinking of years, to see her long-suffering mother as vengeful and destructive. Was it possible? Somewhere in this magpie's nest lay the explanation, not only to this but to everything.

48

Quickly she scanned the two letters from her father, but they gave no clue; polite and stilted, they dealt only with matters of money and might as well have been written by a stranger.

She looked up again at the shelf from which the bag had fallen. There were others there. One by one she brought them down, every handbag she had ever seen Sally use and some she did not remotely recall. She arranged them on the bed, eight of them in all, opened them up and briefly glanced at their contents. Mostly they were emptied of all but dogends of lipsticks, wilted handkerchiefs, anonymous keys, tickets from buses or cinemas, a few coins of pre-decimal currency adhering by verdigris to their linings . . . the detritus of twenty years or more of living, the oddments left behind by the changeover to a new bag. But why not thrown away? In some there were letters, more photographs, one or two Christmas cards signed with an unfamiliar name. In one she found a theatre programme of a long-forgotten show at Drury Lane, the stubs of two tickets carefully stapled to the corner, and wondered: were these things really what they seemed, a hotchpotch of leftover junk that had missed their turn for the dustbin, or did they – could they – each represent something important in Sally's life, a key to the past with which she could not bring herself to part . . .

She stood up, peered into the shadows at the back of the shelf. Revealed by the removal of the bags was a large carton advertising washing powder. Pulling it towards her she saw that it was tightly packed with letters, held in neat bundles by rubber bands. Beside it was another, over the edge of which drooped the blue furry ears of a rabbit she had loved when she was small. Beyond that, the Japanese parasol, a fat envelope stuffed with school reports, two large and shabby photograph albums, a stack of exercise books. She rifled the pages of the one uppermost. It was filled with verses, neatly written in longhand:

Their voices raked and tangled and said nothing.

49

Must have been us, she thought, smiling. Further down the page, a line hit her with dreadful impact . . . she snapped the book shut, closing it, her eyes, her mind to what it could mean.

There was far too much here to consider starting it tonight. She was, she decided, too tired after all, her bruised emotions still recoiling from the threat of further assault. Tomorrow she would go through everything, not only this but the bureau downstairs, read only what she must and see the remainder safely destroyed. Why, she wondered, did the word 'safely' come to mind? Are you sure you know what you're doing . . . she was no longer sure, and for the moment preferred not to know.

She stowed the things carefully back where she had found them, leaving out the two albums to browse through, took a dressing gown from the rail and went to run her bath, her mind still racing.

Later, in the circular bed under the custom-made duvet, she drew one of the albums on to her knees and opened it. The pictures were very old, printed in sepia, the subjects stiff and self-conscious in Edwardian finery. The faces bore a distant likeness to hers or Charles's, but only one or two could she identify. They were long dead, and the next generation wouldn't know who any of them were unless she did something about it. She must find out their names and relationships, record them so that they should not pass and be forgotten . . .

She realized that she could not. There was no longer anyone she could ask. Sally had been the last one left alive who could have told her. Her eyes filled abruptly, flooding her face with the pent-up grief and shock of days. Abandoning herself in the privacy of her mother's bed she found release at last, sobbing quietly far into the night, weeping not only for loss of love but for failure of understanding. When she switched off the light at last and turned her face into the pillow she felt drained, and slid into a numbed and dreamless sleep.

* * *

She was jangled awake by the shrilling of the telephone, a dazzle of sunlight knifing its way between her eyelids, Selina pawing her face to gain attention. She wanted desperately to stay asleep. The first thing to come screaming into her mind was the line she had read last night:

For a terrible moment of truth, I wished them dead.

CHAPTER SIX

Zoë stood swaying and blinking at the downstairs telephone, trying to clear her mind. 'Yes . . . yes, it's me . . . I'm at Sally's . . .'

'I know you're at Sally's,' Mark's voice was patient. 'Are you all right, you were going to ring me, remember?'

'I've just woken up. Give me a chance.'

'Do you know what time it is?'

'Time?' she said stupidly, fumbling for her watch, then realized she had left it upstairs – by the bedside phone, which she had needlessly staggered downstairs to answer. She sank on to a chair arm, her head still swimming. 'What time?'

'Lunch time. Nearly ten to one, to be precise. I was getting worried.' A hesitation. 'Shall I come over?'

'No. No, I haven't got started yet.' It was all rushing in on her like water over a weir, overwhelming her, making organized thought impossible. She made an effort. 'Look, don't worry, I'm fine, just overslept. Mark, there's a lot more here than we thought, I'll ring you tonight, OK?'

She rang off before he could argue and sat still, eyes closed, half hearing the sounds of life in the road outside, the chirping of sparrows, Selina nosing her dish across the kitchen floor, and tried not to know what was hammering at her brain. She did not want today, and only wished she could wash out last night. The others had been right in trying to stop her. It had been a mistake to stay, to stay alone – but she had not believed them. They had known, they must all have known what she had not: that Sally had hated her. Not only Charles – ah, there was the shock, the hurt! She had been prepared, had even in more shaming moments hoped, to discover that Sally had justly hated Charles, however well or wisely she had concealed it – but not her! Was this what they had tried to protect her from . . . recalling the claim she had made yesterday, her cheeks burned in humiliation. She could never have been as 'close' to Sally as she had imagined: no wonder Uncle George had challenged her. What she'd thought herself close to had been an illusion, an outer shell within which, and beyond her reach, a woman unknown to her had lived unseen.

She felt scalded by rejection. She no longer wanted to go through all those papers, dreading what more she might learn. She could destroy it, that damning piece of paper, destroy it and blot it from her mind . . . but then, what else might there not be? If she turned back now, someone else would have to go through Sally's papers, would inevitably read what she had seen . . . she didn't want that. No, she was committed; she could not back out of it now.

She remembered the Valium. That would help, would put a distance between her and the barbs. She drew her hands from her head, moved slowly to find her handbag. It was still in the kitchen, on the worktop, next to the kettle. A cup of tea . . .

Drawing water, she glimpsed Selina through the window, stalking a blackbird. As she opened the door of the fridge the little Siamese erupted noisily through the cat-flap to arch and wind about her ankles, purring and mewing in a frenetic campaign for food.

'All right,' she said wearily, scooping tinned rabbit into a dish. She found teabags in a choice of Lapsang Souchong and Earl Grey, and stood watching the cat at her meal while she waited for the kettle to boil.

'Did you know Sally didn't love me? Everyone else seems to have known but me.' She smiled as Selina glanced up between mouthfuls. 'It's right, I'm not serious.'

Had Sally, in fact, been serious? It could be that she was over-reacting. How, after all, did she know that that verse, half read and as yet unidentified, had not been scribbled in a moment of amused exasperation – that it was not written tongue-in-cheek – even copied from some other source—

A faint throb of hope quickened and died. It was undeniably Sally's voice; moreover, it had the painful bite of truth.

She sighed. How was it possible! How could she have so misjudged her mother? She was not sure even now that she wanted to find out, not confident that she should not make a bonfire of everything, preserve what remained to her of the illusion of a lifetime, and cherish what was left. She had stumbled willy-nilly on the awareness of Sally's rejection, and shrank from the possible discovery that it was total.

The kettle boiled. She carried the steaming tea into the living room, swallowed two Valium and waited for the promised calm. When it came, she knew that there could be no opting out. Questions had been raised in her mind that could not remain unanswered, if they were not to haunt her for the rest of her life.

She looked around her, wondering where to begin. There were the contents of the bureau, the wardrobe, a filing cabinet. Her mind recoiled from the sheer magnitude of the task before her. And there was no knowing what else might be lurking in dressing table drawers, between books, in coat pockets, among trinkets . . . it could take days, even weeks!

Method, that was the answer. She must tackle one source at a time: read, destroy and forget. Since loyalty, she discovered, still stubbornly prevailed, whatever she was about to learn about Sally would end here.

She finished her tea, splashed her face with cold water, dressed again in yesterday's crumpled dress and walked up to the corner shop. It had changed hands since she had lived here, the friendly face of the shopkeeper she remembered replaced by the cool stare of a school-leaver, but the stock it carried was much the same. She bought milk, sliced ham, tomatoes, cat food, as well as the dustbin liners she had really come for: neat black plastic coffins for whatever skeletons might still be lodged in Sally's wardrobe. That, she had decided, was as good a place as any to make a start.

CHAPTER SEVEN

'You were going to ring me,' said Mark. 'Remember?'

Zoë sat still, telephone in hand, hearing his voice as
from another world. In the corners of the living room, the
lavender dusk of summer had gathered like cobwebs. She
looked at her watch. It said 8.35. Was it possible that so
many hours had passed? All around her lay drifts of paper,
neat piles of photographs, sheaves of notes for an unfinished
book . . . she supposed it was.

'Shall I come for you, then?' Mark again. She did not
answer. 'Zoë?' A pause. 'Are you all right?' Did he sound
uneasy? . . . just a shade.

'Yes, I'm all right.' She heard her own voice as from a
long way off.

'Well, then. When shall I come?'

'I don't know, Mark.'

'Tonight?'

'Not tonight.'

'Tomorrow, perhaps?' When she did not answer, he said
again, 'Zoë?'

'I don't know yet. Perhaps not . . .'

Perhaps not at all. She replaced the receiver, quite gently,
before she could say it. When the bell started ringing again
she did not answer it, but sat motionless until it ceased. She
did not want to talk to Mark. She did not want to talk to
anyone. Not just yet. She was wrestling with the eerie feeling
that she had just met her mother for the first time.

55

Part II

The Bark and the Tree

To come between husband and wife is to come
between the bark and the tree.
—*The Gospel according to St Claire*

CHAPTER ONE

Sally had once said laughingly to Zoë that if life had taught her anything it was to know when to let go. This she had sincerely believed: when Gerald announced that he was leaving her for a younger and prettier woman she said meekly, 'I see,' and stifled her grief in her pillow, lest he became angry as well as unloving.

She was wrong about life. What in fact it had taught her was that people who had to be bothered with you hated you for it. Her parents had instilled this lesson into her without any of them being aware of it, and they would undoubtedly have been shocked and offended had anyone suggested such a thing. They merely wanted her, for their separate reasons, to attain to standards beyond her reach: her mother, for her to be a paragon of politeness and good behaviour, an example to her husband whom she thought of as an ignorant backwoodsman. Her father, unhappily aware of this and smarting under constant criticism, longed for her to vindicate him by showing signs of inheriting his own high intellect.

As a result of these pressures and the constant shortfall they produced, she grew up in the conviction that she was a failure, a changeling for some much better child her parents had a right to expect; she seemed to have been sent to them by mistake, a disappointment with which they somehow made do, out of the kindness of their hearts. She knew too that kindness and good nature were not to be taken advantage of.

'You're not to help yourself' – as the party cakes were passed around – 'I'll tell you which one you may have,' and the smallest and plainest would arrive on her plate.

'That's far too good for you to ruin!' – on the confiscation of an expensive doll from her aunt, and she would bite back her disappointment for fear of being accused of throwing tantrums.

'Give Uncle Charles back the sixpence and tell him you're not allowed to accept money.' Whereby the giver was not only deprived of the pleasure of his gift, but was subtly reminded of his sister's opinion that his own children, allowed to help themselves to sweets and indulge their likes and dislikes at the table, were spoilt. Sally, as a well-brought-up child, was rigidly compelled to eat what was set before her, to the last morsel of gristle and whether she liked it or not; when she choked on a beanstring and vomited on to her plate she was banished to her bedroom for defiance.

In vain did her uncle and aunt suggest that she was 'too quiet'; their opinions were discounted. Her mother observed with approval that she hung back at parties, while the other children surged forward to the Christmas tree.

'You're not to ask, wait until you're offered. And don't take the nicest, someone else might like it.'

Sally hardly needed to be reminded, learning early that her place was to take what no one else wanted and pretend it was her choice. Long before she was ten, she knew not only that those who ask get nothing but a reprimand, but that to be tolerated at all one must be self-effacing. She was, moreover, on the way to the conclusion that both she and her father were in some way substandard, and had blundered by mischance into a world whose exacting criteria they could never hope to meet.

Such downward wisdom is not acquired in an instant; all pressures take time to make themselves felt, and the first few years of her life were relatively carefree. The guidelines, however, were being laid down from Day One.

She was born slowly and with difficulty to a middle-aged mother, an experience which haunted her early childhood with nightmares of suffocation and claustrophobia, and which, as she was later to realize, constituted her first unforgivable sin.

Her mother, a fading beauty of domineering disposition, had, after a trail of broken engagements, married a gentle, gauche and somewhat secretive American some fifteen years her junior; it was perhaps understandable that she resented the alteration to her figure, and laid the blame for his fading ardour on the birth of a child she had not bargained for. This, however, was not immediately obvious to a four-year-old; all Sally knew was that Mummy suffered dreadfully from something called 'nerves', which meant that one could not shout, giggle, cry or run about in the house, and as playing out of doors meant that Mummy could not see what you were 'up to' it followed that this also was forbidden.

But the nerves did not happen all the time, and if at the right moment you kept very still and very quiet, she would read you wonderful stories out of a big book or let you watch while she coloured in the pictures. Mummy was very good at stories; you could hear all the people talking when she read to you, and sometimes when Daddy was late home she would sit at the piano and sing song after song: 'Fly home, little heart' and 'Fold your wings of love' were Sally's favourites, and she would imagine a heart with wings wrapped around it like a robin in cold weather. Mummy explained that she was good at these things because she had been on the stage, adding reverently, 'in the West End'. Sally did not know what that meant but it sounded exciting and important; she never tired of listening to the letters from admirers that Mummy kept in the box tied with blue ribbon. Daddy hadn't been on the stage and hadn't what Mummy called 'a voice', but sometimes when he came up to say goodnight he would sing to her softly . . . 'Goodbye Sally, I don't want you to cry . . . I want to see that smile, that wonderful smile . . .' Even if she was feeling sad it always made her smile. It was Daddy's special song, she didn't like anyone else to sing it, not even Mummy . . .

She could hardly wait to be grown-up. When she was, she too would go on the stage and would be beautiful and famous, and crown it all by marrying Daddy, so they would all be together, always.

While she was little there were three things to remember: be obedient, sit still, and never make a noise. For one small girl on her own it was not too difficult to be quiet; all she had to do was watch the grown-ups and try to be exactly the same. In the pre-school years she rarely saw another child, and passed her time with endless dolls' tea parties, solitary games of dressing up and such soundless occupations as the colouring of picture books.

Before she was five years old, she had learnt to read. Trotting at Mummy's side on her daily tour of the dress shops, she identified the prices marked on show cards in the windows; sometimes a few simple words were added, such as 'Stylish' or 'Fox fur', and the daily repetition of familiar words led rapidly to the recognition of others. Her achievement was received with glowing praise.

'I shall tell Daddy when he comes home,' said Mummy proudly. But when Sally pleaded to be allowed to stay up and tell him herself she was promptly admonished. 'You know you have to be in bed before Daddy gets in. He doesn't want you hanging about him when he's tired.'

When Daddy came home he came up to the bedroom to see her, promised her a prize for learning to read, and stayed until Mummy's voice ringing up the stairwell summoned him downstairs. Sally heard their voices for a long time in the dining room below, and noticed with mild surprise that Mummy no longer sounded pleased. Perhaps it was the nerves, she thought, and set herself to trying to go to sleep.

It was never very easy to go to sleep; with the gas fire burning in her bedroom and all her underclothes under her fleecy nightgown she was always too warm, but she knew better than to take any of them off. She had only tried it once.

'If you catch pneumonia, who'll have to nurse you — *I* will!'

She had been angrily stuffed back into them with a smack for emphasis. Now she was resigned to tossing on her over-warm bed, while her thoughts rushed madly about as if trying to make up for all the running and jumping that the rest of her was not allowed to do.

Tonight it was more difficult than usual, because Grandma was coming to stay, and now she had this big important thing to tell her. Grandma's visits were something very special in Sally's life. Grandma was small and bright and bustling, she swept like a spring gale through the uneasy quiet of their home, not on tiptoe but with energy crackling from every strand of her silvery hair. She seemed afraid of nothing and took no notice of Mummy's 'nerves' – 'I haven't got time for all that nonsense!' – talked and behaved as she pleased, took Sally for forbidden walks in the rain and romped with her until she laughed out loud. These visits were looked forward to by Sally with a mixture of excitement and trepidation, their memory cherished afterwards in guilty secrecy and the full awareness that she and Grandma had been defying the rules. No one else, not even Daddy, even dared to do that.

Afterwards, when they saw Grandma off on the train, she would stand, desolated, between her parents on the platform while the big noisy steam engine shrieked and thundered away into nowhere taking Grandma with it, dutifully struggling to contain her dismay. She had to promise not to cry to be allowed to see Grandma off, and the breaking of a promise she was never able to keep made everything that much worse. She would sit sniffling on the back seat of the car, her feet barely reaching to the edge of the leather, and know that she was in disgrace. Not just for crying although that above all things got on Mummy's nerves – but for underhand defection to Grandma's rebel camp.

It was her secret dream that one day Grandma would come to stay for Christmas. Not that Christmas was not perfect as it was, with special food and decorations and no mention of nerves but games and laughter, a huge crate packed with presents from Daddy's side of the family, of which the corners were packed with 'the funnies' from the *Chicago Herald Tribune* and the *Des Moines Sunday Register*. She and Daddy would smooth them all out carefully and try to follow the serials of which parts were inevitably missing; through them she met Popeye, Tarzan of the Apes and the denizens of Gasoline Alley, Daddy reading the text to her while delicious smells reached them from the kitchen where Mummy was preparing the Christmas dinner.

It was a magical time of harmony and shared excitement, building up slowly over the weeks with the secret planning of presents: she would be taken with each of her parents to choose 'her' gift to the other one, helped to wrap it and write on it and hide it until the day, and although she never had any inkling of what her own presents would be they were always beyond her wildest hopes. Believing devoutly in Father Christmas, she would lie rigidly in her bed on Christmas Eve, tense as a clock spring in the knowledge that unless she slept he could not come to deliver the presents entrusted to his care. What if she couldn't, she would think in panic, what if he never came! She could never remember falling asleep, it had seemed impossible. And yet always, somewhere in the shadowy hours before it was properly light, she would open wondering eyes on the lumpy shape of a bulging pillowcase at the end of her bed and know that the Day had really come.

Oh no, there was nothing lacking in Christmas. It was just that she wanted to share it all with Grandma. And tomorrow, perhaps, would be the time to ask.

'No,' said Mummy absently, a letter in one hand while she poured tea with the other. 'She's spending Christmas with Dotty and Louise. You're not the only little girl in the world, you know.'

'But she's always with Dotty and Louise, they have her all the time!' She didn't mean her voice to come out as a wail, but somehow it did.

'That's because she lives with Uncle Charles and Aunt Lucy. And there's no need to look like that.'

Daddy reached over to pat her shoulder. 'Maybe we can ask her to visit with us in the spring. Now, I seem to think it's about time a certain little girl had her own pocket money.' He smiled as Sally looked, puzzled, from one to the other. 'As I recall, it's something that seems to go with starting school. Now, watch carefully.' He moved his hand over the neck of the milk jug, and a bright new penny shone between his fingers. 'Ah – what's that behind your ear? And I think . . . yes, another one just under your chin.' He dropped them into Sally's astonished palm and flipped her playfully with his folded newspaper. 'I must be off, I'll leave Mummy to tell you all about school.'

She was too busy with the mystery of the pennies to take in more about school than that Mummy would get her ready and Daddy would take her, on his way to business.

'And stay with me, and bring me home?' she asked, excited by the thought of a whole day with Daddy, who played games with her on Sundays, lifting her up high above his head, whirling her through the air in 'swings' and 'aeroplanes'.

'Afraid not, darling—' Daddy paused on his way to the door, but Mummy cut him short.

'Daddy has more important things to do than playing with you, you're only a child. Drink up your tea, it's getting cold. And, Erik – Erik!' His face re-appeared in the doorway. 'It's "visit" us, not "visit *with*". Do try to learn the King's English.'

Daddy went quickly, banging the door behind him.

'And don't slam the door!'

Suddenly the fun had gone out of the morning.

'I don't like tea.' Sally stared into her cup, her eyes filling as she thought again of Grandma, the magic pennies forgotten.

'If it's good enough for us, it's good enough for you. I don't want to hear any more of your fads and fancies, just do as you're told.'

Sally knew it was no use to resist. She gulped down the tepid liquid past the lump of disappointment in her throat. 'Will I be all by myself?'

'No, of course not.' Mummy was losing patience. 'You don't think the school's just for you, what next, there'll be other little girls besides you. The Sisters will look after you, Sister Mary Joseph and Sister Mary Sebastian. You're going to the Convent, just across the road. I had a long talk with Sister Mary Sebastian, she was charming. The nuns are so wonderful with children, they have the patience of Job — and they need it.' She rolled her eyes towards the ceiling. 'The sooner you finish those crusts, the sooner we can go and buy your uniform.'

Sally was photographed in her uniform on the day she started school, a solid little girl smiling self-consciously into the sunlight, a miniature attaché case clutched tightly in one hand. Her face was almost extinguished by a panama hat like a chamberpot jammed down over her ears, her knees covered by a gym slip in scratchy navy blue serge, her feet bulging over new shoes bought half a size too small. Shoes for girls, said Mummy, should always be on the small side: in China the ladies all had beautiful little feet, they bandaged them when they were children to make sure they didn't grow too big.

After an initial brush with Sister Mary Joseph, the kindergarten teacher, who was inclined to disbelieve Sally's eager 'Yes!' in answer to the rhetorical question, 'None of you can read, can you?' and challenged it by standing her up in front of the class with a book to prove it, Sally liked school. There were, she discovered to her delight, other children with whom she was allowed to play at break time, it only being necessary to remember which of them Mummy allowed her to speak to, and all manner of interesting things to find out about. She was a quick learner, and having spent her life so far beset by rules, had little difficulty in conforming to more. Occasional problems arose when school rules conflicted with home rules, but she knew what she had to do: 'You just say politely, I'm not allowed to. My mother says so.'

As most of these prohibitions were recreational — playing on swings, on the concrete playground, playing with boys or any game with a hard ball — they posed few serious problems. Sister Mary Joseph would suppress a smile and let it pass. When it came to making the Catholic sign of the cross on waking every morning, that was another matter. Mummy, an avowed Protestant who never went to church, hit the roof. She had not, she declared, sent her daughter to the best, most expensive school in the district to have her converted to Catholicism! Sally, bewildered and tearful, tried to explain to Sister Mary Joseph, who took her to see the great painting of the Crucifixion hanging in the Convent chapel.

'Every time we deny him,' she said in her gentle voice, 'every time we sin, we drive another nail into those hands.'

Sally looked up into the suffering face, the sad, romantic eyes, and knew how wicked she was. Every time she argued with Mummy, every time she broke a rule or pretended to have done something she hadn't, this was what she was doing. And she had not known until now!

'Honour thy father and thy mother,' said the Commandments. That meant you must do what they said. But, then . . . if she didn't do the cross thing, she was banging in nails again. She lay awake for a long time that night, and in the morning made the sign under the blankets.

'What are you doing?' The voice made her jump.

'Nothing, Mummy,' she mumbled, scrambling out of bed.

Mummy looked at her piercingly. 'God hates liars,' she said.

Apart from this and related dilemmas – Mummy insisting that Jesus was not in the golden box in the chapel, when Sister Mary Sebastian had told her that he was – life was enjoyable. She learned to embroider and to paint pictures on leather, there were dancing lessons and a Christmas concert in which she played the fairy Snowflake in pink satin shoes and a white dress with swansdown which Mummy made specially for her. At the end a box of chocolate drops was handed up to her on the stage, and she was chosen to present a bunch of flowers to a lady in the audience.

The lady smiled at her. 'You're a nice little girl, aren't you?'

Sally did not know what to say. Her eyes furtively sought permission from Mummy, somewhere in the audience.

'Well, aren't you?' prompted the lady, holding her hands so that she could not escape.

'Sometimes,' she said uncertainly.

'Sometimes?' repeated the lady out loud, and everybody laughed.

Sally caught Mummy's eye at last, and it was all right, because she was laughing too.

It was not until she was seven that the whole thing fell to pieces.

CHAPTER TWO

Mummy was going away, to stay with Grandma.

'Can I come and see Grandma?' Sally asked eagerly.

'Certainly not. Grandma's not well, she won't want to be pestered with children.'

'But Dotty and Louise—'

'Never mind about Dotty and Louise, that's nothing to do with you. I've arranged for you to stay at school while I'm away.'

But . . . nobody stayed at school, everyone was collected and went home at four o'clock.

'Can't I stay here with Daddy?'

'And who d'you think's going to look after you?'

'Ethel will look after me.' She liked Ethel, who played Snap or Beggar My Neighbour with her when she wasn't too busy polishing the furniture or cooking their meals.

'Ethel has quite enough work to do without running after you. Now, I don't want any more argument, you're staying at school and that's final.'

Sally did not afterwards recall her mother's departure, but the next three weeks remained with her for the rest of her life.

After school she was collected by an older girl she had not seen before, and taken deeper into the walled convent buildings to another and larger classroom. There, she was seated at a desk, given a book of holy pictures to look at, and told to sit quietly 'while the big girls do their prep'.

Nobody spoke during this time, the nuns' rule of silence seeming to extend to cover the pupils, and although the other girls chattered freely during supper in the vast refectory – a meal of soup, bread and butter and small hard pears from the Convent garden, washed down in Sally's case with water because she was too young for coffee – they were all so much bigger than she was that she didn't know how to talk to them. She stared in admiration at one girl, whose pale golden hair hung to her waist like that of the princesses in her fairy tale book.

'Who's that?' she whispered in awe.

'Her name's Coreen,' replied the girl next to her, and returned to her soup.

She was accustomed by now to the appearance of the nuns and did not find them intimidating, but the familiar faces of Sister Mary Sebastian and Sister Mary Joseph, in the voluminous folds of whose habit the smallest children were allowed to play hide-and-seek, were nowhere to be seen; she did not know anyone, and no one seemed to know her. She thought about Daddy, reading his newspaper by the fire in their cosy room across the road, and wondered if he was thinking of her . . .

A Sister she had not seen before took her into a little room off the chapel, and fastened a black net veil over her head. She noticed that all the other girls wore veils, some black like her own and some white, but when she asked the Sister why, she was gently hushed; as they filed into the chapel each girl dipped her finger in a little bowl of water on the wall and made the sign of the cross on her forehead. When it came to Sally's turn, she did the same. The new Sister smiled indulgently. 'Holy water,' she whispered. 'You must be very careful never to spill any.'

Sally liked the chapel; it was full of pictures and a strange, exciting smell, lit with candles whose light bounced and sparkled on the crowns of the statues behind the altar, and everyone curtsied to them before they sat down. It was a bit like the dancing class, she thought, but cautiously said nothing.

By bedtime, she was so tired that she could barely stand. She wondered anxiously where she would sleep, not having been shown a bedroom anywhere. At last, her eyelids already closing, she was led to a room of formidable length, an endless gleaming corridor between two ranks of white curtains. An unsmiling nun parted a curtain on her right, to reveal a narrow iron bedstead and a chest of drawers. A crucifix hung on the wall, and the bed looked hard and unwelcoming.

'This is your cubicle,' said the Sister, eyeing her sternly. 'You must never, never go into any other. Do you understand?'

'Not . . . not even to say goodnight?' Sally faltered. Mummy had said, 'You'll have the other children for company, you won't be lonely.' She was beginning to wonder.

'Especially not for that!' The Sister's voice had an edge. 'Now undress and get into bed. I shall be back to hear prayers in five minutes.'

That was reassuring, at least. Mummy always heard her prayers at home: Gentle Jesus, meek and mild . . . Rehearsing the words in her mind, she began to pull off her gym slip.

'Not with your curtains open!' Sister turned away, shocked, closing the curtain with an indignant twitch behind her, and Sally was alone.

She folded her clothes carefully on the end of her bed and inserted herself like a shoehorn between the bedclothes; they were tucked in so tightly that they might have been nailed to the mattress.

A few minutes later she heard Sister's mannish shoes ringing along the corridor. They stopped, but she didn't come in. Instead, her strong voice lifted in a prayer that Sally did not know, and then from all around her other voices responded, joining in from both sides of her cubicle. She felt better. There were other children sleeping here after all. When Sister had gone, she called softly, 'Are you there?'

No answer. Presently, she tried again. 'What's your name?'

A whisper came from behind the curtain on her right. 'Coreen. We're not allowed to talk. Go to sleep.'

71

'I can't.'

'Yes, you can. Close your eyes and fold your hands on your chest.'

'What for?'

'It's like praying, in case we die in the night. Be quiet now, if Sister hears us talking we'll get a penance.'

Sally closed her eyes very tightly to keep in the tears that were trying to come out. She did hope Mummy would not be away for long.

When she opened them again it was daylight. She lay still for a moment, staring at the white curtains, before she remembered where she was. She was not quite sure what she was meant to do. And her clothes had vanished from the end of her bed. Was she supposed to get up, or wait where she was until someone came to tell her? She listened for sounds of the other girls stirring, but she could hear nothing. Perhaps they were still asleep.

She waited for a long time, but still nobody moved. At last, she whispered timidly, 'Coreen?'

No answer. She climbed out of bed and crept across to the curtain on the side where last night's voice had come from, straining her ears for the sound of breathing from the other side. She could hear nothing. After a moment she tried again.

'Are you there?' Her voice was beginning to quaver. Perhaps the other girl didn't want to be woken up. But she couldn't help it. She tried again, louder. '*Hello!*'

There was only silence, a silence deeper and wider than she had ever known before. It was frightening, as if there were no one else in the world, only her. She pressed her knuckles against her mouth, and tried to think what to do. Perhaps it was very early, so early that no one else was awake. If she could just be sure of that, she could creep back into her bed and wait. But how could she find out?

She knew she must not go into anyone else's cubicle. But if she crept out, opened the curtain just a crack . . . so she could peep inside . . . see for herself . . .

72

There was nobody there. The cubicle was empty, the bed made, the curtains neatly tied back. A loud sob escaped her as she saw that the next cubicle was also unoccupied, and the next, and the next . . . bawling, she ran the length of the dormitory, her bare feet pattering on the polished floor, searching for another child, a Sister, anyone . . . there was nobody.

No one had heard her. She ran back again to her own cubicle, the only familiar thing in a deserted world, and saw that her clothes were there, on a chair outside the curtained entrance. Between sobs, she struggled into them, her jumper inside out, her shoelaces untied, and made her way to the big door at the end by which they had come in the night before. Her small hands made heavy work of turning the handle, but she managed it and stole outside into the corridor.

Perhaps they had all gone to breakfast and forgotten her. She scrubbed at her tear-streaked face and tried to remember how to get to the refectory. She ran blundering down corridor after corridor in her disorganized search, and finally found it—

It too was empty. The tables laid, the benches drawn up, every place vacant. A doorway at the far end stood open. Through it she could see a scrubbed kitchen table, but no people. Her face pulled apart and she was crying again . . .

At length she thought of the schoolroom. Perhaps it was not very early but very late – they had all gone on into class! She sniffed hard, scrubbed her nose on her sleeve. She had only to find her way back to the classroom and everything would be all right, there would be Sister Mary Joseph and Sister Mary Sebastian and all the other children . . .

At last, she found herself in a part of the Convent that she recognized. Through a window she could see the playground, bounded on the far side by the kindergarten building, and the high brick wall with its heavy studded door. She found a way out on to the concrete and ran, sobbing with relief, across it to the kindergarten door. She wrestled with it ineffectively, then stretched up to the windowsill to peer in through the glass. This too, was

73

deserted, the chairs neatly stacked, the blackboard wiped clean, no Sisters, no children, nothing . . .

Panic seized her. Everyone had gone away, and left her here alone. She ran to the door in the outer wall, the one that led on to the street. Out there, just across the road, was Daddy. She tried to open the door but it wouldn't budge. It was locked. But Daddy could do anything. If she could make him hear, he would come and rescue her. She called out, 'Daddy, I want to come home now!' and waited for him to answer.

But Daddy did not hear her either. She called and called, sobbing frantically over and over again, 'Daddy, Daddy come and fetch me . . . Daddy!' Still he didn't hear, or if he heard he didn't know it was her . . . 'Daddy, it's me, it's Sally, it's your little girl . . . *Daddy, I want to come home* . . .' She threw her weight against the door, beating with her fists upon it, hardly knowing what she did, distraught and beside herself . . .

'Now, now, now, what's all this about?' said a voice, and she felt herself lifted up, screaming and struggling, and carried back indoors.

All she could think of now was escape, out through that door and away from this place that had suddenly become a nightmare. Still hysterical, she choked between sobs, 'I want my Daddy, I want to see my Daddy . . .' She wanted to go home now, to tell him how frightened she was, to be comforted and held in his strong, forgiving arms. Most of all, she wanted him simply to *know* . . .

'Sure, you can't see your Daddy today. Not till Sunday, that's when it's visiting day,' said the lady on whose knee she was being held. 'He'll come and see you then, and maybe bring a present, won't that be nice, now?'

Sally stopped fighting. She bent her head and dissolved into a long slow howl of despair. She didn't want a present. She didn't want a formal visit on Sunday. She wanted Daddy now, when she needed him. She was desolate, no longer comforted by the knowledge that he was just across the road. In this dreadful moment he was as far away as

74

the moon. She leaned her head on the white starched bosom and wept.

The owner of the bosom was talking to her, quietly, in a soothing voice. 'Did you wake by yourself and find everybody gone, then? Sure, they're all in the chapel for early Mass, they crept out quietly not to waken you. Wisha now, there's nothing to cry about. Hush now, alannah, 'tis all right.'

When Sally could speak, she jerked out, 'I couldn't find anybody, I was all by myself!' and broke into fresh tears.

'Ah, now that's never so. Just you remember, Our Lord is always with us, no matter where we are. Next time you'll know, and you'll not be afraid. Now, let's wash your face and comb your hair before they all come rushing back for their breakfast, come along.'

Sally suffered herself to be washed and combed, and sat politely at the breakfast table, although she couldn't eat. But it was well into the day before she was able to smile.

That night she did not sleep in the dormitory. Instead she was put to bed in a small room with a section curtained off, not this time in white, but in black. Behind the dark curtains, she was told, would sleep Sister Mary Luke, so she wouldn't be alone. Outside the curtains, on a small bed near the window, lay Molly, her second best doll, and her teddy bear. She rushed to embrace them, consoled by their presence; how they had arrived there, she neither asked nor cared.

In the night Sally began to cough. She coughed and coughed so much that she did not sleep, and a loud frightening noise kept coming from her chest. In the morning she was told not to get up, and Dr Davidson came to see her. She knew Dr Davidson, he came to see Mummy about her nerves and her poor bad back. He pressed down her tongue with a glass thing, and left her some sticky medicine.

'Where's her mother?' he asked Sister Mary Luke, and was taken outside to talk in the corridor. Sally could not hear what was said, except when he raised his voice to call back that he would come again tomorrow.

When he did come back she was no better, and the ugly noise in her chest had begun to hurt. The Sisters brought her lovely things on a tray, but although she tried she could not eat them, lying limp and listless all day until the evening, when the coughing would start again. Coreen came to see her.

'They say you've got whooping cough. You have to be sick, or else you die. They've sent for your mother.'

Sally was more afraid of being sick than she was of dying; in dread, she asked the Sister if it was true.

'No, no, such nonsense,' said Sister Mary Luke. 'Besides, we don't know if you have whooping cough, the doctor thinks it may be croup. Try to drink some of the milk. Isn't there anything you'd like?'

Sally knew she could not ask for what she'd really like. She shook her head and hid her face against Molly's hard side.

Sister Mary Luke was old, and not very well. Perhaps for that reason she did not rise for early Mass, and was an ever-present comfort though rarely seen. If Sally called out at any time, day or night, she was always answered with a gentle, 'What is it, child?' and under her reassuring influence she began at last to improve.

The first time she was allowed up, she asked what day it was. She was told it was Tuesday.

Her eyes filled. 'I missed seeing Daddy.' He must have come and gone again because she was still in bed.

'No, you haven't missed him. Perhaps next Sunday . . .'

Next Sunday he didn't come either; but Sally by that time had turned her thoughts away. Her attention was taken up by adjusting herself to the complicated life of the Convent. The first time she was taken to have a bath, she was ushered into a kind of huge cupboard containing a bath and a chair, and left there to fend for herself. When after several minutes no one came, she undressed and climbed into the big slippery bath, and made some sort of a show of washing herself. She wondered if anyone would come to help dry her, but no one did; when the water began to chill she clambered

76

out and dried herself as best she could. Her nightdress was folded over the back of the chair, and with it a cotton garment she had not seen before. It looked a little like a petticoat, and she wondered whether she was supposed to put that on too. But it was not hers, so in the end she left it behind and padded back to the bedroom in her nightgown.

She was followed by Sister Mary Luke, the strange white garment in her hand. 'This is perfectly dry,' she said reprovingly.

'I dried on the towel,' Sally explained.

'But what did you wear in the bath?'

'Nothing.'

'That was immodest!'

'But nobody could see me,' Sally assured her.

'Our Lord could see you, he sees us everywhere. In future you will wear the bath-chemise.'

Sally was bewildered. If God had made her, as the Catechism said, surely he had already seen her with nothing on? Another mystery to be explained 'when you go to Heaven'.

There were one or two other things Sally was saving up to ask. One of them was how God could be three people at the same time as being one. 'God the Father, God the Son, and God the Holy Ghost,' she was told. She thought about it; so if God the Son was Jesus, God the Holy Ghost must be Our Lady? No, no, no, they told her: the Blessed Virgin Mary was not the same as the Holy Ghost. That made four according to Sally's arithmetic, and in the end she gave up trying to work it out. She would understand everything when she got to Heaven.

On one evening every week they did the Stations of the Cross. Sally loved this. All the boarders formed into a crocodile and walked slowly through a long corridor painted with pictures on the walls; at every picture they paused, while a voice whose owner she could not see told them what the picture meant. The only thing was, the description never seemed to fit the picture. She puzzled over this for a long time, and at last asked Coreen.

'It's because you're last, silly!' said her idol. Which left her feeling foolish but still perplexed.

At the end of the third week, Sally was taken home. By this time she had recovered from her illness, the sharpness of her hunger for her parents was dulled by their failure to respond to it, and she was beginning to revel in the society of other children. Moreover, in the Convent no one shouted at you or had 'nerves', the emotional switchback of home was left behind. She did not want to leave Coreen, or Sister Mary Luke, but when Ethel came for her at four o'clock she went obediently out through the studded door, Molly in one arm and Teddy in the other, to resume her life in the house across the road.

Mummy and Daddy were talking when Ethel took her in. They stopped as she entered and just stood there, one on each side of the fireplace, saying nothing. Then Daddy smiled and lifted her up.

'How's my little girl?' he said.

Suddenly it all came flooding back, that dreadful morning of three weeks ago.

'Daddy, I called you and called you and I couldn't make you hear!' and she burst into tears.

She was plucked from his embrace and seated firmly on Mummy's knee. 'Now then, you can stop that boo-ing and tell me what's the matter.'

She didn't know how to start, where to find words for the anguish, the confusion and terror that had welled up afresh at the sight of Daddy. All she wanted was to get back to him, to end the nightmare in his arms at last . . . but Mummy was holding her fast.

'Come along now,' she was losing patience. 'Stop crying like a baby, you're a big girl now, you're seven.'

She couldn't look at Daddy. She stared at the wall, sniffing and hiccuping, trying to pull herself together. She picked at a loose end in the jumble of her emotions. 'They all went to Mass and left me—'

'That was quite right, they were told not to take you to Mass. You're a Protestant—'

'But I couldn't find anyone!' Now that the words had started they came rushing in a torrent, falling over each other in her need to bring it all into the light, to find understanding and sympathy. Instead, there was silence.

Then, 'So,' said Mummy. 'You couldn't make Daddy hear?' Her voice sounded strange, as though she were speaking not to her but to someone else, over her head.

Sally looked up. She was looking, not at her, but straight at Daddy, who had turned pink, and was staring at the floor. Sally looked from one to the other, waiting for one of them to speak.

'I expect he was still asleep,' said Mummy, and she felt herself eased from her knee on to the floor. 'Go and tell Ethel she can bring tea in half an hour. And stay in the kitchen, I want to talk to Daddy.'

Sally went slowly, oppressed by the growing awareness that she had done wrong in trying to call to Daddy from the Convent. The Sisters, though kind, had been disapproving, the bigger girls had laughed and called her a baby; now Mummy was angry and Daddy looked miserable. Yet no one had told her beforehand that it was naughty . . . suddenly, she remembered Grandma, and brightened. Grandma would understand, and explain to her, Grandma always understood. And Mummy was back, so Grandma must be better! She burst into the living room, forgetting the prohibition.

'Mummy, now Grandma's better, can she come and see us soon?'

They stopped speaking as she came in, and both turned to stare at her as though she were someone they had never seen before. At last Mummy spoke.

'She didn't get better, Sally. She was a very old lady and she died. You won't be seeing her again. Now be a good girl and go back to the kitchen, Daddy and I are still talking.'

'But—'

'Do as you're told!' Mummy's voice was edgy, as it was when her nerves were bad.

She turned in mute appeal to Daddy, who so far had said nothing but was just standing there, looking as though he too were ready to cry. He said unhappily, 'You'd better go, darling. I'm sorry about Grandma. I know how much you loved her.'

Sally felt her face pulling apart. She bent her head and jammed her knuckles hard against her teeth. Never again to see Grandma . . . and she hadn't even said goodbye—

'Don't start again – for God's sake, don't start that!' Mummy's voice was strangled, her hands pressed to her head in a dramatic gesture. 'You can't expect people to live for ever just because you want them to—'

Sally did not hear any more. She ran from the room, hid herself in the bathroom and wept out her grief and isolation into a towel.

CHAPTER THREE

Mummy's nerves went from bad to worse. Night after night Sally would lie awake listening to the voices from downstairs, Mummy's hard and angry, Daddy's an intermittent mumble, while the name Stella Danby ricocheted like a bullet around the walls. Stella was one of three grown-up sisters who lived at the other end of the road, and why they should be arguing about her Sally could not imagine.

She had a part in the Christmas concert, but this time not only did no one come to watch her but no one came to help her dress for it either. When she came to put on her costume only part of it was there and she had to go on in her school knickers without the skirt. The people in the audience laughed all through the dance, and she knew they were laughing at her. When Mummy came to collect her, she tried to tell her about it.

'I've got more important things on my mind than running after you,' she said, looking at her sternly, as if it were somehow her fault.

It was like that most of the time now. Nobody had time for her any more unless she had done something wrong, and the things she must not do were added to daily. She retreated into the story books that opened like doors into another, more inviting world. The one she read again and again was *Peter Pan*, and she daydreamed endlessly about flying away with the children to a land of freedom and adventure where they always won and no one got into trouble. The one thing she couldn't understand was how Wendy could want to go home . . .

In the new year they moved to another town in a distant part of the country, the third change of house since Sally's birth.

Erik Braun, with a stubbornness characteristic of the weak, had resisted his wife's demand that he apply for naturalization, and felt himself as a consequence obliged to cling to the one employment he was sure of, that of branch manager with the American firm as whose representative he had first crossed the Atlantic. He paid dearly for this illusion of security. As it entailed transference from town to town at intervals of one or at most two years, the family was constantly on the move. His wife complained bitterly.

'It's a disgrace that I should have to report to the police every time we change address – as if *I* were a foreigner, and just because I'm married to you!'

Erik's answer was always the same. 'You knew I was an American when you married me, Aimée. If you'd come to the States as you promised . . .' A row would develop every time.

To Sally, however, moving house was an excitement. A new house, in a new place – and this time, a new school! Besides which, as Daddy always went on ahead of them by several weeks, the leaving behind of old associations was more than compensated for by the prospect of reunion with him. He was the magic in her life, a rainbow that appeared too rarely and vanished all too soon, leaving a darkened sky where he had been.

For a while in the new town things were better. Mummy and Daddy were smiling again, they lived in a big house next door to a doctor's family, and Sally was allowed to play with his three children. After two terms at a new school, where the customs acquired at the Convent made her an object of ridicule, she was taken away from it and started at a third, shortly after her eighth birthday.

Mummy had a present from Daddy, a large dog with a long silky coat; she called him 'Boo-boo', he sat on her lap and was fed with chocolates, and snarled jealously at Sally if she came too near. Daddy slapped him and ordered him on to the floor, but Mummy said, 'How dare you hit my dog!' and turned angrily on Sally. 'You're not to tease him,' she snapped, leaving Sally to withdraw, bewildered.

Ethel had come with them, and sometimes looked after her while her parents went out. On an evening just before Christmas Sally, alone in the drawing room, made the mistake of sitting on the sofa already occupied by Boo-boo. He snarled. Sally put out a hand. He bared his teeth.

Sally was aggrieved, indignant. She had done nothing to provoke him, nothing! He was in the wrong, and wrong-doers had to be punished. But how? No one but Mummy was allowed to smack him, she least of all. She thought for a long time. Boo-boo was admired for his looks, something that Sally never was. Suppose she were to spoil them, just for a while, deprive him of all that admiration, in a way that would not hurt . . .

She waited until he fell asleep again. Then she took a pair of scissors from her mother's workbasket and carefully cut a piece of the long hair from his plumed tail. 'It'll soon grow again, Boo-boo,' she told him consolingly. 'But you've got to learn.' That was what Mummy was always saying to her: You've got to learn.

It was a lesson that she, not Boo-boo, was never to forget.

At breakfast the next morning, Daddy said sternly, 'Someone has cut the dog's tail, Sally. Do you know anything about it?'

'Not his tail, Daddy,' she said eagerly. 'Only the hair, I haven't hurt him. He growled at me—'

'You wicked, cruel girl!' shrieked Mummy. 'You've ruined his beautiful coat, it will never grow again! Oh, what have I done to deserve a child like you!'

She began to cry so noisily that Sally was shocked into silence. Rooted to her chair, she looked from one to the other: even Daddy looked angry, his light grey eyes cold as steel. At last he spoke, quietly, without warmth.

'Go to your room and stay there until you're told to come out.'

Too frightened to make a sound, she scrambled down from her chair and ran up the stairs, stumbling and catching her breath in the effort not to cry. When she reached her bedroom she couldn't contain it any longer and flung herself on the bed, rolling her head in the blankets to keep the sound inside.

She waited on thorns for a long time, tensed for the sound of a foot coming up the stairs. No one came. She heard Daddy go out, the front door closing behind him. She heard Mummy go through to the kitchen to speak to Ethel. But still nobody came to speak to her.

She tried to think of a way to put right what she had done. If she cut off a piece of her own hair . . . but there was no way she could fix it on. She fell asleep at last, tear stained on a damp pillow.

She was awakened by a rap on the door. 'Miss Sally, I've brought your lunch.'

'Have I got to eat it?' She was not hungry, not even a little bit. And it was liver, which she hated.

Ethel smiled. 'I daresay I can get rid of it for you. There's blackberry and apple pie, try a bit of that.' She produced a hanky, something that Sally never had. 'Come on, blow your nose and cheer up. All this fuss about a stupid dog – it ought to be out in a kennel, it's spoilt rotten.' She grinned conspiratorially. 'Don't tell your Mum I said that or I'll be in hot water too. Not that I'm not, anyway.'

'Oh, Ethel!' She was threatened with tears again, but Ethel nudged her shoulder playfully.

'Seems I should have been watching you – don't worry, my back's broad.' She flushed the liver down the lavatory while Sally ate the pie, then picked up the tray. 'It's him I'm sorry for, what some men have to put up with—'

'Ethel!' Mummy's voice came ringing up the stairwell, and Ethel was gone.

She waited all the afternoon, wondering if she had been forgotten. As it grew dusk, she crept out on to the landing and peeped through the banisters. A door opened downstairs and Mummy came out. She caught sight of Sally and thundered, 'Go back to your room!'

Sally ran back into the darkened room and cried all over again. Hearing Daddy come in through the front door, she scrubbed her face dry on a corner of the sheet, but still she was not summoned. It was a long time later that Ethel tapped on the door.

'Miss Sally, you're to come down to your tea. Why, what are you doing, sitting in the dark?'

'I can't reach the switch,' explained Sally. 'Besides I'm not allowed to.'

Ethel made a little sound with her tongue, like Grandma used to do, but she didn't say any more.

Sally went into the dining room where the table was laid for tea. Her parents were already seated. When she went to greet Daddy with her usual kiss he said, 'Sit down, Sally. Mummy and I have something to say to you.'

She sat at her place, her stomach tying itself into knots. She looked at both their faces. She was still in disgrace.

Mummy said, 'Well, go on, Erik.'

Daddy cleared his throat. He was not looking at her, but at Mummy. 'We have discussed your punishment for what you did to Mummy's dog. As it is so near to Christmas we thought of not giving you your presents. But as we have already bought them, we decided to let you have them. However, we feel we must do something to make you realize the seriousness of what you have done. So Mummy and I have decided not to accept your presents to us.'

Stunned, she gaped at them both. 'But – I made them specially,' she stammered, her eyes filling. For the first time, she had a gift for Daddy that was really from herself . . .

'That's enough,' said Mummy. 'Nobody wants a present from a wicked girl like you!' She slapped two pieces of bread and butter on to Sally's plate. 'You're very lucky to be let off so lightly. Now eat your tea, Ethel's waiting to clear away.'

Sally stared at her plate in a blur of tears, forcing down

lumps of bread past the painful lump in her throat, scalded by a rejection she was to feel for the rest of her life.

The following summer the family moved yet again, to a house in a more fashionable part of town. Sally missed the children next door, but by then she had built up a friendship with a girl at school called Katey. She liked Katey, who was quiet, with large brown eyes and black hair cut in a fringe. Katey's mother invited her to spend Sunday with them, and Ethel took her in the morning and came back to collect her in the evening, a long ride in the bus to the far side of town. When she came back, Mummy wanted to know all about the visit, what the house was like, what they had had to eat, everything . . . When Sally had told her, she sniffed.

'You won't be going there again,' was all she said.

They waited and waited for Katey to be invited back, but she never was. It was quite enough to have one child to put up with, said Mummy, without having half the school running in and out.

Mummy's nerves were getting bad again, but suddenly one day she was sparkling, her wavy hair newly blonde and wearing all her best jewellery. It was another of Sally's occasional treats to be shown the contents of her jewellery box; each piece would be taken out to be admired, the story retold of who had given it, how handsome and how elegant he had been. Sally thought Daddy was handsome too, but she was learning not to say so.

Mummy would sigh, putting it all away. 'Just to think . . .' But this time, she was not sighing. She took Sally upstairs and dressed her in her best, then looked at her critically.

'Uncle Patrick's coming, you can't let him see you like that.' She took a powder puff and rubbed it over Sally's face, and pinched her cheeks hard to make them pink.

'You look like a death's head on a broomstick,' she said, shaking her head. She heated up her electric curling tongs and tried to do something with Sally's hair, but it was evidently no good because she combed it all out again, and sighed. 'You'll just have to do.'

Sally was relieved, because the hot tongs so near her face made her nervous.

'You'll like Uncle Patrick,' said Mummy. 'He's full of fun. He was my first love, we'd have been married if it hadn't been for Grandma.'

'What about Daddy?'

'Oh, I didn't know Daddy then, I was a slip of a girl.'

'But what about me?'

'You weren't born or thought of.' She laughed, her pretty laugh that was kept for grown-ups. 'You'd have been quite different if Uncle Patrick had been your father, blue eyes and golden curls like your cousin Dotty. Wouldn't that have been nice.'

Sally wasn't sure. She supposed it would, if Mummy said so. But surely, that would have meant not having Daddy . . .

They went downstairs and waited. Presently there was a ring on the doorbell and Ethel went to answer it. Then the drawing room door opened and Uncle Patrick filled the room.

He stood posed in the doorway, both hands extended before him and a big meaningless smile on his face; like a light left on, thought Sally, in an empty room.

'Aimée, *darling*!' he boomed, in a large voice full of music.

Mummy rose from her chair and swept to meet him, putting both her hands in his, fluttering her eyelashes as he kissed her fingers. 'Paddy, how wonderful to see you, after all these years! When I saw the company billed, I just had to ring up and ask if you were still with them—'

'And you don't look a day older!' declared Uncle Patrick. 'Not one day. But wait a minute, who's this? Surely not little Sally? Mm-mm . . . she doesn't look like you.'

'She does take after her father, I'm afraid,' said Mummy.

Uncle Patrick pulled her towards him. 'Come here, let's have a look at you.' He sat down, and lifted her on to his knee. It was embarrassing, because she didn't know him, but she smiled politely. 'And what can you do, sing and dance like Mummy?'

Sally hesitated. 'Not very well,' she said. The dancing lessons had stopped when she left the Convent, and Mummy always said that she sang through her teeth. Not wanting to let the side down, she said, 'I can play the piano a little bit.'

'Don't show off,' warned Mummy. 'You have to have lessons to play the piano.'

Uncle Patrick took no notice. 'Come and show me,' he said, and took her across to the piano.

Very carefully, she played the tune on the black notes that Ethel had taught her while her parents were out.

'I know that one,' gushed Uncle Patrick. 'It's called Chopsticks! Wait and I'll show you the next bit where the tune turns upside down. We'll play it together.' Kneeling on the floor beside her, he showed her how to cross one hand over the other. 'That's very good,' he said as they finished, and when she looked, he was smiling properly, right into her eyes. 'Don't you think she has an ear, Aimée?'

Mummy was standing with her back to them, putting touches to her hair in the mirror. As she turned, the sunlight shafting through the window caught it in a net of gold. 'What?' she said absently.

Sally looked at Uncle Patrick to see if she should play it again, but he was gazing at Mummy and seemed to have forgotten about her. 'Uncle Patrick?' she said timidly.

He seemed to shake himself. 'Mm-mm? What was I saying? Oh, yes. Let's have a look at you.' He stood her up on the piano stool and turned her around. Then he said, 'Yes, you're a nice little thing.' He looked again at Mummy. 'But you'll never be as pretty as your mother.'

Sally got down from the piano stool, because she wasn't really allowed to stand on the furniture, and went quietly out to the kitchen to sit with Ethel. She knew she was neither clever nor pretty. She did wish people wouldn't keep reminding her.

Mummy and Uncle Patrick played songs at the piano all

88

that evening, she could hear them singing and laughing from upstairs. But when Daddy came home, instead of listening in the drawing room he came up to her bedroom and sat for a long time talking on the end of her bed. They talked about her school work, and the coming summer holiday by the sea; but although Uncle Patrick was not mentioned, Sally had the feeling that Daddy didn't like him either.

Next morning Uncle Patrick had gone, but Mummy was still smiling.

'Well, and what did you think of Uncle Patrick? He's charming, isn't he, everybody loves him.'

'Yes, Mummy,' said Sally dutifully; thinking, not really everybody. He was a little bit too charming. Too big, too loud . . . too everything. She sidled towards the door, planning to escape before she was pressed to say more. Mummy was standing at the window, smiling out into the garden, not seeming to have noticed. But as she reached the door, she said without looking at her, 'Sally?'

'Yes, Mummy?'

'If you had to choose, who would you like to live with, Daddy or me?'

Sally was struck dumb by the enormity of the choice. She crept from the room, pretending not to have heard.

CHAPTER FOUR

Sally had a repertoire of recurring nightmares, ranging from a terrifying creature that snarled and slavered in the cupboard she had been sent to open, to the sudden disappearance of everyone in the world, beginning with her parents hurrying impatiently ahead of her through dark, deserted streets to vanish, leaving only their two hats lying on the seat of the car. In the worst and oldest, she was trying to run to Mummy from a bear with slashing claws, and the two kept changing into each other so that turn as she might she always found herself running away from Mummy towards the waiting arms of the bear . . .

From these dreams she would wake screaming, sometimes in her own bed, more often in her parents' room. Her mother, patient by night as she never was by day, would lead her gently back to bed; strangely, it was Daddy who either stayed firmly asleep or was displeased.

Now, to the list was added a new awfulness in which she pursued fleeting glimpses of him through grey empty buildings haunted by cobwebs and broken stairs, a dream from which she woke not screaming but sobbing in deep distress. Of this particular misery she spoke to no one, warned by some dim instinct that it would not be well received.

Her parents were at odds again. They did not quarrel openly in her presence, but it was obvious that they could not agree. Daddy bought her roller skates: Mummy took them away. Daddy gave her a bicycle: Mummy forbade her to ride it. Daddy started teaching her German: Mummy said it ought to be French. Daddy gave her lessons in shorthand: Mummy said Gregg was only used in America and therefore a waste of time: he must teach her Pitman – which he didn't know. Daddy and Sally both lost heart, and the lessons were eventually abandoned.

She was given a recorder and a piano accordion, but no one could tell her how to play them. If you had any intelligence, said her mother, you could pick it up for yourself. In the course of time she was to complain, 'Those instruments were a wicked waste of money, you never play them!'

She was, however, allowed to have piano lessons; practice was restricted to those pieces her mother approved of, and no music allowed which was not defined as classical, anything verging on the popular being condemned as common. Sally, whose taste leaned to the romantic and the imaginative, plodded dutifully through the theorems of Bach and Beethoven without suspecting that music was meant to be fun.

It was not only popular music which was designated as common. The list was endless, and embraced such things as whistling, washing one's face without a flannel, holding one's table knife like a pen, attending chapel instead of church (Daddy was a Methodist), the hanging out of laundry on a Monday (which labelled you as working class), a drink called Port-'n'-lemon, Aunt Lucy, the wearing of headscarves and the beating of children.

This last, however, seemed not to apply to the boxing of ears, and Sally's head rang with increasing frequency as her mother's hand flew out. Sometimes it was justified – 'How dare you defy me!' or 'Because I say so!' when she failed in the unquestioning obedience demanded – sometimes less so, and sometimes, thought Sally in the first stirrings of rebellion, just because she felt like it.

The trouble was that Mummy never forgave anything: once you did something wrong it was dragged up again and again so that you never achieved what the nuns had called a 'state of grace', however good you were trying to be.

Even Daddy's half-hearted protests of 'Darling, do be

reasonable,' slowly dwindled into silence; it was obvious that he was in disgrace too.

To the strictures of 'Don't be inquisitive' and 'Don't answer back' were now added 'Don't tell the girls at school your father's an American' and 'Don't say he has a half-day off, they'll know he's in trade,' from which she gained the insidious impression that Mummy was ashamed of them both. More than once she caught Daddy looking as if he thought so too. She longed to throw her arms around him, but never quite had the courage; she knew he was told of all her misdemeanours – 'and then we'll see if he thinks you're such a nice little girl!' – and she was sure he wouldn't allow her to side with him against Mummy.

The calendar of her sins grew alarmingly, and changed unpredictably from day to day. She would find herself in trouble for breathing into her cup at table, holding her knife upside down, reading in bed, blowing her nose, not blowing her nose, forgetting to flush the lavatory, flushing it and destroying the evidence, or failing to produce the evidence at the specified intervals. This last carried a terrifying penalty: if you didn't go for three days, declared Mummy, you got appendicitis and had to have an operation.

This was more frightening to Sally than anything else. Mummy had once had what she always called her Terrible Operation, which had been the start of all her troubles, leaving her unable to get up in the morning or do anything in the house. Ethel did what was needed in the house and also took Sally to school, while Mummy arranged flowers from the garden and played records or read books, until Ethel succumbed to the dreaded appendicitis and had to go away to hospital. Sally watched with growing alarm Ethel's stomach swelling larger and larger over the months until she could hardly walk, and then Ethel left them and was never seen again.

Katey was making new friends. Sally could hear them talking in a corner of the playground, planning things to do together; but when she tried to join them they walked away. 'It's no good asking Sally, her mother won't let her,' or 'Sh-sh, she doesn't know.'

What Sally didn't know was the answer to the burning question: Where did babies come from? She was not the only child in the class who didn't possess this vital piece of information, and those who did hold the trump card enjoyed tantalizing the unfortunates who didn't. Sally came in for more teasing than most because she was not aware that she did not know, and declared with confidence that she had been found in an egg on a magic island. The others sniggered, but refused to enlighten her. When she asked the question at home, Daddy left the room and Mummy looked nervous.

'I'll tell you when you're old enough. You'd be frightened if I told you now.'

Sally did not like the sound of that. She turned her mind away by asking, 'Why did they laugh when I said I was found in an egg, wasn't it true?'

'Yes . . . in a way.'

'Why only in a way?'

'That's enough,' said her mother sharply. 'Little girls shouldn't ask questions, it's impertinent. And if that's what you children talk about at school, it's just as well you'll soon be leaving.'

'Leaving? But I'll lose all my friends—'

'You can thank your father for that. And it's no good you setting up a wail, you know perfectly well we always have to move. It's no use making friends when you know you'll have to leave them behind, any more than I can plant a proper garden . . .'

Mummy was off again. Sally crept away, busy with her own thoughts. She was trying to reconcile the story about the egg with the mother who had told her 'God hates liars'; there was that other business too, when she was small, about marrying Daddy. She had really thought she could, and Mummy had encouraged her; but when she came home from the Convent crying, 'They laughed at me, they said I can't, and you never told me!' her mother too, had

93

laughed. It was only a joke, she said, adding with a chilling gleam, 'You couldn't have Daddy anyway, he's mine.'

So, if God really hated liars . . . or was it only children who lied, and if grown-ups said things that weren't true it was called joking? It was all very puzzling.

The nuns said God didn't hate anybody, that we were always forgiven because of the nails and the cross. She did hope they were right, because she was still having trouble with that Commandment about honouring your parents; it was no problem loving Daddy, but with Mummy it grew harder every day because of her nerves. At school her teacher took her aside and told her she must be better to her mother; as this happened during a special effort on her part to be good, it was deeply disheartening. More than anything she hungered for approval, and yet it seemed forever out of reach. The harder and more anxiously she tried, the more often she seemed to make stupid mistakes, like forgetting to change her shoes, or leaving her books at school.

'You do these things deliberately to annoy me!' fumed Aimée in exasperation.

'I don't, Mummy, I don't!'

'Don't contradict me!' Bang! and she would retreat with singing ears.

Since her consistent best was never good enough, it followed that there must be some basic inadequacy in herself. Her spirits drooped under the oppressive belief that she was the reason for the state of her mother's nerves, since it seemed she need only be present to make them worse. She wanted to be different, to be acceptable, she really did . . . but how was she to alter herself?

When Daddy, catching her eye, gave her a secret, consoling smile, she looked away, her eyes brimming, aware that as Mummy was disappointed in them both, her constant failures were letting him down too.

'Just try a little harder, darling,' he encouraged her gently. 'Make Mummy proud of you.'

'I can't,' she said unhappily, knowing long before she was

ten that this was something she could never hope for. She was learning to fear the hairtrigger temper, the flying hand.

Sensing that Daddy was proud of her progress at school, she turned her attention to working hard and trying to please him instead. This opened up new and unexpected pitfalls. When he read out the Quiz questions in the Sunday paper and she knew more answers than Mummy did, there were reactions that she could not understand. Mummy accused her of showing off, and then Daddy looked angry and put the paper away.

Why, she asked herself on the verge of tears, what had she done wrong? More and more it seemed to her that she could do nothing right.

They were moving again. Daddy had yet another promotion which had taken him on ahead to a distant town, and Mummy was crosser than ever because she was left behind to pack. Books and china and furniture were disrupted all over the house, and Grace, the maid who had replaced Ethel, gave Sally a friendly warning to keep quiet and stay out of the way.

'Are you coming with us, Grace?'

'Not likely! Not after what happened the other day, I was that uncomfortable!'

Sally had been worse than uncomfortable, she had felt ashamed, even though for once no one could have said it was her fault.

Daddy had come in to lunch and had first gone to the bathroom. Mummy, already at the table, had called to him to come down. When he did not answer immediately, she shouted again.

'Erik, come down here! The food's on the table. Erik!'

Sally cringed. She was calling Daddy in exactly the same voice as she called her, the same way as she sometimes shouted at Boo-boo, as if they were all the same. Grace, who was in the room, had ducked out of the doorway.

'*Erik!*'

The bathroom door opened so violently that Sally flinched,

and for the first time she could remember, Daddy shouted back, the sound of the cistern flushing behind his voice.

'*Yes, what is it now!*'

Mummy drew herself up, and her face went white. 'Sally, ring for Grace.'

Trembling, Sally did as she was told. As she sat down again, Daddy came down the stairs just as Grace reappeared. Mummy put on her most dignified manner.

'Erik, I will not be spoken to like that. You have insulted me in front of the servant. You will now apologize in her presence. Grace, come back!'

Grace, who had tried to escape, hung about uncertainly, looking wretched.

It was Daddy who said, 'It's all right, Grace. I apologize. Now you can go.' When the door had closed behind her he said quietly, 'Very well, Aimée, I've done as you asked. But don't you ever humiliate me like that again.' And he walked out and went back to work without his lunch.

Mummy stormed and shouted after him to come back, and when he didn't she pulled off her wedding ring and threw it across the floor. Then she went stamping up the stairs, crying noisily, leaving the food on the table to get cold.

Presently Grace crept back, and asked Sally if she wanted her lunch. She wasn't sure if she was supposed to eat without her parents, so she said no; when she was alone she wriggled under the sideboard to where the ring had rolled. It shone in the palm of her hand, heavy and brilliant with the soft glow of gold, and as Mummy had thrown it away she supposed she could keep it. She took it up to her bedroom where she cherished it, taking it out at intervals to admire it, not caring that it was far too big to wear. It was beautiful, a crown for a fairy queen, the most exciting thing she had ever owned . . .

The next day Mummy asked if she had seen it, and demanded its return. She handed it back, smarting under a sense of injustice. People shouldn't throw things away if they didn't mean it, it wasn't fair . . . but she was learning the futility of argument. She supposed it was just another of those horrid grown-up jokes.

And now there was a new disappointment, that Grace was not coming with them. She wanted her to come, to be there in the new town, a friendly face and someone to talk to when Mummy wanted her out of the way, which was most of the time.

With Daddy far away and the house in turmoil, she whiled away the long Christmas holidays in exploring the attics, now opened up for the first time. There were trunks and boxes of all sorts, their contents spilling out over the floor. In one of them was a book.

Sally picked it up idly, hoping for a new story that she had not read. It was a volume pleasingly small to her hands, in a dull brown binding crammed with closely printed pages; on the front cover the name ARISTOTLE stood out in a title she could not read. Riffling through the pages she saw that the book was in French, but far beyond anything she had learned at school. Disappointed, she dropped it back into the trunk. It fell open at a double spread of pictures.

She stared, horrified. Four diagrams in colour showed a baby curled inside a woman's body, growing larger in each picture until it seemed the woman must burst. How had it got in there – and worse, how was it ever going to get out? Did it have to be cut out, would it be an operation, would you have to go to hospital, to the appendicitis place where nurses bullied you, strapped up your arms to make you sick and poured boiling iodine over wounds . . . she burned to ask these questions, needed answers but dared not ask, not only in dread of fresh horrors to come but also because she was guilty of having seen a forbidden book.

Was this then, where babies came from, what the girls at school had taunted her with not knowing? She had left the school now, and would not be able to ask them. And she could not ask Mummy. She crept downstairs and nursed her fear for a long time in her bedroom.

At the end of that time she had reached two conclusions:

if that was how babies came, she must never, *never* have one. After prolonged and agonized thought, she consoled herself that only married people have babies.

She would be all right, as long as she never got married.

The repetition of forbidden questions was severely discouraged, and Sally's apparent loss of curiosity about the reproduction of the species went unremarked. For more than two years she hugged her fearful secret, often lying awake into the small hours, trying to come to terms with her anxiety. She was still the target of such phrases as 'when you grow up and get married', and the assumed inevitability of it filled her with dread.

'I might not want to get married,' she ventured timidly. The answer came hurtling back like a boomerang. •

'Of course you'll get married, you don't think Daddy and I are going to support you all your life.'

Her stomach contracted into a cold, tight knot, a knot which her twelfth birthday did little to relieve. Mummy had decided it was time she knew The Facts.

She listened in silence to what she already knew. Now that she was free at last to ask questions, she could hardly speak.

'How . . . how does it come out?'

'You go to hospital and have an anaesthetic.'

She shivered. So it was true. She made herself say it. 'You mean, you have to have an operation?'

'A sort of operation. Yes, you could say that.'

'They cut you open?' She felt herself turning pale.

'If you're too small. Otherwise, the baby comes out without.'

'But how . . . where?'

Mummy looked uncomfortable. 'Where everything else comes out from,' she said crossly. 'From between your legs.'

Sally pressed hers tightly together. 'But how can it possibly!' She was sure she would be too small, didn't see how anyone could possibly be otherwise.

'It all has to stretch. Of course,' Aimée sighed, and

the long eyelashes swept downward in an expression of martyrdom. 'Of course, you're never the same again. A woman who's had a child is like a flower that has gone to seed, its beauty's ruined for ever . . .'

Sally was still wrestling with the mechanics of it. 'It must have to stretch an awful lot. Doesn't it hurt?'

'Oh, does it hurt!' Aimée gave a theatrical shudder. 'That's why you have to have the anaesthetic. They say it's the worst pain in the world; a woman can only stand so much of it, otherwise she goes mad. Well, now you know what it cost me to have you.'

'Oh . . .' Was that why Mummy didn't like her . . . it must take an awful lot of forgiving. Stricken with remorse, she pleaded, 'I didn't ask to be born.'

To her dismay, her mother misunderstood. Eyes blazing, she shouted, 'You wicked, ungrateful girl, after all I went through to have you! Go to your room!'

To try to explain was hopeless, and Sally fled to her room in tears. She stayed there until bedtime, her depression deepening with the dusk. More and more she found herself missing Grandma, the brisk cheerful breeze of her blowing through the house. Grandma had had four children, two of whom had died leaving only Mummy and Uncle Charles, but she hadn't seemed to Sally at all like a flower that had gone to seed. She longed to be able to talk to her about all this, now that she was officially allowed to 'know'. But Grandma was gone.

The next day, when the storm had died down, she ventured one more question to her mother. 'I don't quite understand how the babies get there. I mean, what is it that starts them off?'

Aimée looked first startled, then confused. 'Getting married,' she said shortly. 'You have children when you get married.'

Sally's stomach somersaulted at this confirmation of her worst suspicions, but she stuck to her guns. There had to be more to it than that; the people next door were married, yet they had no children.

99

'But, there's something else, isn't there? I mean, people don't always, do they, like Mr and Mrs Carter, they haven't got any – and Ruth at school said her mother tried for years to have her. I mean, it's not *just* getting married, is it . . .'

'Since you ask, no, it isn't. But that's not for you to know just yet. I'll tell you about it later on, when you're older. Take no notice of what Ruth says; and if that's what you and she talk about in school I'll have a word with her mother.' She poured herself another glass of sherry, lit a cigarette and reopened her book.

Sally went away unsatisfied, and a prey to new misgivings. If the rest was something she was still too young to know, it must be even worse than having babies . . .

She had already formed her own opinion of Ruth and her smug boasting: her mother adored her, she claimed, kissed her goodnight every night and brought her chocolates in bed, and Sally knew perfectly well that mothers did not do things like that. In fairness, she did recall one occasion when she had been taken on Aimée's knee and made a fuss of, but it was either a birthday or Christmas, when visitors were present. And as for Ruth's mother trying, actually trying, to have a baby! No one in her right mind would deliberately do that!

'You're a liar,' she had said to Ruth, adding meanly, 'Anyway sweets rot your teeth.'

Only a few weeks later she had a second gloomy interview with her mother, although it was not until years later that she realized that the two had any connection.

On the first day of the summer holidays she discovered a shameful dark brown stain in her knickers. In dread of punishment, she had rolled them up and hidden them among the shoes in the bottom of her wardrobe, only to find to her dismay that the next pair suffered the same fate. She could not understand it, she was sure she had cleaned herself properly after the lavatory and yet there it was, all over again. What was she to do? She hung about close to the bathroom, nipping in at frequent intervals to make use

100

of the toilet roll, trying to think of a way to keep her mother from finding out.

Her dilemma was ended abruptly by the sound of someone rummaging in her bedroom, followed by Aimée's voice in a tone she had not heard from her before.

'Sally, is this from you?'

She came slowly, reluctantly, from the bathroom, wondering what on earth she was to say. 'I'm sorry, Mummy. I don't know how it happened.'

'It's all right, I'm not angry. Just tell me if it's from you.'

'I'm afraid so.' She hung her head.

'Oh . . .' Mummy was looking at her pityingly, yet at the same time as if she had noticed a bad smell she was too polite to mention. 'Oh, you poor little thing, you've started already.'

'Started?' Sally looked up in shock. 'You don't mean this is going to go on?'

'It will go on for a few days and then stop, then it will happen again every month until you're about forty. I had hoped you would have a few more years of freedom.'

'But, what is it? I don't understand . . .'

'It's blood, Sally. It's because you're a girl, it's called being unwell and you must never let anyone know when you're like it, never, do you understand? And never let a man feel your hand at those times, they can tell. Now I'll go and get you something.'

She came back with a packet of the square bandage things that she kept hidden in the bottom of her own wardrobe. 'Put one of these on.'

Sally stared in horror. 'I haven't got to wear those?' she pleaded, on the verge of tears. She recognized them as the dressings Mummy said she had to use because of her operation. 'It'll show through my swimsuit!'

'You can't wear a swimsuit when you're like that!' It was Mummy's turn to be shocked. 'And you certainly can't go in the water, there'll be no bathing for you this holiday. And no baths or washing your hair until you've finished.'

Sally sat miserably on the edge of the bed. 'What shall

I say to Daddy, he's waiting to take me swimming?' She was only allowed in the sea if he was with her; she would never learn to swim at this rate.

'You'll say nothing to Daddy, what next! I'll tell him you have a headache and have gone to lie down.'

Life, thought Sally, was horrid and was getting worse. She had wished often enough that she had been born a boy, free to romp and whistle and climb trees, to watch Daddy at work on his hobbies in the garage without being removed on the grounds that it was dangerous; now she had reason to wish it as never before.

All in all, being a girl seemed to have very little to recommend it. And then, just as the horizon was at its darkest, without warning the sun came out.

CHAPTER FIVE

Towards the end of the school holiday she was granted permission to leave the house for the first time unaccompanied.

With a lightness of spirit that felt like flying, she went skipping down the street to the nearest sweet shop. Half an hour later, drunk with her newfound freedom, she went again. Twice more in the same day she visited the same shop, and then her mother pounced.

'Where do you keep going off to, all of a sudden?'

'To the sweet shop. You said I could.'

'Four times in one day? Don't tell lies, you've got a boy you're meeting.'

'A boy? No, I haven't, I don't know any boys. Mummy, you know I don't!' She was close to tears, foreseeing already a curtailment of her liberty.

'Right, my girl, we'll soon find out!'

She found herself frog-marched to the sweet shop, where she stood shifting from one foot to the other in humiliation while the puzzled woman behind the counter was subjected to a barrage of questions.

Her innocence was established. But when at last she was allowed to slink home alone, leaving Aimée in possession of her refuge, she knew she could not show her face there again. So in a small way, the prospect of moving to another part of town was welcome.

It all started one morning when Aimée was opening the post, a long letter in an airmail envelope from which a couple of photographs fell out.

'It's from Geraldine,' she beamed. 'They're coming home at last . . . in the spring . . . they're coming to see us!'

She turned to Daddy. 'That settles it, we must take the house in Redfield. We can't possibly have them here.'

Sally looked up, faintly surprised. This was the first she had heard about moving to Redfield. She thought the house they were living in quite nice; it was near her school, and had a verandah, and a long back garden with a tennis court. 'Why not?' she asked.

'Don't interrupt, Sally, I'm speaking to Daddy, not you. But since you ask, this house is not suitable.'

Daddy sighed. 'Not suitable for what?'

'For entertaining. Not people like Geraldine and her husband. He's in the Diplomatic Service, you know, we can hardly ask them to sleep on a bed-settee.'

'Shucks, why not!' said Daddy unexpectedly. 'If she's any sort of a friend worth having she'll be coming to see you, not the house.'

'I daresay.' Mummy's lips twisted in a withering little smile. 'But we don't want her thinking I've married beneath me, do we?'

Sally couldn't look at Daddy. She kept her eyes fixed on her plate, staring hard at the remnant of marmalade, the few crumbs of toast, the knife laid across it.

She hated Mummy when she said things like that, and was constantly consumed with guilt. 'Honour thy father *and* thy mother . . .' She knew she must be driving in nails, and was powerless to stop. The fault, she thought, must be in herself: if the girls at school could get on with their mothers, why couldn't she?

'You're always grumbling about your mother, don't you like her or something?'

'I try, but she hates me. Ever since I was seven, I don't know why.'

Their laughter scathed her. 'Well, you'd better shut up about it, it doesn't say much for you.'

Mortified, she made new efforts to guard her tongue, efforts which were severely strained at moments such as this, when love and loyalty to her father boiled into a murderous emotion she feared to recognize.

She sat silently at the breakfast table, not looking at him to spare him embarrassment, until she heard him go out and close the door.

'Sally!' Her mother's voice cut across her thoughts. 'Sally! Answer when you're spoken to. Pick up those photographs, they've fallen under the table.'

Obediently, she retrieved them. One was of an elegant lady wearing a fur coat. The other made her catch her breath. A beach snapshot of a young man of dazzling beauty, sitting nonchalantly on a breakwater and looking slightly impatient, as if he had not wanted to be photographed. In the darkness under the table she gazed her fill, dizzied for the first time by the heady wine of sexual attraction.

'Who are they?' She tried to sound casual as she handed them back.

'Aunt Geraldine and her son.'

'When are they coming?' She strolled over to the window, keeping her face turned away.

'He won't be, only his parents. He's away at university.'

'Oh . . . I see.' She was careful not to betray her disappointment. Reminding herself that someone like that had no place in her life, she filed him away with Tarzan and the film stars, and slowly he faded from her mind.

Once again the house was in turmoil. Clothes, books, furniture, ornaments – and Sally – wandering from place to place and room to room like displaced persons waiting to be told where they belonged. Sally, transferred to her fifth school in ten years, was desperately trying to find her feet. Boo-boo, the dog, woofed uncertainly at the doorbell, as yet unsure whether he was defending his territory or taking liberties on Tom Tiddler's ground.

The Redfield house into which they had moved was still in the same city, but was much larger and occupied four floors; with so many more rooms it needed two maids instead of one to look after it, and a man who came two days a week to take care of the garden. Daddy seemed tired and harassed, coming home from work even later than

105

before. But Mummy, for the first time, was smiling. Newly installed in the grandest part of town, she directed operations in a flutter of excitement, while Erik looked ever more glum and overstressed.

Sally by now was deeply unhappy. The antagonism between her parents was becoming increasingly overt, and she wilted under the burden of belief that her own shortcomings were the cause of it, a notion ruthlessly reinforced by her mother.

'The only arguments we ever have are always over you,' she complained, adding ominously, ' "To come between husband and wife is to come between the bark and the tree." It says so in the Bible.'

In the Bible! thought Sally despairingly. She searched her school Bible in vain for the quotation, but her failure to trace it did nothing to reassure her. Lying awake in her smart new bedroom she would listen to the distant rumble of trains in the night, thinking, If I really can't bear it another day, I can slip out in the dark and get on one and go away. It was the comfort of that thought that allowed her at last to fall asleep, the illusion that the trap could be sprung.

She had a new nightmare now, although she was too old to cry out in the night; in it she would discover she had committed murder, and would be fleeing from capture through the back gardens of town houses, clambering over fences in the twilight, desperate to escape into open country. There, with no houses and no people, just grass and trees that only belonged to God, she would be safe . . . Sometimes she was caught and killed, only to drift helplessly in limbo, unable to die and yet not allowed to live.

She found little consolation at school except in work. She was long accustomed to knowing her place as 'new girl', it had been her lot for most of her school life; but her latest school was vast and overwhelming and steeped in obscure traditions. Most of the girls in her form had been there since kindergarten and had known one another all their lives, and when told that Sally had attended four other schools were prone to ask her why she had been expelled. Her half-hearted overtures at friendship were rebuffed, and she sometimes thought wistfully of Katey, now hundreds of miles away.

She had written three times to Katey, who had answered only once, a brief account of what she was doing and her marks in the end of term exams. She and the beautiful young man were alike relegated to the mists of the unattainable, and Sally retreated further into an inner life of her own, a fantasy world peopled by flimsy reflections of Peter Pan, Robin Hood and the gods of ancient Greece, figures of impossible achievement who never got married, had babies or were taken to the dentist, but led charmed lives of high adventure, wonderfully different from her own restricted existence. The real world of every day was one in which she saw herself as a misfit, and one in which emotional contact was best kept to a minimum. She must live her life, she decided with defensive arrogance, on a higher plane of existence, where the slings and arrows that Hamlet went on about could not reach her.

It was not a fortunate decision. As an attitude, it could hardly have been better calculated to inflame her mother's temper.

'I won't have you ignore me when I'm speaking to you!'

Bang! As the flying hand made contact Sally, her head ringing, would smile benignly and walk away.

'Come back here!' raged Aimée. 'You supercilious little madam, you – you beastly precocious American! I'll break your spirit for you, see if I don't.'

Sally, her eyes watering, contrived to say loftily, 'I don't know what you mean.'

'It's what they do to horses to make them obedient. I *will not* have you defy me!'

'I see,' said Sally, and bent her head to her book. She was reading about Judah Ben Hur. He too lived his life on a higher plane, despite all the Romans could throw at him.

'I've had about enough of you, my girl, the sooner you're off my hands the better, if you ask me!'

Amen to that, thought Sally, seeing only the promise

of freedom; not recognizing what was implicit in the words.

In her newly elevated state, she hardly took note of the sudden death of Geraldine's husband, or that someone called Gerald was coming with her instead. She donned with indifference the hideous knitted dress her mother chose for her to wear, and dutifully presented herself behind her parents in the hall to greet the visitors. She was totally unprepared for what followed.

'You remember Erik, don't you, Geraldine,' purred Aimée. 'And this is Sally. Say how do you do to Aunt Geraldine, Sally.'

Sally said politely, 'How do you do,' and wondered how soon she would be allowed to escape. Her eyes travelled from Aunt Geraldine's handmade shoes, over her rich fur coat and up to her face, which was smiling in a condescending way.

'Well, dearie, how nice to meet you. My, you do look like your Daddy, don't you?'

Sally didn't know how to reply. She was secretly glad that she looked like her father, but had long since learned the unwisdom of saying so. Rescue came from an unexpected quarter.

'I think she looks like herself,' said a voice from behind Aunt Geraldine, and her eyes flicked upward in gratitude.

Over the fur-clad shoulder smiled the face she had seen in the photograph, but the smile was not patronizing like his mother's . . . she gazed, transfixed.

'Oh, Gerald,' fluttered Aimée. 'Sally was wondering if she ought to call you "Uncle", being so much younger than you are, you know?'

Sally felt her cheeks burn in shame, in excitement, in humiliation. Never, never, never could she call him Uncle – if she had to she would rather never see him again! She lowered her eyes, staring hard at the carpet, fixing its pattern for ever in her mind as she waited to hear her sentence.

Gerald laughed, a young man's teasing chuckle. 'She'd

better not!' he said. 'I'm not in my dotage yet.'

Sally loved him madly, beyond all reason from that moment on.

All through the meal that followed she kept her eyes downcast, not daring to look at his face but quite unable to direct her attention elsewhere, compelled to keep always in a corner of her vision some bit of him, a hand, a shoe, the edge of a jacket . . . she had never felt anything remotely like this before and did not know how to cope with it. It was terrifying, and at the same time delicious. She was totally overwhelmed.

She slept little that night, and in the morning woke early, tense and excited as in the early hours of Christmas. Gerald was sleeping under the same roof, would use the same bathroom, eat at the same table! She could not wait to see him, yet was afraid to show her face.

She wished she had something other than the awful knitted dress to wear; it clung to her developing body in embarrassing places and she was sure that her suspenders showed through. She scrubbed her teeth extra hard, pinched her cheeks in a vain attempt to relieve their pallor, brushed her straight hair until it crackled with static electricity. Still it clung limply to either side of her face, and she exchanged little sighs with her reflection before going slowly down to breakfast. It wasn't that she hoped to make an impression on Gerald; it was just that she didn't want him to notice that she was plain as well as dull.

When Daddy left for the office, Aunt Geraldine announced, 'I think Gerald would like to take Sally to the pictures this afternoon.' Sally looked up in astonishment, and noted that Gerald had done the same. 'You don't mind, dear, do you?' Aunt Geraldine addressed her son. 'Aimée and I would like to talk, and tomorrow dear Erik will be at home. Girl talk, you understand!' she added kittenishly.

So it wasn't his idea, thought Sally . . . of course it wasn't. She drowned in embarrassment.

Again it was Gerald who saved her. 'Perhaps we should

ask Sally if she minds,' he said, and turned to her. 'Would you?'

She did not know what to say. The thought of being taken out by Gerald was breathtaking. But this was not at all how it ought to be.

'Well, say something, Sally,' prompted Aimée, her tone sharp under a layer of cream.

Sally looked at Gerald. 'Not if . . . if . . . I mean,' she faltered. 'Do you want to?' That was stupid. Just asking for him to say No. But at least, he would be able to say it . . .

He smiled, a lovely warm smile. 'I want to. If you promise not to be bored.'

'Oh, no—' she said breathlessly, and then Aimée cut in.

'Of course she won't be bored. It's very kind of Gerald to take her, I think *Mary Poppins* is showing somewhere.' She rustled about, looking through the local paper for the programmes. 'Ah yes, here it is. Don't pay full price for her, Gerald, she still goes in for half.'

Sally felt the hot blood burn her neck. *Mary Poppins* — oh, how could she, a children's film! Of course Gerald would be bored, how could he not be . . . it was going to be awful, she knew it was. He'd probably back out, and who could blame him. It wasn't even as if she'd never seen an adult film, she'd been often enough with her parents . . . Oh, God, she wanted to die . . .

Through her misery she heard Gerald making arrangements, and changed her mind about dying, at least until later. Because, whatever the awful prospects, he was going to take her out.

They set out after lunch in a stiff spring breeze, Gerald striding ahead on his long legs, Sally hurrying to keep up, hampered by the knitted dress which persisted in rolling itself into a ball between her knees and having to be straightened out. She prayed that he wouldn't notice, but once or twice he paused to wait for her, and she knew he must have done. They reached the cinema at last, and Gerald bought the tickets.

'Two, please.' He smiled at Sally, 'I don't think they'd really let you in for half, do you? I hope there wasn't something else you wanted to see, this might be a bit young.'

'What about you?' She smiled with closed lips, careful not to show her uneven teeth. 'My mother seems to have chosen it for both of us, I'm afraid.'

Gerald laughed. 'Well, let's give it a try. We can always walk out if we're bored.'

Walk out! thought Sally. What a splendidly grown-up thing to do, what a grand gesture to make . . . she followed him proudly, to sit beside him in the darkness, breathing the familiar cinema smell compounded of tobacco smoke, air freshener, stale perfume and dusty plush, conscious of other people around them and unable to decide whether to put her elbow on the arm rest between the seats or leave it for Gerald. One or two adult couples near the back seemed not to be interested in the programme but were snuggled closely together; she tried not to see them. A small boy in the next row kept jumping up and down, making a nuisance of himself.

'Children!' she murmured, anxious to dissociate herself from such juvenile antics.

Gerald seemed not to hear. In the interval when the lights went up, he said, 'Would you like an ice cream?'

'Oh – no, thank you.' She said it rather quickly, although her mouth watered. She might drop it down her clothes, lose the spoon, or otherwise disgrace herself.

'Very wise,' said Gerald. 'It's rubbish. Will you keep my seat for a moment?'

He returned with a cellophane-wrapped box of chocolates, which he dropped in her lap. 'I hope you like these.'

'Oh . . . yes, thank you. Very much . . .'

What should she do, open them and offer him one? Share them? Take them home unopened? What did one do? The situation was new to her and she had no idea what was expected. She picked up the box and turned it about to read the label. It contained burnt almonds in bitter chocolate, the expensive kind that her father bought for her mother. 'They look lovely,' she breathed, uncertain what to do next.

'Let me open them for you,' said Gerald. 'I don't know why they seal them up like Fort Knox.' He stripped off the cellophane, opened the box and popped one into his mouth. 'There you are, all yours. I don't eat sweets as a rule.'

Sally's heart swelled with love and gratitude. Not for the chocolates, or even for the afternoon's outing, but for something to which she could put no name, never having met it before.

CHAPTER SIX

When they reached home, Aimée greeted them.

'Well, Sally, I hope you've thanked Gerald for taking you out?'

Sally blushed furiously, recognizing an omission that had nevertheless seemed entirely natural. She stammered something and Gerald cut her short.

'Thank *you*, Sally.' He turned his charming smile on her mother. 'I think you have it the wrong way around, Aimée. By the way, you don't mind if I use your Christian name, I really can't call you Aunt, can I?'

To Sally's surprise, her mother looked pleased and her powdered cheeks glowed pink. 'Of course not, Gerald, you're most welcome to. Of course, one forgets,' she added coquettishly, 'that you and Erik aren't so far apart in age.' Her look congealed as she turned it on Sally. 'You remember that,' she warned.

As soon as she could, Sally escaped upstairs. She wanted to be alone, to fix in her mind every detail of this wonderful afternoon, to be able to take it out and cherish it like jewellery in the drab times ahead. She would ask Daddy if she could have a record of the *Mary Poppins* music for her birthday, so that she could play it and close her eyes and live it all again. She knew that nothing in her life to come would ever equal this.

She spent the rest of the weekend an inch above the ground, and when Monday morning brought the time for departure she was gripped by an exquisite sorrow, a pain only tempered by the knowledge that as Aunt Geraldine was her mother's friend it was likely that some day, somewhere, she would see Gerald again. She reflected that perhaps she would be invited to his wedding, condemned to watch like the little mermaid while he married someone else. She could endure it, she told herself, as long as he was happy. In her reading, she had stumbled upon the legend of a boy and girl in love upon an island; the girl, informed by an interfering deity that the best thing she could do for him was to part from him for ever, made the sacrifice and spent her life in noble solitude. Sally could see herself standing on the shore, one arm uplifted in silent farewell, while Gerald sailed away from her across the moonlit sea . . .

She harboured no resentment of the situation, although she began to see the sadness of never being able to marry. It must be beautiful, she thought, to sleep all night in the arms of the beloved, to wake each morning to the sight of your favourite face . . . at this point she shook herself. Even if she hadn't had to make what she now thought of as her grim resolve, she knew perfectly well that Gerald could never be for her.

She watched as the car drew away, then took her customary refuge in the bathroom. Drying her eyes on the towel, she noticed a tiny bloodstain. Someone, either Daddy or Gerald, had cut himself shaving. She thought back. It was Gerald, she was sure she had seen the mark on his neck as he climbed into the car! Swiftly, she bolted the door and opened the bathroom cabinet. Taking a razor blade, she carefully cut the bloodstained nap from the towel and, carrying her trophy concealed in her hand, went down to the kitchen in search of an empty matchbox. She felt immensely heartened by her find; she had after all a little bit of Gerald that no one could take from her.

Not trusting her relic out of her sight, she took it to school with her. Ruth, who had followed her from the other school, saw the matchbox in a corner of her satchel.

'Smoking?' she inquired.

'Certainly not!' Sally was indignant. Aimée smoked incessantly, her ash falling everywhere, even into the food, and Sally hated it.

'What is it, then?'

'It's private.'

'Oh, yes?' Ruth's hand darted out and snatched the precious box.

'Give it back!' cried Sally in an agony of apprehension. 'You're not to look, it's private—'

'There's nothing in it,' Ruth said scornfully, opening it and tipping it upside down.

'There is, there was—' she scrabbled frantically in the grass and found it at last, a few fragile threads already turning brown. 'Oh, thank God.'

Ruth bent closer. 'What do you want that for, it's just a bit of old cotton?'

'It's not, it's . . . special.'

'Don't see how that can be special.'

'Well, it is. It's part of – of someone,' she admitted, her heart swelling painfully. She glanced at Ruth. She was smiling, but in a friendly way, as she never had before. 'Promise you won't tell?'

'Yes, promise! Cross my heart and hope to die,' said Ruth. She thrust an arm through Sally's and steered her towards the shrubbery. 'Come on, tell all. You're in love, aren't you?'

Hearing it put into words brought the tears welling up. She swallowed hard, blew her nose, and stumblingly told Ruth about the weekend.

'Is that all?' said Ruth when she had finished. 'He didn't kiss you or anything?'

'Of course not!' she retorted angrily. 'That would have been thinking of me as a child, and he doesn't. That's what makes him so special.'

'How do you know he doesn't?' challenged Ruth.

Sally hesitated. How could she explain what she had felt to be shown in so many subtle ways . . . as for instance when they had emerged from the cinema into a dazzle of sunlight, and, about to cross the road, she had felt Gerald's hand, light yet protective, barely touching her elbow. The caring thought of a man for a woman, quite unlike her

115

mother's masterful grasp. 'Well, we had to cross a road,' she began.

'And?'

Ruth was not going to be convinced. It wouldn't sound romantic to her, not enough like Sir Galahad. But she'd started, she had to say something. Wildly, she boasted.

'He picked me up in his arms and half carried me across!'

'Oh, well,' jeered Ruth with an unkind laugh. 'That just proves he thinks of you as a child!'

She had avenged herself for having been called a liar.

Partly because of her preoccupation with Gerald, partly due to her deliberate withdrawal from the emotional torments of her family, Sally was the last to recognize that her parents had reached breaking point.

It was true that she and Erik, in a guilty exchange of confidences, had agreed that life was more peaceful when Mummy was not around to nag them; but that was merely a putting into words of what had always been tacit between them. She failed to attach to it any special significance, since in her restricted experience of family life hostility was the norm.

So when her mother went off to stay with Uncle Charles in distant London, she thought little of it. The whole household seemed to relax, and Sally and her father breathed a different atmosphere.

On his half day the two of them went out together, and on Sunday spent the entire day in the garage while he wrestled with the circuits of a radio he was building. How lovely it would be, she thought guiltily, if Mummy decided not to come back . . .

At the end of a month she came down to breakfast to find Erik with a letter in his hand, a dark cloud troubling his eyes.

'Sit down, darling,' he said soberly. 'I have to talk to you.'

Sally pulled out a chair, perched uneasily on the edge of it. A heavy weight had suddenly formed inside her.

'This is a letter from Mummy. She's coming home on Sunday.' He looked at her, as if expecting some response. When none came, he went on. 'I have to tell you that I won't be here.'

'Oh . . . I see,' said Sally, although she didn't see at all. What was he saying, that he wanted her to do something in his absence, explain to Mummy why he wasn't there to meet her? 'When will you be back?'

He seemed to hesitate. Compressed his lips, lowered his eyes. Looked more miserable than ever. 'I won't be back,' he said at last. As Sally's eyes flew up to his in panic, 'Never. I'm sorry, Sally. I don't expect you to understand and there's no way I can explain. But I'll be in the town and we'll still see each other. Just remember I love you as much as ever.'

Sally was silent for a moment, stunned by the total reversal of her hopes. It was a punishment from God, she thought, for her wickedness in wishing her mother away. Now, she would be alone with her for ever . . . Daddy seemed to be waiting for her to speak.

'I see . . .' she said again.

'No, you don't,' he said. 'I can't expect you to.'

But she did. After all, she thought longingly, if she were Daddy, wouldn't she go too? 'I do understand,' she said. She searched her mind for the right words. 'I think it's – regrettable, but inevitable. Isn't that what you mean?'

Erik looked up, and his troubled eyes lightened. 'Yes,' he said slowly. 'I do believe you do.' He stood up and came around the table to where she was sitting, took her hands and drew her into his arms. 'I'm only sorry I can't take you with me,' he said. 'Take care of Mummy for me, won't you? She's going to need you.'

A hard pain formed in Sally's chest. She wanted to cry out, 'Why, why can't you take me with you?' but she loved him too much to say it. If he didn't want her it meant he would be better off without her, and a pale shadow of the girl on the shore fell across her mind. At least one of them was going to be happy; it was better than nothing.

'I'll try,' she promised him. 'I'll do my best. Only it's not very easy . . .' her voice broke, and he hugged her tighter.

'I know,' he soothed. 'I know, I know . . .'

They stood still for a long time, saying nothing, until he noticed the time and had to leave for work. It was the very last time they were together under one roof.

True to her word, Aimée returned on Sunday. She arrived in a taxi with Uncle Charles, who came forward to greet Sally with a bristly kiss.

'Well, how's Sally?'

'Fine, thank you.' She returned his kiss with a smile, although she had been tying her stomach in knots at the thought of her mother's return. She was thankful that her uncle had come, not only as a means of diluting the tension but also because she was fond of him. He reminded her of Grandma with his brisk cheerful manner, his bag of iced caramels never far from his hand.

Aimée pushed past him into the empty drawing room. 'Where's Daddy?' she demanded.

Sally looked uneasily from her to Uncle Charles. Hadn't Daddy told her . . . surely he must have done . . . 'I don't know, Mummy.'

'What do you mean, you don't know?' Aimée's voice was sharpened by something other than her customary irritability, something that Sally recognized, surprisingly, as fear.

She glanced for reassurance at Uncle Charles before she said carefully, 'He went on Friday. I – I think there's a letter for you. It came this morning.' She pointed to where the envelope in Erik's handwriting rested against the clock.

It was Uncle Charles who went to pick it up. He turned to Sally.

'I'm sure you can find something to do in your room for a little while, ducky.' He winked, his back to Aimée. 'Your Mummy and I have got things to talk about.'

She withdrew, grateful to be relieved of the emotional

storm to come. Halfway up the stairs she heard the first wave break, and hurried on to the seclusion of her bedroom.

Much later Uncle Charles came up and tapped on her door. She looked up eagerly, glad to be released from the tedium of trying to read when she could not concentrate.

'I've come up to say goodbye,' he said. 'Got to get to the station or I shall miss my train.'

'Oh,' she said, disappointed. 'I thought you were going to stay.'

'Sorry, pet. Got to be in the office tomorrow morning. Maybe next time.' He leaned over to drop a kiss on the top of her head. 'I should go down and see Mummy now. I think she's a bit upset.'

Sally nodded, and put away the books. She saw Uncle Charles off at the front door and went reluctantly into the drawing room. Aimée was mopping her tear-stained face in a haze of tobacco smoke, and the room reeked of sherry. As Sally came in she opened her arms in a theatrical gesture. 'Come,' she said.

Sally went, trying to hide her disinclination as she was engulfed in the unfamiliar embrace. She noticed, against her will, that her mother's body overflowed her corsets, and smelled as though she had not washed enough. She was not sure what response was expected of her, but she remembered her promise to Daddy and pushed her arms around her as far as they would reach.

'We must stick together, you and I,' said her mother's voice in her ear. 'You're all I've got left in the world.'

It sounded like a line from a play, thought Sally, and then disliked herself for the unkindness. But the whole situation was beginning to feel unreal. Balanced uneasily across Aimée's armchair, she tried to think of something suitable to say. All she could think of was, 'Daddy wants me to look after you.'

Suddenly everything clicked back to normal. Aimée held her off, to peer into her face with eyes like gimlets.

'So, you knew what he was going to do!' As Sally stared,

she went on, 'I might have known, you had it all worked out between you! He's been poisoning your mind against me for months—'

Promise or no promise, Sally could take no more. She wrenched herself from her mother's grasp and made for her room and the release of tears.

At school, she was sent for by the headmistress.

'So you're leaving at the end of term; we shall be sorry to lose you.'

Sally blinked. 'I didn't know,' she said. 'Are you sure it's me?'

Mrs Taylor's smile said quite clearly that she did not make mistakes. 'You're moving to London, aren't you? I did suggest to your mother that you might board, but apparently she wants you at home. You must, of course, consider her wishes, but I do hope you won't abandon your studies altogether. You have potential, Sally, it would be a pity to waste it. Please give it some thought.'

Sally gave it quite a lot of thought. It was the first time anyone had suggested to her that she had 'potential', although for what had not been made clear. Perhaps, after all, Mrs Taylor had confused her with someone else.

She asked Aimée if she was really leaving school, and if they were moving to London.

'We may go and live with Uncle Charles, I haven't made up my mind. But you're certainly leaving school. How do you think I can afford those fees, now that Daddy's left us?'

'I don't know,' said Sally, somewhat dashed. She hadn't realized that money was involved, either in schooling or in family arrangements, and it did little to lift her depression. Perhaps she could ask Daddy about it, but no arrangements had as yet been made for them to meet. 'I expect I can study at home,' she said.

'If you get a good grounding, you can pick up the rest,' said Aimée with confidence. 'And anyway, when we go to London you'll be going to stage school, there's no point in you wasting your time here.'

Sally was somewhat cheered by this prospect. It sounded exciting, and somehow more grown-up than ordinary school, subtly narrowing the gap between her and Gerald. As casually as she could manage, she said, 'Are we going to see Aunt Geraldine again soon? I thought she was nice.'

'We can't go all that way without the car. Your father took it with him.'

'But they could come here . . .' She realized that she should have said 'she' rather than 'they', but it was too late now.

'We can't invite them,' said Aimée self-righteously. 'Not without your father in the house.'

'Why on earth not?'

'Most certainly not! Aunt Geraldine has a very eligible son, it would look as though I were out to catch him for my daughter.'

She opened her mouth to protest, it was ridiculous – like something out of Jane Austen! Then she caught her mother's gloating eye, and saw what she was up to. She must know about Gerald, she had somehow guessed. And she was trying to use it to make her hate her father . . .

'It was just a thought,' she said artfully. 'I expect you've got other friends.'

She had the satisfaction of seeing Aimée look deflated.

She was taken away from school, just as the rest of the form was preparing for examinations, and they did indeed move house – but not to London. Instead they went into the basement of a damp Victorian house, a 'garden flat' which had no bathroom and an evil-smelling kitchen converted from a cupboard under a blocked-off staircase.

'I must have a garden,' declared Aimée. 'I can't live without my flowers.'

Sally found herself compelled to share her mother's bed, on the grounds that Aimée could not endure to sleep next to an empty space. 'And besides,' she added. 'I'm not wasting money sending two lots of sheets to the laundry.' She looked at the clock. 'The off-licence will be open, you can go round there and take Boo-boo, he hasn't had a walk since yesterday. I'll want—'

'I know,' cut in Sally. 'A half bottle of Johnny Walker and a bottle of sweet sherry.'

Aimée gave her a piercing look. 'Don't be pert with me, my girl.'

'I'm not,' protested Sally. 'It's just that you don't need to remind me, it's the same every time. What about the cigarettes?'

Aimée checked the packet. 'No, I've got enough for the moment, you can get those later on. I shall have some letters for you to post this evening.'

Sally stifled a sigh as she clipped the lead to Boo-boo's collar. At the door, she paused. 'Mummy . . . when am I going to see Daddy?'

'When he agrees to the arrangements.'

'But, Mummy—'

'Once and for all, you are not going to visit him in that house! It's no fit place for a young girl.'

'But you won't let him come here—'

'It would upset me to see him. It's typical of your selfishness that you should expect me to.'

'But you wouldn't have to see him, you could go out.'

'And walk the streets knowing you two were here together, how do you think I'd feel? You're just like your father, no thought for anyone but yourself.'

'Oh, Mummy . . .' Put like that, it made her feel ashamed. Despair assailed her, making her eyelids prickle. Beside her, Boo-boo whined at the closed door. He too was a prisoner; she leaned down and patted him. 'All right, boy, in a minute. Mummy, I'm sorry, but I do want to see Daddy. I know you don't like him, but—'

'How dare you! How dare you say that!' Aimée's face was crimsoned and distorted, but no tears appeared. 'He's my husband, my one great love, you know nothing – nothing!'

Surely that was what she'd said about Uncle Patrick? She viewed her mother dispassionately, the body gross

122

with self-indulgence, the hair unwashed between dyeings by the hairdresser, the fingers stained with nicotine. It was rage, not grief, that made her scream and bang her fists upon the table. I hate her, she reflected coldly. Almost as much as she hates me.

She went out quietly, closing the door behind her.

CHAPTER SEVEN

In the event, they were reduced to meeting in the park. If it rained they sat in Erik's car, chatting companionably or trying to pick out tunes on Sally's accordion, which neither of them had ever learned to play. The meetings always took place on Sunday mornings, because Sally was not allowed out after dark except on errands for Aimée, and Erik had to work on Saturdays. Always she returned home to a barrage of questions.

'Did he mention me? What did he say about me? How did he look when he said it? Sad, wistful, or what? Well, he must have said something, try to remember. He'll be back, you know. It's only a matter of time, everyone says so . . .'

In fact, they never discussed her. It was as though, freed at last to think their own thoughts, they were mutually reluctant to bring her to mind at all. Sally thought she had never seen her father looking so young, so full of life, and was reminded of her mother's coy allusion to his age and Gerald's. The only time she saw him look angry was when she told him that she had left school.

'Why?' he demanded, his grey eyes sparking like steel.

'Well, I think . . .' She faltered, not wanting to foster bad feeling between them. Whatever she felt, she could not forget the dictum of the bark and the tree. 'Mummy said the fees were too high. And I was supposed to be going to stage school, only we didn't go to London after all.'

He looked away, his face unreadable, and an uneasy silence fell. When he turned back to her, he was smiling again. 'Not your fault, don't worry about it.' He patted her knee. 'Have you got Uncle Charles's address? I'd like to send him a Christmas card.'

When Uncle Charles came down from London she had spent endless months at home, doing nothing more exciting than running her mother's errands or walking her dog, which obligation had fallen on her now that Erik was no longer there. She was already nudging the ranks of large grubby girls with hormonal problems and recalcitrant bowels that left appalling odours in the lavatory. Aimée, following behind her with air freshener, was loud in lamentation.

'A young girl should be the freshest, the most dainty thing in the world. Just look at you, pasty skin, hairy armpits, knees like a footballer's − I'll never know why you had to turn out like your father instead of me! Little Dotty's more my child than you could ever be.'

Sally compressed her lips and retreated into sullenness. It was true that she took no interest in her appearance, there seemed to be no point. Aimée chose her clothes, Aimée dictated her hairstyle − just as Aimée had named her dolls when she was small. And she was sick and tired of hearing about Dotty, who slyly tormented her sister Louise, and ran in winsome tears to their mother when Louise hit her back. If you were pretty like Dotty you had it made; if you weren't it was all uphill.

She thought sadly of Gerald with his raven hair, his eyes that changed like the sea . . . she hoped he wouldn't marry someone like Dotty. She went slowly upstairs, took the matchbox from its hiding place and sat for a long time holding it in her hand, thinking of the drop of blood she had stolen long ago, knowing even then that it was all she would ever have.

When her uncle came, he took them both to a theatre. The next day he took Sally out and bought her a new dress, and a pair of shoes to replace the old ones of Aimée's that she was wearing.

'Amy giving you a hard time, is she?'

'Well . . . her nerves aren't getting any better.'

'She's bound to be upset for a while,' agreed Uncle Charles. 'And what about you?'

'Me?' Sally was surprised. It was the first time anyone had asked her that. 'Oh, I'm all right. After all, she's lost her husband. I've only lost my father.' It sprang from irony, from the bitterness growing inside her, from the sense that of the two, her loss was the keener, the less replaceable. Uncle Charles didn't seem to notice, so she added casually, 'Why do you always call her Amy?'

'Because it's her name. You didn't think she was born Aimée St Claire, did you? That's a stage name, your mother was a Simpson like me. I wonder you didn't realize.'

'I never thought about it. But she was in the West End?'

'We-ell . . . in a way, I suppose. She never got further than the second row of the chorus. Most of them don't, you know, it's a very chancy profession. Don't tell Mummy I told you, don't want her to think we talk about her behind her back. But you want to forget about stage school, Sally, go in for something sensible like Dotty and Louise.'

She wondered if Uncle Charles realized how things were between her and her mother, or that he had offered her a weapon with which to strike back. She weighed it for a moment, before laying it aside. It was too heavy, too cruel: the sort of thing Aimée herself would use without compunction. But the last thing Sally wanted was to be like her.

She said thoughtfully. 'Why do you suppose she married Daddy?'

'What a funny question. Because she liked him, I suppose.'

'But she doesn't. She says she loves him but she never says one nice thing about him, ever.'

Uncle Charles chuckled, and patted her shoulder. 'You've got a lot to learn if you think that. Sometimes people take a bit of understanding, specially when they've had it hard as kids. Our home was always breaking down and being patched up again – our father drank, you see, only it's not a thing you talk about. I can remember him waking us up

126

in the night, waving a carving knife and shouting, "Your mother's leaving us, you'll never see her again!" Then the next day he'd gone off and we didn't see him for months. By that time we'd had the bailiffs in and lost all the furniture. It wasn't so bad for me, being a boy, and I was the eldest, anyway. But Amy, she was only little . . . and that sort of thing can be frightening when you're very young. Makes you clutch at people later in life, get them in a stranglehold. And that only makes them want to run away – well, it's understandable. But your Daddy's done it, so you don't want to do it too. Not just yet, anyway . . . you think about it.'

'Yes, of course . . .' She said it automatically. Thinking, if only what one ought to do weren't so far from what one wanted . . .

She thought about it long and hard, trying to imagine Mummy and Uncle Charles as children, startled from sleep and terrified. It must have been awful, like the day she woke up in the Convent. But she still didn't see why it should make you spiteful.

That evening she heard raised voices in the adjoining room.

'You're wasting that girl's intelligence, keeping her at home doing nothing. She should at least be training for something.'

'I'm not wasting good money on educating a girl, she'll only get married and throw it all away. Look what happened to me.'

'At least you had your chance. She's doing nothing – anyway, how's she going to meet anybody stuck at home with you?'

Sally burrowed down under the bedclothes, unwilling to hear any more.

When Uncle Charles had departed for London, her mother announced abruptly.

'Right, my girl! It's high time you started doing something to earn your keep. Go round to the shops and get a local paper.'

When she came back with it, they went down the Situations Vacant column, marking the jobs that Aimée thought were within her capacity. None of them looked very inviting, but the prospect of getting out of the house for several hours every day, escaping her mother's relentless supervision, was pleasing to the point of excitement. She might even, if she could overcome her shyness that crippled her, find friends of her own age.

Not for the first time, it seemed that Aimée had read her thoughts. She folded the paper and surveyed her sternly.

'Now, before you go out into the world, there are things you'll have to know. I'll tell you now, so that you can protect yourself, and then you needn't dwell on them any further.'

It was with some foreboding that Sally sat down to listen; even so, she recoiled in shock. It was as if some floodgate had opened in her mother's mind, as if she had been waiting all these years to pour it all out to her, the clinical facts of sex in the crudest possible terms, festered out of darkness into something unspeakable. Nothing was spared her, from drugged cigarettes through white slavery to homosexual bordellos, with every perversion and embellishment, every lurid detail either known or imagined lingered over with appalling relish.

When the recital was finished, Sally could find nothing to say, could only stare, stunned, into the fire.

'Well, now you know,' said Aimée with awful satisfaction. 'Now you won't be tempted. You'll be able to look after yourself. Make certain you're never alone with a man, a standing cock has no conscience.' She topped up her sherry glass and reached for a cigarette. 'Oh, and don't walk near bushes, you never know who might be hiding there.'

Sally drew a deep sigh. She was beginning to suspect that her mother was prone to exaggeration, but even so . . . How did one reconcile all this with the pictures of smiling brides in their satin and tulle? With the romantic 'stills' outside cinemas, with the magazine pictures of girls in love, their lips poised for delicious consummation . . . It must be that the sweetness and the loving stopped at the altar, that the

128

nastiness only set in after that. Was that why one had to be protected from the knowledge, so that people wouldn't stop getting married? Did the men she knew do such things, people like her father – even, God forbid, Gerald? She pushed the thought away, unwilling to soil her memories.

'You said "tempted",' she said at last, plucking at a crumb. 'Why would I be tempted, if there's nothing nice about it?'

'It's not a question of being nice, it's your duty to the man you marry. You get used to it, it's only the first time that it hurts and makes you bleed. You do it for his pleasure, not for yours. And after the ceremony, not before! That's where you might get tempted, men make promises they've no intention of keeping.'

'Is that what happened to Ethel?' she asked, recognizing belatedly the pregnancy disguised as appendicitis.

Aimée bridled. 'The less said about Ethel the better! A bath in the master's water, indeed – she must have thought I was born yesterday! If you give in beforehand like she did you'll end up the same way. No man has any respect for that sort of girl.'

Sally was not at all sure she wanted the respect of anyone who would do such things to her.

'You make it sound perfectly awful,' she said resentfully. 'What with that and having babies, I'm never going to want to get married.'

'Nonsense!' snapped Aimée. 'Of course you'll get married, it's the normal thing for a girl. And for you with your father's bad blood, the sooner the better if you ask me.'

'Well, you'll be pleased to know you've completely put me off!'

Her mother laughed, a sound of mingled triumph and derision. 'You should have more strength of character, that's all I can say. Here, have a chocolate and stop talking nonsense.' She rattled the box at Sally. 'Anyway, cheer up, there's always birth control.'

Sally picked out a chocolate almond. 'Birth control?' It

had slipped out before she could stop it, and she knew she was going to wish she hadn't asked.

Aimée's smile vanished. 'When a man has a very beautiful wife, if he really loves her . . . he won't let her be ruined. There are things he can do, things to save her from having babies.'

That was a crack at Daddy, she recognized; it also fostered her suspicion that Aimée hadn't wanted her. But it did put a slightly less alarming complexion on the distant possibility of marriage. Although of course, you had to be beautiful enough . . .

For a time they were both silent, busy with their own thoughts. Then Aimée went on inconsequentially, 'Never let a man know you care for him. He'll wipe his feet on you.'

Sally had wanted to refute that, because she knew who was meant.

'I don't think that's true of everybody,' she said.

'You're thinking of your father,' accused Aimée. 'It is true. You're only a child, you don't know what you're talking about.'

'Well, perhaps with husbands and wives,' she persisted unwisely. 'But not with . . . other people.'

'No?' An ugly light dawned in Aimée's eye. 'And when did you see him last?'

'You know when,' she retorted miserably, unable to deny that he was seeing her less and less often. At first it had been, 'I have to go away on business this weekend, honey. I'll give you a call next month.' And then it had been three months, and then five, until it became so rare that it hardly made a difference when he was transferred to another town. They still corresponded, albeit spasmodically. But she had not seen him for over a year.

'Exactly,' said Aimée. 'That shows you how much he cares.'

'He does, he does!' It was there, on all his infrequent letters: 'Ever your loving Daddy . . .'

'Well, I wasn't going to tell you this, but it's better you know the truth. I asked him once, "Erik, don't you even love Sally any more?'' And do you know what he said?'

'I don't want to know!'

'Well, I'm telling you. He thought very carefully, and then he said, ''Not as a father should love his daughter, no.'' '

Sally turned her face away from Aimée's gloating look, determined to hide her pain. It was the last time Aimée was able to make her cry. But the solace of remembering Erik now had so sharp an edge that it hurt her to embrace it.

Gerald too, she pushed to the back of her mind. Although she sometimes saw letters for Aimée addressed in Aunt Geraldine's handwriting, she was never made privy to their contents. She might perhaps have asked, with careful casualness, how they fared; but she did not. She would rather not be told when Gerald got married.

By the time she was seventeen, she had obtained – and lost – three jobs, none of which could by any stretch of the imagination be described as a career.

She had started out by answering advertisements for secretaries, since Aimée considered office work to be suitably genteel. But the interviews always seemed to go the same way.

'No "A" levels, I suppose?'

'I'm afraid not.'

'Well, never mind. How many "O"s?'

'None.'

The professional smiles tended to fade. 'Secretarial training? Experience, then?'

'I could learn . . .'

'Not in our time, dear.'

Sometimes they said it, more often they didn't need to. The result was always the same, and for the first time she saw why Erik had been angered by her leaving school. After a disheartening list of failures she lowered her sights to the more realistic target of unskilled work.

The first success was a disaster. She was engaged, by a harassed works foreman, to pack and label pills in a factory

131

making small animal medicines; he looked her over without enthusiasm and said, 'Oh well, the girls will lick you into shape.'

When her shyness and her private school voice had earned her the epithet of 'toffee-nosed', she became the department's punchbag and was eventually invited to leave on the grounds that she did not 'fit in'.

The next two were little better, although they failed for different reasons. Standing behind a counter selling sweets and cigarettes left her with so little pay, after losing three-quarters of it to Aimée, that she was driven to take an evening job as a part-time usherette. It was tiring after a long day on her feet, and the weight of the ice cream trays made her back ache, but it was more congenial than the factory and the cinema manager was charming. His charm, however, curdled as he noticed her edging away from him; then Aimée took to meeting her to make sure she came straight home, and from then on it was all downhill. The atmosphere deteriorated rapidly to the point where she was called into his office and dismissed as 'unsuitable'. This rejection she accepted without surprise, as she had hardly expected to be rated any higher, but although the sweet shop was next door to the cinema she had failed to realize that it was under the same management, and was crestfallen to find herself unwanted there as well.

After that, her luck turned. She was engaged as receptionist in a hairdressing salon, and found for the first time a niche where her voice and manner did not militate against her. The girls who worked there encouraged her to bring her appearance up to date, swept away her outmoded hairstyle by using her as a model, and taught her that by the subtle application of make-up she could even create an illusion of beauty, given the right day. They might also have fixed her up with dates, had she not been too nervous of men. She did not, of course, admit to this, but made Aimée her excuse.

'My mother doesn't like to be left alone in the evening,' she explained, her fingers crossed behind her back.

It was, however, closer to the truth than she realized, as

she discovered when she wanted to go to a dance with one of the juniors.

'You don't know what goes on in those places, I'm not having you go off after dark unless I know who you're with.'

'But you do know who I'm with, it's another girl.'

'It's not anyone I know or approve of. You're not going, and there's an end to it.'

She was secretly a little apprehensive herself about going for the first time with a girl who made it clear that she was going to pick up boys. So it was not the disappointment that it might have been; but she saw with a shiver where her life was heading.

She tried conscientiously to keep her promise to Erik, telling herself that by taking his place she was freeing him for better things; rather like the women in the war, she thought with amusement, though she hoped her father wasn't still finding life a battle.

Her own struggle was still with her feelings towards Aimée, and not only for Erik's sake, but for her own. She had seen what the venom of hatred did to those who harboured it; one glimpse into her mother's mind had shown her a sick personality. But despite her best efforts, contempt predominated in what she felt for her; and since pity lies uncomfortably close to contempt, and is easier to give than affection, her attitude was largely based on that. It was less difficult to ignore a jibe if she could tell herself that to respond to it was beneath her, and Aimée, who thrived on pity, was slow to recognize that she was being patronized.

Sally herself was increasingly aware of the absurd, the comic element in everyday life. She was also aware that it was never apparent to Aimée; if it were, she would not be wasting her life in futile mourning for the past. She had steadfastly refused to divorce Erik, with the inevitable result that they were not on speaking terms. From time to time a letter would come.

'It's from your father. He's asking me for his freedom again. How do you think I should answer it?'

133

Sally had only once been rash enough to tell her. The storm had gone on for days.

'He's my husband, and he'll die my husband! If he thinks . . .'

Sally made a mental note that her mother could not take the truth, and prepared a list of non-answers in readiness for the next occasion. Life was like that, she reflected, and was getting more like it every day.

She was not, however, prepared for it to go on like it indefinitely. Even Aimée could not reasonably expect immortality, but she was likely to be around for some time. And while it seemed too much to hope that they would ever relish each other's company, it was surely not impossible to live together in peace.

Looking for early snowdrops while Aimée lamented the ravages of winter on her tiny garden, her eye had been caught by a patch of purple glowing through the ice. Kneeling in the snow she had found a rosette of primulas, stemless, leafless, their opening buds pressed tight against the earth, and had marvelled at the tenacity that sustained them. Crushed and stunted, they had doggedly kept on growing, to emerge already in bloom as if winter had never been. Frozen, discouraged, forgotten . . . they had flowered just the same.

She stood for a long time in the fall of rain, only half aware of the faint lisp of the melting snow about her. She too had a life to live. If winter was hard you could fade and succumb, or you could dig in your heels like the primulas. If you couldn't have what you hoped for, you adapted to what you had.

She was not going to be done out of being happy. She could surely find something worth living for if she put her mind to it.

She had no more wish for marriage than she'd ever had. She had only ever wanted Gerald anyway. But she had enjoyed study, and there was something in the air called an Open University, for which no previous qualifications were demanded.

So: if she couldn't be pretty or lovable, to hell with it!
She would try something else – maybe investigate that
potential her headmistress had charged her so earnestly
not to waste.

Setting out to post her inquiry to the BBC, she opened
the front door on to a fountain of pink carnations.

'I'm joining a firm of solicitors in the town,' said Gerald.
'I hope you don't mind, I thought I'd look you up.'

Part III

The Girl on the Shore

Marriage and love are separate subjects.
— *Guy de Maupassant*

CHAPTER ONE

'Ah, here it is.' Aimée was rummaging in her jewel case. 'Here you are, try it on. You can wear it till you get one of your own.' She held it out, a gold ring with a sparkle of tiny diamonds.

Sally took it hesitantly, perplexed by this unexpected generosity. 'It's lovely . . . but no, I'd be afraid of losing it.' She threaded it experimentally on her right hand.

'No, silly, the other hand. It's an engagement ring.'

'But I'm not engaged.'

'As good as, it's only a matter of the announcement. I saw Ruth's mother in the hairdressers, she said Ruth was getting engaged, so I told her you were too.'

'Oh, you didn't! You mustn't go round saying things like that, suppose it got back to Gerald—' Quickly she removed the ring and handed it back. 'I'm not engaged or likely to be, he hasn't even asked me.'

'Well, he will, it's an understood thing. So you'd better have your answer ready.'

'I'll have it ready if and when he asks me, not before,' she answered with unwonted sharpness. If this did get back to Gerald, she wanted him at least to know it wasn't her idea. For good measure, she added, 'I don't consider myself bound to Gerald in any way, any more than he is to me. Anyway, I don't want to get married yet. Not to anyone.'

That was true enough. She did not want harsh reality crashing in on her wave of euphoria.

It had been the realization of a dream when Gerald had arrived on their doorstep, seeking not Aimée but herself. When a few days later a junior looked out and said, 'There's a gorgeous man outside on the pavement, looks like he's waiting for someone,' she had glanced up and found it hard to believe her eyes.

'Oh . . . I think he's waiting for me.'

A chorus of good-humoured teasing had followed her as she went out, pink with pride. Since then, she had been carried from day to day on airs above the ground, sustained by the secret fancy that Gerald, unbelievably, was floating there beside her. It was all so delicate, so beautiful, that she wanted nothing changed.

'What do you mean, you don't want to get married!' Aimée's outraged voice cut across her thoughts. 'I suppose you want to be a good time girl, play around with half a dozen like your father? Well, let me tell you, my girl, if you think you're going to play fast and loose with the son of my oldest friend, you've got another think coming. I'll queer your pitch for you, you see if I don't!'

Sally fled, slamming the door behind her, her mother's voice still ringing in her ears.

It was a fortnight before she saw Gerald again, by which time she had convinced herself that Aimée had somehow carried out her threat. When he did at last appear, she could not meet his eyes, but ushered him towards the living room where Aimée sat picking over a box of petit fours. In the doorway he checked, put a finger under her chin, tilting her face to make her look at him.

'What's the matter?'

'Nothing.' She smiled brightly, hoping he would not see through it to her grief.

He leaned past her to close the door. 'There is something, what is it?'

'Oh . . . nothing really. I haven't been getting on so well with my mother. We have a little spat occasionally,' she added, and smiled again.

He drew her towards him. 'Don't forget, I know your father,' he said softly. She leaned against him, her head on his chest, listening to the soft, slow rocking of his heart, struggling to suppress the tears that threatened her.

'Come for a walk,' he said at last. 'I've something to say to you.'

They walked through the late spring evening to the park, and sat down on a bench under a cherry tree, its petals falling about them like pink snow. It was the same bench where long ago she had come on Sunday mornings to meet Erik. Gerald took her hands in his. She felt herself beginning to tremble. He smiled.

'Don't be frightened, it's nothing bad. At least, I hope you won't think so.' He paused for a moment, cleared his throat, as though he were about to make a speech. 'As you may have realized, in the past weeks I've become very fond of you. And I hope, in due course, to ask you to marry me.' He put an arm around her, cleared his throat again. 'And now, I should like to kiss you.'

He tilted her chin, bent his handsome head towards her. She closed her eyes, thinking, This is the moment, the first kiss that everyone dreams about . . . she could not remember ever being kissed on the mouth before. His lips felt incredibly soft, dry, cool . . . she felt her own wanting to part, to taste his mouth . . . but as she began involuntarily to press upward towards him, just as her hand moved to touch his hair, he drew away and sat back.

She was left bewildered, wondering what had gone wrong. They were meant to be on cloud nine, she was sure they were . . . but everything had fallen unaccountably flat. It must be something to do with her; there could be no flaw in Gerald. He was speaking again.

'I didn't come to see you last week because I had to write to my mother for her approval. I only got her answer today.'

She was taken aback. This was Jane Austen all over again. Surely nobody nowadays had to ask their parents' approval – surely not men, and not at Gerald's age? She asked thoughtfully, 'What did she say?'

'Oh, she was delighted, she thinks you're very sweet. I knew she would, of course.'

'That's nice,' said Sally, mindful that not many people

did. It was reassuring to know it had been merely a formality . . . hadn't it? 'But supposing,' she said carefully, 'just supposing she hadn't?'

The answer came as something of a shock.

'Well then, I suppose, we'd have to think again. But she does, so we don't have to worry.'

They strolled home through the dusk and broke the news to Aimée, who, when Gerald had gone, said, 'There, what did I tell you!' with every sign of satisfaction. Then she added darkly, 'That's one in the eye for your Uncle Charles.' But when Sally asked what she meant, she merely said meaningly, 'Never you mind.'

It was not until some hours later that it occurred to Sally, falling asleep at last on the outermost edge of the double bed, that nobody – not even Gerald – had asked her if she was pleased.

Not of course that she wasn't pleased – oh, of course she was! Gerald was clearly in no hurry for marriage, and meantime she saw him almost every day. He would come after supper most evenings, and spend the time chatting companionably with them both, discussing music and books with Sally and theatre with Aimée, who was on her best behaviour and out to impress him. She even agreed that Sally need no longer call her Mummy since Gerald was using her Christian name; it would be rather nice to have Sally call her Aimée. 'Like sisters,' she explained, fluttering her thickly painted eyelashes at Gerald.

Her new amenability did not, however, extend to allowing them out together after dark. 'I can't bear to be left alone in the evenings, Gerald. After all I've been through, it's such a sad time of day. And Sally's very young to be out at night with you alone.'

Not too young to be sent to the pub when the off-licence is closed, thought Sally with some resentment. Since Booboo the dog had gone to the happy hunting ground she had been the target of catcalls and worse. But she said nothing, not wanting to complain in front of Gerald.

He said with charming politeness, 'Of course, we understand. Don't we, darling?'

'Of course,' echoed Sally automatically, the disappointment assuaged to some degree by his having called her darling. But since he went home every weekend to see his mother, it meant that they hardly ever saw each other alone.

Of course, of course . . . she found herself saying it more and more often, without even thinking what she said. Rigorously trained not to argue, not to answer back, not to complain, she heard herself complying without question with whatever was suggested.

She reminded herself that she had nothing to complain about. In fact, she had what she had always wanted and never dared to hope for. It was just that it was no longer quite the same . . . yes, that was it. It was no longer her own private dream, a special thing to be hidden and cherished in secret, but somehow thrown open to the public and made official. As though, she thought, you were to take a chrysalis and break it open before its time. The butterfly inside would still be there, but some of its bloom would be lost.

As the weeks went by, she found herself pushed further and further to the edge of the group, as Aimée, with a vivacity that astonished her, began to take over.

At first it was her old theatre programmes, then her souvenirs, then her ponderous albums of photographs of herself in costume for the various shows she had been in. 'Starred in,' she said, and Sally, afraid of appearing mean-spirited to Gerald, held her peace.

Gerald was encouraged to arrive earlier, and special meals were set before him. 'It's so lovely to have you in the family,' purred Aimée, whipping up delicacies she had formerly maintained they could not afford. 'As the man of the house, would you like to carve? Sally, darling, pop and get the wine out of the fridge.'

Sally, startled to hear herself addressed as 'darling', glanced at her sharply, and was rewarded with an enigmatic look. Surely, she reasoned with herself, surely she must be wrong. Aimée was, after all, her own mother; even she would not stoop to such a thing. But when she found the conversation deftly turned to Madame de Pompadour, and from her to an elderly French courtesan who had found her newest young lover to be her own grandson, she became a prey to doubts she could confide to no one.

On the pretext of having his photograph taken for Sally, Aimée made an appointment for Gerald at a fashionable studio. But when the pictures arrived she kept the large framed portrait for herself, and gave Sally a small print in a pocket folder.

'Oh dear,' smiled Gerald, 'how embarrassing. Well, I suppose, as she's paying for them . . . never mind, darling, you've got the original.'

'Yes,' replied Sally, trying to return his smile. She didn't know what else to say.

It all came to a head with her eighteenth birthday. Gerald, to her delight and relief, insisted on taking her out for the evening. He had tickets for a show, and had booked a table at a restaurant.

'So you won't need to cook for us, Aimée,' he said. 'You can put your feet up and have an evening off.'

'Oh, lovely!' said Aimée, a gleam in her eye.

When he came to collect Sally, Aimée, her hair newly blonded and decked in her best jewellery, was ready too.

'Of course I'm invited,' she replied to Sally's protest. 'Gerald wouldn't leave me out, don't be so silly.'

'But you don't understand—'

At that moment the doorbell rang. Sally ran to answer it. 'Oh Gerald, I'm so sorry . . .'

'What's the matter, darling, aren't you ready?'

'Oh yes, quite ready, but—'

'Well, that's all right then. Cheerio, Aimée, don't wait up for us.' And he drew Sally out through the door and closed it behind them.

In the car, he said, 'Don't worry about your mother, she'll get over it. This is our evening and nothing's allowed to spoil it.'

144

Over dinner, he took her hand across the table. 'I haven't given you your present yet.' He reached into his pocket and brought out a jeweller's box. 'I hope you didn't want diamonds, I always think they're rather cold.'

Sally opened the box with trembling fingers. Nestling in the velvet was a ring. It was beautiful; a cluster of sapphires on a silver-coloured band. But the significance of it made her stomach catch. She looked up at him with questioning eyes.

'Platinum,' he said. 'It won't turn your finger black. And you can choose the finger.' He smiled, then was serious again. 'But I hope you'll consider it. I had a letter from your father today. And now that you're eighteen, I think it's time we thought about getting married.'

'Of course . . .' She had said it, as she always did, her automatic response. But when she came to mull it over that night, lying awake with Aimée snoring beside her, she knew it was the right, the only thing to do. For one thing, if she didn't take Gerald now, she was in danger of losing him to, of all people, Aimée! There could no longer be any doubt that her mother had been out to win him; when they returned, she had already gone to bed, the door on the catch and the fire and lights extinguished. And when Sally came at last to join her, she was ostentatiously asleep.

She and Gerald had stayed talking for a while, side by side on the shabby sofa. Then Gerald had laid his arm along the back.

'May I kiss you?'

'Of course . . . do you really need to ask?' She did wish he hadn't. It would have been so lovely to be taken by surprise.

He kissed her. Softly, lightly, as he had before. She plucked up courage.

'Gerald?'

'Yes, dear?' He smiled indulgently.

'I've always thought . . .' She faltered, went on shyly. 'Would you like to kiss the back of my neck?'

'I'd love to.' His eyes were teasing, amused, as he bent towards her. She felt his lips brushing her skin, and a flame shot through her. His fingers fumbled with the zip at the back of her dress, sliding it down, down, his lips following . . . her eyes closed, her bones melted . . . she anticipated the journey to the small of her back . . . over her hipbone . . . oh Gerald, my darling . . . darling . . .

'Well, let's make you decent,' said Gerald primly, zipping up the two inches or so of his exploration. 'Don't get up, I'll see myself out.' He dropped a kiss on the top of her head and was gone.

She lay there for a time, her eyes closed, clinging against the back of the sofa as if it had been her lover. If this was the nice part of making love, it was worth whatever might follow. Nothing you wanted in life was free, and if you wanted it badly enough . . . she was going to marry him, come what may. She would escape from Aimée, live the rest of her life with lovely, wonderful Gerald . . .

The change from a harsh tyranny to a bland one may be seen as an escape to freedom; but a benign dictatorship is nevertheless a dictatorship. Sally, who in her eighteen years had never been allowed a decision of her own, made a smooth transition from one authority to the other.

When Gerald took her to see the flat he had chosen for them to live in, she said breathlessly, 'Oh, it's lovely!'

As indeed it was. Spacious and airy, on the top floor of a newly converted mansion, it commanded a view across the park and was in every way preferable to the one in which she lived with Aimée.

'There's only one thing,' he explained. 'No children or pets allowed. But I daresay we could smuggle in a kitten.' And he smiled conspiratorially.

To Sally, that was a blessing, and she squeezed his arm in bliss. She stood by deferentially as he chose the furnishings, proud of his taste which was so much better than hers, and when he arrived one evening in a smart new Morris Minor, her response to his 'How do you like my car?'

was a happy, 'Oh, it's wonderful! Will you take me for a ride?'

It was always to be his flat, his car, his 'little wife' . . . but if she saw it then, she accepted it as perfectly right and proper. She was disappointed though, when he announced that he did not want 'his' wedding in a church. She had daydreamed a white wedding, surrounded by friends and orange blossom, complete with full length dress and diaphanous veil. She had even thought of whom she would throw her bouquet . . .

It was best, said Gerald, to start as you meant to go on, not in the artificial atmosphere of a party.

'Quite right,' agreed Aimée. 'Besides, I told your father I'd consider a divorce when you grew up and got married, so I want it kept as quiet as possible.'

'You don't mean he's not to be told,' protested Sally. 'Who's going to give me away?' It was the wish of her heart to have Erik there, whatever the circumstances.

'I don't think you need any one in a Register Office. If you do, you can ask Uncle Charles.'

For the first time in her life, Sally defied her. Without telling anyone, even Gerald, she wrote to her father and asked him to be present. Two days before the wedding her letter was returned to her, the envelope marked 'Gone to USA'. Erik had gone home at last, and she could only wish him well.

They were married by Registrar, with only Aunt Geraldine and Uncle Charles as witnesses.

'I'll get you Daddy's address,' Uncle Charles managed to say to her under his breath. 'Then you can write and tell him. I know he'll be glad for you — as long as you're happy.' He seemed to hesitate. 'Ducky, is this really what you want?'

'Why of course . . .' What a funny question.

'You're quite sure?' he persisted, so that she smiled, and kissed him on his bristly moustache.

'Of course . . .' Her mind was already on other things.

147

Aimée, having punctuated the short ceremony with sighs and the artistic mopping of tears, waved them off in the little Morris. 'Bye bye, Gerald! Goodbye, Sally,' she embraced her extravagantly, and added ominously, 'Take care of yourself.'

That was among the other things on Sally's mind, and she could have done without being reminded. There were things a man could do, Aimée had told her; she hoped Gerald hadn't forgotten they were not supposed to have children. Sitting beside him in the car, moving inexorably towards a shared bed, she tried to recapture the moment on the sofa, and found it eluded her. If only he'd done it then, she thought, when I didn't have time to get nervous! We'll be able to go all the way, she told herself, desperately trying to ignite the spark. That was what the girls at work whispered in corners, giggling, their eyes still warm with remembered joy . . .

It was no use. By the time they arrived at the hotel, she was silent with tension.

All through the meal which she could barely eat, she worked on a formula, a ritual to see her through. As a child, about to have a tooth extracted under gas, she had repeated to herself, 'Wendy had a house in the treetops, Wendy had a house . . .' hoping to combat her fear with the promise of dreaming she was there. Now, she said to herself: I shall get into bed in my new nightgown, and start to read a book. And Gerald will smile, and take it gently out of my hand, and say, 'You don't really want that with me here, do you?' And he'll take me in his arms and kiss me all over and − she could not force her mind any further than that.

When they had finished their coffee, he said, 'Shall we go upstairs and unpack?'

'Yes, of course . . .' What was she saying, when all she wanted was to run away!

They unpacked, and then Gerald disappeared into the bathroom, to return wearing elegant silk pyjamas.

She looked at her watch. It was only half-past eight.

'It's hardly worth going down again,' he smiled. 'Let's read in bed.'

She stole a small postponement in indulging in a long, warm scented bath, a luxury denied her in Aimée's flat. The girls at work had dressed her hair, and would doubtless have lent her a bathroom had she not been too embarrassed to admit she didn't have one. But when she had tried to remedy the lack at the bedroom wash-stand this morning, Aimée had been vitriolic as rarely before.

'Just like some totty, getting herself ready for a customer!' she said witheringly.

Too late, it occurred to her that Gerald might think the same. She clambered out, dried herself and changed into her one new nightie, to emerge feeling exposed and vulnerable.

She could not look at Gerald. As she took up her book and slid carefully into the bed, he put out the light. She lay in the darkness, rigid with apprehension, trying to identify a soft, barely audible sound, lip, lip . . . lip, lip, lip . . . coming from the other side of the bed.

Then she heard his voice beside her.

'I should like to make you my wife now,' he said politely.

Which, with considerable fumbling and the minimum necessary force, he did.

CHAPTER TWO

And that, by and large, was how the marriage went. Gerald always asked, and Sally always complied, and after the first few times and a visit to the doctor, who lent her a textbook and told her that it was she and not Gerald who should be taking precautions, she no longer found it actually painful.

She was, however, a long way from finding it pleasurable. The book had confirmed her suspicion that she was supposed to enjoy it too, but she did not want that great piston banging about inside her, and the moment of penetration invariably snuffed out her little candle. She remembered Aimée saying, 'You do it for his pleasure, not for yours,' and that seemed to her not unfair. Her share of the bliss was in holding him close and seeing his eyes begin to shine, in knowing at such moments that she was filling his every thought. Once or twice she attempted to prolong the perfunctory foreplay, but soon realized that she was being selfish, because he was inclined to take it as a refusal and turn away to sleep, looking wounded. She loved him far too much to hurt his feelings, so she gave up trying and settled for what she had.

After all, what she had was better than anything she had known before. Gerald was consistently kind, never shouted or bullied her, and always kissed her good morning and good night. True, he expected her to keep the flat immaculate and to have his meals ready on the dot, and after Aimée's bohemian household there did seem to be rather a lot to learn.

'Darling, where's my towel?' called Gerald from the bathroom.

'Isn't there one there?' she called back, wrestling with the complexities of cooking eggs and bacon without setting fire to the toast.

'Only yours,' he replied, and Sally, who had never seen more than one towel in a bathroom in her life, added one more mental note to a fast-growing list. Geraldine, shocked by the state of her parental home since the departure of the maids, had undertaken her domestic training the first time she had come to spend the weekend with them, instead of their going to her.

'Windows are best cleaned on Fridays – the insides being wiped over every day – and silver on Saturdays.' She had presented them with all Gerald's sports trophies from his schooldays, as well as a handsome silver tea tray complete with teapot, cream and sugar vessels. 'Always start upstairs and work down. I know you've only a flat at the moment, but if everything is done on the right day you know that nothing has been missed. And it takes twenty minutes to iron a shirt correctly. I'll give you a little lesson before I leave, dearie, and next time I'll help you take the curtains down and wash them.'

'They've only been up three months,' Sally offered timidly.

'High time they were done, then. The longer they're left the harder it will be. Oh, dear . . . when did you last wash this paint?'

Aimée, who had complained of neglect because they were always away at weekends, had had to be invited too, and promptly took up the cudgels in defence of her way of life.

'Really, Geraldine, you can't take a thoroughbred and expect it to pull a cart! The women in our family aren't bred to manual work.' She looked sidelong at Gerald, and added, 'You have to remember, you and I had servants.'

Currents of angry electricity flashed between the two mothers throughout the meal, and Sally and Gerald relaxed into laughter over the washing up. Then Geraldine appeared in the kitchen and took the tea towel from Gerald's hands.

'You go and sit down, darling, little Sally will do this.'

151

And Sally found herself alone at the sink.

After the initial shock, she was a willing pupil. Learning for the first time how clean furniture could shine, discovering that a kitchen could smell of fresh baking instead of stale dishcloth, she found that she too abhorred dirt. But she was not entirely convinced about polishing the bathroom taps with car wax, and the thought of cleaning the oven before she served the meal left her as cold as the waiting roast.

Besides, Gerald had started inspecting window frames for signs of dust, and when he came home unexpectedly, on a day when she had hurried through her chores to read a book, and remarked, 'Isn't there anything else you should be doing?' she did begin to wonder: perhaps after all it hadn't really been such a good idea to have Geraldine come to stay, because if she hadn't realized that her housekeeping left so much to be desired, maybe Gerald hadn't either. But it was such a long drive over to Geraldine's every Friday evening, and it took a big bite out of Sunday to drive back, and she had so longed for a weekend in their very own home.

Also, she did wish Geraldine – 'Gerry', as she was now supposed to call her – wouldn't always refer to her as 'little Sally', as if she were still a child. But in that, she supposed she was being unreasonable. After all, she had wanted desperately to be allowed to call Gerry 'mother', wanting to share Gerald's family and, she had to admit, to put Aimée's reign behind her. So although she had felt deeply hurt when told not to, she had no right to complain. Not that she ever would complain, of course. She had had enough of being unhappy: whatever life might bring her now, she was determined to enjoy it.

There was only one real problem, and that was that there didn't seem to be any arrangement about the renewal of her clothes. Her best jeans had shrunk in the wash, and it made her feel sick to do up the button, especially bending over to clean the bath first thing in the morning. She had saved a little money from her working days, but most of it had gone on buying Gerald a wedding present, and now she had no pocket money left. Was she supposed to ask, she wondered uneasily, remembering all too clearly the prohibitions under which she had grown up. She hated to have to ask, anyway, especially for such essentials as toothpaste and tampons; these last were still a source of acute embarrassment to her, as modern as she was trying to become. She consoled herself that she didn't really need many new clothes . . . yet. But her hair was hanging straight and limp again, now that the juniors were no longer using it to practise on.

'Darling, what's happened to your hair?' asked Gerald. When she explained that she could no longer have it styled free of charge, he didn't offer to pay for it as she hoped, but merely said, 'Oh, I see,' and smiled indulgently.

She had lost the job at the salon, because it was over on the far side of town, and as Gerald took the car to his office half an hour later than she needed to leave, she had no means of getting there on time. She couldn't squeeze anything from the housekeeping because the shopping was ordered and delivered on credit, leaving Gerald to pay by cheque at the end of the month.

She wasn't complaining, of course not . . . she didn't really need any money . . . It was just that some of her other clothes were also getting a little tight; she must be still growing, she thought. Or perhaps it was being married, and so much happier these days.

When she noticed that her usually heavy period was sparse – she knew now that it was only Aimée who called it 'being unwell' – and that toiling up four flights of stairs was making her feel dizzy, she thought perhaps she wasn't so well, after all. When she was suddenly seized with stomach cramps, Gerald called in the doctor.

He ordered her to bed for a rest, ran the rule over her, and smiled.

'Nothing to worry about,' he assured her. 'Just normal pregnancy. I'll send in your husband, I expect you'd like to tell him yourself.'

153

'Oh, no!' said Sally quickly. 'I mean – I'm not sure he'll be pleased. Would you tell him? Please . . .' She was so seized with dread she could not trust herself not to betray it in the telling. And it was true that she wasn't sure how Gerald would take it.

Geraldine had been campaigning for a baby since the wedding, and Gerald's response had been understandably irritated. She would have to be patient, he had countered; they had not been married five minutes, and anyway, they couldn't have a baby in the flat. He had smiled reassurance at Sally. 'I'm not that keen on squalling brats, anyway,' he said teasingly.

She had never had the courage to raise the subject herself, but had skated along from day to day in the vague hope that if he ever did want a child, perhaps she would be able to feel better about it by then. Now the whole thing had been sprung on them both, and she wasn't even sure he would not be angry. Perhaps he would see it as her fault, due to carelessness, since prevention had been left to her. She knew that she had been careful, desperately careful, since the doctor had told her what to do . . . but it now seemed his advice had come too late.

Gerald came into the room looking grave, but still pleasant. He came and sat on the edge of the bed. 'So,' he said. 'You're going to make me a father?'

'Yes,' she said breathlessly. She looked anxiously into his face. 'How do you feel about it?'

He considered for a moment, then looked not displeased. 'I think I might get used to the idea. Though we'll probably have to move.'

'A honeymoon baby,' trilled Geraldine. 'How romantic! Now, dearie, you won't let them fill you up with anaesthetic, will you? I didn't when I had Gerald. I was on my knees on the floor but I refused everything, I wasn't having my baby poisoned with drugs—'

'Sally will have what the doctor advises, no more and no less,' said Gerald, seeing, perhaps, that Sally had

154

turned pale. But Geraldine was not to be stopped.

'Well, we women are very brave, and little Sally won't let you down, you'll see. You won't, will you, dear?' she pursued relentlessly, so that Sally was forced to turn the conversation.

When Aimée was told, she clapped a hand to her brow, causing Sally's stomach to turn an obedient somersault. 'Oh, my God!' she moaned. 'I shall have to go away where I don't know anything about it. Don't tell me, Gerald, when they take her away, I'll never have a moment's peace if I know she's in labour—'

How could she be such a hypocrite, thought Sally, before she realized that Aimée was, as usual, playing a role. This time it was called 'devoted mother'; she wondered if Gerald saw through it.

'If that's how you're going to be,' he answered unexpectedly, 'I think it's best if you're not around. There's no reason to get worked up about a perfectly natural function.'

Aimée stopped abruptly, her mouth still open. When she got Sally alone, she said slyly, 'He doesn't seem very concerned about what he's done to you. Still, that's men . . .'

Sally said loyally, 'Of course he's concerned, he just doesn't want me upset.' She couldn't help thinking how sweet it would have been if he had been the one who feared for her. But then, Gerald didn't go in for pretty speeches. He never said anything for effect.

Time pushed her inexorably towards her Waterloo. A bed had to be booked for the birth, and they were faced with a choice.

'There's the hospital,' suggested Dr Wright, and Sally shook her head vigorously, reminded too sharply of childhood terrors. 'But they'll only take you there if you have complications. Or the two private nursing homes, but they're pretty expensive. Or the maternity home, that's as good as any, and it's free.'

'Would you be looking after me?'

'If you want me to, though the staff are quite competent.'

'Oh, yes . . . please!' The thought of having a baby without even a doctor escalated her alarm.

'Very well, then,' said Gerald. 'The maternity home it is.'

On his next visit, the doctor said, 'How about the confinement? Not frightened, are you?'

He spoke with such confidence that she felt unable to admit to cowardice. So she said, 'I'm trying not to think about it.'

'Well, you'd better think about it, get yourself in the right frame of mind, we don't want you panicking at the last minute. You know what happens?'

She nodded. She had read through the book he had lent her; but the diagrams were no more reassuring than Aristotle's, and already she was growing enormous.

'That's all right, then. Just don't listen to any old wives' tales. I'll see you again in a month, I'm not sure I can't hear a second heart.'

Twins, she thought! How would she manage . . . although, perhaps having two small babies might be easier than one big one . . . and oh, what bliss! with a ready-made family, she need never have any more.

When the suspicion was confirmed, they broke it to the two mothers one at a time.

'Oh, you clever, clever boy!' cried Geraldine, embracing Gerald ecstatically. 'I always wanted a grandchild and you've given me two!' She took out a lace-edged handkerchief and dabbed a tear from her eye.

'Actually,' laughed Sally, by way of whistling in the dark, 'he's given them to me.'

She waited for Geraldine to share the joke, but instead she got a sharp-edged look.

'I hope you're not going to be possessive, dearie,' snapped her mother-in-law.

Aimée's response was predictably different.

'When I tell anyone I'm about to be made a grandmother, they always say I don't look old enough. I don't know how I shall feel about having two.'

'Better send one back then, hadn't I?' said Sally drily. 'I'm going to the shops, do you want any cigarettes?'

Aimée looked shocked. 'You're not going out in the street, in that condition? It's not decent!'

156

Sally lost her temper. 'Well, I don't see you offering to do it for me. And I'm getting very tired of your nasty remarks, if you find it so disgusting, why don't you go away where you don't have to look!'

Aimée regarded her coldly. 'I see you haven't changed,' she said. 'I had hoped that marriage might soften you, but I should have known better. You'll cut yourself on that razor tongue one day.'

Damn! thought Sally, aware that she had let herself down. She was still working on her attitude to Aimée, and now that she was out from under her, could no longer be used as Erik's whipping boy, it should have been getting easier. She could, she thought with a touch of the old arrogance, afford to be kind, to view her mother with compassion; it was easy enough to be kind when you were happy, and she saw with dawning insight that Aimée was spiteful because she was not. Perhaps she never had been, and whether or not she had brought it upon herself was immaterial.

Sally recalled the day she had rashly advised her to divorce Erik, adding, 'Then you could marry Uncle Patrick, couldn't you?' Aimée had turned on her eyes that glittered with angry tears. 'Uncle Patrick's dead. Daddy knew he was dying and asking for me, and he kept it from me. That's your wonderful father for you! And you ask me to release him, after that . . .' She had been sad for Uncle Patrick, whom she had not liked very much; and ashamed for her father, whom she had loved a great deal, learning slowly the painful lesson that we are not loved according to our deserts.

She was still faintly astonished that she herself should be loved by Gerald, and felt the need to repay God's bounty by keeping his commandment with regard to Aimée. The rule of the Convent, though brief, had left its mark.

Now, with a conscious effort she reached over to touch her mother's hand. 'Sorry, I didn't mean it like that. I'm just a bit tired.'

Aimée was not fooled, and gave her a look so quizzical that she retreated, smiling and shaking her head. Sometimes she had the oddest feeling that it was she who was the mother, Aimée the child.

She was moving imperceptibly towards a changed attitude to life. She was no longer driven by the obsessive need to win approval, since her marriage to Gerald had given her a degree of approval she knew she had done nothing to deserve. Her deepest concern was not to lose it, to merit his affection by becoming worthy of it. She was still haunted by the belief that no one who knew the worst of her could love her, still nagged by the remembered: 'I shall tell Daddy, then we'll see if he thinks you're such a nice little girl . . .' She had moved from darkness into such a blaze of light. With so much to lose, she did not dare to be complacent.

She wanted to be all the good things for Gerald, to be beautiful, and clever, and passionate, although this last was becoming daily more difficult as her size increased. She felt less glamorous than ever trying to manoeuvre her bulk over the edge of the bed, and frequently ended with closed eyes and bitten lips, causing him to say, 'Are you all right, dear? Not hurting you, am I?'

'No, darling, of course not.'

Of course not . . . she could only hope he was enjoying it more than she was.

Being beautiful wasn't getting any easier, although she had never been in Gerald's league from the outset; and maintaining the flat to Geraldine's exacting standards didn't leave much time for being clever. She had only to catch the note of doubt in her mother-in-law's prompting, 'You do want to make Gerald happy, don't you, dearie?' to redouble her efforts no matter how tired she was, reminded that she wasn't very efficient either.

So there weren't really too many alternatives. But one thing she felt she could be, if she really put her mind to it, was nice. Kind and unselfish, understanding and sympathetic. Because behaving well was open to anyone, and needed no special talent. All she had to do was think back to what she had learned at the Convent.

CHAPTER THREE

'Gerald,' whispered Sally. 'Gerald . . . are you awake?'

She had been lying awake in the darkness, alone with the pains that were coming and going inside her, saying nothing until she was quite sure what they were. A few moments ago, she had felt a small warm seepage between her thighs, and now she knew. 'Gerald,' she whispered again, and very softly shook his shoulder.

'Mm-mm . . .' Gerald mumbled, turned, and put his arm across her. 'Go to sleep.'

'No,' she said, 'I'm afraid I can't.'

'What?' Blinking, he raised himself on an elbow, reached to put on the light. 'What's the matter? If it's just another nightmare—'

Sally said carefully, 'I think . . . I think by this time tomorrow, there may be four of us.' She had rehearsed that speech for weeks, and was pleased that she had been able to say it, calmly, just the way she planned. That she had not broken down and confessed her panic, seeking solace in his arms. The truth was, she was not quite sure that solace would have been forthcoming. Gerald was always so calm, so unruffled; and at this particular moment she did not want her shortcomings underlined.

He sat up, rubbing his face. 'What are we supposed to do?' he asked.

'We ring the doctor,' she told him. 'Then the maternity home, to tell them I'm coming.'

He got out of bed. 'I'd better get dressed and take you. While I'm shaving, you can have a shower.'

She showered and dressed with shaking hands and then,

159

smiling through clenched teeth, stowed her spongebag and comb in the suitcase that had stood, ready packed, in the bedroom for the past two weeks, a daily reminder of the ordeal to come. She had wondered fearfully what some of the things were for: tape, safety pins, lanoline, scissors – were they for the baby or for her – but no mention of the baby clothes she had lovingly put together.

Now Gerald carried it down for her – 'I'll go and start the car' – and she was suddenly alone. Aimée, true to her word, had scuttled off to stay with Uncle Charles until it was all over, while Geraldine, in a flutter of excitement, waited at home for the telephone call which would summon her to come and look after Gerald. She wished she had either one of them near her now, women who had been through the same experience, who could tell her what to expect . . . yet, thinking of Aimée, perhaps not.

She closed the door of the flat behind her and leaned against it, trembling, for a moment. She wished she could run back inside, and hide herself in a dark cupboard, could shut her eyes tightly and open them to find it had all been a mistake . . . she drew a deep breath, pulled herself together, and started down the stairs.

On the second landing she was seized with a pain much stronger than before, and had to wait for it to expend itself before she could go on. Two more assailed her on the next flight; she reached the bottom crouched over the stair rail. Gerald was waiting for her in the hall.

'You've been a long time,' he said. 'Are you all right? I thought I might have to come back for you, only I couldn't leave the car where it is.'

'Oh, Gerald . . .' gasped Sally. It was the nearest she had yet come to a reproach.

They eased her somehow into the Mini, and the drive to the maternity home was a nightmare. Pains were coming fast and strong, and at one point she had to plead with him to stop.

'I – I think this might be going to be one of those quick jobs,' she managed to gasp before the next one seized her. 'It must be the car, just let's rest a minute.'

Gerald let the clutch in slowly. 'We'll go slowly. Don't want you having it in here,' he said. Despite herself, Sally began to cry.

She was still crying when they reached the Home. She managed to crawl out from the car and stood wilting on the impressive doorstep, with Gerald looking slightly embarrassed beside her. The door was opened to them by a beefy middle-aged woman in a nurse's uniform.

'Ah, Sally Hammond,' she said. 'We weren't expecting you until next week.' She looked so severe that Sally half expected to be turned away. Then she turned to Gerald. 'You can run along now, Father. Go and get some sleep, there'll be nothing happening yet. We've got your phone number?'

Gerald repeated it, and asked about visiting hours. Then he turned to Sally.

'Right, then, love. I'll see you this evening.' He dabbed a brief peck on her cheek, and was gone.

Sally stared after him through a blur of tears, thinking, If I died today, I'd never see him again . . . Then another pain gathered like thunder inside her, pulling her almost double.

The voice of the beefy nurse cut across it, barking like a sergeant on parade.

'Come along, Mother! And stand up straight, you haven't started yet.'

She was wrong about it being a quick job. She and her suitcase were installed in a tiny room containing only a narrow bed and a locker, and a brisk young nurse about her own age came in, shaved off her pubic hair, gave her an enema reminiscent of the suppositories to which she had been subjected as a child, and ordered her into a hot bath.

'That'll get you going,' she said cheerfully. 'How often are your pains?'

'I don't know,' said Sally, bewildered. It had not occurred to her to count.

'Well, you must time them,' said the girl. 'When they're every five minutes, ring the bell.' And she too, disappeared.

Sally wasn't sure how long she was supposed to stay in the bath, so she stayed in until the water began to cool and then got out. It was then that she realized that the pains had stopped.

As she dried herself on the big scratchy towel, she saw that over the back of a wooden chair was folded a white cotton garment with fastening tapes . . . suddenly she was back in the Convent, arguing with Sister Mary Luke about the bath chemise. She smiled, putting on the surgical gown, climbing up with difficulty on to the high, hard bed, laying her face against the glacial pillow, composing herself to sleep. There was now no turning back, and where there is no hope, there is no fear. She was safely arrived, in the right place, and it was all out of her hands. She closed her eyes. Immediately, the pains started again.

All night and all day they went on, fierce enough to be frightening, yet a good twenty minutes apart. From time to time, a nurse would put her head around the door. 'How are you getting on?'

'Nineteen minutes, I think . . .'

'Oh, you haven't started yet. Relax, you must relax . . .' A glass ear trumpet would be pressed against her stomach, a rubber-gloved finger thrust up her anus, and she would be alone again, staring at the dark green shiny walls, the light green shiny ceiling, the netted window through which she could see nothing. She longed for someone to sit with her, even for the spurious company of a radio . . . there was nothing. At some point during the day, Dr Wright dropped in on her.

'Well, young lady, how are you feeling?'

'All right,' she lied bravely, because if she started to tell him how she really felt she knew she would disgrace herself. 'A bit tired,' she conceded. 'Will it be much longer?'

'Mm . . . mm . . . let's have a look.' He too, went through the rigmarole, then checked her blood pressure, sitting on the edge of the bed. 'That's fine,' he said. 'Well, it might be tonight, but it's not very likely unless you get a move on. We'll give you some pethidine, that'll help you to relax and get some sleep.'

For the next few hours she drifted mercifully out of, and fearfully back into, the dark waters of pain. As dusk was falling, there was a tap on her door and Gerald's voice said, 'May I come in?'

A nurse burst in ahead of him. 'Come along, Mother, sit up, you've got a visitor!' She lugged Sally into an upright position. 'Come on, you're not ill, you know.' She smiled brightly at Gerald and went out, leaving them alone.

'Hello,' said Gerald, dropping a kiss on the top of her head. 'I haven't brought you flowers yet, I'm waiting till you've earned them.' He smiled teasingly.

Sally clung to his hand. 'You will stay with me . . . until they turn you out?'

He glanced at his watch. 'Well, just for a while. I promised to ring Mother in half an hour. When do you think it will be?'

'They don't seem to know. Not yet . . . oh, Gerald, they're saying I haven't even started—' Her voice cracked and she turned away to hide her face in a tissue.

'Now, now,' said Gerald kindly. 'You must be braver than this, you know. After all, it's a—'

'I know!' she burst out. 'It's a perfectly natural function! So's dying! And it hurts, it hurts dreadfully and it just goes on and on!' She burst into tears, sobbing helplessly.

Gerald reached across her and rang the bell for the nurse, who came in tutting, told her not to be a baby, and went to fetch her a cup of tea. When she looked up for Gerald, he had gone.

Towards midnight the level of pain had built so high that she could not lie still. The pethidine had worn off hours earlier. Timidly, she asked if she could have some more.

It was the beefy nurse who had first admitted her who answered the bell. 'We'll see what the doctor says when he comes in the morning. Just forget about it and try to get some sleep. You'll need all your strength for tomorrow, mark my words.'

'But I can't sleep,' she pleaded. 'Every time I try it starts up again. Couldn't I possibly have some tonight?'

The beefy nurse glanced at her watch. 'I'll give you some chloral, then we'll all get some peace. We've got three of you queuing for the delivery room, so perhaps it's just as well.'

When she returned with the claret-coloured liquid, she added, 'You young primips, you're all the same, spoon fed! You don't know what a good labour's really like. Now settle down, and don't let me hear from you again until you're every five minutes.'

She makes me sound like a bus service, thought Sally, and she cares just about as much as if I were. How can a woman be so callous towards another one? How can Gerald . . . she doused her train of thought in the chloral, turned her face into the pillow and tried to relax.

The following day was much the same, only more so. Dr Wright came, and gave her pethidine in the morning, and in the evening she was told by the nurse she could have no more, because she had already had too much.

Gerald came again, sat politely by her bedside for a few minutes, and as politely left. This time she did not complain, or entreat his sympathy; but then this time, for the first time ever, she had not been longing to see him. In the warm, vital spot where he had lived within her, there was now a terrible numbness. Perhaps the drugs had damped down her emotions; she turned her thoughts away from him, towards the job in hand.

By the afternoon of the third day, the pains were still a full seven minutes apart, so it was with some surprise that she became aware of something bulging between her thighs. She reached down a hand. It felt hard, and was certainly not any part of herself. She rang the bell.

It was answered by the young nurse she had seen before.

'Oh, lord, it's the baby's head!' she cried. 'Come on, we've got to get you upstairs.'

'Upstairs?' echoed Sally faintly.

'To the delivery room. Come on, there's not a moment to lose.'

Somehow, Sally struggled to her feet, and with the girl's arm around her went out through the door for the first time since her admission.

'Come on,' urged the young nurse. 'It isn't far.' And she steered her towards a long flight of stairs.

'I can't get up there,' gasped Sally. 'Isn't there a lift?'

'We can't use that,' said the girl. 'It's not for patients. Come on, I'll help you, you'll be all right.'

Halfway up, a fierce contraction dragged Sally to her knees.

'Oh, come on!' Ahead of her on the upper flight, the girl turned back towards her. 'You don't want to have it on the stairs, do you?' she pleaded, in evident agitation.

'Just a minute,' groaned Sally. 'Just wait till I can walk . . .'

She did make it, in fact, but only just in time. Suddenly, everything was happening at once. She was hoisted on to a bed even higher and harder than the last, thick white bed-socks were pulled over her feet, Dr Wright appeared from nowhere and a smelly rubber mask was put into her hand.

'Put your finger over the hole and breathe deeply when you need it,' he said. 'And push really hard when I tell you.'

Afterwards, she couldn't believe it was all over so quickly. She pushed so hard when she was told that she could feel it all moving inside her, and after the second heave there was a blessed rush of relief, and a tiny voice squalling amid the tinkle of instruments.

'It's a boy,' cried the doctor, holding up a slippery plum-coloured monkey with tight-shut eyes, wide-open mouth, tiny body quivering with rage. 'Here you are, nurse, clean him up while we get the other one.'

'Oh, poor little fellow, he looks furious!' laughed Sally, tears of reaction pouring down her temples in the interim between births.

'Have you chosen a name for him?' asked Dr Wright.

'Charles,' said Sally promptly. 'After my favourite uncle.' She had intended that Gerald should choose the name, but he had shown so little interest that she had now changed her mind. 'Ah – here we go again.'

After twenty minutes more, small Charles had an even smaller sister. She was tiny, and quite beautiful, with a heart shaped face and delicate hands, every finger finished with a perfect filbert nail. Sally wanted to hold her and admire her, examine her little body, see the colour of her eyes . . . as the doctor left, both babies were taken away to the nursery, wrapped like tiny mummies in lengths of yellowing, well-washed calico.

'Oh, couldn't I have them with me?' she pleaded. 'Just for a little while.'

'Certainly not!' she was told. 'How do you think we can look after the babies if they're scattered here, there and everywhere? You'll see quite enough of them once you get them home, believe me.'

'I suppose so . . .' she conceded weakly, blinking back her disappointment. Their attitude implied that she had already taken up more than her fair share of their time, and if she was honest she knew that what she needed now was sleep. She lay with closed eyes while someone sponged her face and hands.

'That feels nice,' she said gratefully.

'We only do it for you once,' said a cheery, no-nonsense voice. 'You're not ill, you know.'

'Oh, no . . . of course . . .'

She did wish everyone didn't sound so censorious, as if by some piece of thoughtless conduct she had given them all a great deal of trouble. Anyone would think she had been doing it all for fun . . .

As she was wheeled from the delivery room, Dr Wright reappeared.

'I can't get hold of your husband, he's not in his office. What's your home number?'

Sally gave it to him. In a few moments he was back.

'No answer from there either. Where's he likely to be, did he tell you?'

Sally tried to think, her brain still fuzzy from drugs and lack of sleep. 'What day is it?'

166

'Friday.' The doctor smiled, but a frown was gathering between his eyebrows. 'Any help?'

'Friday . . . of course! He's probably gone to his mother's,' she told him. 'If not, she may know where he is. You could try ringing her.'

The frown took over. 'This is very bad! He shouldn't go off like that, suppose I'd needed his consent for an emergency operation—' He stopped, seeing Sally's distress. 'Never mind, it's not your fault. Have you got her number?' She heard him mutter as he turned to go, 'Good God, fifty miles away!'

She found herself unloaded on to another high, hard bed, and propped upright on a glacial sheet barely covering a thick chilly rubber one.

'Actually . . .' she said timidly, 'I'd quite like to go to sleep. If I may . . .'

The nurse rallied her with a laugh. 'What? At half-past three in the afternoon? It's not bedtime for hours yet, there's visiting time before then, you don't want to be asleep when your husband comes, do you?'

When she had smiled her way brightly out of the ward, a girl in one of the other three beds said, 'They're like that here, right bloody cattle market. You go to sleep if you can, love, don't take any notice. What time's your old man coming?'

'I don't know . . .' Sally's eyes brimmed over. Abruptly, she lost control and the next moment she was sobbing helplessly. She heard sounds of response from the other beds, and then there was an arm around her.

'Don't upset yourself, ducky, we all have a little weep. You'll feel better when you've had a bit of a rest. Come on, cheer up! What have you got, little girl or a little boy?'

'B-both,' she managed to stutter.

'Well, aren't you the clever one, twins! Here, d'you hear that, girls, she's got two, one of each!'

She heard other voices joining in, congratulating her, saying how lucky she was. And she knew it, really she knew it . . . she just couldn't feel it, because Gerald wasn't there, and didn't seem to care. While his babies were being born, he had been miles away with Geraldine instead of here with her. Like her beloved Erik, he had failed her when she needed him most . . .

By the time the doctor came back she had dried her eyes. He had tracked down Gerald, who had said he was bringing his mother back with him this evening, and would 'pop in and see her at visiting time'. And he sent his love. Sally smiled dutifully, wondering how much he had to send . . .

By the time he came that evening she was too exhausted to feel anything. She wilted against the iron pillows and tried to make conversation. How was Geraldine, had he telephoned Aimée, had he remembered to increase the milk order . . . no, of course she hadn't expected flowers because the shops were closed. Already, he was beginning to glance at his watch.

'Have you seen the babies?' she asked him at last.

'Not yet,' he smiled. 'Mother was quite indignant that they wouldn't let her see them, she's waiting in the car, fuming.'

She laughed weakly. 'It's fathers only, I'm afraid. But please have a look at them, I want to know what you think.'

'What are they like?'

'The little girl's beautiful . . . she's just like you, oh, do go and look!'

'I'll have a peep on the way out.' There was a silence. 'I suppose we'll have to think of names for them.'

'Zoë,' said Sally with unwonted firmness. Although she had snatched the name out of the air she knew with absolute certainty that it was right. 'And the boy's Charles.'

'I don't know about that,' Gerald laughed uneasily. 'Mother wants him called Gerald.'

'He can have it for a second name,' said Sally. 'But to me he's Charles.' She closed her eyes and wished he would go away.

'I must be off,' he said brightly, and she guessed he had checked his watch. He dropped a peck on her forehead, and was gone.

168

CHAPTER FOUR

Sally let herself in at the cottage door and went straight through to the garden. Pausing only in the kitchen to put the kettle on for coffee, she sat down in unaccustomed stillness on the sunlit doorstep to wait.

She felt strangely disorientated without the twins underfoot, squabbling, demanding this or that, and, always, her undivided attention. This was her first day of freedom, long awaited and looked forward to, the promised luxury of a day of her own, and already it was tainted by a nagging guilt, a feeling of meanness, a sense that her own enjoyment was being taken at their expense. She wondered how they were coping with this, their first day at school. She could probably guess.

Charles, born so angry that he had screamed and arched his back when held to her breast, had changed little. He was constantly frustrated in his efforts to overreach his budding abilities, yet furiously resentful of help or guidance and unable to tolerate restraint in any form, even affection. Zoë, soft and submissive, had fed contentedly and thrived on love. Gentle and a little oversensitive, a child whom the lightest rebuke would reduce to tears: Zoë, to whom her heart went out, and whose own heart leaned so touchingly to Gerald.

For reasons oddly at variance considering their twinship, they were equally difficult to deal with, if only because it was impossible to treat them alike. In them she saw all too clearly reflections of long ago: hearing in Charles's bullying tones the echo of Aimée's, so that only too often she had to stay her hand, for fear all that anger, all that hatred she

169

had had to suppress might rise up and destroy them both. And Zoë, little, put-upon Zoë, how often did she get away with murder because of the sympathy evoked by her situation . . .

Perhaps she should have warned their teacher, that cool, impressive young woman with the over-confident voice . . . but no, this was being silly. They had to start school some day, go out into the world, learn to accept discipline outside the home. That was what Gerald would say. He had selected their school with great care, an exclusive and quite expensive kindergarten recommended by one of the senior partners; Gerald had been flattered by this man's invitation to call him George, and Sally knew that nothing would have induced him to go against his recommendation. As she herself had not come into the district until she was ten, she had no means of assessing the local nursery schools and was forced to leave the choice to those better informed.

Aimée was visibly impressed, and was already rehearsing the role of Aristocratic Grandmama in readiness for prize days. Geraldine, too, had approved it; not that she knew anything about the schools in the area, but she held that a promising young solicitor with an eye to a partnership must be seen to be successful, and an outward show of affluence could do nothing but good. It was only Sally who had reservations about starting them both together, and so young: Zoë who feared to leave familiar things, and Charles who could not wait for new horizons. But feeling her opinions to be of no account, she had hesitated to voice them.

She sighed. Geraldine, surprisingly enough, was proving more of a trial to her than Aimée. She was always on hand to remind her of what she ought to do, Gerald of what he ought to expect; sniping in ways so subtle that she could not be faulted. 'Not still in nappies at a year, dearie? My Gerald was clean and dry by the time he could stand, I wasn't going to have him grow up bow-legged.' And Sally, totally lacking in experience, had wrestled inexpertly with the problem to no avail, provoking a crossfire from Aimée, who accused her of cruelty. Depressed, she thought: If only they'd both go away, and leave us alone to manage on our own . . .

And yet, in an obscure way, she saw that that would be admitting defeat. She still clung to the conviction that difficult people were best dealt with by rising above them; you had to resist retaliation, meet malice with humour, the soft answer that was said to turn away wrath. She held stubbornly to the tenet that if you could stay calm enough to smile and be pleasant, if you dropped your end of the rope and walked away, sooner or later they would tire of the boring game and leave you in peace. You had to be stronger than they were, more patient and more determined. In the end you would win, and things would go your way. And you could take satisfaction from knowing that you had bested them.

Leaving aside parental interference, she and Gerald rubbed along together very well. In six years – longer than that, if you counted back to their first meeting – they had never had a row. There had been no raised voices, no slammed doors. She wondered how many people could say as much.

It was true that they never reached any great heights in bed. And she knew from her reading that there were couples who did. The Indians, the Spanish – perhaps also the French, although that seemed unlikely as they appeared to be more concerned with their stomachs – and of course the Poles, the great romantics of Europe, as one journalist had called them. Americans had a poor track record, and the English were the butt of jokes from Bordeaux to Bombay, so as she and Gerald were both near the bottom of the league, it hardly seemed worth worrying about.

He treated her with a kind of amused tolerance, seeming to enjoy her occasional observations which made him laugh. She regarded him with tranquil affection which was what remained of her girlhood's consuming passion. She had known since the birth of the twins that he could not give her the depth of love she had felt for him: the love that

171

worries, that cannot endure separation, for which absence means the imminent threat of loss . . . it was not his fault. He was what he was, incapable of feeling to that degree of intensity. He was too separate, too self-contained to give away so much of himself; a man in a glass case, like one of those French clocks that you could see and hear but never touch.

It was perhaps providential that he had married someone like herself who, knowing that she did not inspire great love, could not hold him to blame for not providing it. With one unlovable, the other unable to love, how could anyone come between them? She smiled. They had something far more durable, a friendship stronger, closer and more lasting than any romantic emotion. Above all, she wanted their marriage to last, to endure and be peaceful, to provide the children with the safe and loving background she had lacked. They at least would never have to suffer the misery of divided loyalties.

And there was really nothing to disagree about. Gerald made perfectly good decisions, and she was happy enough to abide by them. When Aimée pointed out that he changed cars and even decided on houses without consulting her, and Geraldine retorted with flashing eyes that 'it was his money, and his little wife was very lucky,' she would smile and leave the arguments to them. She did consider herself lucky, on the whole; Gerald had never yet chosen anything she didn't like, and moreover she had a kind, reliable husband whom she could trust implicitly. She felt safe with Gerald, finding his even temper, his unruffled calm ineffably reassuring. She was sure that if an earthquake befell or a nuclear war broke out he would be just the same, that she and the children would draw strength from him and be unafraid while he was there . . .

It was true that she would have liked to go with him when he went out. But there was no one to look after the babies. Neither of their mothers had ever offered, and when they came as guests expected to be entertained themselves. It couldn't be helped. It was not as though she hadn't enough to occupy herself with in the evenings. There was gardening in the summer, and when the nights drew in she baked cakes to Geraldine's exacting standards, or made little dresses for pretty Zoë to wear to charm her beloved Gerald . . .

Despite, or even because of, their often exasperating behaviour, the children absorbed her completely. Their developing personalities engaged her fascinated attention, so that she hardly cared about her lack of social life. Their physical beauty never ceased to surprise her; when strangers paused to admire them in the street her heart swelled, and she knew that having found her way safely through child-birth she would have liked to have more, a real family on which to lavish her love, all that bottled-up affection that her parents had not had time for, and which even Gerald seemed unable to accept. But he had made the decision for her, along with all the rest. Two, he maintained, were quite enough, and more than he had bargained for. And now that they were starting school, she would be free to do some entertaining for him . . .

Well, at least she knew that if he said he was taking a client to lunch, or working late, or going on a weekend conference, she could believe him. He was too honourable, too conventional and, it had to be admitted, too dull for anything else. It was impossible to imagine prim, slightly prudish Gerald – the Gerald who had forbidden her to use the word 'passion' and cautioned her not to get out of bed without her nightdress – indulging in the amorous pecca-dillos of other men. She had been able to laugh at the busybody neighbour who insisted she had seen him with a blonde; it could not have been Gerald, she was confident of that.

She was duly ashamed of her own occasional, albeit hypothetical lapses: the daydreams that left her mind and body glowing, the turbaned bus conductor whose velvet eyes had swept her briefly, bathing her in dark fire that dissolved her bones like wine. If only, oh, if only . . . but then, it would have to be Gerald: she knew she could never really go to bed with another man. It would be far too embarrassing,

all that preparation, all that fumbling, with a stranger . . .
she had banished the hunger to the back of her mind, and
spent more energy on the garden, planting roses with names
like Happiness, and Peace.

The kettle shrilled, inviting her to coffee. She rose and
went indoors, noting with pleasure how the sunlight warmed
the new pine fittings of the kitchen to a golden glow.
Counting her blessings, Geraldine would call it. Blessings
. . . or compensations? She pulled herself up. They were
blessings, of course they were. She loved the cottage, and
earnestly hoped that this was where she could put down
roots, and live for the rest of her life. This home had been
bought, with help from Geraldine; this one was not rented,
they could not be asked to leave it on someone else's whim.
It was their third since the flat, and she had begun to
think she was destined to be a nomad, to spend her life in
wandering as she had as a child. Like Aimée before her,
she had planted gardens, only to have to leave them, and
began to have an inkling of how her mother had felt.

Not that Aimée had settled in one place now that she no
longer had to travel with Erik. It seemed that wherever she
was, she wanted to be somewhere else, either the next place
where the grass looked greener, or the one she had just come
from and now knew she should never have left. Back and
forth she shuttled between one flat and another, her curtains
and carpets never fitting anywhere, her precious piano and
her oddments of furniture growing ever more battered and
shabby, herself a pathetic misfit, unable to call back the past
and unwilling to settle for less. Sally felt sad for her, just
as she had felt sad for Uncle Patrick, and wished she could
think of something that would help.

It seemed such a waste, for Aimée, whatever her emotional
flaws, was a woman who could yet have made something
of her life. Widely read and talented, she could still when
occasion demanded be charming company. Sally had
poignant recollections of a time when, coaxed by some
means into an expansive mood, she had read with her
through the whole of *Omar Khayyám*, explaining its philo-

sophy, illuminating its lyricism in a way she remembered still, an oasis in the desert of rejection. Now that Aimée was a free spirit, with no obligations and an adequate income still loyally provided by Erik . . . why, oh why could she not let herself be happy!

Even as she asked herself the question, Sally suspected that she knew the answer. Her mother, although in her sixties, was stuck in an adolescent fantasy: the knight on the white horse, the handsome young man who would fall madly in love with her. This was the one, the only occasion to demand that she rise and shine. She had come to life briefly for Gerald, hoping perhaps that by attaching him to her daughter she could bring him close enough to make the conquest for herself.

Sally knew she had disgraced herself irreparably by winning him away, and it was without much hope that she cast about for interests to brighten her mother's life. She had once made the mistake of suggesting that she join a dramatic society, offer her knowledge and experience where they would be appreciated, make new friends . . . Aimée had been insulted. What could she be thinking of, to suggest her associating with amateurs! It was then that Sally realized all she wanted was sympathy; baulked of her unattainable desire, she was determined to embrace martyrdom. As long as she fed on self-pity, no plan for positive living would be acceptable, and least of all from her daughter.

But Sally was not giving up, not least because it had become a point of pride. Aimée might play-act to her heart's content — if so listless a heart could ever be contented — but she had no right to allocate roles to others. Erik, labelled heartless philanderer, would no doubt be reviled to the end of his days, but she was not accepting her role of undeserving child. Aimée could do as she pleased about it, complain all she liked to the milkman, the baker, anyone else she could persuade to lend an ear: Sally did not have to live up to that reputation. Some buried streak of stubbornness decreed that she should give the lie to it; and since someone had pointed out that you don't have to like a person to love him, she had decided her mother was going to be loved, and whether she liked it or not.

Her ideas of religion were no longer as cut-and-dried, as picturesque as they had been at the Convent. They had expanded and become diluted, were veering into the realms of the nebulous and the unexplained. Her early struggles with the fifth Commandment had led at one point to her throwing the whole thing overboard. If there had really been a God who demanded that she love her mother, she had reasoned, he would have given her one with whom it was possible. And how could you equate an ever-loving God with the dreadful sufferings of innocent children, a God who was supposed to be an ever-listening ear . . . and yet, in the extremity of labour, she had prayed unashamedly. She still did not know why. Religion, as it had been offered to her, was as much of an enigma as ever.

Now, she held that if there ever was a miracle it was the uniqueness of the human spirit. That of the millions upon millions crowding the earth, no two were exactly alike. People and their foibles, she thought, how fascinating they were. The tattered exercise book in which she jotted her observations and tried to sort them into verse was filled with her reflections on how this or that person was dealing – or failing to deal – with one problem or another. She sometimes daydreamed another existence, one in which she played a useful part, did some kind of work worth doing; maybe something like Gerald's, sorting out legal wrangles, or a doctor's or a nurse's, saving life and relieving pain . . . as it was she was sitting on the sidelines, making comments that were of no practical use to anyone.

Even so, it was the only thing she did that was more intellectually demanding than making custard. She was sometimes a little sad about that, since she had done nothing to justify Erik's belief that she was capable of better things. Although he never hinted at it, she knew in her heart that he had always hoped she might do something brilliant and extraordinary, something that would vindicate them both. Something to leave a little mark upon the world, however faint and easily scratched out.

Whatever either of them had hoped, it had all come to nothing in the end. Or rather to a very little, since here she was, restricted to her immediate family and seeing no one else. Maybe after all there was Someone Up There, reminding her that charity begins at home . . .

She laughed, drank up her coffee, and went upstairs to sort out the linen basket.

Halfway down the stairs, her arms overflowing with sheets and towels and assorted underwear, she heard the telephone start ringing and rushed to answer it. She always rushed to answer it, still conditioned to instant obedience when called.

'Hello . . . hello, Gerry?' she said breathlessly, recognizing the voice.

'You sound out of breath, dearie. Down the garden again?' Was the inquiry really tinged with reproof . . . perhaps not. 'I rang to say I'll be coming over to give you a hand with Friday.'

'Friday?' She searched her memory but couldn't think of anything.

'The dinner party.'

'What dinner party? What are we talking about?'

'Oh, hasn't Gerald told you?' A tinkling laugh. 'Well, he will. It's that nice partner, George something. He's coming to you for dinner on Friday with Diana, his fiancée. So to make up the numbers I'm bringing an old friend, I'll have the spare room and he can spend the night at the pub—'

'Are you sure it's this Friday . . . I mean, absolutely sure?'

'Of course I'm sure, dearie. I'll come over on Thursday afternoon and Gerald can pick me up from the station. We'll have all day Friday to make our preparations. Now I suggest . . .'

Sally hardly heard what she was suggesting, being too preoccupied with her own thoughts. Geraldine's help would be welcome enough with the first dinner party she ever had to give . . . but, how typical of Gerald to have asked his mother first!

177

CHAPTER FIVE

Sally sank into an armchair and closed her eyes. The bus had been hot and crowded, Charles over-excited, Zoë tearful as usual, and her own head and feet were both throbbing.

'Now, dearies,' said Geraldine cheerfully. 'Up you go and change out of your school clothes, while I make little Mummy a nice cup of tea.'

They went, still protesting noisily, jostling one another on the stairs. When Sally opened her eyes again a fresh cup of tea stood at her elbow, and Geraldine sat facing her, smiling expectantly.

'I've got everything worked out,' she said with confidence. 'We have twenty minutes before we need to start the vegetables. And I've made eggy sandwiches for the little ones' tea, all cut in pretty shapes with the biscuit cutters.'

Oh dear, thought Sally. Charles hated eggs, and Zoë ate hardly anything but fruit. She wondered whether to warn Gerry now, or whether she would be seen to be raising objections. There were going to be tantrums and bruised feelings either way; she might as well let it find its own level. She passed a hand across her forehead.

'Thanks, Gerry, that was sweet of you.' She drank her tea gratefully and fished in her handbag for aspirin. 'I'll just make a few banana ones as well. In case they're extra hungry.'

'You stay where you are, dear. Eggs are better for them, I can easily make a few more.'

Oh, well, I've tried, thought Sally, closing her eyes again. No one can ever accuse me of not trying. Dear God, she could have done without this party tonight. With the children fractious from their first week of school, and the threat of her period dragging like a weight in her inside, she would have given anything to crawl between cool sheets and sleep. Instead, she was going to have to force the twins into early bed, do her share of the cooking and try to look her best for Gerald's guests. That reminded her.

'Where's your friend, has he arrived, or is he coming later?'

'Oh – didn't I tell you? He couldn't manage it, so I've got a surprise for you. I rang dear Aimée to see if she could come, and your nice little cousin's staying with her. She's coming too, and bringing her young man!'

'Louise?' cried Sally, brightening. She had a special affection for her younger cousin, the occasional companion of her childhood. Louise the tomboy, the rebel, the un-favoured child. Louise, who had also grown up in the shadow of Little Dotty. 'I haven't seen her for ages, not for years.'

'Not Louise, dear. Dorothea's the name. I think they call her Dotty, such a pity, I always thought. Oh, and a letter came while you were out, with an American stamp. Looks like your daddy's writing, here it is.'

Sally swallowed her disappointment and glanced at the letter; took in the postmark, the familiar handwriting like long looped copperplate that seemed universal to Americans, and dropped it into her handbag. She would read it later, when she had time to savour it . . . she hauled herself to her feet as the twins, still squabbling, began their descent. 'Come and have tea,' she called, her head wincing. Then to Geraldine, 'That makes eight of us. Will there be enough?'

'Trust your Auntie Gerry, dear! I've been planning it all while you went to get the babies. By the way, I'm sure Gerald would lend you the car to collect them in – if you asked him the right way. So much better for them than coming home on the bus.'

What bliss! thought Sally, to drive home in comfort with the shopping in the boot. 'It would be nice,' she conceded. 'But it's only insured for him, I haven't got a licence.'

179

Geraldine smiled archly. 'Your trouble is, dearie, that you don't know how to get round a man! You must have driving lessons immediately. I'll ask him for you tomorrow.'

Sally thanked her a little ruefully, reflecting on the undeniable fact that Gerry was far more likely to plead successfully than she was.

Four hours later, she sat nursing her weariness at the dressingtable, dressed in her best, her hair carefully combed, her body bathed, powdered, perfumed . . . if only it hadn't been Dotty who was coming to dinner! Tonight of all nights, when she felt herself to be particularly on trial, she was going to feel more inadequate than ever. Dotty had always had that effect on her, and with Aimée there as well . . . She sighed, straightening her aching back. It couldn't be helped, and she must do her best with whatever came of it. She opened the scent that Gerald had brought her back from his last trip to Paris, dabbed it on her wrists and throat. The pulse points, Aimée called them, and she should know. She had good taste in such things, although she often wore too much jewellery in Sally's opinion. She looked critically at her reflection, and decided to leave off the earrings. Lipstick, she must not forget lipstick.

Dipping into her handbag to find it, she saw the letter. This time, something about it caught her attention. Something unexpected, something not quite as usual . . . she looked again. The handwriting was not Erik's, although uncannily like it. The returning address was correct, right down to the zip code, but there was something different about the name . . . '*Mrs* Erik Braun . . .'

For a moment she stared at it stupidly, her brain fogged by aspirin and fatigue. But, Aimée was here . . . not in the States. She never had been. Suddenly light dawned. Of course! Erik must have got his divorce out there, and married again. She was pleased for him, of course she was – yet there was a faint twinge of something . . . not jealousy, not that. What then, rejection? Perhaps, though she was not sure. Of course she did not want him to be alone all his life, she wished him happiness, she always had, and yet . . . yes, that was it. She wished he had written to tell her himself, instead of leaving it to a stranger. Well, of course, to him it must not seem like that, his new wife was no stranger to him . . . but only to her. She glanced at her watch, wondering if she had time to read it. Five minutes. She ripped it open.

> Dear Sally,
> I do not know how best to tell you this, as I believe you thought a great deal of your father. The truth is, there is no good way to tell bad news . . .

Sally felt herself turn cold. Her eyes raced over the page, the lines blurring before she could take in their meaning.

> . . . I have to tell you that Erik has gone from us. It was very sudden, a heart attack from which he did not recover, and I personally am still in a state of shock. I don't believe he had told you we were married, your mother convinced him not to, as she said it would be upsetting to you. I am only sorry that you had to learn this way. Please forgive me for being the bringer of such sorrow . . .

Sally could not read any further. She sat rooted to the dressing stool, her hands and feet like stones, unable to move or speak, even to think. All her brain could register was that she had to go through with the party. She could not afford to give way, because Aimée was downstairs and would disgrace them all with a display of histrionics. She was not ready to share her grief, least of all with Aimée. It was good, in a way, to have to dissemble; it gave her a few hours to pretend to herself that her father was still alive . . .

She stuffed the crumpled letter back into her handbag, applied the lipstick to her numbed mouth. And when Gerald put his head around the door to say urgently, 'They're

181

here!' she stood up without a word, and followed him downstairs.

Geraldine, busily handing drinks and salted peanuts, gave her a two-edged smile as she appeared.

'Sally believes in wearing out the old ones first!' she quipped, drawing faintly embarrassed laughter from the guests.

'Sorry,' murmured Sally automatically, going to help her.

Aimée leaned forward in her seat as she passed. 'You look like a death's head on a broomstick, go and put some colour on,' she whispered fiercely.

Sally didn't answer. 'I thought Dotty was coming, isn't she here?' Keep to trivialities, she reminded herself, then you'll be safe.

'She's coming later, with her young man. Come here!' She reached to pinch Sally's cheeks but missed.

'Darling, come and meet George and Diana.'

Sally dragged her face into the semblance of a smile, shook hands with Diana, a slightly overblown English rose, and found herself looking up into the face of a very large, rough-hewn man with bright blue eyes, untidy hair and a solid, comfortable frame. He swallowed her hand in a massive paw, smiled down at her, and she was overwhelmed by a longing to cling to his shapeless tweeds and weep. Somehow she mastered the impulse. She heard herself say, 'How lovely to see you . . . I've heard so much about you . . .'

Where would she find enough meaningless words to fill the rest of the evening . . . she was saved for the moment by a knock at the door, and hurried to answer it.

Dotty stood on the doorstep, her silver blonde hair catching lights from the porch lantern. Her azure eyes were sparking and a spot of rose glowed angrily in the centre of either cheek.

'Come in . . .' said Sally, looking past her for a companion. 'Where's your friend?'

Dotty strode past her. 'He's not my friend any more!' she snapped. She held up a hand for silence. 'Don't ask me, I'm in no mood to talk about it.' She took off her coat and thrust it at Sally. 'Where's Aunty Aimée?' She swept on into the living room, all eyes turning to greet her entrance.

Sally carried her coat upstairs, laid it on the bed and came straight out again. Not looking towards the dressing-table, not daring to be alone with the handbag, the letter, the moment . . . It had pierced her like a knife and all she could do was hold the wound together. Once it started to bleed she knew there would be no staunching it . . .

Downstairs Dotty was on form, entertaining everyone with a light-hearted dissertation on the vagaries of young men, her own uniquely successful methods of dealing – or dispensing – with them.

'I can't be bothered with that nonsense,' she was declaring brightly to a chorus of delighted laughter. 'If they can't behave there are plenty more where they came from.'

'I can well believe that,' said Gerald gallantly, while enormous George leaned back in his chair, his eyes alight with enjoyment, and Aimée looked on admiringly. Never in Sally's life had she won such a look from her mother.

But Dotty at the moment was fulfilling Sally's duty of amusing her guests, so perhaps she should be thankful for small mercies. She smiled bleakly and left her to it, taking refuge with Geraldine in the kitchen.

'Come along, dear,' Gerry rallied her. 'Don't leave it all to me.'

'No . . . of course. Only, I'm not sure what to do with the avocados.'

Dotty came breezing in. 'Oh, good old Sally!' she laughed. 'Never knows what to do – here, give them to me.'

She hacked them up anyhow, but being Dotty, would no doubt get away with it. She sailed in, bearing the first two aloft. 'Come along people, it's ready!'

They leaped to their feet, anxious to please her by being the first to obey.

Sally lived through the meal like an automaton. Her hands, even her face, did her bidding, seemingly unaware that her mind was switched off. Her stomach received the

183

food and did nothing with it, sulking, as if it had forgotten what it was for. She smiled, endlessly and without reason, her eyes palpably glazing, unable to blink. She babbled, mindlessly, unable afterwards to recall a single word she said, her thoughts constantly swerving to avoid perilous confrontations. Lemon meringue pie . . . her one speciality, her recipe direct from Erik . . . his 'receipt', as he had called it . . .

She felt her control wavering, and in desperation sought Gerald's eyes. They were on Dotty. Inevitably. So were everyone's. She gritted her teeth. Quickly, think about something else . . . she turned to George, beside her. Said idiotically, 'Do you know any jokes?'

He looked startled, then amused. 'Not the sort you'd appreciate, my dear. Why do you ask?'

'I – I don't know.' She blushed. 'Just, I need to laugh.' Quickly . . . for God's sake, somebody make me laugh . . .

Something in her face, in her look, must have spoken to him.

'What is it?' he spoke under his breath. 'Has something upset you?'

'My father . . .' She spoke in a small, tight voice, surprised to find she could say it at all, that no storm of tears had broken to undo her. 'I'm sorry – no, please don't say anything! I don't want to spoil the party . . .' She felt herself trembling violently. Perhaps, after all, she was going to break down. She must have been mad. What was she thinking of, to tell George, of all people – George, to impress whom the whole evening had been designed! 'Excuse me,' she stammered. 'Please forget what I said. I must see to the coffee . . .'

She stumbled blindly to the kitchen, leaving him staring after her. But she was past coherent thought. She took cream from the refrigerator, aimlessly put it back; moved cups about, on to the tray and off again, seeing only Erik, conjuring pennies from teacups at that long ago breakfast table . . . Erik, oh Erik . . . it couldn't be true, it couldn't . . . he couldn't be dead . . .

Water was pouring down her face like rain down a window. She couldn't see through it or past it . . . the edge of a glass was pressed to her mouth, a fiery taste of brandy scorched her tongue . . . she tried to speak but nothing came out, though she could neither close her mouth nor open her eyes . . . an arm encircled her, pressing her streaming face against fabric . . . a hand was rubbing her back . . . sounds of wonderment reached her from a thousand miles away. Then from under her head a voice boomed, 'It's a damned disgrace, you ought to be ashamed! Expecting your wife to give a party in the state she's in—'

It was only then that she realized the man holding her was George.

CHAPTER SIX

'I feel so heartbroken,' sighed Aimée, fluttering faded lashes in an expression of studied pathos.

Oh God, thought Sally, here we go again! Twelve years of separation and malice, and now we're expected to console the sorrowing widow. She looked on dispassionately as her mother dug among her relics, the now tattered love letters, the faded photographs, searching for something with which to whip into life her decaying emotion. Play-acting, she thought, she's always play-acting. The real Aimée only pops out on occasion to lash out at some poor wretch who's missed his cue.

'More tea?' she offered drily.

'I couldn't eat a thing,' said Aimée reprovingly. 'As you'd know if you had any finer feelings.'

Sally kept a straight face. 'I thought perhaps, after eighteen months . . .'

Aimée had turned from her and was delving again. 'Did I ever show you this miniature of me when I was four? The artist did it for nothing, he said I was such a beautiful child.'

'No, I don't think I've seen it.' She held the picture in her hand; it was indeed a beautiful child, more so even than Dotty. The eyes deep violet, set in, as Gerry would say, 'with a sooty finger', a luxuriance of bright hair escaping from under an Edwardian velvet hat smothered in ostrich feathers . . . in fancy dress, thought Sally, even then. But it was something about the expression that caught her attention, a look she had seen so often on Aimée's face. Here it was, on this lovely child in the borrowed plumes, swamped by the ill-fitting hat: the eyes mistrustful, the

186

delicate lip about to quiver . . . she remembered what Uncle Charles had told her about their childhood. Was this what it had done to four-year-old Amy Simpson, made her afraid to grow up? Was that perhaps what had drawn her to the stage, the search for a character in which to hide herself, a mask for the frightening suspicion that there was really no one inside . . .

In her sixties, she remained a little girl trying on hats, tossing each aside in favour of the next in a fruitless search for the one that fitted her . . . poor Aimée. Poor little Amy . . . the trouble was, they were all grown-up hats. Not one of them was ever going to fit a little girl. Had she tried the bridal head-dress in mistake for the Fairy Queen? Alas for King Oberon, whose natural behaviour had outraged and frightened her.

It was hard, in any case, to imagine people of the Thirties having sex. Especially women. It didn't seem to go with Oxford shoes, long shapeless clothes, directoire knickers, stays of boned pink cotton worn over the vest. And yet sex there must have been, since procreation did not stop. Those prudish women, those shamefaced men must, despite their scraped haircuts and obliterating tweeds, have indulged their appetites, disown them all they might, since a whole generation had emerged to embarrass them.

And it was perhaps understandable that Aimée admired Dotty – admired, maybe even envied. Dotty, who as early as seventeen had been whole and self-assured, a projection of Aimée's self to a success she could never herself achieve. Dotty, bursting with confidence and cheer, who was always happy because she always had her own way. Aimée who was never happy, because however often she won, she could never be sure it was what she wanted . . .

All those roles, thought Sally, one after another for as long as she could remember: star-of-stage-and-screen, martyr-to-ill-health, lady-of-the-manor, deserted tragedy-queen; even ageless-charmer when Gerald came on the scene. She wondered how she had reconciled that one with devoted-parent and mother-of-the-bride.

'Well?' prompted Aimée, hungry for the expected compliment.

'It's very like you, anyone could tell . . .' She looked with compassion at her mother, at the spreading figure, the grey hair where the dye was growing out . . . she was never going to grow up now. She was one of life's walking wounded, and would have to be humoured as she was.

Sally pushed the biscuit tin towards her. 'I'll make some fresh tea,' she said.

'I told you I couldn't eat anything, why can't you understand,' said Aimée pettishly.

'Understand what?' She had been miles away.

Aimée snorted. 'There, you see! You don't even know what I'm talking about. Your father and I were devoted to each other for sixteen years, until that bitch got her hooks into him. Then just when he was trying to get free of her he died, before he had the chance to come back.'

Caught off guard, Sally looked at her in surprise. 'Was he coming back, did he say so?' As so often with her mother's monologues, she had been guilty of not listening. Perhaps she had missed something that had not been said before.

'Of course he was coming back! I've told you a thousand times, before he left, he looked deep into my eyes and said . . .'

'Oh, that . . .' She should have known, have remembered what had become little more than a ritual incantation.

Aimée looked at her sharply. 'Is that all you can say? Well, I suppose you couldn't be expected to understand, you're only a child – what are you laughing at?'

She rearranged her face. 'Just that you always say that.'

'Then don't talk about things you know nothing about,' snapped Aimée, her fat fingers rummaging in the biscuit tin. 'Aren't there any chocolate ones left?'

'I expect the children have had them.' She had nearly said 'the other children'.

'They shouldn't be allowed to pick out the best,' said Aimée tartly.

Sally felt her patience beginning to slip. Her grief for Erik was not sufficiently healed for her to feel comfortable in the presence of what she felt to be Aimée's sham; for all her resolution, the obligation to suffer it stroked a finger over the raw edge of a nerve. She stood up abruptly, slapped the lid on the biscuits, tacked on a determined smile.

'I'll get some more tomorrow. I'm a useless mother, what else would you expect? Just give me up, I'm past praying for—'

'There's no need to speak like that!' retorted Aimée. 'I was only passing a civil comment.' She reopened the tin, found a biscuit with jam in the middle and proceeded to nibble at it. 'Gerald's very late tonight, isn't he?' she said slyly.

Sally controlled the snatch in her stomach. The one that came of the fact that these days Gerald was late nearly every night. 'He has to see a client,' she managed to say calmly.

'Oh? I didn't think solicitors had to do business late at night.'

Neither did Sally. But she had no wish to discuss it with Aimée. 'No? Things must be changing then, because they do quite often now.'

Aimée lifted an eyebrow. 'If you say so.'

'I do say so,' said Sally firmly. 'Now, I've got to think about dinner.'

There was a silence. Then Aimée said nonchalantly, 'Have you heard from Dotty lately?'

'No, have you?' She was glad enough to steer the talk away from a loaded subject. 'We don't write very often. How's she getting on?'

'Oh? I thought you must have been seeing her, she seems to have all your news.'

Sally looked up from the recipe book to surprise a look of triumph on her mother's face. Was she merely being mischievous . . . or did she know something? Not Dotty, she prayed. Anyone else, but please, not Dotty. She felt a sudden chill. Was that why she hadn't heard from Louise for so long, did she too suspect and, unlike Aimée, want to avoid carrying tales?

'Oh well, of course,' she lied bravely. 'I write to her from time to time. It's just that she doesn't answer very often. You know Dotty, too busy living to put pen to paper. Oh—' She pretended to have remembered something. 'I promised Gerald some fresh salmon tonight, it's his birthday. Can you remember how to make that sauce he liked, I can't find it in here . . .' She was babbling, as she always did when nervous. Aimée would not be fooled, for who knew her better. But she had long ago learned to keep her anxieties to herself.

'Did you know he was going to be best man at George's wedding?' she called back through the doorway. 'Next month it would have been, if it hadn't been for the accident. Poor George, he's still terribly upset, he's hardly been in the office since it happened.'

Aimée followed her through into the kitchen and looked about her for somewhere to sit.

'Haven't you got any chairs out here?' She settled for a stool, and went on talking. 'I never really heard the details. Was he driving when it happened?'

'So Gerald said at the time. Apparently they'd been to a party, he'd had a few drinks, the road was icy and that was it.' She felt mean, diverting Aimée's attention by running down poor old George. But he'd never know. And it did happen to be true. And it was infinitely preferable to discussing Gerald. 'Thank God, it was instantaneous. At least she didn't have time to be frightened.' Had she, she wondered; could anything really be quicker than the intuition of death . . . one could only hope so. 'It's George I'm sorry for, it's really hit him sideways.'

'I heard he'd been drowning his sorrows,' said Aimée. 'He's like me, a person of deep feeling. Too grief-stricken to be able to think of work.'

'I don't think he has to worry about that. According to Gerald he has private money, he could manage quite comfortably if he wanted to retire. I don't think it would be good though. I mean, it's better to have something to occupy your mind. It doesn't help to sit and brood.'

Aimée surveyed her coldly. 'You always were a callous little madam,' she observed.

She was still there when Gerald's key turned in the lock. It was noticeable, thought Sally, that her mother, who was always busy elsewhere when her presence might have been helpful, none the less contrived to be at the cottage whenever her son-in-law came home. Even Gerald had commented on it.

'Can't you drop a hint to your mother?'

'Well . . . I've tried, but she doesn't seem to catch on. It's a bit difficult, short of saying outright, Don't come.' The truth was, she had not yet learned a way of saying No to Aimée. The habit of deference was still too deeply ingrained. 'I suppose I could pretend that you're bringing work home,' she offered weakly.

'No – don't say that, it doesn't matter.' The look on his face had been enough to warn her that the subject was closed.

Now, Aimée put on her most ingratiating face, and sniffed appreciatively. 'Mm – mm, smells lovely. You've turned out a good little cook, Sally, I'll say that for you.' She smiled at Gerald. 'Can I stay and have a little bit? Then you could run me home.'

They exchanged glances above her head. Short of churlishness, there was no way of refusing. Gerald returned her smile without a tremor. 'Why not?' he said smoothly. 'We'll have a bottle of wine to mark the occasion.'

Was he telling her, in his tactful way, that this was to be regarded as a one-off? Sally caught his eye and turned away to conceal her amusement. Thank heaven for Gerald, she was thinking, he could always be relied on to carry things off when she was out of her depth.

Over the cheese, Aimée said inconsequentially, 'Are you taking Sally to the ballet next week?'

'No,' said Sally quickly. 'We can't fit it in.'

She sent a little frown, a small shake of the head, across the table to her mother. Aimée ignored it.

'If it's the matter of a babysitter, I'll come over if you

191

get them to bed first. As long as it's only the once, I wouldn't mind. It seems a pity to miss it.'

'Then you take her,' suggested Gerald evenly. 'I'll come home early so that she can go.'

'She doesn't want to go with me,' protested Aimée. 'She wants to go out with you, of course she does. She wants a romantic escort.'

Sally said nothing, willing herself not to look at either of them. It was bad enough that Gerald didn't want to take her, without Aimée pressing the point. For once she was not sure if she was stirring up trouble deliberately, or trying in some clumsy way to help; either way it was making matters worse.

'Then I suggest you find her one,' said Gerald pleasantly. 'I'll pay for the tickets.'

Aimée gasped audibly; but when Sally looked up she had recovered herself and was smiling coquettishly. 'You're teasing her, aren't you?' she suggested, but she didn't sound too sure.

'No, he's not,' said Sally, smiling brightly before he could answer. 'He's teasing you. I've already told him that I don't want to go. It's just a sort of joke . . .'

'I'm quite serious.' Gerald gave her a look so cold and hostile that she was silenced. 'If Sally can find someone who wants to take her out, I will willingly pay his expenses. Now, did you have a coat? I have just time to run you home.'

In bed that night, doggedly sawing away, he said irritably, 'Can't you pretend to enjoy it? Imagine I'm somebody else, or something . . .'

Stung, she retorted, 'I wouldn't know how to, would I? You can't fake something you've never experienced.'

If that was below the belt so was nis blaming her, when clearly both their minds had been elsewhere.

'You mean, you don't like me making love to you.'

He sounded offended rather than hurt. She said quickly, 'No, of course I don't mean that . . . not really. It's just that . . .' She tailed off. What she had wanted to say sounded so – so unacceptable. An enormity, even. She could imagine Geraldine throwing up her hands in outrage.

'Well?'

His voice in the darkness above her was a quiet challenge. She would have to answer him, so why not with the truth. You were supposed to talk about these things, it was unfair not to, all the magazines said so. And perhaps this was the moment, one that might not come again. She screwed up her courage. 'It's just that – well, sometimes, I feel I'm being entered – sort of, against my will . . .'

He stopped. Withdrew, moved away in an angry silence. Then he said frostily, 'Do you realize what you're saying, that you think you're being raped?'

'No, no, of course not – not that, you know I didn't mean that—' She reached out to him but he moved further across the bed. 'Oh, Gerald . . .'

'It is not possible,' he annunciated the words carefully, as though he were in court, 'for a husband to rape his wife. Assent on marriage is considered to be final.'

'Yes, of course . . . of course . . .' She lay abandoned beside him, her nightdress up under her arms. 'Gerald, please come back. I'm sorry, I didn't mean to upset you, forget what I said. Please . . .'

Although she had little pleasure in the act, she needed the closeness of it, the reassurance that their marriage was not really, alarmingly, beginning to crumble. One wayward tear was beginning its descent over her temple when at last he spoke.

'Don't ever say a thing like that to me again.' His voice was full of suppressed indignation. After a pause he returned to blunder his way back into her; but there was no more warmth in their union than there ever was, and she did not feel forgiven.

What was happening to them, she asked herself as she lay awake watching daybreak stain the sky. She could hardly recognize in her chilly, perfunctory husband the enchanting Gerald who had come between her and her wits when she was fourteen. Was it he who had changed, or was it herself . . . she did not know. She was only sure that then, so long ago, she had known for a certainty that she had only to be with him to be happy. And that now it was no longer so. She wanted, needed, something more than his mere presence − although even of that she was seeing less and less. She wanted closeness in marriage, a measure of warmth and affection, and every day that passed told her more surely it was not to be. Did he still love her . . . had he ever loved her? The truth was, she did not know. She could not remember his saying it to her in so many words. What she remembered with devastating clarity was his Spartan edict, delivered with all the authority of a papal bull, that since no one could promise to love for ever, neither was ever to ask the other if he still did . . .

She sighed and turned over, searching with her face for a dry place on the pillow. Unable to escape the nagging of the suspicion Aimée had sown, teasing her brain for evidence to either support or deny. The thought of Dotty scalded her more than at any time during their childhood; if Gerald, God forbid! was falling in love with her, it would be bitterly hard to live down. And lived down it would have to be, if Charles's and Zoë's lives were not to be scarred as her own had been . . .

At times like this, assailed by doubt and disappointment, she was not even certain that she was still in love herself. The only thing she was sure of was that, in terms of her personal happiness, of the shared laughter, the tactile delights she had so fondly imagined, her marriage to Gerald had proved to be a mirage.

When she woke in the morning, heavy-eyed, he was already out of bed.

'Gerald . . . about last night,' she began tentatively. 'Before the children come in, I just wanted to say—'

'I don't wish to discuss it any further,' he said politely. 'Are we having any breakfast?'

'But we must discuss it—'

'Not just now,' he said. 'The trouble is, there's no mutual

194

affection between us. And when affection is left hanging loose, it's liable to be taken up elsewhere.'

'Gerald . . .' Her voice came out little above a whisper. Her stomach had turned cold. 'Surely, you don't mean that . . .'

He indicated the clock. 'It's quarter to eight,' he reminded her pleasantly, and disappeared into the bathroom, locking the door.

When she returned from taking the children to school she made straight for the exercise book in which she habitually unburdened herself. She had to set down the fragment that had been running in her mind since last night. It was not complete, she could not think of it as a poem; it merely said what she felt. She fished in her bag for a ballpoint and scribbled it down.

> My tides of love run down
> To still small pools of pity where you stalk
> Aloof as a heron on the edges of my life
> And care no whit for where you walk.

She sat for a while, thinking about it. She could not extend it, or develop the idea. It didn't matter. Already she felt eased by having committed it to paper. It was pity, not anger, that she felt for Gerald, for anyone who knew so little above love and was missing so much in life.

She sighed, and put the book away. She wished she could have been a real writer; it must be so satisfying.

CHAPTER SEVEN

She was aware of him long before she met him. Before a word or a look had been exchanged, she was conscious of his presence – or his absence – in the library where she stopped after taking the children to school, to indulge her taste for other people's poetry – real poetry as she thought of it – or in the second-hand bookshop where she rummaged in the bargain box; once she saw him from the corner of her eye, buying wine at the far end of the new supermarket.

It was not that his physical appearance was particularly striking. He was, she judged, of medium height, and neither fat nor thin; but there was something about him that spoke to her. Something in the quick, decisive movements of his hands, the lively eyes that seemed alert to everything – even her own unwarranted interest – the oblique of dark hair that slid forward across his brow as he looked down . . . she was hard put to it to say what had first compelled her attention. Not his looks, surely, since he was not especially handsome, and far less so than Gerald. It was more that his was a face you had to keep your eyes on for fear of missing something if you looked away. As if it were a mirror, or perhaps a window, in which thoughts and emotions were reflected so swiftly, or briefly, that to blink might mean the loss of something fascinating.

Before she realized what was happening, she found herself watching for him. About the town, in the library, near the bookshop . . . when she caught herself looking for him at the bus stop, she pulled herself up short. This was ridiculous. It could even be dangerous, in a way she was not quite sure about. She reminded herself sternly that she was a married woman. And he, quite probably, was a married man. She was unsure why that should make her spirits droop. But there was no denying that it did.

And then, for a whole week, she did not see him. Then it became a month. When it lengthened into weeks, she knew that he must have gone away. In one way, it was sad and disappointing; his presence had brightened her solitary treks from school to shops, from shops to home, even though they had never spoken. But in another way it was something of a relief. Now she could safely build him into her sexual fantasies, the daydreams with which she indulged herself while endlessly mowing grass or ironing shirts . . . unnamed and unknown, he became the cipher for all she was missing in life.

Was he a newcomer, she wondered, or had he always been around? Even as she framed the question she knew the answer: if he had been, she would have noticed him. Free to fantasize, she invented a background for him, and a nationality; he was not English, she decided, not with those high cheekbones, that lean ascetic face. He was no boring Smith or Jones, he would have some exotic name like Anton, or Ivan or . . . she did not know many foreign names and quickly ran out of alternatives. It didn't matter; it was only as a lover that he had significance. Perhaps he was a sultry Latin – or a Pole, one of those great romantics she had only read about. He might touch her here, and here . . . his mouth would caress her most secret, hidden places . . . she would close her eyes and drown in sensuality.

She had attained a stage where she had only to think of him to feel her body begin to glow when, alarmingly and without warning, he was back.

It was in that most romantic of settings, the supermarket, that it happened. She was waiting at the checkout, two places behind a woman who was having problems in finding enough money, first taking out a giant pack of soap powder to reduce the bill, and then, finding that was not enough, trying various combinations of goods before deciding that she couldn't do without them and asking if she could pay by cheque. Only then, she couldn't find her cheque book, it must be in her other handbag—

'Next, please!' The cashier swept her groceries back into the basket and turned her attention to the queue.

The woman hovered, dithering. 'I'll come back in about half an hour, do you think you could keep them for me . . .'

'Plenty more on the shelves, madam.'

'Oh, but . . .'

The cashier ignored her in favour of the next shopper, turning her eyes towards heaven as a murmur ran through the queue behind Sally. It was hard to tell if it meant sympathy with the cashier or with the customer, or merely impatience at the delay.

As Sally turned to see which, her eyes were met by his, smiling faintly in just the degree of amused tolerance as her own. She felt her face burn scarlet.

'Next, please!'

It was her turn to fumble. She threw her purchases into the carriers anyhow, dropped her change and had to scrabble for it on the floor, where it had scattered among the dust and scraps of paper.

'Also, these.' He was down beside her, in the shadows between the counters, holding out a handful of coins.

'Oh . . .' She took them, hot from his hand, stuffed them loose into her pocket, and fled, barging ungracefully through the swing doors, hampered by shopping in both hands.

A furtive glance over her shoulder told her that he was still standing there, watching her. He was smiling . . . or was it laughing? She bolted like a rabbit, not relaxing until she was safely on the bus.

You stupid, stupid idiot! she thought angrily, her face cooling as the bus bumped and growled on its way. You've really made a fool of yourself now. What must he think of you – you didn't even thank him, just rushed off like some silly schoolgirl with a crush. And that smile, of his, that knowing smile – yes, knowing! That's what it was, he knows, all about you and your imagination, that sort of man always does . . . because of course, you're not the first. Or the only. I bet he has dozens of women panting to jump into his bed. He's the type . . . and he finds it funny! God, I hate men like that! I don't ever want to see him again, why couldn't he just stay away and leave me my fantasies, that's probably all he's good for. He's ruined everything, coming back like this – and laughing. How dare he laugh!

By the time she had reached home and stowed her shopping, she had it all worked out. Since she could not meet him again without the most acute embarrassment, she must make sure that such a meeting did not take place. Unless and until he disappeared again, the only way was to avoid the places he was likely to be; she would do her shopping further afield, at different times. Better still, hermetically sealed in the car.

When Gerald came in, she said, 'Darling, now that I've passed my test, could I borrow the car to take the children to school? I could drop you at the office first and—'

'It wouldn't be very convenient,' he said smoothly. But she noticed that he was frowning a little. 'I might need it during the day.'

'You could ring me. I'd bring it in at once—'

'N – no . . . I think not. If I needed it urgently, you might be out.' He dropped a kiss on the top of her head, gave her his charming smile, and went upstairs to say goodnight to Zoë.

It was always Zoë he went up to see, never Charles. She would see the little boy hover longingly in his bedroom doorway and wish she could even things out. Often she had gone up herself, only to find him tucked firmly in his bed, ostentatiously feigning sleep. Bending above him, she could sense his withdrawal. It was not her blessing that he hungered for, but aloof, elusive Gerald's.

She sighed, and set about the business of preparing the evening meal. Life had been easier of late, since Gerald had unaccountably returned to coming home at a normal time.

Nothing had been said, but she had felt instinctively that whatever had kept him away from home was over, at least for the time being. She supposed she should be glad – well, of course she was glad. Of course – except that, since there had been no quarrel, there had been no kiss and make up to sweeten it. It was more a sort of cool resumption of normal service. Until, she supposed, the next time. But things had eased in other ways: perhaps conscious that she was owed some compensation, he had taken to letting her handle the housekeeping money unsupervised, even allowing her the occasional use of the car. And it was heartening to know that since she had survived the hazard once, she could hope to do so again: the marriage would remain intact, the children safe, for as long as she chose to turn a blind eye.

It could be worse, she reminded herself, it could be a great deal worse. She loved her children, she loved her home, and in her own way and for reasons she could not have explained, she realized that she still loved Gerald. You had only to look about you to see the relationships of others falling apart like packs of cards. But you didn't have to let yours do the same. It was a little like sticking out a routine job when all around you were becoming unemployed.

She smiled now, remembering her panic over the man in the supermarket. It was not, after all, an incident from real life. If she couldn't have the car, so be it. And if she saw him again . . . she would just ignore him.

For all her good intentions, it did not work out that way. She had managed to avoid the supermarket all that week, and then she had to go in there for Charles's favourite blackcurrant drink. She could not buy it anywhere else because it was the supermarket's own brand. She gritted her teeth and marched in, looking neither to right nor to left as she bore down on the drinks section.

As chance would have it there was none on display. She found a youth stocking up shelves, and was obliged to wait while he went to find out about it. She felt like a sitting duck, unable to escape or hide herself from view. And she

200

was right here by the drinks display; suppose he came in to buy wine as he often did — where she had seen him before—

'Hello, again!'

His voice came from behind her, and she started violently. She had been staring so intently after the stockroom boy, willing his immediate return, that she had forgotten to keep an eye on the door. Panic seized her afresh.

'Oh — forget it,' she blurted aloud, and barged past him towards the exit, conscious that the stockroom boy had reappeared carrying a carton. But she couldn't wait, he would have had his errand for nothing. And Charles wouldn't get his blackcurrant . . . damn, damn, damn! she thought, tears of humiliation stinging her eyes, hearing in her mind Dotty's lighthearted 'Good old Sally, she never knows what to do . . .'

Outside on the pavement, she stopped, trying hard to make herself go back. Perhaps, if he had gone . . .

He hadn't. When she looked, he was still standing where she had left him, an expression on his face that took her by surprise. He looked . . . yes, that was it, crestfallen. Almost, she would have said — had it been anyone else — hurt.

She walked slowly to the bus stop, feeling unaccountably depressed. Dotty was right, she never did know what to do. She blundered about like a half-grown colt, kicking the people she most wanted to impress. And the more strongly she was attracted, the more inept and hopeless she became.

Lying awake that night, she reminded herself that she really knew nothing about this man. She had no justification for investing him with the character she had invented for him; he was just as likely to be a nice ordinary person looking for friends in a strange town. What right had she to bruise the feelings of someone who was trying to be pleasant? It was time to grow out of blushing and giggling, to lay her schoolgirl imaginings away with the *Girl's Own Paper*. To behave like a responsible adult instead of scurrying about like a frightened rabbit.

Gerald, she was convinced, had friends of his own, a social life that she knew nothing about. Why shouldn't she do the same?

The next day was Saturday. The children were at home, and Charles was asking for his blackcurrant drink.

'They didn't have any. I'll go in again on Monday.'

Gerald looked up. 'You could have the car if you want to go today.'

'Now, Mummy, now!' demanded Charles.

'Not now, I'm busy.'

'Oh, Mum!' wailed Charles, and Zoë chipped in.

'Mummy said she's busy,' she said self-righteously. 'Anyway, I want to stay with Daddy.'

'It's no good going today,' lied Sally. 'They won't have any more till Monday.'

She felt herself blushing and turned her guilty face towards the sink, where she scraped away ferociously at the potatoes, aware that she had taken at least one step on the downward path.

On Monday, she made a point of going back to the supermarket. There she saw only the usual slow trickle of shoppers like herself, stocking up on the oddments they had run out of over the weekend. With a slight sense of disappointment, she bought the drink for Charles, and deliberately came away without the butter on which they were running low at home: it would provide a pretext for another visit tomorrow.

It was only a quarter past nine. She might as well drop in at the library. She had rehearsed in her mind what she would say to him next time they met. Quite casually, she would say, 'So sorry I had to rush off the other day, I suddenly remembered I had to catch a train . . . you must have thought me very rude . . .' Or was that a bit old-fashioned, did anyone bother about being rude these days – and did one 'suddenly remember' to catch a train, perhaps it should be 'realized I was going to miss it'. And then, suppose he asked which train . . .

This was too silly, what did it matter, it was only something to open the doors, make it possible to talk . . . he was going to laugh at her. Well, if he did, if she took a dislike to him, that would be it, and it would solve everything.

At the library she took out the first book that came to hand, her eyes flitting constantly in search of him. After that, feeling deflated, she wandered on to the bookshop, though by now she hardly expected to see him today. It was only Monday, she reflected, trying to stave off the depression that afflicted her from time to time. There would be other days.

At the end of two weeks, she knew that he had disappeared again, perhaps for good this time, taking all sorts of intriguing possibilities with him. It was her own fault, she had brought it on herself. It served her right for being such a fool, behaving like an idiot. Dotty was still maddeningly right. She would never know what to do, and life would continue to pass her by because of it. Listlessly, she took back the unwanted book to the library.

'Are you taking out another?'

'Not just now.' She no longer felt like reading. It was hard to find anything she did feel like doing. Even the garden was getting away from her, the grass overgrown, the bindweed poking unwelcome noses up through the soil of the rose bed.

She waited in silence while the assistant wielded her rubber stamp and put the book away. As she put out her hand for her card something alighted on the desk in front of her, and a voice at her elbow said, 'Also, this?'

It was a bottle of blackcurrant drink.

CHAPTER EIGHT

'Your hand is shaking.'

Little lines of laughter crowded the margins of his eyes, as if they could not wait to join in. The irises were a rich warm brown, the colour of the *fundador* brandy Gerald had brought back from a meeting in Madrid. Like the eyes of a fox, she thought, or like amber, with dark rims melting into the reddish brown like smoke . . .

She tried to set down her coffee cup without rattling it in the saucer. 'It's nothing, they always shake.' She suppressed a nervous giggle. 'I'm the ruination of gramophone records.'

The laughter lines increased. 'I think, no. I think you have fear, just a little.'

'Should I have?' She felt very daring, teasing him, as if she were another person. As if she were Dotty, she thought with a little lift of the spirits; and so far, she was carrying it off . . .

'Of me?' He shook his head. 'You should fear nothing. You must enjoy, enjoy. Like me. I enjoy everything.'

Enjoy . . . what was he thinking of? She had no business to be here at all, drinking coffee with this man. Only, he had made her laugh at her own inept apology, and pretended to be devastated, insisting that she make amends with an hour of her time. And it was only an hour . . .

'Everything?' She hid her unsteady hands beneath the table. 'Surely there are some things nobody enjoys.'

'Such as?' Amusement tugged at the corners of his mouth. It was very finely cut, she noticed. Very expressive.

'Well . . . like being ill, or whatever.'

204

'I am never ill.'

'You're very lucky.' If that sounded slightly sardonic, it was meant to.

'I make my luck and so must you. Good things don't fall from heaven, they're made on earth.'

'I'm glad you think so,' she said primly. She was on the point of dismissing him as conceited and cocksure; too free with his 'you must' do this or that on first acquaintance . . .

'I do!' He laughed disarmingly. 'And so, how do you amuse yourself?'

She stared, confused. 'How do I what?'

'Amuse yourself. To enjoy, what do you like?' He narrowed his eyes. 'I think you dance.'

'Dance?' Ah, if only . . . 'What makes you think so?'

'You walk like a dancer, move like a dancer, like a tree in the wind. I know, I see you about the town. I too. We dance together some time.'

In spite of herself, a fierce thrill shot through her. So, he had watched her about the town . . . as she had him. She was gripped by an overpowering urge to say Yes, to look out at the view from some window he was opening in her life, to lean out and fill her lungs with new air, even at the risk of falling . . .

'No,' she said quickly. 'I'm afraid that's not possible. If you've seen me in the town you must know I'm married. With two little children,' she added, not giving herself time to weaken.

He shook his head in mock despondency. 'Alas!' He reached across to pick up the hand that wore the wedding ring. 'Why do you do this thing so I cannot marry you?' He bent his head and his lips touched her fingers. When he looked up, the red-brown eyes were bubbling with amusement. 'Since I cannot have you, madame, you have seen the last of me. I shall go and shoot tigers—'

'You're making fun of me!'

He laughed again. 'I tease you, I am bad. But you blush

so very charmingly.' He stood up, leaned across the table, and before she could recover herself, planted a swift kiss on her cheek. '*Ciao*,' he called back.

Before she could speak he was gone, leaving his touch still tingling on her skin.

When she reached the cottage, Aimée was waiting on the doorstep.

'Where on earth have you been? I've been here since half-past nine!'

'Oh . . . sorry.' She jerked her mind to attention. 'I thought we said lunch. It's only quarter to twelve.'

'Yes, but where did you get to, you're always back by ten. Did you have to go somewhere else?'

She was aware of being skewered by one of her mother's suspicious looks. An imp of mischief entered her. 'Sit down,' she invited. 'I'll tell you all about it. You remember Gerald saying he'd pay someone to take me out? Well, I've found someone.' Aimée leaned forward, a look on her face that warned her to swerve before the moment of impact. 'I'm in love with an Indian carpet salesman, we stopped to book our trip to the Taj Mahal.'

Aimée stared at her blankly for a moment, before dawning realization twisted her face into an uncertain smile. 'You're not serious?'

Sally patted her arm in reassurance. 'It's a joke, Mummy. I am bad, I was teasing you.' Echoing his words . . .

'Just for that,' laughed Aimée reluctantly, 'you can make me a cup of tea.'

Sally went to fill the kettle, reflecting with pleasure on how much better they were getting on these days. It must be years since she had called her mother Mummy. At the sink, she turned back.

'Actually, I stopped at the Cadena for a coffee.' It had not been the Cadena. Why had she said it was? She went on quickly. 'Then I decided to walk home instead of coming on the bus.'

'You walked? Five and a half miles, you must be mad!'

'Not really.' She smiled blissfully. 'I enjoyed it. It was such a lovely day.'

Later, alone, and with the euphoria wearing off, she reflected that he had said nothing about seeing her again. He hadn't even asked her name – and she hadn't asked him his. Oh, damn! She sank down despondently on the kitchen stool. It was just another fiasco after all, one more bubble bursting on the stagnant pond of her life. And yet . . . he had said they would dance together. Well, of course they couldn't. Couldn't do anything, really, not even meet, not deliberately.

Did Gerald mean what he had said, about there being no affection between them . . . she wished she were sure. But just to remember it gave her a cold, sad ache of isolation, and she couldn't ask. They didn't seem able to talk any more. In the early days they had talked endlessly, discussing everything under the sun, but then it was all hypothetical, they hadn't been touched by emotional problems themselves. Now that they were, it was different, every subject seemed loaded with dynamite.

When he came in, she asked him, 'What does "*ciao*" mean, do you know?'

'Why do you ask?'

'Oh . . . everyone seems to be saying it. Sort of, instead of goodbye. Is that what it means?'

'It's Italian, I think,' he said maddeningly. 'Just another fad, I suspect.'

'Yes, but what does it mean, exactly?'

'I'm not certain, you should look it up. Why do you want to know?'

'Because—' She stopped. Why not tell the truth, it was innocent enough . . . so far. 'I came across it in a book I'm reading.'

Gerald smiled, and picked up the evening paper. 'Then I should read on, and find out from the context.'

'Shall I?' She gave him a long, sober look; an opportunity to challenge her.

He returned it enigmatically. 'Why not? It's what I'd do.'

It was almost as if he knew, she thought, hurrying towards the library the next day, as if he knew, and did not care. As if it were what he wanted, the freedom to go his own way while she went hers. They had talked about that kind of marriage in the old days, the kind where partners stayed together without love, pretending nobody knew. They had agreed it was more honest to make a clean break . . . but that was then. Then there had been no children, no solicitor's reputation to be considered, and even now, in the so-called Swinging Sixties, such things mattered. Now, she cared about the children. And Gerald, presumably, about his career. She was sure, or fairly sure, that he no longer cared about her. She put the ache to one side, and hastened her steps.

There were a few familiar faces at the library, but not the one she looked for. She sauntered the aisles with diminishing optimism, then repeated the exercise at, first, the bookshop, then the supermarket. After that she went to the park, seated herself on one of the benches, and tried to read. At the end of two restless hours she went to the Cadena and drank a solitary coffee, unable to bring herself to go straight home.

By the end of the week, she knew there was no point in looking. It had been a flash in the pan, a passing amusement for him, perhaps – she coloured hotly – a joke. The window she had longed to jump through had been just another mirage; Gerald would be the one to have his fling while she remained stuck in the kitchen, trying to allay her boredom with new recipes for jam.

It was so much easier for a man; he could go out and search for what he wanted; a woman could only leave herself lying around and hope to be found. It wasn't fair. She wondered if it would be any better for Zoë when she grew up, but there seemed little hope of it. The girl who dared to use initiative was battling against the wind, not so much from the men as from the jealousy of other women. She knew very well that if she had a wild affair with Anton or Ivan or whatever he called himself, it would be not Gerald but Geraldine who would want her horsewhipped, and Aimée who would hold her while it was done. She sighed philosophically; the whole thing had become academic.

She stared in perplexity at the second bottle of blackcurrant. She was sure she had picked up only one from the display, yet here she was at the checkout, unloading two.

'Did you want two, madam?'

'No . . . yes. I suppose I might as well . . .' She tried to remember. She had left the trolley while she went back to the cheese counter. Perhaps when she came back, she had picked up another bottle . . . stupid. She had been doing stupid things in the past week or two. She went on unloading her purchases. At the bottom of the trolley was a scrap of paper, the sort that might have been torn from a shorthand notebook.

On it was roughly scrawled, 'Coffee in half an hour? Adam.'

Adam, Adam! Of course, the name was perfect. It fitted him exactly, though it gave no clue to his nationality, gave no more away than the faint trace of accent that she couldn't identify . . . she would be able to ask after all, would find out all the little things she had wondered about—

'Three pounds, please!' The checkout girl's voice was tinged with impatience. She pulled herself together.

'Sorry . . .' She paid and hurried away, to be called back at the door to collect her forgotten shopping.

In half an hour, the note had said. But not where he would be. Should she go to the same place as before – or did he mean he would meet her here – and why in half an hour, why not speak to her there and then? There was a flavour of cloak and dagger that set her pulses racing, adding a spice of the clandestine, the romantic – almost as if he knew. Perhaps he did know, she thought, slowing her steps. Perhaps he did this sort of thing all the time. She remembered what she had thought that first time, when she looked back and saw him laughing . . . she checked her watch. She had twenty minutes; time to sit in the park and think it over before committing herself. Best not to be there first, anyway, she would feel such a fool if he didn't turn up after all.

She sat on the edge of the hard bench under the cherry tree, wrestling to reconcile her inclinations with her principles. Was she really in danger of letting herself in for an ill-advised liaison? Had she thought it through to all possible consequences – already she was lying, before there was anything to lie about. Not that there was likely to be, she told herself with confidence. It was one thing to fantasize, even to fall in love, quite another to do anything about it.

No, why shouldn't she go and have coffee with Adam? She was sure that Gerald had gone a lot farther than that! And if he didn't care – which he didn't – why should she? All the same, two wrongs didn't make a right . . .

A shadow fell across the path in front of her.

'I thought I might find you here,' said Adam. 'You are telling yourself you must not meet me for a so decadent coffee.'

Despite herself, she had to laugh with him. 'How did you guess?'

'I tell you something else.' He seated himself beside her and folded his arms. 'You will next remind me that you are a happily married woman.'

She made herself say it. 'You're absolutely right.'

He smiled at her sidelong, and slowly shook his head. 'I think not.'

Suddenly she felt angry, her privacy invaded. 'What makes you think you can say that! You don't even know me!' Such things were for her to tell him, not the other way about. If, and when, she decided to . . .

He stopped smiling. 'Because if you were, you would not be here with me.'

She felt her face beginning to tingle. 'You approached me,' she retorted.

'Yes. And you have not run away.' He reached for her hands, turned her to face him. 'You know what I want. And you do not run away.' He released her, turning playful again before she could reply. 'Ah, now I see that charming blush. I think we have coffee in the bosom of your tribe, you will feel more safe in a crowd.' He commandeered her shopping and she had no choice but to follow.

By the time they reached the restaurant she had recovered some of her composure.

'And in the bosom of which tribe do you belong?' She had sorted the words out carefully first, to have them in the right order.

'Ah! Now there's a question.'

But he did not seem disposed to answer it. Perhaps something awful had happened in the war. Perhaps she shouldn't have asked. Quickly she framed a different one. 'What language do you speak – I mean, most easily?'

'You mean, my English is "not so hot"?'

'No, no, I didn't mean that. Although it isn't.' She laughed a little unsteadily, uncertain how he would take it.

'Now, that is better!' He clapped his hands together once in a gesture of delight. 'You begin to tease me back, now we are friends!'

'So tell me, what is your language?'

He seemed to consider. 'French. Italian. Spanish. Serbo-Croat. Some Russian. Oh – and a little English . . .'

She tried not to look impressed. 'No, I meant your own language, your nationality. Where you were born?'

'Trieste. But this is not interesting, tell me about you. Tell me your name.'

'Sally,' she said. Not yet trusting him with more than that. 'I know yours . . . Adam.' Speaking his name made her feel unaccountably shy.

'Sally,' he repeated. His intonation gave it a slightly exotic sound. 'You know what it means?'

'I didn't think it meant anything.'

'Oh, yes.' He leaned forward. 'It means, would you believe, "an escapade"?'

Their eyes met and held like a charge of electricity. Flustered, she reached for her handbag, and stood up. 'I don't believe it,' she said breathlessly. 'You made it up.'

'Try me,' he said under his breath. Then he smiled and rose to his feet. 'Look it up when you get home. Now, I think we go back to the park, we have much to tell each other, no?'

They talked on and on, exchanging ideas and opinions, comparing their likes and aversions, their beliefs or lack of them, exploring one another's personalities instead of merely supplying data. The questions she had longed to ask no longer seemed important; on the practical side she learned only that he was a journalist, some kind of foreign correspondent, which was why he disappeared from time to time; that when he worked at all it was far into the night, and that he was based in London. So, what was he doing here, she asked. He meditated before replying.

'Something awaited me in this place.'

Did he mean her, she wondered; afraid to ask in case he said no. As if he had overheard her thoughts, he put a hand on her shoulder as they strolled, not saying what did not need to be said.

'It must be nearly time for lunch,' she said, for the sake of changing the subject. 'Good God! It's twenty to three, I must fetch the children!'

He did not make conventional apologies for taking up her time.

'See you tomorrow.' He bent his head to kiss her swiftly on the mouth, and walked briskly away across the park.

She sank down on the nearest seat for a moment in which to collect herself. She felt dazed, disorientated, disconnected from her normal way of life; the Sally who had to pick up two children from school was someone from another planet. She herself was a different person with a life of her own, a woman involved in a flirtation with a foreign correspondent . . . she got slowly to her feet at last, and walked in the direction of the school.

She arrived ten minutes late, to be met by the school secretary.

'Oh, Mrs Hammond, I've been trying to reach you all day! It's Zoë, she's been quite sick, and she's running a temperature.'

CHAPTER NINE

All the way home in the taxi Zoë whimpered, her small face burning and tearstained.

'Mummy, where were you? I wanted to come home and they couldn't find you. I was ever so sick—'

'All over the tablecloth!' Charles bounced excitedly. 'And it was beetroot—'

'Don't shout,' pleaded Sally. 'Zoë's got a headache. We'll soon be home and then it's straight to bed.'

'Not me!' he wailed indignantly. 'I wasn't sick, I want my tea. Can we have toast with lots of butter – oh, not again!'

'Just be quiet, can't you?' snapped Sally, her nerves fraying as she tried to mop up Zoë. 'You should have more sense than to talk about tea just now. How would you feel if it was you?'

He subsided, his face reddening angrily, and turned away to sulk in the far corner of the seat. Sally wound down the window and tried to make her daughter comfortable, thinking: Talk about coming down to earth with a bump!

As she paid off the taxi she could hear the telephone ringing.

'Where on earth have you been!' demanded Aimée. 'I came all the way over on the bus and there was no one there. I've been trying to ring you all day . . .'

'Sorry, I can't explain just now, I've got to get the doctor. I'll ring you back later, 'bye for now.' She rang off without waiting for a response.

As she was looking up the doctor's number it rang again. She lifted it only long enough to identify her mother's voice and, with a stronger sense of guilt than any she had felt that day, replaced the receiver.

By the time the doctor arrived, Zoë had slept for an hour and was looking better, although she was still feverish. He examined her for rashes, felt behind her ears and looked inside her mouth.

'Hmm . . . looks like measles, there's a lot of it about. Can't be sure until the rash appears, I'll look in again tomorrow. Meanwhile keep her warm and quiet, and you'd better keep the boy at home. If it is, it's three weeks' quarantine, I'm afraid.'

Three weeks' quarantine! Sally saw him to the door in a daze. All she could think of was, Adam . . . oh, Adam . . .

Dr Wright turned and smiled his encouragement. 'Don't look so worried, it's not bubonic plague, you know. They're past the age for dangerous complications.'

'Oh, yes . . . yes, I'm sure. Thank you for coming out. I'm sure they'll be fine.'

She watched him down the path. Then closed the door and stood with her back against it, savouring what she knew must be the last of her ephemeral romance. Oh, Adam . . . Adam! If she was not there tomorrow, he would think she had backed out. She would never see him again . . . against all common sense, she felt the tears begin to form . . .

'Sally!' came Gerald's voice from the living room. 'Aren't we going to have dinner tonight?'

Zoë's illness dragged on for ten days, her restless little body refusing to stay quiet, repeatedly exhausting itself and having to give in and go back to bed. And on the last day of quarantine, Charles developed it too. Sally was too busy to brood, her every moment occupied with nursing, washing constant changes of bedlinen, trying to create dishes to tempt their capricious appetites. Aimée's ruffled feathers had to be smoothed – she was not accustomed to being spoken to 'like that', she declared – and Geraldine was forever on the telephone for what seemed like hourly bulletins; her chief concern seemed to be that Gerald had not had measles as a child, and 'everyone knew it was much worse for adults'.

Sally could not recall having had it either, but no one seemed to be worrying about that. If she did become ill, presumably one of the mothers would come and help; it was soon obvious that neither was going to offer unless she did. As for Gerald, it was clear that he felt he was making his contribution by not nagging if his meals were a little late . . . she smiled wryly, and got on with the job.

But at night, while Gerald slept, she would lie wakeful, wide-eyed though weighed down by weariness and anxiety. If only she could have got in touch with Adam, explained to him – why, oh why hadn't she asked for his address! Or a telephone number, anything, even the name of the paper he worked for! She had learned so much about him, knew his taste in music, that he too loved Janácek and witty unpredictable Prokofiev – even that he had once seen Ulanova dance . . . but not his second name. She was so angry with herself she wanted to scream and beat upon the walls. Night after night her anger would build, only to end in silent choking tears.

The poems built too, the little unfinished scraps that eased her as did nothing else, filling the pages of the book with such intimacies that she dared not leave it about, had to carry it always with her where she could keep an eye on it; a poignant reminder of the matchbox she had cherished with its drop of Gerald's blood. Even now it filled her with pain to think how far they had travelled since then.

It was pointless wishing you could bring back the past, pointless and destructive; she had watched Aimée destroying her life like that. The thing to build on was the future – if only she had not let it slip through her fingers . . . and there she was, back where she started on the long slide into depression.

By the time first Zoë and then Charles had finished with their illnesses and the endless quarantine, and it was clear that neither she nor Gerald was going to catch their measles, only three weeks remained to the end of term. Checking off the days on the calendar, she saw with dismay that the long summer holiday was about to break over her like a tidal wave, that for another six whole weeks she would be unable to go out on her own . . . it was then that she realized she hadn't quite lost hope.

On their first day back at school she dropped them at the gates and made straight for the park, walking with a swinging step and a heart grown unaccountably light, her face upturned to the sweet June haze of early morning. She had not yet convinced herself that it was silly to mourn the loss of a man she had hardly known . . . oh, but she had, she had! . . . but she was working on it. And anyway, the park was lovely at this time of year. And it had been a place of happiness for her, if only for a day. And she could sit there in peace, and write in her little book.

So that was what she was going to do. She had brought a flask of coffee, and a bag of crumbs for the birds, and she had warned Aimée that she would not be in all day.

'Where are you going, can I come with you?'

'Not really, it's business.'

'What business, what are you going to do?'

'Wait and see,' she had said mysteriously; trying not to feel mean about throwing Aimée back on her loneliness, buttressing her resolve with the knowledge that she was motivated only by curiosity.

She sat on the seat where they had met before, near the great bank of azaleas. They were over now, their fiery blossoms burnt down to shreds of rag, but they had been in full flower when she was here with Adam . . . she took out the exercise book and sat with it in her lap. She closed her eyes, sorting out in her mind the words she wanted to write . . . for once, nothing came. The sun was warm on her eyelids, the heavy scent of lilac wafted towards her from somewhere nearby . . . a bee zoomed past her face so close that she felt the breeze of its wings. She relaxed, allowed herself to drowse, revelling in the peace of solitude . . . conscious from time to time of the leaves of her book gently riffling in the wind.

A child ran past her with clattering feet, pursued by a barking terrier. She woke refreshed, and opened the book. From between the pages a scrap of paper fell out. She picked it up and read, 'Forgive me . . .' in a familiar rapid scrawl.

Adam! He had been here – and she had missed him! Frantically, she looked around her, hardly hoping to see him, yet compelled to look—

He was there, sitting on a bench on the far side of the lawn, and he was watching her. As she looked he raised an arm in greeting; then, as her face broke into uncontrollable joy, rose to his feet and started towards her.

'Adam, oh Adam!' she blurted, when they had met halfway, had handclasped, had hugged each other without thought and then, with thought and a little self-consciously in that public place, had drawn apart to sit sedately on the bench.

'I thought I'd never see you again.' She laughed unsteadily, and wiped her eyes which seemed to be watering.

'I am sorry,' he said. 'I was called away. When I couldn't come that day I said, "Adam, she will not forgive you."' He squeezed the hand he was still holding. 'Then I see you here today, and I have a little hope.'

Her laugh felt a trifle shaky. 'I'm quite good at forgiving, I've had practice.' She hesitated, torn by temptation to tell him how deeply she had felt. 'Anyway,' she said lightly, 'it's like kissing, it goes by favour.'

She felt the pressure of his fingers on hers increasing relentlessly, drawing her towards him. She was helpless as a mouse, her body moving of its own will while her conscience hid its eyes . . . her lids drooped, her lips parted as she felt his breath on her face . . . then his mouth took possession of hers, drowning her in a rich sensuality that set her blood on fire. Her fingers caressed his face, roamed through his hair, she forgot everything in the first taste of real sexual pleasure she had known . . . she became aware that his hand was under her skirt, moving smoothly upwards between her naked thighs . . .

Her eyes flicked open abruptly, crying No! Her hand flew to arrest his wrist. It felt strong, hard and determined; but it stopped. He took his mouth from hers, his amber eyes still burning.

'Come to London.'

Flustered, she broke away and stood up. 'No – I can't, you know I can't. It's impossible.'

'Please—'

'No, no, no!' She snatched up her belongings and fled.

She was halfway home when she realized that she still did not know where he lived. Why did she need to know, she demanded angrily of herself, what was she thinking of, the whole thing was crazy, had gone too fast for her and got totally out of hand. She had not wanted to be involved in some steamy affair that would leave her ashamed, she had wanted a friendship, a flirtation, a romance . . . not this. Fantasies were one thing, putting them into hole-and-corner practice quite another. She was angry, angry and disappointed, in Adam, in herself and – yes, in Gerald. It was he who had laid her open to this, Gerald, in his glass case, denying her his warmth and affection. It was unfair to her. It would serve him right to be betrayed, to be cuckolded, to learn how it felt to be hurt . . . except that he wouldn't be hurt, because he didn't care. He was invulnerable behind his glass.

Adam was right, she admitted reluctantly: if she had been happily married . . . He was right about so many things. And she couldn't in all fairness blame him for jumping to conclusions.

By the time she had reached home, her agitation had subsided. She poured away the flask of coffee, made a fresh mugful, and took a pad and a pen into the garden to write him a letter. 'My dear Adam,' she began. No, that assumed too much. She crossed out 'my', leaving 'Dear Adam'. That was too formal, like a business letter. Maybe just 'Adam' – or did that sound angry? It was going to be more difficult than she thought. She took a swig of her coffee, tore off the top sheet and started again.

If we are to go on seeing each other we must reach a proper understanding, not go off at half cock—

Oh no, not that! She giggled, tore off the second sheet and started yet again.

If we are to go on seeing each other we must reach a proper understanding. I'm sorry if you misconstrued my remark about forgiveness as an invitation to more than I'm free to give; but you did know I was married and it's something we must both remember and respect.

Now it read like Aimée and Geraldine rolled into one. As prim and frosty as something from a hundred years ago – Jane Austen again, she thought: how the woman seemed to haunt her!

Yet it had to be said, and how else could she put it? How did other girls say these things; she wished she had a friend to confide in. She wasn't close enough to anyone, except perhaps Louise. But Louise was too young, and anyway she was in London, while Dotty – she realized with a shock that Dotty would probably not trouble to say it at all. She bent her head and forged on.

Please, please don't imagine I don't love you—

She crossed out 'love' and put 'like'. Considered a moment, changed the phrase to 'want us to be friends'. Then she went on:

I know we could have wonderful times together if only we don't ruin things. I've never known anyone quite like you, dear Adam, I truly don't want to lose you and I know that's what would have to be if we let things go too far . . .

She pondered for a long time whether or not to sign it

'love, Sally'. Even friends did that. That was not very terrible, was it . . . She recalled Aimée's bitter advice, never let a man know you care for him . . .

Aimée had had it all wrong; that was why her life was in such a mess. She was not going to be like that. She signed it 'Your loving friend'.

The next problem was how to get it to him. She couldn't post it without an address. The only way was to give it to him the next time they met; give it to him, and smile, and walk away, so that they wouldn't talk until after he'd read it. Yes, that was the way. She slipped it into an envelope and tucked it into the back of the exercise book.

She had a whole empty day ahead of her. The thought struck her that he might be called away again without warning, might have to go tonight – she might lose sight of him again! Suddenly, the thought was unendurable.

She went through the cottage like a whirlwind, shutting windows, locking doors. She would not risk another spell of misery, she would go now, while he was still in the town, make sure he got her letter and at the same time secure his address. She slammed the door behind her and hurried to the bus stop.

She wandered about the town all day without a sign of him. It was hardly worth going home for lunch, and she could not bring herself to go while there was still a chance of seeing him. She had left things so badly, so badly! She had to put it right today, before it was too late. She made her way to the coffee bar where they had gone together; she would have a sandwich, might even find him there.

What she found was Gerald. He was with a girl, their heads leaning close across the tea stains and spilt sugar, in an attitude that made it clear they were not discussing business.

She stood on the pavement outside, watching them through the steamy window, clearly oblivious of her and the rest of the world. For a moment she was struck dumb, not by surprise, but by the simple fact that she did not know what to say, or how to deal with it. Then she walked slowly away, her anger mounting with every step. So this was the marriage she had been at such pains to protect; while she was denying herself, he was doing no such thing.

So be it. She would stay with the children and keep them happy, would never be the one to break up the home. But one thing she knew: if and when she saw Adam again, she was not going to give him the letter. And if he asked her again to go to London, somehow, come hell or high water, she would go.

CHAPTER TEN

'I've had such a sweet letter from George in France,' purred Aimée. 'He's bought a little villa near Biarritz, and he wants us to go over.'

'Us?' queried Sally without interest.

'Well, Dotty and me. Of course, I could never cross the water, but I'm sure Dotty'd love to go. He was very taken with her, you know.'

Like everyone else, thought Sally, thankful that at least she'd had no chance to enthral Adam. Even though he was fading back into a fantasy, he was hers alone, her memory of him intact, unspoiled by scalding comparisons with Dotty. And it looked as though memory was all there was going to be.

Week after week had gone by with no sight of him, no sign that he even wanted to see her again. Yet he had seemed so eager, so passionate . . . maybe that was the trouble. Maybe she had resisted him so vehemently that he had taken it as final, her rejection of him total. So that, she supposed, was that. And, as usual, it was her own fault, her own failure to cope with the situation that had left the whole thing in ruins. Perhaps it was just as well . . . she shrugged mentally, trying to resign herself to his loss.

It was not easy. More and more she felt that she was living the life of a much older woman, perhaps even a nun. She would have to be at least forty to be able to dwell happily in peaceable domesticity, to revel in it as Geraldine did, to content herself with it and long for nothing more. And maybe even then . . . she sighed.

She felt that she had lived all her life in a darkened

cave; Adam had been a hand stretched to draw her out to play in the sunlight. Why she needed to be led out she was not sure, except that she felt the need of permission, of absolution from whatever sin it was that had confined her there. In the back of her mind still lurked the conviction that she was not in the world by right but only on sufferance. The sunshine was there but it was meant for someone else, like the parties and the Christmas trees of her childhood; she could not just stroll out and join in without an invitation.

In the intervening weeks her anger against Gerald had cooled, slowly melting down into one more layer of depression that was only occasionally warmed into resentment. Lacking the temerity to tackle him about what she had seen, she was almost ready to concede that it had been her imagination. His regard for her appeared to be no less, his behaviour towards her no different from the way it had always been; he remained polite, pleasant to the point of indifference, only a little less warm than in the beginning. Only, they rarely met each other's eyes, and never laughed together. She could laugh with the children, could even chat companionably with Aimée . . . but she could hardly bring herself to smile at Gerald. And he scarcely seemed to notice the omission. He was, she reminded herself, just a very cold man. Or was he? That girl . . . but then, one fond meeting in a coffee bar did not amount to much. The girl could have been anyone, or no one. Either way, she was probably best forgotten . . .

'What are you thinking about?' Aimée's eyes skewered her as she pounced with her habitual question.

'About George,' she lied quickly. 'Thinking how lucky he was to be able to retire when he did. I mean, he couldn't have, without his family money to fall back on.' She went to the window to gaze out across the valley. She never tired of the view, watched it lovingly throughout the seasons, the spring a symphony of uncounted different greens, the autumn when the oaks blazed gold against the dark wine of the beeches. If she ever wanted to die, she thought, this view would be enough to hold her back. She remembered Aimée, and said, 'So, are you going?'

'There, I knew you weren't listening! Of course I can't go, you know I'm terrified of water. But of course Dotty can't go alone; I was hoping Geraldine might go with her.'

'Perhaps,' said Sally vaguely, reflecting that she was never the one to be asked. Of course, if she were, she could not go because of the children. Of course . . .

Life seemed set to amble on again at the old speed limit; after her brief excursion into the fast lane she was already coned off, back among the crawlers, hemmed in by grocery lorries and furniture vans. It was hard to feel much concern for Dotty's disappointments: she had so few of them. She returned her attention to the garden where a squirrel flickered across the grass, his coat a glowing halo in the sun. 'Why don't you ask her?' she said.

'Oh, I have,' said Aimée. 'But she didn't seem very keen. Such a shame, poor little Dotty to have to miss such an opportunity. Geraldine's so full of having the children to stay, she doesn't seem to want to talk about anything else.'

'Is she?' Sally was startled out of her reverie. 'It's the first I've heard of it. What did she say?'

'Oh, she was going to tell you, only I rang up in the middle of her making plans – oh dear, I wasn't supposed to say anything!'

'Well, never mind, I'll pretend not to know. And don't worry about Dotty. If she wants to go, I'm sure she'll find a way.'

Aimée looked at her piercingly. 'You always were jealous of Dotty,' she said knowingly.

When Geraldine telephoned that evening, Sally feigned a surprise which quickly became genuine.

'What I was thinking, dearie, is that if Charles and Zoë are coming to me for the last week of the holidays, then you and Gerald could go to France with Dotty. How would that be? I'm sure it would do you both good, and it would be so nice for Gerald to see his old partner again. Now don't say no, because I've got my heart set on it, you just tell

Gerald to let me know his arrangements. Tell him, I won't take no for an answer.'

Sally stood by the telephone in stunned silence, unable to believe her luck. A holiday in France . . . and without the children! She could hear Geraldine's voice at the other end, going on to elaborate what she had said, then repeating her name when no response was forthcoming. She pulled herself together. 'Yes, I'm still here. Look, it's a lovely idea . . . oh, yes . . . yes . . . I think you'd better talk to Gerald yourself, he's just come in.'

She handed the phone to him, thinking: he's more likely to agree if she asks him than if I do. Then watched the frown gathering between his eyebrows with growing misgivings. She could hear Geraldine's distant persuasions, could see them falling on stony ground as he said merely, 'Yes . . . yes, but . . .' and finally, 'I'll have to think it over. I'll let you know. I'll give you back to Sally.'

She took back the receiver with a sense of deflation. 'Hello, Gerry. I'm afraid he doesn't sound very keen.'

'Don't you worry, dear, I know how to handle him if you don't. He's tired now, you give him a nice meal and leave the rest to me. Don't say anything more and I promise you, everything will come right.'

Whatever her methods, Geraldine prevailed. Almost imperceptibly Gerald, although omitting to actually discuss it with Sally, started talking as though it were a foregone conclusion. She began to feel elated despite herself, filling out her passport application, rummaging through her meagre wardrobe for suitable wear, encouraging Charles and Zoë to look forward to staying with their grandmother. They were going to be spoiled, there was no doubt of that, and would probably return unmanageable. But who cared . . .

By the time they were ready to go she was exhausted, having spent the intervening days preparing and packing clothes for four people, clearing out perishable food from the cupboards, mowing the lawns, stopping milk and papers and attending to the hundred and one little things that had to be remembered, while Gerald stood by looking faintly irritated by her lack of efficiency. Asked if he could not be the one to ferry the children over to their grandmother's, he politely declined.

'If you were only a little better organized,' he reproved her gently, 'you wouldn't have this rush at the last minute.'

'Oh, Gerald!' She felt her tolerance beginning to slip, and carefully moderated her tone. 'Couldn't you do this one thing to help – just to please me?'

He smiled at her over the edge of his evening paper; a smile of indulgence, even forgiveness. 'I'm taking this whole trip to please you. Air fares to the south of France don't grow on trees, you know.' And with the smile only faintly tinged with reproof, as it might be for Charles or Zoë, he retired again behind his paper.

Sally compressed her lips as she bundled the children into the car. With Dotty as one of the party it was unlikely that he was making the trip purely out of self-sacrifice. She drove the fifty miles to Geraldine's in silence, while Charles and Zoë bounced and squabbled in the back.

'Why aren't you taking the ferry and driving down?' asked Geraldine. 'You could have picked up Dotty and all gone together.'

'I don't know,' she said thoughtfully. 'It does seem sensible when you think about it.'

Late that night, falling wearily into bed, she asked Gerald.

'Because I may have to come back before you if this Fordham case blows up. I wouldn't want to leave you stranded there without the car.'

'I'd be stranded anyway.'

'Not if you had your return ticket. At least you'll have the means of getting home, and George will see you on to the plane.'

He seemed to have it all worked out.

'But . . . surely I'd be coming back with you?'

'And cut short Dotty's visit, too? You seem to be forgetting why you're going.'

You're obviously not, thought Sally with dawning cynicism. Oh well, at least she was going. A little consolation

227

prize for the loss of the enchanting Adam . . . if only she could have been going to Biarritz with him! If only she had waited for him, instead of rushing into marriage with Gerald, or with any Englishman. Perhaps she had quite simply married the wrong half of her nationality. What was wrong with her that, married to Gerald and the envy of her friends, she still wasn't satisfied? There had to be something, for there was no longer any blinking the fact that she was not. Adam had seen it the very first time they talked: 'If you were happily married . . .'

So, why wasn't she; could it be that she still wasn't trying hard enough? On an impulse, she turned towards Gerald.

'Would you like to make love?' she suggested.

He looked at his watch. 'It's too late now, I have to get up in the morning.'

He spoke with as little emotion as if she had offered him a second cup of tea.

They arrived in the midst of a deluge, to be collected from the airport by George in a vintage Daimler. The windscreen wipers beat frantically back and forth across the screen, inadequate to clear more than an intermittent peephole for the driver. Sally had never seen such rain, it beat like thunder on the metal roof and obliterated the windows as if flung from a fireman's hose, reflecting back the car's headlights in white circles of light that showed them nothing.

'Just as well we didn't come by car,' remarked Gerald, glancing slyly at Sally.

'Dotty made it all right,' George hunched over the steering wheel to peer through the windscreen, his eyes screwed into brilliant slits beneath bushy greying eyebrows. 'She's got some spunk, that girl!'

'You mean, she drove herself down? I didn't know she had a car.' She might have guessed Dotty would have a car as soon as she could drive.

'Hasn't had it long, apparently. Her father bought her a second-hand MG and she couldn't wait to try it out. But it's a hell of a way for a girl to drive on her own – and on the wrong side of the road! You've got to take your hat off to that cousin of yours.'

'Yes,' said Sally without conviction. The qualities people admired in Dotty tended to leave her cold. Without pausing to think she said, 'Did you know she was coming by car, Gerald? We might all have come together.'

Too promptly, he answered, 'It's only a two-seater.' As she turned her head to look at him he added, 'All MGs are, aren't they? So I've heard.'

They drove on in silence until George took a turning off the road and boomed, 'Here we are, welcome to Liberty Hall! Don't get out, my dear, I'll go in and get you a brolly.'

They sat side by side in the back of the car, saying nothing. Sally tried to see Gerald's face, but he turned it away to stare stubbornly out of the window.

Dotty appeared on the porch of the villa, fetchingly attired in a bikini and floral wrap.

'Hello!' she called exuberantly. 'Seen my car? It's parked alongside you, look!' She ran prettily through the downpour to open the car doors, making Sally feel dowdy and matronly, as she never failed to do. 'Do come and see,' she seized Gerald's hand, dragging him out into the rain. 'I've christened him White Lightning, you absolutely must come and admire him!'

Sally remained where she was. She was not interested enough in Dotty's acquisition to be willing to stand out in the weather, and in any case what pleasure she had taken in the trip had abruptly evaporated. She watched them chatting and laughing through the streaming windows until George reappeared with a gigantic umbrella to escort her into the house.

'Come in, come in, don't worry about them, let them catch their own pneumonia, we'll go in by the fire. Let's have that coat, it's soaked already, I bet you've never seen rain like this in England. Now, what would you like to drink?'

Ensconced in a vast wicker armchair by an open hearth

229

on which pine logs blazed, holding the largest brandy and soda she had ever seen, she thought what a cosy man George was; how sad for Diana to have missed all this, this lovely home in such a beautiful place, with this kind, adoring husband. That she had been adored was plainly in evidence; her pictures were everywhere, huge photographic enlargements in heavy silver frames, each with its tribute of roses or bougainvillaea. It was almost as if the villa were a shrine, each picture with its flowers a little altar.

'You're looking at the photographs.' George came back to the fire with his second brandy. 'This place was bought for Diana, she chose it for the honeymoon, and then we never spent a night in it. I couldn't stand the thought of strangers here, so when . . . well, afterwards I went ahead and completed the purchase. Do you think that was silly?'

'I think it was lovely,' said Sally. Her eyes misted suddenly and she had to swallow a lump in her throat. It was probably just tiredness. And the brandy. Yet as she looked out through the rain to where Gerald and Dotty still lingered, she couldn't help thinking: lucky, lucky Diana to have been so loved. Even though it had been cut short . . . perhaps that was the best way in the long run, to have it cut short like a flower before it can fade.

She became aware that George was watching her, his eyes among their crows' feet warmed with something she could only describe as tenderness; as if he knew what was passing through her mind.

'Drink up,' he said softly.

She pulled herself together. 'We must be quite near the sea. Is there a view?'

'You'll see it from your bedroom window if the weather lifts. When it does, we'll drive down the coast, I'll show you Juan-les-Pins and maybe Socoa, there's an interesting rock formation there.' He got to his feet. 'I'm going to fetch those two, my housekeeper goes mad if we're late for meals.'

'Your housekeeper?' She hadn't envisaged anyone else being here.

He chuckled. 'Quite a character, old Sabine. Heavily disguised as an earwig but her cooking's superb.'

He left to plunge out again into the rain, where she heard his voice cheerfully rallying the others, who came in meekly, smiling like children confident of boundless forgiveness.

They ate their meal to the accompaniment of Dotty's inexhaustible chatter, which was, as always, sufficient to keep both men entertained and release Sally to enjoy her food in silence. Only when Sabine appeared to serve them, narrowly sheathed in shiny black satin from throat to shiny black shoes, did she catch George's eye in mutual amusement, and look away before she could disgrace herself.

The downpour did not lift the next day. They pottered about the villa, pestered the windows, tried to decipher French weather forecasts on the radio that only George understood. By the evening, Dotty was showing signs of impatience, and it was clear that boredom could not be far behind.

Next morning, Gerald rang the office.

'The Fordham case?' inquired Sally drily.

He looked at her uncertainly, as if caught off guard.

'You warned me, remember?' She smiled faintly. 'Don't forget to leave me my passport. Assuming, of course, that you want me back.'

He laughed and kissed her cheek, 'Of course I want you back, silly girl!'

But it was only for the benefit of the others; the displeasure in his eyes was unmistakable. She didn't care. Every hour convinced her more that she had been manipulated, that he was leaving her here deliberately for reasons of his own. At least, she reasoned, this would seem to show it wasn't Dotty, since she too was to be abandoned to George and the rain.

At the airport he kissed her goodbye, his usual perfunctory embrace.

'Have a nice time,' he said, and pressed a traveller's cheque for fifty pounds into her hand.

She looked at it, torn between automatic gratitude and mounting bitterness. Finally, she smiled.

'Isn't it rather a lot, for going to play in the next street?'

Again his eyes challenged her. Then he laughed. 'How you do tease,' he said pleasantly. He turned on his heel and was gone.

For two more days, she and Dotty waited for the weather to improve, while George, kindly but unexciting, struggled to keep them entertained, Sally wrestling with her inner anger and Dotty with the boredom that was never far away. When they had been driven around the tortuous streets of Biarritz, and taken to see the slate cliffs above Socoa, where the mysterious blue-grey plates slid layer upon layer down into the invisible sea, melting into the mist without the sun to show the way, George was apparently bereft of ideas.

'I thought there was lots of nightlife in the South of France,' pouted Dotty. 'I hate staying in every evening.'

'Not my scene, I'm afraid,' said George firmly. 'I'm a walking man myself.'

That night, Dotty came in and seated herself on the end of Sally's bed.

'Do you really want to stay on here with boring old George?' she whispered. 'Frankly, I've had enough. I'm going back to London tomorrow, why don't you come with me?'

CHAPTER ELEVEN

Early the next morning they were on their way, leaving a slightly puzzled George waving them off on the steps of his villa. It was a shame, thought Sally; they must seem to him very ungrateful for all the efforts he had made, and she squirmed under an all too familiar burden of guilt.

'Don't be daft,' said Dotty. 'You should never do things you don't want to do, it's no good to anyone. Reluctance always shows. Don't tell me you'd rather stay there on your own for the rest of the week?'

'Not really,' she admitted, but refrained from adding that she was nervous of flying back on her own. 'Will you be able to take me the rest of the way home?'

Dotty grinned across her shoulder. 'You don't want to go home yet, you're off the lead for a few days. Shake a loose leg in London while you've got the chance.'

'Well . . .' She wasn't sure she had a loose leg, or even how to shake it . . . not now.

Dotty laughed. 'Your trouble is, you don't know how to enjoy yourself, never did. Well, you'd better start learning before it's too late.'

Sally smiled ruefully. 'Now you're going to tell me it's later than I think.'

'How did you guess,' replied Dotty, and pressed down her foot on the accelerator. 'Let's see what this beast will do.'

They roared through France in the white sports car at a speed that at first caused Sally to shrink into her seat, but quite quickly began to exhilarate her strangely. She sat in silence, savouring the scent of pine trees in the first sun after rain, fascinated by the grapevines bordering the road between Bayonne and Bordeaux, their ranks opening and closing like fans with the movement of their passing, their wet leaves glittering in the bright September light. It was beautiful and unfamiliar; she wanted to keep the scene fresh in her mind, to press it like a flower and take it home with her.

'Scared?' challenged Dotty, her eyes sparkling with mischief.

Sally settled herself more comfortably in her seat. 'Not me. Let me know when you want a rest from driving.'

'No fear, you wouldn't go fast enough!'

They stopped for lunch at a bistro outside Tours, buying charcuterie food and washing it down with cheap French wine and aromatic coffee, Dotty so eager to be back on the road that she could hardly wait to eat.

'What's the rush,' asked Sally. 'It's so lovely here, I wouldn't mind staying for a bit.'

'Got to get on the ferry tonight,' replied Dotty, in a voice that brooked no argument.

'Why have we?' Sally was a little disappointed that they were in such a hurry to leave France. It was her first – perhaps her only – visit, and she was just beginning to enjoy it.

Dotty avoided her eye. 'Oh . . . travelling's such a waste of time. You want to get it over as quickly as possible. Come on!' She was already back in the car, still chewing her last mouthful.

Sally, already prevented from stopping in Montelimar to buy nougat for the children, said nothing. It began to look as if Dotty had better fish to fry in London.

They arrived at the flat in the small hours of the morning, having driven from Dover in a fine drizzle that penetrated Sally's summer clothes. She had not been prepared for the return in an open car, particularly one on which the folding roof no longer functioned. Dotty, cheerfully protected under a plastic mack, had teased her as a matter of course.

234

'You don't want to worry about a drop of rainwater – makes your hair curl,' she laughed.

'Like carrots?' Sally quipped dutifully, anxious not to fall short by complaining. Dotty seemed to get so much out of life; if only she could be a bit more like her . . . By the time they reached the outskirts of London she was wretchedly soaked, huddled in stoical silence, determined to say nothing that could be construed as moaning.

They toiled up three flights of stairs, hampered by the weight of their wet luggage, to a flat that appeared to have been converted from an attic. It consisted of two enormous rooms, one of which had an end divided off to serve as a kitchen; over the stable door Sally could see an assortment of empty wine bottles and dirty glasses. The second room, almost equally spacious, boasted a built-in double bed, some assorted shelving and a corner screened off to take a shower, lavatory and a wash basin adorned with a grimy rim.

Large paintings showing varying degrees of talent splashed their vibrant colours over the walls, clothes and books littered the floor, brilliant shawls lolled artistically over decrepit armchairs, cupboard doors hung wistfully from broken hinges and the litter of an abandoned breakfast sulked upon the table. The whole thing was reminiscent of a set for *La Bohème*.

Sally peeled off her damp coat, and rolled up her sleeves. 'Did you have to leave in a rush?'

'Not particularly,' Dotty looked at her in surprise. 'Why do you ask?'

Sally turned away to hide a smile and went to the sink to run the taps.

'There's no hot water till the morning,' Dotty warned her. 'If you want to make a drink you can use the kettle.' She yawned prodigiously. 'I'm going to hit the sack. You won't have to mind sharing, otherwise it's the sofa. 'Night, don't be long.'

Sally looked about her helplessly, wishing she had had the strength of mind to stay in France. She had been a fool to let Dotty talk her into leaving – but then, that was her

235

trouble, she had always been a fool. Now here she was in cold, grey London, in a flat that looked as if a bomb had hit it, and no idea of how they were going to spend the rest of the week. Some of Geraldine's house pride must have rubbed off on her, she thought, for she couldn't stay here without doing something about the mess. But there was little she could do tonight, and anyway she was far too tired. She felt the sofa: it was as hard as iron. She couldn't see any blankets or cushions, and Dotty had, characteristically, gone off to bed herself without telling her where to find them. She sat disconsolately on the hard seat, staring at the crumbs trodden into the carpet, cold, hungry and too tired to do anything but think, until after a while she began to shiver.

With an effort, she gathered her resources and followed her cousin into the bedroom. She stood looking down at her for a moment, bright hair tumbled over the only pillow, the blankets rolled about her slender form, leaving the rest of the mattress bare.

She sighed and, shaking her head, lay down close beside her to glean what warmth she could.

She woke late the next morning, with a full bladder and a blinding headache from the sunlight that streamed into her eyes from an uncurtained window. She reeled to her feet and staggered to the lavatory, wondering vaguely where Dotty was. She must have got up first. Perhaps she was making breakfast.

'Dotty?' she called. There was no answer.

She went through into the living room but there was no one there; it was just as they had left it last night, the dirty dishes on the table, their cases where they had set them down. No . . . only her cases. Dotty's were not there. She ran to the window and looked out. The white sports car was no longer parked in the street below.

For a fleeting instant she knew panic. It was the awakening in the Convent all over again, the world suddenly emptied and nobody left but her. She felt her face pull apart as one childish, noisy sob that she could not control broke from her . . . she didn't know what to do, where to run

. . . she was abandoned, lost in a strange city with no means of getting home . . .

She pulled herself together. Of course she could get home, she had the money Gerald had given her, she had only to get a taxi to the station, and then a train, and she would be home. Besides, she told herself sternly, 'Don't be a fool, she's only gone to the shops . . . but with her suitcase? No, Dotty had gone off somewhere without her. It was just typical of her to do a thing like this.

She buckled the armour of her anger on and marched back into the bedroom. She would get dressed, make some coffee and decide what to do. That was when she saw the note.

It was pinned to the pillow on Dotty's side of the bed.

> Have fun – back in time to drive you home on Saturday. *Do something exciting!*
> Love, Dotty.
> PS Make yourself at home, help yourself to anything.
> PPS Not much food in the house, but G. left you some money, didn't he? Enjoy it, and *don't be a drip!*

For a long time she sat on the edge of the bed, speechless, just staring at the paper. Then the telephone began to ring. Automatically, she got up to answer it, unearthing the receiver from under a pile of ironing.

'Hello . . . Sally speaking . . . hello?'

From the other end, no answering voice; only the paytone from a public call box. Then the dialling tone as the caller rang off. A wrong number, she supposed. Or perhaps someone for Dotty, not wanting to waste the call when they found she wasn't there . . . but how did they know she wasn't there? She stood thoughtful, her hand on the telephone. Then she sat down, and dialled the number of Gerald's office.

'Is it possible to have a word with Gerald Hammond, please?'

'I'm afraid Mr Hammond's not in the office, would you like to speak to his secretary?'

'No, I'll ring again later. When will he be back?'

'Not until Monday, I'm afraid. Who shall I say called
. . . hello?'

Sally felt an anger so cold that she did not trust her voice.
She replaced the receiver without another word. You bastard,
she was thinking, you shit! Her hands drove deep into her
hair, clawing her scalp as if it had been Gerald's. You rotten
conniving *shit!* She searched her mind for stronger, fouler
words to hurl, drumming her elbows in frustration on the
table while the tears of rage splashed down . . .

Afterwards she felt drained.

She thought again of Dotty's note. 'Do something exciting
. . . don't be a drip.' There must be something to do in
swinging London. Why should she be the only one not to
enjoy it?

Tension demanded activity. And if she was to spend the
next few days in this pigsty it was going to need cleaning
up. She took a quick shower and dressed, and tore into the
mess like an avenging fury.

By early afternoon it was unrecognizable and she was quite
pleased to be there. She had purged the refrigerator, thrown
out rancid butter and mouldering cheese, and expelled a
bottle of milk that had turned to yellow curds and whey;
when the breadbin revealed a cut loaf with a long grey
beard, she decided it was time to investigate the shops. She
wondered whether Dotty had had the foresight to leave her
a door key. If not, she was going to be in trouble. A brief
search revealed a Yale key hanging on a nail beside the door,
with another note attached.

> I'm leaving you my only key so you'll have to let me
> in when I get back!

She knew another moment's indignation. What right had
Dotty to keep her penned here when she might either want
or need to go home before Saturday! It was just like Dotty
. . . but perhaps it was just her cock-eyed notion of seeing
that she had 'a good time'.

238

She found a corner grocery within a couple of hundred yards, and stocked up with necessities for her stay, including some expensive frozen meals. Since she was here on her own she was not going to waste precious time on cooking. Not far down the road she noticed a bank. She hesitated, but only briefly. Then she went in and cashed the fifty pounds' worth of travellers' cheques.

She felt no guilt about it, as she would once have done. 'A penny to play in the next street . . .' It hadn't been far from the truth.

She returned to the flat feeling pleasantly naughty, and unpacked her purchases. She looked inside the oven – dear God, no! The pie she had meant to warm up would have to be eaten cold. She unwrapped the lettuce from its newspaper and tossed it into the sink. As she went to throw the paper in the bin, a photograph caught her eye, a small rectangle at the head of a column.

It couldn't be . . . she didn't believe it. She straightened it out, smoothing the crumpled sheet to read the print. It was headed 'HERE AND THERE' by Adam Niklaus.

She sat down, staring at it, unable to believe what she saw. It was Adam's face. She would have known it anywhere. Her Adam . . . the very phrase started a tingling in her blood. And now, of all times. It was fate. An omen. It couldn't be otherwise. After so many chances and mischances, they were to get together despite everything. It was meant to be. And why not, she asked herself fiercely. The children were being cared for. No one knew where she was except Dotty, who wouldn't be back before Saturday. And nobody cared – Gerald, least of all. So why not, *why the hell not!*

She searched the paper for a telephone number, but found only an address. Directory enquiries gave her a number and, her voice already trembling, she rang it. No, the speaker at the other end regretted, they could not divulge the address of their correspondent. But if it was urgent, they could give her the number of his answering service.

She was beginning to weaken. So many other people

involved, all knowing she was trying to ring him, probably guessing . . . sniggering . . . she must brazen it out, try to make it sound like business . . .

'Yes, please.'

She scribbled the number, dialled it before she could change her mind. She was answered by what sounded like a very efficient secretary, who asked her for the message she wished to leave. For a moment she was stumped. What to say that would convey anything to him, without sounding totally trite and ridiculous?

At last she said, 'Please tell him Sally called. Ask him to ring this number as soon as possible, if he's interested in blackcurrant cordial.'

CHAPTER TWELVE

They were to meet under the clock at Charing Cross station.

Sally arrived a few minutes early and hovered about the bookstall, keeping her head down as she flipped through unwanted magazines, stealing furtive glances in the direction from which she expected him to arrive. She was not sure why she didn't want to be there first; perhaps it was pride, or the unexpressed fear that he would not turn up. What would it matter, she asked herself sensibly, since nobody would know if he stood her up? She had no answer; but she hid behind the bookstall just the same.

A hand touched her sleeve. 'I guessed you would be here . . .'

He was there, smiling, the amber eyes gently teasing her.

'Hello . . .' She could think of nothing more to say. It didn't matter, she thought happily. It would never matter again. Nothing mattered now, except that they had found each other at last.

Adam put a light hand on her shoulder. 'I thought we'd have a drink somewhere, and a meal. Then maybe a theatre?'

'Lovely,' she smiled. 'Anything, whatever you like.' She blushed, realizing what she had said.

He laughed, hugging her briefly. 'Maybe a drink first. You know what they say, a journey of a million miles starts with a single step.'

He took her to a Spanish wine cellar in the Covent Garden area, where they ate snails in paprika and chicken al ajillo, and drank long draughts of an innocuous-looking wine punch packed with crushed ice and fresh fruit.

'Sangria,' Adam explained, recharging her glass with the sparkling rosy liquid. 'Don't worry, it's half lemonade.'

'And the other half's blackcurrant cordial, I suppose?' Already she felt an alarming tendency to giggle.

'Ah, no! We have that later. Where are you staying?'

'In a borrowed flat. It's Hampstead, I think.'

'You think?' His expression was quizzical.

'I shall take a taxi, that way I can't get lost.'

'What a pity,' he said, suddenly sober. 'If you never get lost . . . how can I hope to find you?' He picked up her hand across the table, turned it over, touched his mouth to the inside of her wrist.

She found herself trembling violently. She wanted him to find her, to take her back to the flat, to stay the night, whatever that night might bring. She wanted a memory to cherish all her days, a memory of Adam, of sleeping with a man who desired her, of waking to find him still beside her in the morning. She could not speak. She bent forward, laid her cheek against his hair, inhaling the faint foreign scent of it, like bracken on an autumn day . . .

He raised his head at last, their eyes met from only a few inches apart. When he spoke, his voice was husky. 'Let's find that taxi,' he said.

At some point during the night she woke briefly, aware of a sheltering arm laid across her. Gerald? she thought, in faint surprise. And then she remembered . . . Adam. She sighed contentedly, nestled into his embrace, and slept again.

In the morning she woke refreshed and with a sense of happiness, as though something good, of which she did not instantly recall the details, had happened. She turned her head on the pillow. Adam was still asleep, his dark hair rumpled, his face relaxed, a bluish shadow darkening his jaw.

Very gently, carefully, she lifted the fall of hair away from his eyes, and lay on her elbow, watching him. She knew now that what she had believed were fantasies had

242

not been fantasies at all; they were intuitive guesses at a reality she had somehow missed with Gerald, and which she had managed to convince herself was a figment of her own overheated imagination – until last night. She closed her eyes and let her mind drift back – to the weightlessness with which their two bodies had moved in a unison almost mystic, to the way they had dispensed with the need for words, either of asking or of giving . . . how even thought had melted at last in a crescendo of sensation, soaring, soaring – urgent, exciting – wonderful – terrifying – glorious . . . ah, glorious – ah! – ah . . . alleluja-aah . . .

Afterwards, she had lain speechless, sightless, her body still throbbing softly with the first joy it had known, absorbing through her pores rather than consciously hearing his whispered endearments, his whispered caresses . . . until they both slept. Now she wanted it again. To live it again, to be sure it was not just another dream to be lost and never recalled . . .

She opened her eyes. His were still closed, but he was smiling faintly. Was he dreaming . . . of her? She gazed at him steadily, trying to will him awake. She had heard that if two people were close enough . . . his smile increased.

'Good morning,' he said, and rolled over to take possession of her.

This time it was not the fiery volcanic eruption of last night's explosion, when they had devoured each other with bodies arching and writhing, his tongue curling hotly about her nipples . . . but it was still good, still sweet, with a new quality that sprang from remembered intimacy, relaxed yet satisfying in a new and delightful way.

She was drowsing off again when he dabbed a quick kiss on her lips and abruptly left her. She heard him splashing in the shower, and a roar of protest as the water came through too hot, or perhaps too cold.

She called sleepily, 'Shall I make coffee?'

'No time. I have to go.'

She sat up, vaguely alarmed. She had not thought of him leaving her, had imagined them spending the day together.

243

Ridiculous, she reminded herself, of course it was. Of course . . . She jumped out of bed and threw on something, a shawl from one of the chairs. 'I'll make coffee while you shave.'

'I cannot shave here — unless you have a razor,' he teased her. 'Don't worry, I have to rush.'

She was already filling the kettle but she put it down again, and went back into the bedroom where he was fishing under the bed for his other shoe. 'Will I see you tonight?' she said diffidently.

He looked up. 'Do you want to?'

She felt for some reason, hurt. 'Of course I want to.' Did he think he was a one-night stand for her, that she was in the habit of taking men home, just anyone . . . Pride came to her rescue. 'Unless you don't, of course.'

He sat back on his haunches. 'Why would I not?' He sounded faintly surprised. 'My darling, you were wonderful.'

My darling . . . She felt herself blushing. 'Do you mean that?'

He rose to his feet and faced her. He tilted her chin with a finger and looked into her face, his eyes smouldering. 'You should not ask that . . . unless you are prepared for the truth.'

So he had meant it . . . his darling. He too was falling in love. She raised her lips to his and kissed him, passionately, longingly. A kiss to bring him back.

'See you tonight,' he whispered. And was gone.

All day she could think of nothing else. She went back to bed and lay luxuriating in her memory of the night before, daydreaming the hours away, her only interest in pushing them behind her until his return.

The telephone rang twice. The first time it was another wrong number, or more likely, she thought, someone checking to see if she was still here. The second time she didn't even bother to answer it. About four in the afternoon, she got up, showered and dressed, and made herself a sandwich, which she forgot to eat. Adam . . . Adam . . . Adam was all of her thought.

At six o'clock she set the table for two, rummaged in the

refrigerator for the makings of a meal and set up the coffee machine. She wished she had bought candles, and some wine would have been nice. But there was not time to go to the shops, in case he arrived while she was out. She realized that, true to form, they had not pre-arranged a time.

By eight o'clock she was becoming agitated. Had he had to go off somewhere – perhaps he had tried to ring her. Why, oh why hadn't she answered the telephone, she should have known it might be him! Now she did not know what to do. Yes, she did; she must wait and trust him. He would not just disappear, without a word . . . would he?

At half-past ten she cleared the table and went to bed. He was not coming, and she could only guess at the reason. Perhaps in the morning he would ring to tell her why . . . perhaps.

At twenty past eleven, tearstained and dishevelled, she heard a ring on the doorbell. She sat immobilized, her crying checked as always by the dread of disclosure. Another ring, closely followed by a knock. A discreet knock. Then Adam's voice.

'Sally . . . are you there?'

She scrubbed her face hurriedly on the sheet, wound it around her and ran to the door, her heart flying up to meet him. She opened it quickly and turned away, eluding him to hide in the shower room. 'I thought you weren't coming,' she called, splashing her face with cold water. 'I've taken off my make-up, wasn't that silly.'

'Don't bother for me,' he called back. 'I like you without it.' He had followed her through, coming up behind her to take her in his arms. 'What happened to your eyes?'

'Oh, nothing . . .' she lied without thought. 'Hay fever, I get it sometimes. It goes off. Do you want something to eat?'

'I have eaten. And you?'

'Oh . . . yes.' Another lie. Why was she afraid to be honest, even with him; afraid to ask where he had been, why he was so late. 'I could make some coffee.'

He was already peeling off his clothes. 'I have brought

champagne.' He laughed, and with a single deft movement stripped her of the sheet. 'Never better than when taken in bed.'

They padded about naked, finding glasses, opening the champagne, searching for the runaway cork for Sally to keep as a souvenir, their eyes upon each other all the time, asking and answering, inviting and responding. Not the questions she really wanted answered; but after the second glass of champagne, they no longer seemed important.

In the morning, he was up and dressed before she had opened an eye. He bent above her and kissed her lightly. 'Shall I come tonight?'

She struggled out of sleep. 'Yes . . . of course. But what about today?' He was going again, she was waking to another disappointment. She had vaguely supposed that once together they would stay together, had not envisaged spending her days alone. 'Do you have to work?'

He smiled. 'Are you here tomorrow?'

She cleared her brain, did a rapid calculation. Dear God, it was already Thursday! 'Yes, but my cousin may be back. She's going to drive me home on Saturday.'

'In a pumpkin, with four white mice? Poor Cinderella.' He kissed her again, his tongue flicking between her lips, stirring her blood . . .

The telephone rang and he drew away. 'Are you going to answer it?'

'Nobody answers. It's just someone checking up.'

He looked at her shrewdly. 'Your jealous husband, no?'

'He's not jealous!' She had blurted it out without meaning to. She averted her face for fear it should give her away.

Adam bent forward, kissed her softly and with great tenderness. 'Tonight, I come earlier,' he said. 'Please, no more hay fever.'

He went. She was alone again, the telephone still jangling in her ears.

When he had gone, she got up and washed her hair,

unearthed Dotty's drier from the back of a broom cupboard. Then she went to the shops again, coming back with wine and candles, peaches in brandy and an expensive bundle of out-of-season asparagus. She had let herself down last night, in her own eyes at least; she would not do it again. She went round the flat once more, busy with duster and polish, and arranged the hothouse roses she had bought in the only vessel she could find, an elderly stone jam jar which had housed the dish mop and scourer. She was reminded inconsequentially of George and his lost Diana, the ubiquitous photographs in their silver frames. Poor George, living on his memories . . . after tomorrow, she supposed, she would be doing the same.

She still had half a day to kill. She thought of all the things she could be doing in London: galleries, museums, concert halls. She could not go. He had said he would come 'earlier', and she didn't know when that might be. She would rather miss everything the capital had to offer than her last chance of his company.

She sat down with her little book and prepared to write, to press the moments with Adam between the pages like dried flowers – she recalled saying something like that to Dotty while driving through France, or had she only thought it – but as soon as she tried to crystallize her memories she was lost in them, drowned in a sensuality that was still too new to her. After a while she closed her eyes and gave up the attempt. There would be time enough when she went home, enough and too much, and then too much again . . .

Adam returned at six o'clock, brandishing two tickets for the Theatre Royal, Drury Lane.

'We are very lucky, I got these from our theatre critic who must be somewhere else tonight.' He swung her around, pulled her towards the door, tossing her coat towards her. 'He has written the crit, we only have to warn him if the theatre burns down!'

'What, really?' she was incredulous, taken by surprise.

He laughed delightedly. 'I am bad, teasing you again. Come now, there's a taxi waiting.'

'I've prepared a meal—'

'Later.' Moments later, they were on their way.

Afterwards, she could remember nothing of the show they saw, only that there was music and colour, and Adam there beside her. She remembered his every word, every gesture, each movement stamped indelibly on her mind. When it was over they went to a wine bar somewhere nearby, and sat talking across a scarred table in an alcove, their faces lit from below by a stub of candle in a Chianti bottle, not hurrying to go home, prolonging the anticipation of pleasure like children saving the best until last.

When at last they drew up in the taxi outside the flat, their hands lightly joined, their senses already gently kindling, she looked up to see a light in the living room window.

'Did we leave a light on?' she asked Adam.

'I don't think—' he began, but she cut him short, seeing the white sports car at the curb in front of them.

'My cousin's back. Oh Adam, I'm so sorry . . .'

He squeezed her hand. 'I think it's best I don't come up.'

'Yes . . . yes, I'm afraid it is.' She fought down tears of disappointment, torn between longing to keep him with her a little longer and dread of the outcome if he should meet Dotty . . . she shook her head. 'Darling, I'm so sorry,' she said again. 'Will you write to me?'

'Write to you!' He drew back, astonished. 'Oh no, that would be unwise. You have my answering service. When you come to London again . . .'

'But I never come! This is the first time ever, I have children at home. Oh, please say you'll write to me, please!' She felt the tears brim out of control, and dashed them away quickly.

'Look, darling Sally. It has been beautiful, no? We must not spoil it by ruining your life. If I write to you someone may see a letter, your husband—'

'He would not mind.'

He laughed, a cynical, worldly laugh. 'This, I must see, my dear. No man cares to be cuckolded!'

'Not even if—' She broke off. She felt humiliated by

248

Gerald's infidelity, and no less stung that Adam could laugh in the poignant moment of parting. Suddenly cold, she gathered her coat and bag. 'If you don't want to write to me, all right. But don't tell yourself that it's because of my husband.' She opened the door of the taxi and stepped out. 'He told my mother,' she said bitterly, 'that he'd pay someone to take me out!'

She slammed the car door and fled up the steps to the flat, not looking back to see the impact of her words. Unwilling to break down sobbing in Adam's arms; unwilling for him to imagine she had said it for effect.

Plodding up the long staircase, her days of joy behind her, she asked herself why she had said it at all. She hadn't really wanted to, hadn't wanted Adam to know. It was as if it had been forced out of her by some pressure building up inside that she could no longer contain.

CHAPTER THIRTEEN

Dotty was sitting at the table with an empty mug in her hand, fish and chip papers spread before her on the table. She looked tired and strained, as though she had not had enough sleep.

'I thought you didn't have a key?' said Sally, trying not to frown as she saw her roses obliterated under the greasy wrappings.

Dotty laughed. 'Just making sure you stayed to do something exciting. Did you?'

'I went to the theatre.' She was thankful she had that to fall back on, that she didn't need to lie. 'How about you?'

'You know me,' said Dotty. 'I always do something exciting. And who was that you came back with?'

A throb of panic made her say quickly, 'Just a man I shared a taxi with.'

Dotty smiled knowingly. 'All that time talking to someone you just shared a taxi with?'

'We were sorting out the fare.' She looked straight into her cousin's eyes, defying her to persist. It was not for Dotty to spy on her, to question her comings and goings – certainly not in the light of her own defection.

Dotty leaned back and lit a cigarette. 'Oh? I thought perhaps all this' – she swept a hand to embrace the candles, the roses, the table laid for two – 'was for a romantic rendezvous. No?'

She was watching, thought Sally, like a cat watching a mousehole.

'Oh no,' she smiled, taking pleasure for the first time in

a lie. 'It was a little welcome home for you, to thank you for all your hospitality.'

For a moment they regarded each other with thinly-veiled hostility. Then she had the satisfaction of seeing Dotty colour and look away.

They did not question each other further about the ways in which they had spent their time, but retreated into trivia or silence. They slept uneasily, both restless and uncommunicative, and woke to a day without zest for Sally, and which even for Dotty seemed to offer less than its usual attractions. With Sally's suitcase in the boot of her car, she said half-heartedly, 'Look, do you really need me to drive you home?'

'You promised,' said Sally firmly, and climbed in and sat down.

'Only, I'd rather just take you to the station . . .' her voice trailed off with diminishing hope.

'Tough.' Sally smiled. 'Don't forget to lock the door.'

As they drew out of London into the autumnal country-side, she reflected that whatever else, she had drawn strength from her interlude with Adam. Hesitant though she might be to presume that she was loved, she was confident at least that she was wanted, that one other person was glad that she was alive. Since the death of Erik, the increasing chill between herself and Gerald had done nothing for her confidence. Even the children pre-ferred their father's company, couldn't wait to go and stay with their grandmother; in moments of doubt she had asked herself if they could all be wrong. Now, because of Adam, charming cosmopolitan Adam, she was aware of herself as an individual, with a right to voice her wishes, to make demands of her own. For the first time ever, she had imposed her will on someone else – and of all people, on her insufferable cousin! She sat smiling quietly beside her sullen chauffeuse, during all the long drive home.

'I won't come in,' said Dotty when they arrived. 'I've got to get back.'

'But – you must want to rest and freshen up, surely. It's such a long way—'

'No, I'd rather go straight back.' She was already handing out Sally's suitcase, glancing at the cottage door as if she expected an ogre to jump out. 'I did tell you I was pressed for time.'

As the door opened, she was already back in the driving seat, roaring away up the lane with a wave of her hand as the children, closely followed by Geraldine, came pelting down the path to meet them.

'Mummy, Mummy, where have you been, what have you brought us back?' yelled Charles, the gravel spinning out from beneath his feet.

'You're not supposed to ask!' reproved Zoë self-righteously. 'Are we, Gran?'

'Gran said she would,' retorted Charles. 'Didn't you, Gran?'

'Now, now, dearies, don't greet little Mummy with an argument!' She bent forward to greet Sally with the ritual kiss on the cheek. 'I'm sure Mummy has, haven't you, dear?' She smiled a confident reminder and turned to lead them into the house.

Oh God, she had forgotten! How could she have forgotten? She thought quickly. 'I couldn't see anything I thought you'd like in France. So I thought we'd all go into town tomorrow and you could choose something yourselves. How's that?'

'Oh, yippee!' yelped Charles, galloping back into the house, excited by the prospect.

But Zoë was not deceived, and her small face dropped in disappointment against her mother's hand. Sally squeezed the little hand in hers, ashamed for the first time of the way in which she had spent her week.

Gerald came in later that evening, dropped a perfunctory kiss on her brow and said cheerily, 'Well, how was France?'

'Wet,' she said briefly. 'And how did the Fordham case go?'

'Fordham . . . Fordham . . .' he muttered, half to himself.

'Oh, yes – fine, they settled. Only after that, it wasn't worth coming back.' A pause. Then, it seemed to her, a deliberate casualness. 'Did you and Dotty enjoy yourselves?'

Clearly, they were going to pretend, both of them. So be it. Pretence, acceptance . . . trust. Maybe that was how marriages were made to last.

'We came back early.' If she didn't tell him, he would no doubt hear it from George. 'I tried to ring you.'

'Oh?' The note of alarm was unmistakable.

'Yes.' She smiled mercilessly. 'They said you wouldn't be back until Monday. I expect it was a mistake, don't you?'

For a split second only, he looked flustered. Then the crack in his composure sealed to perfection. 'Oh, no. I'm glad they remembered, I said I was not to be disturbed. After all, I was supposed to be on holiday.'

'Oh . . . of course,' she agreed smoothly, and turned her head to conceal her amusement. You had to hand it to him, she was thinking; he was not a successful solicitor for nothing.

So this, then, was how it was going to be. She would not question Gerald, and he would not question her: a hollow marriage, rather than a stormy one. On balance, she felt that she could live with it. It would endure, the children would be safe, and no one was likely to get hurt.

Divorce, she knew, was not in either of their minds. She could never consider breaking up the home; and Adam, being Catholic, would be unable to marry her if she did. As for Gerald, it was not long since he had told her of a junior partner whose career had been wrecked by the scandal attending his divorce; she had no illusions about the value he placed on his own career.

For a time the euphoria sustained her, and then, inevitably, it began to fade. Three days did not add up to enough of a memory to live on for the rest of her life, and before long she was casting about for ways to contrive another visit to London. Not that she was keen to involve Dotty again, although the privacy of the flat had been a joy. But if only she could get the children looked after, she might find a cheap hotel, or a boarding house. Or maybe wherever Adam lived . . . but she couldn't take that for granted. She couldn't even be sure that he would be there, since his work was likely to take him abroad without warning. All she could do was arrive in London, ring his number and hope.

Two weeks before Christmas, she rang Geraldine.

'I want to do some Christmas shopping in London, for the children. I don't want to take them for obvious reasons, and I'd have to stay overnight. Do you think you could possibly . . .'

Geraldine could, and would be delighted. And refrained from teasing her until just before she rang off. 'You won't forget their presents this time, dearie, will you?'

For an instant, she caught her breath. Then let it go again. Of course Geraldine did not suspect, how could she? And for that matter, what would it matter if she did; it was Gerald's concern, not hers, and if he did not mind . . . It was not that she was ashamed of her liaison with Adam, on the contrary, the thought of him filled her with happiness. It was cowardice, the lack of whatever was needed to confess to breaking someone else's rules, checked even now by the fear of anger, of the loss of esteem, even when she was reasonably sure there was none to lose.

She arrived in London in time for lunch, ate a quick snack in a sandwich bar and did her shopping, bumping and jostling her way down Regent Street in a blaze of Christmas lighting. It had not occurred to her that the world and his wife would be there too, all with the same intent. When she had made her purchases, looked at all the windows, had another coffee . . . she could not put off the moment any longer. She made her way to Charing Cross station as the only place she knew, found a telephone booth and squeezed herself into it. This way at least, she had told herself, if Adam was not in town she could still go home, would not be condemned to a miserable night in a strange hotel alone. She rang the number of the answering service and waited.

'May I have your name, please?'

'Oh . . . yes, I suppose so. It's Sally. Sally Hammond. Does it matter?'

'Ah, Miss Hammond, I thought I recognized your voice. Mr Niklaus would like you to ring another number. It's only for you, that's why I had to ask. Ready?'

She wrote it down with shaking fingers, then fumbled for more coins for the extra call. At last she was through, at last to the right extension, at last, after an interminable wait while she fed the box with coins, she was rewarded with Adam's voice.

'Sally! This is wonderful, where are you?'

'I'm at Charing Cross.'

'And I'm in Fleet Street – don't go away, I'll be right with you!'

She was trembling as she pushed her way towards him through the crowd, trembling and laughing and crying – no, surely not crying! It was just that her eyes were watering, so much laughter and the coldness of the air.

In the morning they woke early, and lay companionably chatting in the shabby hotel room. He wanted to know all about her, the names of her children, whether they looked like her, who was taking care of them. When she told him, he said sharply, 'She doesn't know you are with me?'

'No, of course not. But I told you, it wouldn't matter.'

He cocked a quizzical eyebrow, and reached for a cigarette. 'You don't mind, I smoke in bed?'

'No, I don't mind what you do.' She smiled, reminiscing. 'I used to hate it when my mother did.'

'Tell me . . .'

She found herself telling him about Aimée, about Erik, and her up and down childhood. About her stay at the Convent, the incident of Boo-boo and the scissors, sparking it up to make an amusing story, pleased to find that she could relate it lightly, even raise a laugh . . .

'She is a monster, your mother!'

She looked at him, expecting to see the familiar teasing look. He was serious.

255

'Oh, no . . .' she protested. 'No, she isn't. I didn't mean that.'

'This is lies, then, that you tell me?'

'No, of course not—'

'Then it is true, she is a monster.' He reached across her to stub out his cigarette. 'You have to understand this, not feel guilty about telling the truth. Bad people do not become good, simply because they have given birth.'

But she did feel guilty, there was no escaping it. You ought to be loyal to your parents whether you thought they deserved it or not. Besides, backbiting was cowardly, her own worst character fault; and now she had betrayed it to, of all people, Adam. She was silent, at a loss to undo the damage.

Adam smiled, and rolled on to his elbow.

'You are too complicated. People should be simple. Some day, I marry someone very simple, someone easy to understand.'

She felt a chill. It came as no surprise that she was not the one he planned to marry; he was Catholic, she was married to Gerald, no divorce could ever alter that for him. But that even had she been single he wouldn't have considered it, was something she would rather not have known. At this precise moment, she could do without being told that she was something transient in his life.

It must have showed in her face, for he reached across to kiss her.

'Some day,' he repeated, his eyes smiling into hers. 'Not yet. Not while I have you.' He slipped an arm under her, pulled her into his arms. 'Perhaps never . . .'

She turned to pillow her face on his chest, keeping it hidden, swallowing determinedly. She knew it was meant to make the hurt go away; she didn't want him to know that it hadn't. But he was not to be fooled. His arm under her twitched playfully.

'Come on,' he teased her. 'Cheer up, it's not as if you were in love with me.' When she didn't answer, his arm twitched again. But when he spoke his tone was subtly changed, tinged with something all too close to apprehension. 'You're not . . . are you?'

The chill deepened to a sliver of ice, a sliver that pierced her painfully in an old, old wound. He didn't even want her to love him, didn't want that responsibility hung about his neck.

'No, no, of course not—' she said with forced brightness, springing out of bed to escape his scrutiny. 'We'd better get up or I'll miss my train . . .' She made for the wash basin and turned both taps full on, splashing her face vigorously while groping for the towel.

He put it into her hand and turned her to face him. 'We must talk about this,' he said gravely.

She had herself under control now. 'It's all right,' she said coldly. 'I understand. Perhaps it's best if I don't come any more.'

He spread his hands. 'If you wish. But you are hurt, that is not good.'

'Oh, no,' she smiled, angrily. 'I can only be hurt by those I love.'

Adam pursed his lips. Then he said gently, 'Like your husband.'

She had opened her mouth for a stinging retort when she saw the truth of it. She stared. He nodded. And now, maddeningly, the tears got the better of her, rushing into her eyes, pouring down her face, splashing in great drops off her chin, while she stood stubbornly compressing her lips, still telling herself that she was not going to cry . . .

Adam took her in his arms. 'Darling Sally, come and sit down. We talk, understand each other, yes?'

Blindly she nodded, allowed herself to be led back to the bed, sat silently, weeping, listening to his voice.

'If we are wise, we can give each other much and no one will be the loser. You have your problems, they are not for me to solve. But I can give you, perhaps, something that is missing from your life, yes?'

She assented, her face against his neck, her eyes on the little hollow at the base of his throat, where a few dark silky hairs encroached from the forest of his chest. 'But I don't know what I can give you, if you don't want . . . love.'

He took her shoulders and held her away, forcing her to meet his eyes. 'I don't talk about my work. I tell you now, and then no more. It takes me to war zones, to famines, to earthquakes. Wherever there is death, despair, torture and oppression, there is Adam Niklaus, growing day by day more jaded, more isolated, more cynical . . . I spend my life among the dying and the hopeless.' He paused, and for a moment they were both silent. Then he cupped her chin in his hand, and smiled. 'Now comes Sally, still believing in fairies, to fall into my arms: this young, fresh, silly, romantic girl, throbbing with life and passion. What more could I ask . . .'

His smile had changed subtly, haunted by something undefinable. After a moment she wound her arms tightly about him, saying nothing, and before long they made love again.

Having decided that she would catch an afternoon train, they made a lightning tour of the West End, already sparkling in its Christmas finery. She bought a thankyou gift for Geraldine, and then one for Aimée who, like the children, must not be allowed to feel left out. In the pet department of Harrods, a solitary Siamese kitten mewed in its pen.

'Oh, poor little thing,' mourned Sally. 'It's all alone, it must be so unhappy.'

Adam smiled. 'You want it?'

'I'd love it — only I'd have to ask Gerald.' She blushed, aware of his amusement. 'I mean,' she added defensively, 'they're very expensive.'

'You must learn to manage your life. You do not ask, you tell. Just tell, without shouting. And smile, be charming. Then, you find that you have won.'

He was moving on, and she followed him, her eyes still dragged to where the tiny creature climbed the bars, one paw reaching through in a desperate effort to retain her attention.

'Come, we have lunch.'

Reluctantly, she went. When they had eaten, falling silent in the shadow of the imminent goodbye, he pressed her hand briefly.

'Wait here for me.'

He returned carrying a large perforated carton from which issued faint sounds of scrabbling.

'Oh, Adam—'

'The pedigree is in the envelope. Also, they tell me, a diet sheet. One more baby for you, one that you may spoil.' He laughed. 'It is for this, no? that the English keep pets, so as not to spoil their children?'

'Oh . . . Adam!' she could think of nothing else to say. 'Oh . . . but I have nothing for you!' She was delighted, distressed, confused, altogether overwhelmed. She took the box on her knee and tried to peep in through the air holes. 'Oh, I'll never forget this!'

'Then I have all I want,' he said lightly. 'Now, to your train.'

At the station, she leaned through the window to drink her last sight of him as he stood smiling, unconcerned. She said it before she could stop herself. 'Oh, Adam . . . I do miss you.'

'And I you.' He laughed. 'When I have time – no, I tease you, I'm bad. Of course I miss you.'

He drew her down towards him and they clung briefly.

'I'm always afraid I'll never see you again.'

'You will always see me.' He drew back to look at her. 'You don't believe it now, but time will show.' He released her and took an envelope from his pocket. 'Does anyone in your family read German?'

'What an odd question.'

'Well?'

'No, not as far as I know. Not even me.'

'Then you will have to look it up. I think it's Goethe.'

'What is?'

'Your Christmas card.' He handed it to her. Doors were slamming along the length of the train. He kissed her quickly and stood back. 'Give love to the little cat.'

'I'd rather give it to you.'

He smiled, shaking his head. 'I'd only lose it. Love is like possessions, you have to have somewhere to keep it. I'm always on the move.' He raised an arm in salutation as the train began to move. 'Enjoy life, see you soon. *Ciao . . . au'voir . . .*'

'Goodbye . . .' She stood waving at the window for as long as she could see him, still standing motionless in an ocean of movement; faintly amazed to watch him being bumped and jostled by the crowd who saw in him nothing unusual, while to her he was so extraordinary, so special. Perhaps it was simply that he was Adam, and all those others were not . . .

She sat back in the corner seat and opened her card. It was a print of Dürer's praying hands. Strange, she had never thought of Adam as being religious, not in everyday life. It was not signed, but inside he had written: '*Alles vergeht, aber die Liebe siegt.*'

She could hardly wait to get home and look up the translation. Because she had recognized one word, the one that everyone learns first, or nearly first, in any language. '*Liebe.*' She knew that that meant love.

The kitten had settled quietly now, and she guessed it was asleep. She laid a protective hand on its box, and allowed herself to drift into a drowse of bitter-sweet content.

When the train pulled into her home station it was snowing, thin spiteful flakes that stung her face and left a miserly coverlet on the ground. She telephoned Gerald to collect her from the station.

'I've got a kitten in a basket and a load of shopping, I can't bring it all on the bus.'

'Oh, very well,' he said. 'I'll come and get you.'

While she waited she tried to work out a feasible story to explain her acquisition: how she had somehow stretched her miniscule dress allowance to make the purchase – or perhaps she should say she had been persuaded to give it a home. But it didn't seem likely that pedigree-cat breeders

260

gave away their stock, and anyway, how would she explain her having met one? She stood gnawing her lip in the biting cold, shifting from one foot to the other, sheltering the kitten in its box under a fold of her coat.

When Gerald drew up in the car he was smiling. He took the box from her and stowed it in the back with her shopping.

'Did you say you'd brought a kitten,' he said. 'How nice.' And that appeared to be the limit of his curiosity.

The children were enchanted by the little Siamese and argued endlessly about what she was to be called, until Sally proclaimed flatly and finally that her name was Selina. Aimée's was the only eye in which suspicion briefly winked, and even that was quelled by Geraldine's blithe assumption that her son had made his 'little wife' a handsome Christmas gift, a notion of which Sally was careful not to disabuse her.

The festive season came and went uneventfully, and was followed by a cold late spring. Sally ordered from the newsagent the paper in which Adam's column regularly appeared, and devoured it hungrily, her only, albeit impersonal, link with him. Every week she cut it out, with its small familiar photograph, and hoarded the cuttings in the back of her poetry book. At the library where she had first seen Adam, she had traced the quotation: 'Everything is forgotten, but love endures,' and although at first she had been slightly disappointed, longing as always for something more personal, more committed, less enigmatic, with time it had grown into a knot of warmth that she embraced in the coldness of long nights.

Three more times, not counting the occasion when she went to London to find that he was out of town, after which she learned the wisdom of ringing from a call box in the village before getting on the train, she went winging to meet Adam and together they took what he laughingly called their 'four steps in the clouds'. Then one week his column was missing from the paper. Perhaps, she thought, puzzled, he was taking a holiday — what a pity she hadn't known.

But for the next four weeks his column failed to appear, and at the end of that time his photograph reappeared over the caption: 'Among the Disappeared', and a brief paragraph below it stated that he had gone to Argentina on an assignment, and that so far all efforts to contact him had failed.

CHAPTER FOURTEEN

She had had no premonition of the disappearance of Adam. No sixth sense had warned her that this was the last, the one and only time left that she would see him. Nothing more than the sense of loss she always felt as her train drew out, the ache of longing for what was past that melted imperceptibly into the longing for what was yet to come, the anticipation of a future as yet unforeseen but none the less certain, promised. 'You will always see me,' he had said, and she clung to that reassurance against all the odds. Now, without warning, it was all over, finished, gone.

For a long time she did not believe it. He would come back somehow, some time . . . only, it would be much longer this time. It was difficult enough not to betray her anxiety in snapping at the children, to keep the mask of contented wife and mother nailed to her face; once allow herself to accept that he was gone, once let the anxiety become despair . . . she dared not contemplate the consequences.

Gerald, mercifully, seemed to notice no change in her, any more than he had noticed any other variation in her mood since they had married. Even the vigilant Aimée, apart from the occasional sniping which seemed to be part of her nature, was too preoccupied with her own affairs, as was Geraldine with the budding achievements of the children.

But the children noticed; oh yes, they noticed. Discovering fresh power to drive her to the end of her shortened tether, they vied with one another in devising new and devious ways of fraying her patience, while Sally, aware as always that she was herself to blame, ground her nerves to a pulp in her efforts to resist the urge to retaliate.

At least she was spared the ordeal of watching for the post. Adam, she knew, would never write to her, whatever the circumstances. She had pleaded in vain, he was immovable. He would do nothing to endanger her marriage.

'We can have much, if no one is the loser. We meet, we give each other all the good and beautiful things, and then we go back to our lives, I to my work, you to your family. No problems, no decisions, no agonies of choice. It is better, you will see.'

Now she saw, albeit unwillingly, that in this as in so much, he had been wise. The letter that failed to arrive had never seriously been expected, and for a while she was able to cling to the illusion that one day she would ring his answering service to find that he was back. One day . . . She rang it twice a month, no more, from a call box in the village, and although she always met with the same negative reply, when she replaced the receiver she could console herself that perhaps by the time she next rang he would have surfaced and left a message for her. Adam was so capable, so cosmopolitan . . . she couldn't imagine him being lost anywhere for long.

When she was politely but firmly requested not to ring again, as Mr Niklaus was no longer a client, she felt the first real chill. She pushed herself to ring his office number in Fleet Street, and asked for the journalist who had written the paragraph reporting him missing.

The voice was male, youngish, briskly competent. 'Were you a particular friend?'

The use of the past tense was unnerving. 'Sally,' she faltered. 'Sally Hammond. Perhaps he mentioned me?'

'Oh . . . yes, I believe he did.' It was clear that he didn't remember. 'Well, Sally, why don't we meet for a drink? We can't really talk on the phone.'

'Oh, yes – please. Only, I'm a long way out of town. Can I ring you later?' She didn't want to tell this stranger that she had children, a husband, arrangements to be made, in case he'd guessed that she was trying to trace a lover.

'Any time,' he said airily, and rang off.

So, that was it. Somehow, she must go, and in a small way she felt heartened. At least, she was going to hear something, and anything was better than nothing, better than going on like this indefinitely, not knowing what had happened to Adam or how long he might be gone.

They met a few days later in a coffee bar in Villiers Street, just off the Strand. He was a rangy young man in a shabby Burberry, with the same alertness of eye that had characterized Adam.

'Sally?' He smiled briefly, hand thrust towards her in greeting, and motioned her towards a seat. 'I'm Guy, we spoke yesterday. You don't know me but I've got something for you. Sit down, I'll get us a bite. Coffee?'

He returned bearing sandwiches, which he balanced on the narrow shelf that served as a table; there they perched on high stools, hemmed in by the crush of other customers, conversing with each other's reflections in the long mirrors that lined the walls.

'Adam left this for you.' He indicated a small black case which he had set down at their feet. 'It's been standing about in the office with your name on, that's why I asked you to come, hope you didn't mind?' He flipped the luggage label tied to its handle. 'No address, you see, we couldn't send it on. He seemed to think you'd call sometime.'

'Yes . . . what is it, a suitcase?'

'His typewriter.' He seemed to hesitate. 'Said he wanted you to have it, if . . .' He did not finish.

'If what?'

'If he didn't get back.'

Sally stared. 'You mean . . . at all?'

'He didn't tell you?'

She shook her head. It came to her that she had known next to nothing about Adam's pursuits when he wasn't with her. Whatever else they had discussed, it was never his work. And as for Argentina, it was just a name on a map.

'Tell me,' she said. 'Please, tell me what you know. Are you saying that he went to this place knowing it was risky – how risky was it?'

Guy pulled his mouth to one side in a wry gesture. 'Let's say, it's not the place to go if you have dependants. Or a weak constitution.'

Oh, God . . . She pulled herself together enough to ask, 'What was this assignment he went on?'

'Ostensibly, to report on the country's economy. Actually, to try and trace another journalist who disappeared a year ago. It's a dangerous business, poking sticks into political hornets' nests.'

Her heart seemed to stop, then start again with a heavy thud. 'Are you saying . . . he may never come back?'

He lit a cigarette, drew on it deeply, regarded her through the haze. 'Put it this way. Prisons in the Argentine are not like prisons here. It has to be faced that the inmates don't always survive.'

Suddenly the heat in the tiny place was too much for her. She stared hard into her cup, trying desperately to keep it in focus. She was aware of Guy saying something, then of his hand under her arm, guiding her out into the street, into cooler air, and the rattle and fume of traffic.

'Sorry,' he was saying. 'I didn't realize. Of course, he has the language, he may have gone underground. It's always possible. In which case . . .'

She found herself in a bar, being steered to a corner seat, a balloon of brandy put into her hand. Now she was cold, shaking, her teeth trying to chatter. Guy sat down beside her, a half of bitter in his hand.

'If he's gone underground, we'll hear something sooner or later. I'll be in touch.' He pressed a card into her hand.

She collected herself enough to say, 'Don't write.' It was less necessity now than loyalty to Adam, who had always been so assiduous not to compromise her. Even when he must have known where he was going, must have wanted to warn her . . . 'I'll ring you from time to time, if that's all right?'

'Of course.' Was he suppressing a smile, knowing or guessing her circumstances . . . it hardly mattered now.

She swallowed the brandy, a fiery core of strength. 'I'd better be going.'

'I'll see you to your train.'

In the taxi, he said, 'Sorry if I've been tactless. Didn't realize the situation, all I had was your name on the label, it didn't tell me much. Sorry,' he said again.

'There's nothing to tell.' She heard her own voice through the numbness in her mind. 'Just a name on a typewriter. Thanks for your help.'

'Such as it is.' He sounded deprecating, almost apologetic. 'Adam was a mate, so if there's anything I can do, anything at all at any time, you've got my card.'

She nodded. 'Thanks again, I won't forget.' They finished the short journey in silence.

In the train, she took the typewriter on her knee and opened it. Perhaps after all he had left some message inside. A single sheet was in the roller, bent in a curve from being shut in for so long. She turned it up and read:

> Don't forget to write . . .
>   A.
> PS I read your poems

She wanted to laugh, cry, scream with frustration, strangle him for being so maddeningly flippant when what she wanted, needed from him was something so much deeper . . . but even as the tears came pouring, driving her to flee for the privacy of the grubby toilet, she knew that she could not be angry with him now, or ever again.

He was not really being flippant. He was simply being Adam.

She reached home in a state of nervous exhaustion, in a damp summer dusk that turned the valley to mist. Through the lighted windows she could see Geraldine reading to the children, and knew in a moment of dread that she had to face them all. As she fumbled the key in the lock, the door was opened from within by Gerald.

267

'Back so soon?' he said drily.

Wearily, she set down the typewriter. 'I won't be going again.'

She tried to meet his eyes, she really tried. But she could see nothing but Adam's face, fading out of her life. She smiled blindly, and walked on. As she moved forward, his hands arrested her, taking her by the shoulders and turning her towards him. She stood leaning against him as she had long ago, hearing his heartbeat as she wrestled with the grief, obscurely thankful that she had him to come back to. Gerald, kind, patient and uncurious, an everlasting refuge in the turbulence of her life . . . she knew she could never have left him, had never once seriously considered it; she had needed Adam for something quite other, something that was missing from her life with him, had needed him as well as, never instead of Gerald. Adam in his wisdom had seen it from the start.

'I'm sorry,' she whispered, choking, not even certain that he heard. 'I'm just tired.'

She felt his arms encircle her, a touch, perhaps a kiss, on the top of her head.

'Better go and freshen up,' he said, releasing her.

'Yes.' She dashed a hand across her eyes, straightened her back. 'I've got a typewriter,' she said brightly, snatching words from the air in her desperation. 'I'm going to be rich and famous, how about that?'

He smiled back, giving her strength, showing his approval with a little nod. Approval, not of her intent but of her bravery. Gerald, who was always embarrassed by a show of emotion.

She would make it up to him, she resolved as she wearily climbed the stairs, must give herself back to him without reservations, find ways to compensate him for her defection even though he knew nothing of it and would never know . . . she wished she could have told him, would have given much to be able to unburden herself, to lay her guilt and her anguish in his uncritical hands. But that was a monumental self-indulgence that would rob him of her gift, would abnegate any sacrifice she could make. It was no good being half-hearted about it; love was not love, if not given with both hands.

She felt no disloyalty to Adam in making this commitment; he had known from the beginning, had understood better than she, that some part of her would always belong to Gerald; Gerald, who had rescued her from the fear and loneliness of her childhood, had enabled her to live it down and come to terms with her mother. It had been a hard lesson to learn that her husband had no more use for her affection than Aimée had − he hadn't even wanted sex with her for months − yet it was none the less his by right. And if by some defect of his nature he was unable to accept love, it was nobody's fault and there was little she could do about it.

She remembered with a twist of pain Adam saying, 'You have your problems, they are not for me to solve.' That was equally true of Gerald and herself. No, thanks, might be his signal: it need not stop her making the gift. The fringe benefits at least could sweeten his life, albeit unrecognized.

She set herself to believe in the loss of Adam as final and irrevocable. It was perhaps a punishment, God's judgement upon her, as the nuns would have said. So be it, she thought; but if she must do penance, let her at least do it cheerfully, privately, not spread her misery to those around her.

Steeling herself, she applied herself to the study of cookery books, set about redecorating the cottage, worked herself to exhaustion in the garden . . . she would not, she resolved, ring Guy for possible news of Adam. It would be better that way, because no hope meant no suspense. If Adam did return, he would surely find a way . . . she would not allow herself to dwell upon it.

Yet try as she would she could not delete him from her mind. His presence haunted her dreams, images of such reality and vividness that she would wake believing him back with her, to be wounded afresh with the impact of his loss. Warm in his arms, she would be torn from sleep by the voices of the children, quarrelling as always, demanding her adjudication. In the tattered exercise book that was her only solace, she wrote what she could confide to no one, her secret shameful longings, her unjustifiable anger . . .

I dreamed of my love and they awakened me
The little importunate children that are not his.
Mother! they shouted, and Mother! and Give me! and
  Mother!
Their voices raked and tangled and said nothing . . .
Their monkey chatter drowned his quiet words
The breath of their quarrelling drove him from my knowing
His eyebrows melted from beneath my fingers
His image irretrievably lost in darkness

And I was cast up upon the loveless shore
Only the children, and the bitter light;
Their voices like the swords of hate cut through me
For a terrible moment of truth, I wished them dead.

She felt a little eased for having written it, could not bring herself to destroy it as she knew she should. It remained in the book with everything else, against the time when she might feel strong enough.

One other indulgence she allowed herself, and only one. When the time came, she would mate Selina instead of having her spayed; that way there would always be a Selina, a flesh and blood link with Adam, the only one . . .

Weeks later, she stood in the call box in the village, shivering despite the heat of the day.

'Guy . . . I'm sorry to ask you this, but . . .' She hesitated, unsure even now that she could bring herself to say what had to be said. But she must, she had no choice. She swallowed, tried again. 'It's just . . . there's no one else I can ask, no one I can tell . . . I do hope you understand. You – you must feel free to say No, of course, only—' She felt her voice crack and cleared her throat noisily. 'You see, I can't tell anyone here, and I'm desperate – I don't know what I'll do if you can't help me . . .' Again she faltered.

There was silence at the other end. 'Are you still there?'

'Yes.' He sounded cautious, and a little tentative. 'What is it, are you in some kind of trouble?'

'Oh, yes, yes, I am,' she blurted. 'Oh Guy, I'm so sorry to ask you, but you're like Adam, you know so many people, and I can't go to my own doctor – oh Guy, I need an abortionist!'

Shamefully, without warning, she burst into tears, her head pillowed on the tattered, evil-smelling directory.

CHAPTER FIFTEEN

The year that followed faded to a dark blur in her memory. Afterwards, it was as if her mind recoiled from the pain, the misery, the unattended illness about which she had been forced to lie. She who abhorred deception now had a whole area of her life which had to be buried, which she hardly dared recall herself. She plodded on through day after day, at worst an hour at a time, blinkered against anything that might assail her emotions, might trigger a disaster, a descent into suffering too awful to contemplate. Her smiles, when they eventually returned, were of tolerance, of patience . . . they were rarely of joy. In the absence of comment from Gerald, she was able to persuade herself that she was winning.

Until one day lightning struck. She was washing dishes when it happened, up to her elbows in suds at the sink, and thought she must have misheard. She straightened her aching back and turned to look.

'What did you say?'

Gerald shifted his feet. 'I said, I think we should consider a divorce.'

She stared. 'If that's a joke . . .'

But she knew it wasn't. When she saw his face, she knew. She felt as though she had been punched in the stomach, numb and faintly sick.

'It's not a joke,' said Gerald. 'Leave that and come and sit down, I want to talk to you.'

She picked up a tea towel and followed him slowly through to the living room. 'But you always said . . .'

He shook his head. 'I've been thinking it over. Things

are changing, it's not such a mark against one as it was.'

She sank on to the sofa before her knees could let her down. 'Gerald . . . you're not serious. You can't be. Look, if it's something I'm doing . . . or not doing . . . surely we can talk about it? I mean, we don't have to break up the home. Think of the children . . .'

She felt herself floundering in the dark, as if she had been pitched into a midnight sea, as if the ground had opened without warning under her feet and dropped her into an abyss. From a long way off she heard Gerald say with faint derision, 'Think of the children. That's all you ever do.'

She could not believe what she was hearing, what was happening, could see no reason for it. Her first thought was that he had somehow found out about Adam. But that was all over, lost without trace . . . and he wouldn't have cared, had never valued her fidelity anyway. Hadn't he callously invited her to find someone else when his own eyes roved elsewhere? No, it had to be something else. She felt bewildered, twenty years back in her childhood, disgraced and rejected and not knowing why.

'Gerald,' she protested at last. 'What have I done?'

He shook his head again, but he was not smiling. 'Nothing. It's nothing to do with you, it's me.' He cleared his throat. 'There's someone else.' Unbelievably, he added, 'You'll laugh when you know—'

'Someone else . . .'

She felt cold, her voice was flat, expressionless. But as she brought her eyes to his face her anger was beginning to build. So, this was the marriage she had tried so hard to save. For this she had destroyed her child – Adam's child, perhaps his only one – had lived like a nun for more than a year, doing penance for a single fall from grace. And now, because Gerald had found metal more attractive, Gerald, whose needs were paramount, the whole thing was to be tossed into the dustbin. It was not to be borne! She dried her hands slowly on the tea towel, staring at the words, 'Pure Irish Linen' woven into the border. She moistened her lips.

'I see,' she said icily. 'So one of your passing fancies has decided not to pass. Is that it?'

She had never spoken to Gerald in that tone before. She was surprised at herself. He was clearly surprised too, for a tiny frown was gathering between the perfect eyebrows.

'No,' he said crisply. 'No, it's not like that at all. I'm in love for the first time in my life. I have had girlfriends in the past, though I thought you were too wrapped up in the children to notice. But this is different, I never really knew what love meant until now.' He looked at her in mild reproach. 'I thought you'd understand. I thought, you of all people . . .'

'So I'm supposed to understand?' The words tasted dry and acid in her mouth. 'What I don't understand is, if this is your first love, why did you marry me?'

The frown deepened. He was not used to being challenged, not by her. 'That was different,' he said again. 'I thought it was what you wanted. That's what your mother said.'

She looked up, startled. 'What my mother said?'

'Well . . . not in so many words.' He smiled at last, a little nervous rictus. 'She pointed out that you were very young, and I mustn't — what was that old-fashioned phrase she used — "trifle with your affections".'

Sally clenched her teeth, remembering Aimée's words to her on the subject. Had she thought to bring Gerald closer by a marriage to her daughter, or merely been eager to get Sally off her hands . . . whatever the motive, it was a wasted effort now.

She compressed her lips. 'My mother has a lot to answer for.'

'Be that as it may, you were glad enough to get away from her.'

'But it wasn't why I married you!' She was appalled. 'I don't know how you can say such a thing or even think it!'

He raised a cynical eyebrow. 'I know what I believe.'

What you want to believe, thought Sally. So you needn't feel bad about it, don't have to carry the burden of betrayal, or whatever we're supposed to call it now.

'You know that's not true!' she burst out, her voice cracking with emotional frustration.

'I know you never wanted me,' he accused.

'In bed, you mean?' So that was it, he'd found some red-hot sexy piece who'd set him on fire at last. It was hard to believe, she couldn't imagine him getting excited over anything . . . 'I couldn't help being frigid,' she retorted. 'I did my best. You never made me feel you really wanted me, I felt anything with the right plumbing would have suited you just as well!' She didn't want to say these things to him, they sprang from the hurt inside her and she could not bite them back. 'I suppose you were making do with me until the right one came along!'

He spoke with dignity, unruffled as always. 'That was unworthy of you. We'll talk about it some other time, when you're feeling calmer.'

'When I can behave myself, is that what you mean?' She twisted anguished hands in the tea towel. 'I've heard it said that a man will leave a woman he loves for one who's better in bed,' she said with quiet bitterness. 'Are you telling me it's true?'

Gerald turned away from her, paused with his hand on the door. 'I don't wish to discuss it any further,' he said.

She let him go, remaining where she was, immobilized by the turmoil of her thoughts. Then suddenly she jumped up, remembering something left unsaid. 'Gerald?'

He was in the kitchen, quietly finishing the dishes she had started to wash. Something he would never normally do. She stood in the doorway and watched him.

'There was something you started to say and didn't finish. What was it you thought I'd laugh at?'

He turned, thought a moment, looking puzzled. Then his brow cleared. 'Oh, yes! I remember, I started to tell you who it is. You're never going to believe this.' He smiled again, nervously. 'It's your cousin Dotty.'

They did, of course, discuss it further, and it was Gerald and not Sally who decided the time. But by then she had, by a mighty effort, brought herself to come to terms with the situation.

Gerald, after his initial displeasure, displayed a lightness of heart, a disposal to joke, that she had not seen in him since their earliest days. He was happy, she realized; there was no blinking the fact.

For herself, she hardly knew what she felt. Dismay, certainly, for Charles and Zoë, innocently expecting their safe world to continue, their cocoon to remain intact. And a certain dread of the future on her own account, since when Gerald left her she would have to manage the household affairs, she who hardly knew the procedure for paying the rates.

She could not rid herself of a bitter resentment of the abortion to which she had subjected herself, a renewed remorse for the unseen baby she had lost, so painfully, so shamefully and with so much grief; pretending, after she had crawled home with the lethal drugs at work inside her, that no such thing was happening and that nothing was amiss. It was resentment less for herself – since she had after all brought it upon herself – than for the child robbed of its life, sacrificed to save something destined only to be thrown away.

The knowledge that Dotty was taking her place had buried her heart in ice, and what she felt towards Gerald evaded definition. In that area she was totally numb, as if scar tissue had formed so deep that there was nothing more to be felt there, ever again. It was abundantly clear that he had made his decision to go. Refusal to co-operate in the divorce he had set his heart on would avail her nothing and would merely engender hatred. She remembered all too well the consequences of that.

It was no good feeling angry with Gerald: if he couldn't love her he couldn't, and he'd made it clear enough that he never had. You couldn't love someone because you felt you should. No doubt he had tried, done his best within his limitations . . . he could not be blamed.

It was like herself with Aimée, she thought sadly. She

had wanted to love her mother, and God knew she had tried. But emotions could not be forced. You could behave as though you loved, do everything you should, even add that little bit extra, but no power on earth could make it flow from the heart. At best you were only going through the motions.

So however bad she might feel about it, all in all, it was best to cut losses and let him go free. At least they needn't end in hating each other. And the children wouldn't be staked out on a battle ground between them.

The mothers had to be told. Next to telling the children, the worst bit was breaking it to the mothers.

With Aimée away on a visit to Uncle Charles and the children safely invited to a beach weekend with friends, Sally, her stomach in knots of apprehension but determined that Gerald should do his own dirty work, rang Geraldine and asked her to come over. Gerald, she promised, would collect her and take her back, an arrangement which did not please him when she told him of it.

'You do ask me to do some horrid things,' he complained, climbing into the car at seven o'clock on a Sunday morning.

'Tough,' said Sally drily, and closed the door on him.

It was late morning when they returned, early autumn with the scent of woodsmoke drifting across the garden, Geraldine slightly ruffled at having been bidden at their convenience rather than her own.

When Sally caught Gerald's eye with a questioning look, he frowned and shook his head. So, he hadn't told her, hadn't taken the opportunity of the long drive to break it to her quietly and in private. She greeted her mother-in-law with the customary kiss.

'Come in, Gerry, sit down and I'll make coffee – unless you'd prefer sherry? I'm afraid Gerald has something to tell you.'

Geraldine came in, looking from one to the other as though she sensed impending disaster.

'What's the matter?' She looked about her anxiously.

'Where are the children? What's happened, are they all right?'

'The children are fine, they're at a party,' said Sally, and retired to the kitchen, closing the door.

Within seconds, Geraldine appeared in the doorway, a man-o'-war with all guns blazing, her eyes flashing with celestial fire.

'Whose fault is this? Who's responsible for this dreadful thing, surely not my Gerald. Is it you? I can't believe it's my Gerald.'

Sally, taken off guard, stammered and blushed. 'I hope not.' She could not look back over her marriage with any sense of achievement. 'I've tried, but who knows . . . I suppose I've failed.'

Gerald appeared behind Geraldine. 'Of course it's not her fault,' he said loyally. 'It's mine, I take full responsibility. I want to marry someone else.'

In the moments that followed, Sally felt for the first time a genuine compassion for Geraldine. Since her widowhood she had moulded her life about her only son, had set him on a pedestal impossible to maintain; now her idol lay in shards, and her loving pride lay with it.

'I can't believe you'd leave those lovely children,' she wept, again and again. 'Sally, can't you forgive him and try again?'

'I don't want to be forgiven,' snapped Gerald. 'You're not listening, Mother. I've told you, I want a divorce.'

The rest of the day was one Sally could well have done without.

But at least the dreaded confrontation with Aimée was spared her. Aimée had already been told the news, via Uncle Charles, who had had it from Dotty. She rang Sally the same afternoon and she, too, was in tears.

'I can't believe little Dotty could behave like that, did you know she was with Gerald that time you went to visit George in France?'

As long ago as that, thought Sally: so it was Dotty all the time.

'And when I said to her, Dotty, you're surely not going to break up a marriage, think of Sally left to bring up the children alone, d'you know what she said?'

'No,' said Sally obediently, although she did not really want to be told.

'She said, "Well, it's her own fault, if she'd made him happy he wouldn't want to leave her for me." ' There was a pause at the other end, during which Sally could hear her sniffing and blowing her nose. 'I've never been so shocked in anyone, Sally, I'd never have believed little Dotty could be so wicked . . .'

We all had our disillusionments, reflected Sally; now Aimée's idol had been shattered with the rest. She wondered if she was going to have to prop up the two grannies as well as trying to console the children. She had not told them yet, and they would have to be told soon if they were not to stumble on the truth from some unwelcome outside source. She tried over and again to find the right words to take the hurt away. There were none. And at length she decided it was Gerald's responsibility to tell them, to try to explain his decision. She could find neither the words nor the heart to tell them. It was up to him.

In the event he too failed to find the words. On the day he left, he kissed them goodbye in the morning and said lightly, 'I won't be home tonight.'

It was left to Sally after all, to break the news and dry the tears.

Hearing him leave the house for the last time, she felt a sudden desolation she had not bargained for. It took her by surprise, causing her to turn her face into the pillow to stifle tears of her own. 'I didn't want you to go, I wanted you to love me,' she sobbed into the linen . . . Then she dried her face, nailed a smile to her mast, and took the children to school.

They were forced to move out of the cottage. Sally dreaded going; she had hoped to live there undisturbed for the rest of her life, loved it and the garden she had made, spent the last few minutes of her occupation in cutting every last flower to take with her . . . but Gerald needed the money from the sale to set up his new home, as Geraldine, quickly won over by Dotty's indisputable charm, was quick to point out. Sally, striving to be sensible, reminded herself that with only a third of their former income they could not afford to stay there anyway, particularly since Gerald had departed with the car. It was becoming a toss-up as to whether to pay the gas bill, the electricity bill or the water rate in any one month, new clothes were out of the question and when school fees fell due she spent sleepless nights wondering how she was to pay them at all. But she was determined not to make more changes in the lives of Charles and Zoë than were unavoidable, and a certain stubborn pride was growing in her, demanding that she prove herself able to look after them without Gerald to hold her hand.

They moved into three furnished rooms and a 'kitchenette' – a glorified cupboard with a sink and a power point – and she stepped back on to the treadmill of job-hunting to make ends meet. It had not been easy before; now it was even more difficult. Not only had she no more qualifications or training than she had ever had, but she was older, which meant that she was expected to be experienced, and had children, whose needs demanded that she be home by mid-afternoon and free to look after them throughout the school holidays. Part-time work seemed to be the answer, but it was only available in catering, and she found herself at one point working for three employers in different kitchens to keep ahead of the bills. After six months and the sale of her precious engagement ring, followed by the Hoover and what silverware remained, she was totally exhausted and hard put to it to hide her despair.

She wrote tentatively to Gerald, whom the children had seen only twice, asking if he could possibly help out with their school fees. He replied that they could go to a state school free of charge, adding that he would prefer her not to write to him again because Dotty, now his wife, did not like it.

Although still smouldering bravely with defensive anger, she found this answer unexpectedly hurtful, seeing in it a rejection not merely of their marriage, but of more than ten years of her friendship.

Aimée was sympathetic, a fact which surprised Sally until she became aware that the sympathy invariably drifted into an aren't-men-beasts session, with Erik as the villain of the piece. Asked if she would consider babysitting to free Sally for a better job, she launched into a tirade about the plight of abandoned wives that effectively deflected the subject from the danger of having to say Yes. After a couple of efforts, Sally recognized defeat.

One evening when she had fallen asleep over the task of lengthening Zoë's school dress she was startled by the telephone ringing in the hall, followed by her landlady's voice calling up the stairs.

'Mrs Hammond, it's for you. Would it be your husband?'

The woman's voice was informed with curiosity. Sally started to reply, 'I haven't got a husband,' before deciding not to satisfy it.

She stumbled down, half asleep, picked up the receiver left hanging by its cord. 'Hello?'

'Hello, Sally! This is George, remember me? I stopped by the office the other day and they told me about you and Gerald. It occurred to me, perhaps you and the children would like to come back with me to the villa for a little holiday?'

CHAPTER SIXTEEN

Sunday morning. She knew it was Sunday morning, because George was still in bed. She could feel him breathing softly, interestedly, on the nape of her neck.

Instinctively, she stiffened. Why was it that she felt a repugnance to George, poor kind bumbling George, that she never felt to cold, uncaring Gerald? Was it because Gerald had been — and in fairness, still was — beautiful to the eye . . . if so, it was mortifying to think how shallow, how trivial, the attraction must have been. She would have liked to feel more warmly towards George, more as he deserved her to feel. But she did not feel truly married to him, could in no way bring herself to contemplate having a child, even had she been physically up to it, which since the dubious abortion with its absence of aftercare, she had reason to doubt. It would be, she felt dimly, a betrayal of Adam, that not content with destroying his child she should put someone else's in its place. Yet her empty womb felt like a mausoleum . . .

Her thoughts dwelt relentlessly on the child she had lost. She had needed the cleansing of natural grief and was unable to focus it on a faceless, nameless foetus she had never seen. She had only her anger. When Zoë whimpered over trifles, she had to stop herself from snapping. 'You're alive, aren't you? Stop complaining and be grateful!'

Yesterday, it had taken all her forbearance to say gently, 'I wish I could help you not to be so unhappy.'

Zoë had said nothing, merely looked resentful.

'Why are you? Nothing's ever right for you.'

'I want Daddy.' The lower lip drooped. Sally pulled

her into her arms, where she stood, unresponsive.

'You've still got me,' offered Sally, conscious that it was a poor exchange.

'You married Uncle George!'

'I thought you liked Uncle George.' After the long, lovely stay in France that had lasted the whole school holiday, the tireless story-telling, the uproarious romps on the beach, the extravagant present, the illicit sweets . . . surely, it had seemed so.

'I didn't want you to marry him! He doesn't like me any more, he's horrid when you're not looking. He says I'm spoilt.'

She began to wail, and Sally felt her patience shortening. Perhaps she was spoilt . . . but it was hardly her fault. Favoured and then abandoned by Gerald, having to adjust to George, however kindly, taking his place. It couldn't be easy. She tried another tack.

'There's still Charles – no, I know you don't get on together. But a brother's something special, something no one can take away.' If only she herself had had a sibling . . .

'Worse luck!'

'Zoë!'

'Well it is! It's awful having a twin, nothing's ever just you.'

'But surely that's good?'

'No, it's not, it's horrible, you're only half a person. And my other half's all wrong!'

Remembering the exchange, Sally sighed, and turned restlessly. George, who had been lying in wait, slid his hand over her thigh. Oh no, she groaned inwardly . . .

'I thought I heard the children,' she said lightly, and moved towards the edge of the bed. George pulled her back, his hand moving purposefully higher. 'It doesn't matter, does it? We are married, for God's sake.'

'It's not that,' she said uneasily. 'It's just . . . embarrassing. They might come in.'

'Soon settle that.' He bounded out of bed, his greying hair on end, his flannelette pyjamas sagging to his knees.

'There, I've locked the door,' he announced triumphantly, kicking off the pyjamas.

Involuntarily, she closed her eyes as he turned back towards her. It was not for his aesthetic impression that she loved him.

'Open your eyes, darling. Look at me, I like to be looked at. Diana always did, she enjoyed seeing me, it turned her on—'

'I'm not Diana.' She smiled, her eyes still closed, held out her arms to him. 'Just come back to bed.'

If only he could leave Diana behind him, she thought. Just in bed, would be something. Just to be able to enter one room without encountering a shrine . . . was it so unreasonable? Her picture was everywhere, a constant reminder that she, Sally, was expected to emulate her. At first she had found it touching, a tribute to the depth of George's feelings, a welcome contrast to what she felt to be the shallowness of Gerald's. But as time went on she saw it increasingly as not only somewhat morbid, but a perpetual slight to herself, a daily comparison which she could well do without.

'I'm waiting,' said George, his voice thickening.

'If you want me,' said Sally evenly, 'come back to bed. Look, George, I've told you, I'm not Diana, I'm me. People are all different, they react in different ways. I can't be somebody else, you have to accept me as I am.' She was surprised at herself, at the alacrity with which she was speaking. 'And while we're on the subject, I do find it a little off-putting to have Diana's photograph on the bedside table.' She essayed a laugh. 'Makes me feel she's watching me in bed with her man.'

'Well,' said George, quite seriously, 'so you are in a way. I mean, after all, this would have been her bedroom, if the poor darling hadn't died. You surely don't begrudge her a little photograph, do you?'

He managed to sound so reproachful that she felt obliged to retract.

'Well, no . . . of course not,' she said half-heartedly, aware that he had left her with no alternative. 'It's just – look, come back to bed, I want to cuddle you. That's better,' as he settled his head on her shoulder. She tightened her arms about him and went on, 'What I mean is, don't you think we should be starting a new life on our own, rather than trying to recapture the past?'

But George was not listening, intent only on achieving his original objective . . .

'Mummy!' A plaintive voice came distantly through the door, and the handle turned ineffectively. 'Mummy, I can't get in—'

'Go back to bed,' growled George.

'We want our breakfast,' Zoë's voice. Then, in a mutter behind it, Charles's resentful one, 'Come away, they don't want us.'

Sally, between two fires, contrived to glimpse her watch. 'Oh, dear . . .' she smiled apologetically. 'It's half-past nine.' She attempted to rise but George held her fast.

'Go and help yourselves,' he called out.

'I can't reach!' protested Zoë tearfully. 'I'm not tall enough.'

'I'll have to go,' said Sally. 'Sorry, love.'

'Surely they can make themselves a piece of toast. Charles can reach if she can't.'

'They're only young,' Sally reminded him. 'We don't really want them fooling with the hot stove, they might have an accident.' Seeing his sulky expression, she smiled. 'Well, I don't anyway. I'll go and see to them, and then come back.'

She was prompted less by inclination than by goodwill, hoping to coax him back into good humour. But as she ducked her head to kiss him he jerked away from her and dived out of bed. Before she could restrain him he had wrenched open the door and flung it wide.

'Well, come on in, then, it's Liberty Hall in here! Come in, if you must,' he boomed in a boisterous attempt at jollity.

Zoë, her small face on a level with his hairy naked loins, checked momentarily, her wide eyes startled, and then

285

ducked past him to hurl herself on to the bed where her mother lay.

'Oomph!' grunted Sally, the air knocked from her lungs by the impact.

'Get off!' barked George, and was ignored by the child who straddled her mother's body, giggling and bouncing up and down.

'No, Zoë, get off,' remonstrated Sally. Then, more urgently, 'Darling, you're hurting me!'

'Get off, I said!' roared George, and his heavy hand landed with a thump across Zoë's back.

'Don't do that!' Sally struggled up, blazing. 'Don't you dare do that, don't you ever do it again! If anyone has to hit my children, it'll be me and no one else.' She saw Zoë, transfixed, her eyes squeezed shut, her mouth wide open with no sound coming out. 'Just look at her,' she raged. 'You don't know your strength, you're much too big and heavy to hit a little girl!'

'She was hurting you,' blustered George. 'She's spoilt and disobedient. She's got to learn!'

She's got to learn, thought Sally: that old refrain again . . .

'Perhaps,' she retorted smartly. 'But not from you.'

As Zoë caught her breath and began to bellow, Sally reached to draw her into her arms. But the child fought her off and ran away, still yelling out her shock and indignation.

Distressed, she reached for a dressing gown and stared after her, but George grasped her painfully by the arm.

'No!' he rapped.

Turning to meet his eyes, she saw them hard as sapphires, glinting for the first time with naked jealousy.

'George . . .' she breathed.

He said nothing. After a moment he released her, snatched up his clothes and disappeared into the bathroom.

Sally sank down again upon the bed, her head in her hands. 'Oh George,' she sighed. 'George, George, George . . .'

It had seemed such a wonderful thing, a gift from heaven, when George had come back into their lives. Since the holiday in France two years ago, they had hardly been out of each other's company, a time of pleasures shared and troubles halved. The resultant marriage had been long predicted as a blending of two lonely people in happy companionship; and it would be so good for the children, everyone said. Geraldine had welcomed it as a lessening in some degree of Gerald's guilt in having left them: everything was going to work out for the best, she said cosily. And Aimée, to whom for a woman to remain unmarried was a stigma, could hardly wait to see the knot tied again. It was only the twins who failed to appreciate their apparent good fortune.

After a brief honeymoon period in which 'Uncle George' was a novelty, playing with them, reading them bedtime stories long past their normal lights out, and encouraging them to do things that their mother had not allowed, they sensed a change in him, a bewildering change for which they could see no reason. Already threatened by his declared intention of adopting them, they were puzzled by the unexpected withering of his generosity, by complaints of how much they ate, how much petrol he had to put into his car to take them to school. They were beginning to resent his always being there when they wanted to confide in Sally, and his abrupt demand that they call him Daddy was the last straw.

'You're not our daddy,' Charles had said stubbornly, his eyes dark and stormy.

'I am now, like it or lump it.' George's were bright and flinty, his smile fixed. 'So that's the answer to that one.'

Sally, foreseeing trouble, had made efforts to mediate, attempts which each had construed as her having sided against him. Baffled, she withdrew, unable to do more than look on as their hostility increased.

It was the first open crack in the relationship that had promised so much. George, warmhearted and funloving, had seemed to her like the sun breaking through after the long grey chill of life with Gerald.

She still could not think without pain of Adam, his charm

extinguished and his vital spirit sapped, lost or imprisoned in the remote, unimaginable Argentine; but she knew now, had accepted at last, that she would never see him again. When Gerald had gone, before George came on the scene, she had telephoned Guy in the faint hope of news. He had met her in London and taken her to the Martini Terrace high above New Zealand House. There, looking down over the gold embroidered darkness of London, he had broken it to her that Adam was officially listed as missing, presumed dead.

She had stood with an untouched drink in her hand, unable to speak, the great panorama below her swimming in lakes of black and gold, while Guy's voice went on quietly talking her through it, sustaining her gently until she could again sustain herself.

It was over, a brief and unreal rapture like the song of a bird in the night. The Americas had swallowed him, as they had swallowed Erik; what was it about America, that no one ever came back? In her imagination it crouched like some monstrous kraken beyond the Atlantic, devouring those she loved. It had taken Adam, and she had to accept that she would never see him again.

Yet the interlude, doomed as it was, had given her the knowledge that she could be loved, the confidence she needed to start again, to build a new life with George. And, give or take a few problems, it had started well enough. Although he had, undeniably, an embarrassing tendency to drink too much at parties, and it was true that household bills were regularly left unpaid until the threat of disconnection, she told herself that everything had its price. What if she did have to ring their hostess the next morning to apologize, what if she did have to nail the bills to his forehead until with good-humoured grumbling he produced his cheque book — didn't it always end in laughter, in everything working out all right in the end?

The matter of the children, though, went deeper and was much more serious. Relationships had already been strained by the needless legal wrangling with Gerald over their maintenance. Lawyer against lawyer, Greek meeting Greek, they had tried to beat each other into submission out of court, fighting back and forth over the same ground month after month like France and Germany in World War One, battling not for possession of the twins but for the privilege of disowning them; a war of attrition felt most keenly by Sally, in the unenviable position of having produced two children nobody wanted. A war, moreover, of which Charles and Zoë were undoubtedly aware despite all her efforts to keep it away from them, staked out as they were in the middle of no man's land . . .

When the wrangling had dragged on for eighteen months, and Gerald in exasperation had stopped payments altogether, there had seemed nothing for it but to get married and hope for the best.

That, she saw now, had been a disastrous error of judgement. But by that time she had reached the point of no return financially; her slender resources already strained to breaking point, she had lost her employment and fallen behind with the rent in trying to keep up with George's lifestyle, a fact which seemed to cause him no concern.

'Oh, that'll be all right, darling, don't you worry, we won't let you get into debt,' he had assured her cheerily, but without offering any practical remedy for her problems.

He had also, to her great disappointment, sold the French villa.

'Can't afford Biarritz and a family as well,' he had told her jovially, leaving her nevertheless with a sense of being trapped, since for her sake he had parted with it and she therefore owed it to him not to back out.

And there had been Aimée. Inevitably, Aimée . . . Her health beginning to fail, she had somehow inveigled George into inviting her to come and live with them, in the rambling Edwardian house he had bought with the proceeds of the French sale.

'Don't you want your mother here, where you can look after her?' Reproof had been evident in his tone. 'I should have thought you'd be pleased. It's not every husband who'd do as much, you know.'

'No, I know . . . don't think I don't appreciate it. It's just . . . well, we haven't always got on, you see. And then, she's not all that patient with the children . . .' He had looked at her speculatively, and she guessed that Aimée had put in what Erik would have called 'her two bits' worth'. She was left with nothing more to say than, 'It's very good of you, love. Of course she must come.'

'So I should think.' He had frowned at her, mockingly, his eyes teasing and full of humour, then pulled her into his arms to jolly her into agreement.

It was going to be all right, she had thought then. But now, the doubts she had been pushing to the back of her mind were growing more insistent by the hour.

She raised her head from her hands, aware of someone watching her. It was Charles, gravely handsome, an unsmiling presence in the bedroom doorway.

'Mark's here,' he said with dignity. 'You'd better get dressed.'

CHAPTER SEVENTEEN

Sally sighed. Mark, another legacy from Diana, her 'baby' brother who had taken to spending his school holidays with them instead of with his middle-aged parents; because George had extended an open invitation which Mark, at eighteen, had little conception of keeping within bounds. And Mark, at eighteen, was no longer a baby, with a disconcerting habit of gazing soulfully at Sally when he thought George wasn't looking. She could have done without this particular complication today.

'All right, love. I'm coming,' she told Charles, and reached for her clothes. 'Close the door, will you, so I can get dressed.'

The boy hesitated. It was strange, she thought, how in her mind he was already a boy, never a little boy, as Zoë a little girl; not yet nine, he was as gravely self-contained as his father, as though he already carried a man's responsibilities. Was he feeling now, as a man might, rejected?

'You can come in if you like,' she offered. 'Just shut the door behind you.'

Charles did not answer. He merely went out, his face as firmly closed as the door.

She worried about Charles, far more than she did about his sister. Zoë was all right, would always be all right, she could scream or whimper, give vent to her temper and let the devils out. Charles had turned his anger inward. He seemed locked within himself, an animal bleeding in its lair, not to be reached by the most loving hand. He never spoke about Gerald, never complained about George. It was baffling to guess what he thought about either, or of the situation in which he found himself.

Only once had he said anything about it. When Gerald first left them, he had asked when he was coming back. Sally had steeled herself.

'I'm afraid he's not.'

'Not ever?'

'He'll come and see you. But he's gone to live with Cousin Dotty.'

He had turned on her with glittering eyes. 'You let him go,' he accused her. 'You let him go, and you never even told us!' He turned his back, and something in his attitude told her that he was crying. She wanted to comfort him but he shook her off, and marched high-headed from the room.

It was since then that he had, in Aimée's words, 'gone sullen'. He no longer bullied his sister, but ignored her. To Sally's persuasion he was unresponsive, to George's boisterous jollity he turned a deaf ear, while Aimée, by dint of repeated questioning, elicited an occasional Yes or No before he could escape her coils. Only with Geraldine he seemed to come to life, perhaps because she reminded him of Gerald or, more likely, because she spoiled him outrageously; a fact which Sally was prepared to blink on the precept that he needed to respond to someone and the end justified the means. Here, in the home that had been forced on him, he plodded through life like a small bulldozer, looking neither to right nor to left.

She sighed again, shrugged into her dressing gown and went along the landing to the bathroom. The door was locked. George was still in there, probably having a long slow soak in the bath, unmindful of the fact that everyone else was waiting for the lavatory. Every single member of this family seemed to pose a problem! She smiled ruefully, and went down to the kitchen in search of coffee.

Aimée was there, sitting in the rocker by the Aga. 'About time,' she said, only half in fun. 'What time do you get breakfast in this house?'

'When I'm ready,' Sally said pleasantly. 'What about you?'

'This is your kitchen, I wouldn't want to take liberties in it. The children are both hungry, I told them they must wait for you.'

Sally put the kettle on. 'You could have made a drink,' she smiled. 'I'd have forgiven you.' It was so much easier than starting an argument. If she once began quarrelling with Aimée there would be an end to peace. 'Tea or coffee?'

'You know I never drink coffee.' Aimée sounded aggrieved. 'I don't feel well this morning, I think I'm getting what Zoë had. That's the trouble with children, they're always bringing something home from school.'

'I don't think you'll have caught her tonsilitis. Didn't you tell me you'd had yours out – oh, there's Mark, cutting up logs. I expect he'll want a cup of tea.'

'You can make tea for Mark, I notice.'

'Yes,' said Sally patiently. 'And for everyone else. It won't be long.'

Mark's curly head bobbed past the window and almost at once he appeared in the doorway with an armful of logs. 'Thought you'd want these for the fire later on.' His cheery glance took in the kettle, the cups, the teapot. 'Making tea?'

'Yes, it won't be long, there'll be a cup for you.'

'I've got a better idea, I'll make one for you. I'll just get rid of these.'

He disappeared into the drawing room and the sound of logs thundering into the hearth came through the wall.

'He didn't offer to make one for me,' said Aimée. 'And your legs are younger than mine.'

'Maybe that's why,' smiled Sally, goaded into mischief. An impulse which she immediately regretted.

Aimée looked at her slyly. 'What does George think about him coming in here with you not dressed?'

Damn! thought Sally, aware that she had missed her footing on the eggshells.

'George is very broadminded and he won't think anything at all,' she said firmly, and went and called up the stairs, 'George! Do you want tea brought up or are you coming down?'

'I'll take it up,' said Mark as he came in. 'Did I hear Zoë crying?'

'Probably.' Sally pulled out a stool and sat down. 'She had a little brush with Uncle George. I suppose I ought to go and see if she's got over it.'

'I think you'll find she's all right,' said Mark.

As he spoke, a nightgowned figure appeared in the doorway. 'I'm not all right!' Zoë pouted.

'I think you are,' said Mark, unperturbed as he poured boiling water on the tea.

Zoë started up a wail. 'I'm not! I've been crying for hours and hours and hours . . .'

'Oh, ducky,' began Aimée, intent on showing up Sally.

Still goodhumoured, Mark cut her short. 'I don't think you have,' he said reasonably. 'Shall I tell you why?'

Zoë glowered.

He smiled, an engaging schoolboy grin. 'Because I heard you through the bedroom window telling Charles where he gets off. And he was definitely coming off worst.'

Zoë's tear-stained face became a battleground between pride in having bested Charles and determination to milk the situation for the last drop of sympathy. When she could no longer suppress her pleasure she ducked her head to hide it, and lunged out, half in play, at Mark. He parried her neatly, and perched her on his knee.

'Suppose you go and wash your face, then I'll tell you the new joke I got from school? It's about an African chief who wanted a throne . . .'

'Tell me now!'

'Not now, go and get dressed first.'

As she scrambled down, George appeared.

'Hello, finished bleating, have we?' he inquired tactlessly, and was treated to a glare as the child left the room. 'Oh dear, oh dear, oh dear . . .' He glanced at Mark, as if for support. 'Well, if you've had a girl on your knee, I want one on mine.'

As he pulled Sally on to his knee she put an arm around

his neck, something she had never felt free to do with Gerald, and felt his answering hug.

'Where are your top teeth, love? Do wish you'd wear them,' she teased.

'They're not comfortable.'

'You could get them altered.'

'Oh, I can't be bothered with things like that. Either you love me or you don't, silly things like teeth don't matter.' He grinned up at her, toothless.

'Oh, George . . .' She laughed reluctantly, and dropped a forgiving kiss on his wiry hair.

Mark, across the table, smiled in sympathy, his strong young teeth shining. She switched her eyes away.

'I must go and get dressed, then I can start the vegetables.' She disengaged herself with difficulty from George, and realized it had been a mistake to sit on him. 'Let go, love, I want a bath before I start the cooking.' At times like this, she regretted the loss of Sabine, whose dismissal had coincided with the sale of the villa.

'Aren't you coming to church?'

'Well . . . if I have time. Only, there'll be eight of us to lunch and it's after ten already. You don't mind, do you . . . just this once?'

In fact, she hated going to church with George, who regularly settled down to snore loudly through the sermon, and had once insisted on going in his bedroom slippers. Today she was not sorry that Gerald was coming with Dotty to visit the twins; not because she relished the prospect of seeing him with Dotty – whom Aimée had quickly forgiven, though she could not – but because it gave her the excuse not to go.

'I shall have to explain to the vicar,' grumbled George without malice. 'I don't know how you can get through the week without going to say your prayers.'

'I don't need to go to church to do that,' she said lightly. 'What about that inner room, with the door locked?'

'Can't say my prayers in the lavatory,' said George. 'Everyone to his taste, I suppose.'

295

When she came downstairs again, bathed and dressed, Mark was standing at the sink, quietly peeling potatoes.

When Gerald arrived, she was standing at the cooker, her face harassed and steamy and her hair hanging in wisps.

He halted in the doorway, greeted her politely. As if they were strangers, she thought. It was hard to imagine that they had ever shared a bed. Perhaps, to outsiders, it had always been hard . . . and yet still her pulse had flickered at the sight of him.

'Good morning,' she returned his formality. 'The children are in the garden—'

He turned away, and Dotty breezed in past him.

'Hello! Hello, everybody! When's dinner, I'm starving!' She opened the door of the refrigerator. 'Give me the cream and cherries and I'll decorate the trifle.'

'We're not having trifle.' Sally shut it quickly and stood with her back to it. 'Why don't you go up and see Aimée, she's not feeling very well.'

'Yes, we are, you always make trifle. I saw it in there.' She stared curiously at Sally, amusement slowly spreading over her face. 'Aren't you funny?' Her scorn was thinly disguised as teasing. 'I suppose you want to do it yourself? You know I'd do it better.'

'That's right,' said Sally pleasantly, aware that she was being childish. I don't care, she thought. 'You go up and see Aimée, she's been looking forward to it.'

At that moment Aimée appeared at the head of the stairs, still in her dressing gown. 'Is that you, Dotty?' she called in her best frail-invalid voice. 'Thank God you're here, I've been feeling dreadful.' As she disappeared into her room with Dotty's arm about her, Sally heard her say under her breath, 'D'you know, I had to wait three hours for a cup of tea this morning . . .'

Sally shook her head as she tackled the cauliflower, reflecting that even Dotty had her uses; with Gerald occupying the children, she could be left to absorb Aimée's complaints while she and Mark got on with the cooking. She could not help noting the difference between Dotty's notion of helping and his. While she demanded to trim the trifle, he looked for the most useful job and did it.

'This is very good of you, Mark.' She smiled in his direction. 'You don't have to, you know.'

It was a mistake. His brown eyes warmed, and he coloured. 'I happen to like you rather a lot,' he mumbled.

There was a moment of deep embarrassment. They both stopped what they were doing, not looking at one another. Then Sally spoke.

'I didn't hear that, Mark.'

'I said—'

'No, you don't understand. I said, I didn't hear that.' She picked up her knife and began hacking indiscriminately at the creamy florets. When she stole a glance at the boy, his neck was crimson, his eyes suspiciously bright. As George's big feet were heard tramping down the gravel towards the house, he mumbled something inaudible and hurried from the room.

'What's up with him?' George poured porridge oats into a pudding basin, soused them with cold water from the tap and began to eat, the wet mixture dribbling down his chin from between his missing teeth.

'Nothing,' said Sally. 'Darling, do you really need that, we'll be eating in half an hour.'

'If I'm eating it, I need it,' said George with irrefutable logic. 'Don't nag, dear. Mustn't be nagged, don't like it. Where's young Zoë, off with Gerald, I suppose?'

'They've gone for a walk. It's nice for them to have him to themselves.'

'What's that supposed to mean?'

She looked up in surprise. 'Without me around. Or Dotty, for that matter.'

'Without me, don't you mean?' His voice was flat and angry. 'They only want me as a useful provider, when darling Daddy comes I can go hang!'

'Oh, George . . .'

297

His eyes met hers, cold as flint. 'Oh George! Oh George!' he mimicked. 'Is that all you can say—'

'They're only children, can't you make allowances? You can't expect them to understand.'

'Perhaps not. But is it too much to expect you to?'

'What do you mean by that?'

'I mean that you put them before me every time – yes, every time! Look at this morning. I want to make love to my wife and what do you do? You get up, and go running after them.'

'I'm sorry, I'm sorry!' With an effort she forbore to remind him that he habitually tried to waylay her when she needed to get up for the twins. 'You just have to realize I'm not only your wife, I'm their mother as well—'

'Oh, no! Not "as well", not by half. You're their mother first, last and in the middle, you're only my wife if you have a few minutes left over!' He glared at her, the skin about his mouth a greenish white. 'It was never like that with Diana.'

Sally, already on edge from the tensions of the day, felt her patience snap at last. 'I don't want to hear another word about bloody Diana! I'm not her, I can't be her, it's no use you trying to turn me into somebody I'm not!'

George drew back, his blue eyes hostile, his mask of anger settling into something close to satisfaction, as though, having made a point, he was glad rather than sorry.

'No,' he said slowly. 'It isn't. I should have seen that from the start.'

'If that's all you wanted,' said Sally, her eyes smarting, 'you shouldn't have married me.' She waited for the accustomed touch of his hand on her shoulder. It did not come.

'Perhaps I shouldn't,' he said. He pushed past her to pour the rest of his porridge down the sink. 'I'll be lunching at the pub if I'm wanted. No place for me here.'

Oh, God . . . she thought. And today of all days, with Dotty and Gerald here. It was all too much. She stood still, her hands gripping the edge of the sink, a hot tear running down to join the cauliflower.

Only one . . . why didn't she feel more? Was George right in saying that she didn't really care? She remembered her searing grief for Adam, the numbing shock of Gerald's desertion . . . could it be that she was putting less into each succeeding relationship, growing a kind of armour to keep her from giving of herself too much . . . if so, how selfish . . . and who did she think she was? She knew that in the beginning she would willingly have died for Gerald. Would she, for Adam? It had never crossed her mind. Now, at this moment, she felt only disillusionment over George. That and disappointment . . . and yes, a degree of exasperation! The truth was, she was no longer sure that the game was worth the candle. Maybe love was an overrated luxury, after all. Or maybe she was just emotionally worn out . . .

She opened her eyes, aware that someone else had come into the kitchen. It was Mark. He gently moved her away from the sink, fished in the water for the knife.

'I've put the kettle on for a coffee,' he said. And carried on trimming the cauliflower.

The next few hours crawled by like flies in treacle. Aimée declined to come downstairs, and had her lunch sent up on a tray, a diversion which Sally welcomed as an escape from having to explain George's absence, at least to her. To the others she said merely that he had been called away.

Dotty gave her a glance that said clearly, 'You don't get *me* out of the way that easily,' and Sally saw with amazement that she was jealous.

She hoped Gerald didn't think it was a manoeuvre to get him alone . . . She had been relying on the presence of Aimée and George to dilute the tensions between herself and Gerald, between her and Dotty, between Dotty and the children . . . in the event there was nothing; even Mark ate in silence, enclosed in his own thoughts. Perhaps she should go up and sit with Aimée, she thought, and leave the rest of them to themselves. But she could not face Aimée just now, or the need to parry her probing questions.

Her hopes of packing them all off to the park were thwarted by a sudden downpour, and the afternoon dragged by, with Charles insisting on watching his favourite television programme while Gerald played endless card games with Zoë – a privilege he had rarely accorded her in the past – and Dotty sat drumming bored, beautiful fingers on the arm of her chair.

'We'll have to go when we've had a cup of tea,' she announced. 'Don't forget we have a party tonight.'

Sally saw Gerald scowl at her before he had time to rearrange his face. 'We don't need to go just yet,' he said evenly as Zoë looked up in dismay. He smiled his reassurance. 'Your move next.'

Dotty, as always, had her way in the end. They left before six, a tear-stained Zoë waving them off at the end of the drive while Charles sulked ostentatiously somewhere out of sight.

George was still missing. Sally watched from the doorway, struggling to control the feeling of abandonment she always felt on seeing Gerald leave for home with someone else. She saw Zoë's arm return to her side, saw her head bow and her slight shoulders convulse as she turned back towards the house, and started out to meet her.

As she did so she saw Mark appear from somewhere to approach the child. He spoke to her, she nodded and reached up her arms to him, her face distorted. He picked her up and carried her back towards the house, talking to her soothingly as he came. He was a nice person, thought Sally; kind and unselfish. He deserved something better than abortive calf-love for a broken reed like her . . .

As she reached out to take Zoë from him, Charles's agitated face appeared on the landing.

'Mum! Come quick, up here! It's Grandma Aimée – she's making a funny noise and I can't wake her up!'

CHAPTER EIGHTEEN

Aimée did not survive the journey to hospital, and it was hard to know if she regained full consciousness. She never spoke again, only fixed her gaze on Sally all through the interminable ride in the ambulance, staring at her with dreadful accusing eyes.

Sally was devastated. Not merely because she had failed in her duty, had been too busy and not willing enough to give time to her mother when it was needed, but because it was her fault that Aimée – poor silly, damaged, pathetic, impossible Aimée, who had insisted on taxis all over London because she was frightened of the Underground, who had refused in panic to go with Erik to America because she 'could not cross the water' – had had to face the ultimate fear alone.

It was this for which she could not forgive herself.

In vain she reminded herself of the fate of those who cry Wolf! Of the innumerable times when Aimée, sneezing twice, had pleaded in all too genuine apprehension, 'I'm not going to die, am I?' She could not escape the knowledge that when the alarm was real she had failed to answer it. She had been selfishly absorbed in her own concerns, and no amount of excusing it could take away her guilt.

Remembering how she had been glad of Dotty's presence 'to absorb her complaints' she was scalded with shame and remorse. The fact that she had felt so little affection for her mother made it not better but worse; for a long time she was silent, preoccupied, unable to talk, not knowing how to relate to anyone. She felt disgraced, worthless, undeserving of attention as she had not felt since she was a child.

Unpredictably, she missed Aimée; less as one missed a loved one, for try as she might she could not persuade herself of that, than as one misses a piece of important and unfinished business, a completion at once desired and unachievable, a need to go back and get it right which can never now be fulfilled.

With the approach of Christmas she found herself deliberately recalling how Aimée had loved it, trying to feel sadness, refusing to recognize how much easier it was going to be without her, as though she had a duty to carry guilt. When the children, particularly Charles in his capsule of self-containment, appeared not to miss their grandmother she felt it was somehow her responsibility to see that they did, as if she had infected them with her own indifference, and was inclined to keep reminding them of an obligation to mourn.

'Can't understand you,' grumbled George. 'Didn't seem to care about the old girl when you had her, now we get crocodile tears.'

'She was my mother,' she said, unable to offer a better explanation. The truth was that she did not understand herself.

George in these days was with her less and less. At first he offered pretexts: he was going to visit a cousin, an aunt, good old Harry in Timbuktu or his old pal Cyril from university. After a while he just went, and his absences grew longer, his presences – and his temper – even shorter.

Zoë, her insecure world still further shaken, took to invading Sally's bed, and George, returning unannounced in the small hours, found himself displaced. The drinking problem which had become evident after Diana's death was growing steadily worse; debts mounted on all sides while essential repairs to the old house were neglected.

Sally's depression deepened. The fact that she cared less for George as time advanced did nothing to abate her sense of rejection. It was as though he had taken over from Aimée the task of keeping her in her place . . . and that place was at the bottom of the class. She asked herself repeatedly why she couldn't make a success of the simple achievements of other women, the ordinary domestic affairs of husband and home. Was she really so much uglier than others? She knew others better loved who were less attractive. Did she try less hard, make less of an effort . . . no, that was not true either, she worked tirelessly in the overgrown garden, the dusty half-carpeted rooms that were never warm enough because the fuel bills were left unpaid. And yet both her marriages had failed, her son was beginning to eschew her company, even Erik had gone without warning, had never invited her to visit him . . . had Aimée been right about her after all?

And yet . . . and yet there had been Adam. Adam, whose memory even now cost her a twist of pain. Adam . . . who had shown her that she was not, as Gerald and now George had labelled her, frigid. It was noticeable, she thought, that men who failed to arouse their wives never seemed to blame themselves; it was as though, having pressed the right buttons, they felt safe in assuming that the woman's mechanism was at fault.

Of course, Adam hadn't known her as long as the others; he had never tried living with her – was that the difference? Perhaps, if he had . . . she sighed. Maybe after all, it was better to love and lose. Only Mark seemed to want her now, and he knew her only from a distance. Besides which, he was barely out of adolescence and seeing her through the rose-coloured lens of youth. He would grow out of it . . . they always did.

It was Mark none the less who helped her through the darkness that now fell. He said nothing, asked no questions, yet was always there. It was as though he eavesdropped on her thoughts, with a sensitivity peculiar to those who love; she would reach for an object and find it put into her hand.

For a time she forgot the need to keep him at a distance, simply comforted by his presence. She knew that sooner or later she must ban him, send him away and bar the door, if only because should George reappear and turn ugly he could find himself caught up in a messy divorce . . . but she could not. Not yet. Not quite yet, not until things were easier. She would miss him, needed his schoolboy jokes to make her smile at moments when she thought her face had forgotten the way.

And Zoë would miss him. Zoë loved him in her immature way, could be won round by him when no one else would do. It would have to be explained to her why he didn't come any more, Mark whom she hero-worshipped, who helped her with her homework, who listened patiently to endless rambling accounts of how everything had gone wrong for her at school . . . it was not to be contemplated, at least for the moment. One could only cope with so much at a time.

'Where will you go when the house is sold?' he asked her.

'The house, what house?'

'This house.' An uneasy pause. 'You don't mean you didn't know?'

'I don't know what you're talking about. You must be mistaken.'

But he wasn't mistaken. George was heavily in debt and had fallen behind with the mortgage, as he told her that same evening.

'But why, George? I thought we were all right, what's happened?' His drinking, she thought privately, what else . . .

He said gruffly, 'I have expenses you know nothing about—'

'Then you shouldn't have! I'm your wife, George, I'm here to help, you should be able to tell me anything.'

'Well, I can't. Now, if you'd been Diana—'

'Oh, God, give me strength!' For once it was her turn to storm out, slamming the door.

What was happening to her patience, all that forbearance she had been so proud of! She did not know, only that she had been too patient with too many, and for too long; that in future what was left – and there was none too much of it – would be reserved for dealing with her children.

Tight-lipped, she watched the removal men pack up what little of their belongings would fit into a flat, sent Aimée's precious piano, her one relic, into storage, sorrowed over her roses and azaleas while trying to parry Zoë's anxiety about where they were all going to sleep and how Selina would manage without a garden; and when George drifted off to the pub at the height of the chaos, prayed shamelessly that he would not return.

At eleven thirty that night, filthy and exhausted, still unpacking china and saucepans from the tea chests on the landing, she received a note, scrawled in a drunken hand on a crumpled piece of paper. It was, inevitably, Mark who brought it to her, apparently unaware of what it said. 'Staying with friends for a few days. George.'

'Shall I go back and dig him out?' He grinned. 'Lend me an apron, I'll carry him home in it.'

'No,' she said slowly. 'Leave him where he is. I'll manage.'

Mark said nothing, only watched her closely for a moment. Then he rolled up his sleeves and set to work.

Months passed before they saw George again, by which time she had had formal notice from his firm of the arrangements he had made about the flat. The rent would be taken care of by the office, and a sum 'for housekeeping' would be paid monthly into her account; they were unable to say whether or not he would be joining her there, but any letters addressed to him in their care would be forwarded.

Sally knew better by now than to attempt to get information from a lawyer who did not mean to give it; the only person she could conceivably have asked was Gerald, and that she felt to be impossible. She turned her attention instead to making ends meet, which they did only by dint of considerable juggling. Gerald was still sending money for the twins, but if they were to be spared changing schools at a crucial time in their education they would all have to tighten their belts. She considered looking for a job herself, but she knew that the old stumbling block of lack of training was still there, and decided that for the little she could earn she might as well remain at home and carry out what economies she could.

In any case, Charles and Zoë had had enough upheavals in their lives without having to adjust to their mother being out all day. She sat up into the small hours to make their clothes, even parts of their school uniform, at home; it was Geraldine who took them with her on annual holidays, and bought them each a winter coat at Christmas. Sally herself, once her own began wearing thin, made do with an extra sweater or stayed indoors.

She was angry with George at times, but she never once wished him back. From time to time she would receive a greetings card, telling her how well and happy he was; and that was all.

Gerald saw the children at increasingly long intervals, usually picking them up on a Sunday morning and dropping them back in the evening, when Zoë would regale her with unsought stories of how Daddy and Cousin Dotty were having rows, and Charles would scowl and tell her to shut up.

Sally did not want to listen, but neither could she entirely suppress her amusement: Dotty's bohemianism and Gerald's obsessive tidiness always had seemed to her unlikely bedfellows, and she would not have been human not to smile.

Mark had long ago left school, and, to his parents' fury, flatly refused to go on to university. It was not until much later that he let it slip to Sally, foreseeing perhaps what her reaction would be. That anyone could be offered such an opportunity and fail to grasp it was beyond her comprehension.

'Mark, you must have been mad, how could you!'

Mark coloured, but said nothing.

'Didn't you realize what you were throwing away? I'd have sold my soul to go — at least, I would now. I suppose I didn't mind at the time, I was young and silly and thought leaving school was the same as growing up . . .' She stopped, seeing the expression on his face.

'It wasn't that,' he said defensively. 'I'd have had to go to Keele.'

'What's wrong with Keele?'

He opened his mouth to speak, closed it again. Then he looked at her steadily. 'You know what's wrong with Keele. It's too far away.'

'Oh, Mark . . .' She turned away, embarrassed by the trap she had laid for herself and then walked into.

'It's all right.' He smiled. 'It's not your fault, you couldn't help what happened. I'm quite old enough to make my own mistakes.'

'I know, but . . .' She could think of nothing adequate to say, nothing that would have held any conviction.

'No,' he said quietly, surprising her. 'You don't know. You're saying that because you think it's what I want to hear. And I don't think you really know what's happened between us.'

'I don't want to hear this, Mark.' She went to a drawer, took out knives and forks at random, anything to occupy her hands, to change the subject.

Mark followed her, took the implements from her, put them back into the drawer.

'Too bad,' he said lightly. It was the same tone he used to Zoë, half bantering, half inflexible. 'Sally, I'm not the lovesick boy you choose to think me. I'm a man. I can vote, I could be charged with murder – I could join the army, go out and die for you. But I'd rather have it the other way.'

'Mark, I'm not listening to you. Please, stop.'

'No. You can't tell me what to do any more, still less what to think. I know what I know, and that's that you'll never be happy with George. Get free of him and give yourself a chance.' The hesitation was barely perceptible. 'Give me a chance.'

Sally sat down at the kitchen table, her head in her hands. Panic had seized her, not only at the thought of life with someone as young as Mark, but at the thought of it with anyone at all. He was speaking again.

'I've watched you all these years, I know you better than anyone. I understand you, don't you see? I know I could make you happy, only try me.' With a hint of desperation in his tone, he repeated, 'Give me a chance.'

'I'm trying to give you a chance, Mark, I am fond of you, I want to see you happily married with children. I'm not sure I could do that for you, not by the time I was free, anyway. I want to see you happy with someone your own age. Maybe even younger, someone like Zoe . . .'

In Mark's jaw a muscle tightened and relaxed. Tightened, relaxed again.

'You'd have to be long gone,' he said at last.

And what about Zoë, she thought, remembering Aimée and Gerald. How would she feel to see her idol borne off in triumph by her mother. 'Oh, Mark . . .' She sighed, shook her head, distraught.

He smiled, wanly. 'Just stop saying, "Oh, Mark" and say you love me.'

'It's not as simple as that.'

She felt the tears rising. To be offered the gift of love so late, so unsought . . . and be afraid to take it! And she couldn't, not at the price of spoiling his life. He was young, untried, and dazzled; she had to be wise for them both. If she wasn't, she would have another cause for grief in place of his friendship that she valued so much . . . 'I can't,' she said. 'Dear Mark, I can't. I only wish I could.'

'I don't understand,' said Mark. 'Explain to me.'

'I can't explain, it's just – it would be wrong for you. And I know it's wrong for me. I daren't, if you like.'

Mark took her hands. He looked miserable. 'Try me,' he said. 'Just try to explain. You owe me that.'

She tried. It was something she hardly understood herself. 'It's . . . I don't know.' She shook her head. Started again. 'I'm like a stray cat the children brought in once. The winter was bitter, yet when she came indoors she seemed afraid to stay. She'd come in and get warm, and then cry to be let out. She'd never stay longer than an hour, though she was glad of the fire and the food we gave her. Yet she panicked if we tried to keep her in. I thought at the time she must have kittens somewhere, but we never saw any. I think now, she had a kind of wisdom; it was as if she knew that if she let herself grow soft, she wouldn't be able to survive the cold outside.'

'Sally . . . Sally! You're not a stray cat, you don't have to live like one. Trust me! Come in by the fire.'

'It's no good,' she said patiently. 'It wouldn't work.'

She had learned her own wisdom, would make no more sorties on to Tom Tiddler's ground; better the desert, where she knew her way. Gently she withdrew her hands, smiled into his troubled eyes. It was with a strange sensation of peace that she said, 'You see, in the last analysis, that's where we live, the cat and I. It's where we feel at home. In the cold, outside.'

Mark averted his face. He was silent for so long that she rose, and touched his shoulder. 'I'm sorry, Mark . . .'

He straightened, turned to her with a smile that told her poignantly that he was indeed no longer a boy.

'Don't worry about it,' he said lightly. 'Can we afford a coffee or are we down to water?'

'Coffee, we're rich today,' she had returned equally lightly. 'You put the kettle on, I'll wash the cups.'

They drank it in silence. As he left, he kissed her for the first time, sedately on the brow. 'See you.'

Watching him go from the upper window, his curly head bobbing with his lithe young stride, she felt a perverse sense of loss. Had she been wrong to send him away, was she a fool . . . no, of course not. She might have made a different answer if it had been Adam . . . but it was Mark.

She knew she had been right. Even had the match been suitable — which it wasn't — the world of loving relationships was not for her; it was too fraught with risk, with the dreadful traps of misunderstanding and heartbreak. In all her life it had brought her more sorrow than joy, and she turned her back on it now with something akin to relief, like the climber with no head for heights whose feet feel the welcome kiss of terra firma.

Mark continued to visit, and although she occasionally caught him watching her, he never again made an overt approach.

As Zoë grew past her ugly duckling stage and budded into beauty, he paid more attention to her and less to Sally, endorsing her conviction that she had made the right decision, quelling any lingering wistfulness she might have felt. And as Zoë became increasingly susceptible to the charm of her childhood hero, Sally withdrew to leave her field clear, mentally turning her back on all things past.

It was true, too, that a resolve was growing in her mind that should she find herself free of George, she would rather keep control of her own life. She had barely survived two crashes riding pillion: hereafter, however bumpy the ride, she would be in the driving seat.

Bumpy it certainly was, financially. If only, she thought, some unknown relative could pop off and leave them rich! But money, like her marriages, seemed to melt at her approach. At this point, she would shrug mentally: at least she was her own woman. And yet . . . if only she could earn enough to live on!

It was not, however, with any thought of gain that after years of penny-pinching she first wrote a letter to a newspaper. ' "Tug of love"!' she exploded, slamming the paper down on the table. 'It's nothing to do with love, it's nothing but a power game between the parents, with the poor bloody kids as pawns!'

Mark looked up, startled and faintly amused. 'Why so vehement?'

'Because all this cant in the papers makes me sick! Look at this,' she waved the paper under his nose. 'This poor little four-year-old, snatched in the street by a father she hasn't seen since she was a baby, carried off to God-knows-where in some other country, now her mother's saying, "She's mine and I'll get her back if it takes the rest of my life." If either of them really cared they'd stop fighting and think of the child – tug of love, my arse!'

Mark laughed. 'Never knew you could be so coarse.'

'I feel coarse, it makes me bloody angry!' She controlled herself with an effort, attempted to laugh. 'Sorry, you wouldn't understand, how could you? It's just that I've experienced it both ways and from all sides, and I know it's the child that suffers, every time.'

Mark thought for a moment. 'If you feel that strongly about it, why don't you say so? Write to the paper, tell them what you think. They might just publish it.'

'Who wants to know what I think?' Feeling foolish now, she pulled herself together. 'Take no notice, I was just letting off steam.'

'Somebody might. Try letting off steam where it'll do some good.' He handed her a pen from his pocket. 'Don't wait to cool down. Do it now.'

Their eyes met and held, hers uncertain, his challenging. Then, with a little nod, he turned away.

Sally sat thoughtful for a moment. Then she found a sheet of paper and began to write.

Part IV

The Centrifuge

A person can be lonely even if he is loved by many people, because he is still not the 'One and Only' to anyone.

—*Diary of Anne Frank*

CHAPTER ONE

'So here you are, a boss-cat now,' smiled Louise. 'Come on then, fill me in with all your news.'

'That's a tall order.' Sally smiled back across the polished desk at her favourite cousin, bright hair cropped to a burnished helmet, nails immaculate, clothes expensively casual. They might have been sisters. 'I forget, how many years have you been abroad?'

'Put it this way, when I went to Belgium you were thinking of marrying George. A lot seems to have happened that I've missed.'

'Try writing letters,' Sally teased her. 'It works wonders. Well, Zoë's married – you remember Mark, Diana's brother? – and Charles was, only he's getting a divorce. And there's Tiggy, Charles's little boy, he's nearly six. He's a bit lost, with his parents splitting up. He stays with me a lot, and cuddles the cat, but it's not the same.' She sighed. 'I don't know what it is with this family . . .'

Louise lit a French cigarette, exhaled the smoke in a pale blue cloud. 'And what about you?'

The scent of Gauloise drew her back across the years. Adam had smoked black tobacco. Somewhere she must still have two that she had cherished, foolishly . . .

'Sally?'

'Me? Oh, free at last, thank God.'

'And?'

'And nothing. That's the way I like it.'

'Don't give me that.'

'It's true. I'm, what's the phrase, wedded to my career.'

'Spending your life sorting out other people's affairs,

315

never having any of your own, what sort of an achievement is that?'

'It's enough,' she said defensively. 'It's what I wanted, what I've worked for. I enjoy it.' She sat twisting Aimée's emerald, which had taken the place of the wedding band on her finger. She did not remember when she had taken to wearing Aimée's jewellery, like a quiet banner on her hand; a denial to the outside world of the rift between her and her mother, a gesture of negation against her own uneasy sense that she had not mourned her enough.

Louise raised a quizzical eyebrow. 'And you're fulfilled?'

'Yes,' she gave herself the chance to waver. 'Yes, I'm fulfilled.'

'So, tell me about it. How did it happen, the good old rags to riches thing? From what I heard you were having a tough time, now I come and find you in a posh office with lackeys and your books on every bookstall.'

'Only one book, it just did very well for me, that's all. It was topical, I suppose, about the children of divorce. And controversial. It came out at the right moment and sort of took off.'

'But how did you come to write it? I never knew you did things like that.'

'Neither did I, it all came from a letter to a newspaper. I was furious when I wrote it, really steamed up, and when it came out it triggered a correspondence that went on and on for months. Then someone suggested I did an article for a magazine, they liked it and it became a series . . . the whole thing snowballed.' She decided to say nothing about the phone-ins and the television chat shows; Louise was family, not business, it would sound like boasting. 'I started working for *Gloss* magazine, and they suggested the book. Apart from the odd poem when I was feeling down, I'd never written anything in my life until then.' From somewhere, the words floated through her mind, *Don't forget to write* . . . It must be the Gauloise. She smiled, her new professional smile. 'So it is an achievement of a sort, at least for me. Anyway,' she challenged playfully, 'what about you, you've never married.'

'That doesn't mean I spend my life alone. You're behind the times, if you think you have to make it legal.'

'I wouldn't hold down my job for long if I were! If I'm alone, it's because I'm happy that way.' Salving her pride, she added, 'Anyway, I've had my moments.'

She smiled wryly at the memory. She had sampled uncommitted sex, briefly persuaded by a colleague that she might be missing something. The first time she had had a one-night stand she had mistaken it for a relationship, and had been bewildered when the man next appeared, acknowledged her with a nod and spent the evening with his back to her, assiduously engaged in picking up her successor. True to form she had made no challenge, but retired from the field to wonder where she had gone wrong. It hadn't taken long to reach the conclusion that casual sex was overrated; having known the real thing, she was not prepared to settle for the wandering attentions of uncaring men whose noses were forever up some other woman's skirt. She was cynically aware that what she demanded was too much. But if it was not on offer, she was not interested in the bargain counter.

'I'm fine,' she said, an assurance that brooked no argument.

Louise's smile suggested she was not convinced. 'I'll believe you. Never mind, I've teased you enough.' She looked suddenly wistful. 'What a shame Aunt Aimée didn't live to see your success. She'd have been so proud of you.'

Sally smiled. 'You reckon?' She could not have done any of it with Aimée looking on.

'Oh, she would!' persisted Louise. 'She thought the world of you, you know, she was always talking about you.'

'You've got it all wrong,' said Sally. 'It was Dotty she liked.'

'No, Sally, it was you. Oh, I know she nagged you, but didn't you realize? She just loved you so much she wanted you to be perfect.'

317

Sally turned away, her emotions jolted uncomfortably. 'We'll have to be going. I have to collect Tiggy from school on the way home. You'll come back to the house, won't you, my car's in the basement car park?'

Louise said no more, but came with her in the lift to where the white Lotus waited.

'Going one better than Dotty?' She joked. 'Can't say I blame you in the circumstances.'

'Where is she now, do you see her?'

'Hardly at all. Paris, I think. You knew she'd left Gerald?'

'Yes,' said Sally drily. Gerald had passed on to another new lady without a backward glance. Not that she wanted him back — and if she had it would have had to be on very different terms — but it would have been nice to think she had at least been considered in passing.

'I never felt happy about it,' went on Louise. 'That's why I've been out of touch with you for so long. I felt . . . embarrassed for her. I won't put it more strongly than that.'

Sally smiled her affection, her forgiveness. 'I don't know. On reflection, perhaps she did me a good turn. I know I'd never have attained all this with Gerald, or even with George. I've done more for myself than either of them did for me.'

Louise regarded her thoughtfully. 'I wonder if that's not a faulty attitude. I mean, perhaps one should be attracted to what someone is, rather than what he does.'

Sally felt herself blushing. She knew the truth of that, of course she did. And yet, the old style of marriage had surely been based on such a premise: Give up everything, hand over to me and I'll look after you. She was not sure she could explain that to Louise, whose thinking was conditioned by a different world. Aunt Lucy had been more modern, more forward thinking, while Aimée, though only a few years older, had clung stubbornly to the Victorian ethic.

'You're right, of course,' she quipped in self-defence. 'Some agony aunt I am, "Don't do as I do, do as I say".'

But the train of thought had led back to Adam. Who was

to say if that had been the right relationship? As she nosed the gleaming car through the traffic and out of central London, he was back in her thoughts for the first time in years. How would he have looked by now if he had lived, greying at the temples, a little thickened at the waist, but still . . . ah yes, still Adam. Lines drifted into her mind, poignant and painful, the last poem she had written more than ten years ago.

Did you ever know how much I loved you?
How the sound of your footfall in another room
Where you moved unseen set me curiously at peace
Knowing you near . . .

Did you ever know how deep I loved you?
Deeper than other loves or the fear of death
There was always one small part within my being
Turned towards you . . .

Did either of us guess for how long after
My voice could not be trusted with your name . . .
That your going away would diminish my spirit and leave me
No longer the same?

She suspected even now that had he remained in her life, she would have asked for nothing more.

Tiggy's face brightened as the car drew up at the school gates. He was waiting in his usual place in the window of the Principal's office, from where he could watch the road. He could never be persuaded to interest himself in any activity that would divert his gaze but would sit there with his eyes glued to the traffic, his small face growing pinched and anxious as the minutes passed.

His mother had been erratic in this respect, as often as not sending taxis to collect him from nursery school when at last she thought of it, often half an hour late. Sally made special efforts not to keep him waiting, even to the extent of working from home on days when she was responsible

319

for him, aware that in his disordered life even a small tension was the last thing he needed. As it was, ten minutes past the appointed time had produced a face at the window which was taut and white with strain.

He jumped up and ran to meet her at the door.

' 'Bye, Mrs Raines!' he flung over his shoulder, and raced down the path to the waiting car. There he checked at the sight of an unfamiliar face, and looked uncertainly back at Sally.

'This is your cousin Louise. You haven't met before, she works in Brussels.'

'Hello,' he said shyly. Then corrected himself. 'How do you do.'

'Hello, Tiggy. It is Tiggy, isn't it?'

'Yes. Well, Daddy says it's Theodore.'

'Which shall I call you?'

He hesitated, wriggled, smiled self-consciously. 'Don't know.'

'He gets called Tiggy at home,' said Sally. 'But he's Theodore at school.' She winked at Louise. 'It's more grown-up.'

The little boy fidgeted with suppressed excitement on the drive home, and she knew he was itching to ask the one question she could not answer. Before long it was out.

'Is she coming? Did she ring up while I was at school?'

'Not yet,' she answered evenly. 'You know she's a very busy lady, she has lots of things to do.' Damn her! she was thinking. Damn her, beautiful, thoughtless Jenny. She was just as likely to forget. 'If we don't hear by this evening, I'll ring her again.'

Tiggy's face fell a fraction before he manfully hitched it up.

'She will come, won't she?' he pleaded, his grey eyes smoky with doubt.

'Of course she will, if not tomorrow then another time. She won't break her promise, you'll see.' She answered Louise's unspoken question with a single mouthed word, 'mother', and wished she had the confidence in Jenny she was trying to inspire in her son. 'But Daddy'll be there.'

'Yes,' said Tiggy without interest, accepting it for the consolation prize it was.

It was sad, thought Sally, how it was always the abandoning parent who grew the halo, never the one who stood by them, set personal desires aside and struggled to bring them up alone. It was understandable. The remaining parent was the one who had to impose discipline, became tired and unlovable and was always boringly there. The deserter, on the other hand, shone with the nostalgic aura of lost love and had a scarcity value with which no amount of loyal devotion could compete. You couldn't blame the child. But it was ironic that the more stoically you concealed your resentment, the more likely you were to find yourself passed over if the wanderer elected to drift back, to bask in all that backlog of adoration he'd done so little to deserve.

She recognized that she too must have viewed her parents through the biased eyes of childhood; it was only now, in observing Tiggy, that she saw how little she had known of what passed between Erik and Aimée behind the locked doors of their marriage . . .

She became aware that he was sitting in silence with drooped head, and made an effort to cheer him.

'Zoë and Mark are coming to dinner this evening, you can stay up and see them for a while.' He looked up and smiled dutifully. 'And Selina will be waiting for you. Will you feed her, you know she likes her supper best from you?'

He brightened, and turned to Louise. 'Do you know Selina?'

'I'm not sure, is that the Siamese you had years ago?' she asked Sally.

'Her granddaughter.' The first Selina was sleeping her long sleep beneath a flowering cherry in the garden. Other cats had flickered in and out of their lives from time to time, but only the present Selina now remained, a souvenir to Sally and an ever-present comfort to her grandson. 'This Selina's really Tiggy's, she only lives with me.'

As she pulled on to the short steep drive and parked, she

noticed that Louise looked mystified, and laughed. 'I know what you're thinking, the house doesn't go with the car.'

'Oh, no, I—' Louise began to protest, then, reminded perhaps that they had been children together, gave in and laughed. 'Well, yes, if I'm honest, it's not what I expected. What made you choose it?'

'I was sick of being moved about, and I wanted to get Aimée's piano out of storage. As soon as I had a bit of money I couldn't wait to get a place of my own, something nobody could take from me . . . this was available.'

'But you don't have to stay here, why not move?'

'Foolishness, perhaps. But . . . do you remember the cottage – no, it was Dotty who came there. Well, I loved it, I really did. And that's what I want, to buy it and live in it and never have to move again. Don't laugh, one day it will come on the market again, and when it does . . .' She stole a glance at Louise. 'Do you think I'm an idiot?'

'Not an idiot, no.' She remained in her seat, staring thoughtfully ahead of her. 'Only, I can't help wondering. Are you sure you'd be happy there, after all that's happened? Wouldn't you be better somewhere fresh than trying to live in the past . . . you can't really bring it back, you know. What's gone is gone.'

'I know that!' Who better, she thought. But she hadn't meant her reply to come out so sharply. She softened her tone. 'It's not a question of bringing back the past. It's just . . . a place I've been happy in, if you like.'

'And you're not happy now?'

'I am happy now. And I'll be even happier in my favourite place, that's all. What's wrong with that?'

Louise regarded her fondly. 'Nothing. And it's your life. I just want what's best for you.'

Sally smiled. 'I don't want what's best for me. I want . . . what I want.'

'Who doesn't?' Louise met her eyes and smiled back. 'I reckon it's your turn.'

My turn? thought Sally as they strolled into the house, yes, perhaps it is, though it's a fat lot of good to me now.

I'd want to be young and slim and active again, to have the enthusiasm to do the things I used to want to do, learn to ski, dance the stars out of the sky . . . I've used up the best of my life just waiting for my turn. Why did I do it? Nobody wanted me to. I've got maybe twenty more years – thirty with luck – in which to start living my life. And they're the thirty least productive years, the dregs, before my brain begins to atrophy and my body goes to pot . . . No, nobody really wanted me to. They just expected it. And because it was expected, I felt the obligation.

Tiggy was indoors ahead of them, hopping with impatience. 'Come and see Selina, how she rides on my shoulder! And I want to show you my room.' He took Louise by the hand and led her upstairs.

As soon as they were out of earshot, Sally played back the messages on her tape. One from her editor; an angry tirade from Mahlia Rhys whose copy had been clipped to make more room for hers; another from the rival magazine which, according to the grapevine, was looking to headhunt her; at last, one from Jenny in Milan, with a string of all too familiar excuses.

She switched off, too angry to listen to more. Why had Charles chosen to marry a fashion model with a career that meant more to her than both of them put together! Well, they both knew why: the classic slip between the sheets that had been the beginning of Tiggy. But surely to God there must have been a better solution than a wrongheaded marriage doomed from the outset to divorce. She could have suggested a dozen alternatives, would herself have adopted Tiggy, given half a chance. But Charles was still Charles. He played his problems close to his chest, his troubles were his own, his griefs inviolable, his mother the last person he would confide in. Well, perhaps the last but one. As a result, small Theodore Gerald Hammond had been born to be one more displaced person in a cold and confusing world. She hoped to God Zoë wasn't making the same mistake . . .

There was little she could do for her waiflike grandson, other than simply be there, a stable and unchanging presence in his lonely, unstable life. She did what she could to soften the blows for him, but she was always aware that he was not her own, was lent to her only when Charles allowed him to be; and the fact that she tried to keep him in touch with his mother did not help the situation. She could not blame Charles for that; while it was easy enough to conceive of his being cold and unresponsive as a husband, Jenny herself had been far from a model wife, and as a mother all but non-existent. But a child must be allowed to love his mother whatever her shortcomings, and Sally could not lend herself to schemes to keep them apart.

Zoë, her childhood miseries outgrown, had matured into a lovely and sympathetic young woman, a godsend to Tiggy, who adored his aunt. And while Sally, in more cynical moments, occasionally wondered if her efforts were not based on an echo of sibling rivalry, a not entirely worthy desire to show her brother how it was done, she consoled herself that the reason was immaterial, since the benefit was none the less genuine for that.

Certainly, she was thankful that Zoë was coming tonight; she sighed, faced with the necessity of breaking it to Tiggy that he could not hope to see Jenny for yet another month.

She was spared by the arrival of Charles, who announced that he would not be staying but had come to take his son away for the weekend.

Caught off guard, she blurted, 'Couldn't you stay to dinner first? He was looking forward to seeing Zoë—'

'He can look forward to seeing Tina. It's time they got together.'

'And Louise is here.'

'Louise?'

'Dotty's sister.'

A faint twitch of the lips. 'Give her my regards. Theo!' He called up the stairs. 'Put the cat down and pack your pyjamas, we're going fishing.'

Tiggy appeared on the landing, hugging Selina as Charles had predicted. He looked startled, his face a battleground

324

between pleasure and disappointment. 'But, Daddy—' he began, before Sally caught his eye and silenced him.

'I'll go and put his things together,' and she hurried up the stairs.

In the little spare bedroom that he had made his own, she whispered. 'It's all right, Mummy couldn't come after all. So it'll be nice to have something else to do, won't it?'

He nodded obediently but didn't speak, and while they searched drawers and cupboards for suitable clothing she saw that a large droplet of water had splashed down on to Selina's coat.

'I expect Daddy's been looking forward to taking you fishing,' she rallied him. 'He wanted to go fishing when he was a little boy, but his Daddy was too busy to take him. So cheer up, have a lovely time, and I'll see you Sunday.'

She hugged him briefly, tightly enough to let him know his feelings were understood, then released him and led him downstairs to his father.

As she stood with Louise, smiling and waving them on their way, she reflected that Charles, whether consciously or not, appeared bent on giving Tiggy the attention he had missed from Gerald, which could be no bad thing.

A factor that Zoë, perhaps predictably, failed to appreciate.

CHAPTER TWO

'You don't mean to say he just marched in and took him away!' Zoë was indignant. 'I think that was very rude, especially when he'd been invited to dinner. Typical!'

'Louise, you won't recognize Zoë,' Sally said brightly. 'You haven't seen her since she was in her pram.'

'Don't say I've grown,' laughed Zoë, successfully diverted. 'I know I'm carrying all before me.'

'When's it going to be?' smiled Louise. 'What are you hoping for, girl or boy?'

'Oh, I don't care, I shall love it whatever it is.' She tossed a mischievous smile towards Mark. 'Now that we're married. I do believe you're blushing,' she teased him, hugging his arm.

Sally went through to the kitchen to see to the food. And also, to escape the expression on their faces as they met each other's eyes. Even Mark . . . she was thinking. He never sought her eyes any more. Well, wasn't that what she had wanted, what she had said? She had avoided his for longer than she cared to remember. More or less, since being told with such relish of his response when George had accused him of being in love with her: Good God, no, she was old enough to be his mother . . . She wasn't of course, though the fact had been beside the point. She knew, had known even then, that it was a panic denial, that probably even at the time, he hadn't meant it. It had served just the same to strengthen her resolve; she consoled herself with it in rare moments of weakness.

Damn Louise! coming out of the blue to disturb her peace

of mind, talking about fulfilment, suggesting that there was something missing in her life. Delightful as it was to see her, she had ruffled the still waters of her contentment, as a breeze blows over a lake. She looked up from preparing salad at the sink to gaze through the window into the cherry tree. Even the birds were in pairs . . .

'Can I do anything useful?' Zoë strolled into the kitchen, her heart-shaped face warm with happiness.

'Not really, darling. Unless you like to put some music on, you'll find the discs on the music centre. Oh, and you could ask Mark to deal with the wine. Ice in the freezer, bucket over there. I thought we'd have champagne as Louise is here.'

'Ma, you've got everything,' Zoë laughed admiringly. 'You're filthy rich these days!'

'You're only jealous.' She pulled a face of comic pride, because that was what Zoë expected. But she thought, surprising herself: It's I who am jealous. I've only got things, you've got people.

Throughout the evening the thought remained in her mind, running under her practised conversation like an underground stream. When Zoë and Mark had left she said to Louise, 'Can't I persuade you to stay over? You can have my bedroom and I'll sleep in Tiggy's room.'

'Nonsense!' said Louise. 'If you've got a double bed we'll share it, it wouldn't be the first time.'

'Jolly chats after lights out? Oh yes, do let's. And no Aunt Lucy to bang on the wall and tell us to go to sleep.'

They creamed off their make-up and told each other how little they had changed, blinking the fact that they could well have passed each other in the street unrecognized. But there was something appealingly cosy about indulging in mutual kindness, in ignoring each other's responses to the inexorable passage of time. By the time they doused the light and settled to sleep, both were in the frame of mind for sentimental nostalgia.

'Louise . . .' Sally spoke softly in the darkness.

'Yes?'

327

'Remember this afternoon, when you said Aimée had liked me, really?'

'Yes, I remember.'

Sally turned restlessly. 'Are you really sure? I mean, you didn't see much of us, when you think about it.'

'I did until Grandma died.'

'Ah, yes . . . but that was when it all changed. When she came back from looking after Grandma.'

'Looking after Grandma?' Louise's voice held a note of surprise. 'She didn't look after Grandma, Mummy did.'

'She didn't?' It was Sally's turn to be surprised. 'But surely, that was why she couldn't come back when I was ill. Because she was looking after Grandma. They sent for her from the Convent, but she didn't come, not until after the funeral. I think you must have forgotten.'

'No, I haven't!' Louise sat up and switched on the light. 'Aunt Aimée was there, but not to look after Grandma. She went out every evening, I remember Daddy saying so. And on the night Grandma died there was an awful row. Dotty and I were in bed in the next room and we could hear them, Grandma crying, and Daddy's voice coming through the wall: "A promise is a promise, Amy, you've got to go back for the sake of the child." And then we heard Aunt Aimée come out and go into her room, and she was crying too. She was still crying when we went to sleep. The next day Mummy told us that Grandma had died in the night. Aunt Aimée stayed on a whole week after the funeral, until Daddy sent her home.' She fell silent, and Sally became aware of her cousin's eye on her. 'Perhaps I shouldn't have told you that, it must be hurtful for you. But it's all a long time ago . . . are you upset?'

'No,' said Sally slowly. 'No, I'm not upset . . . just relieved. I wish I'd known years ago.'

'Relieved?' Louise looked puzzled. 'I don't understand.'

'Yes, don't you see? I always thought I couldn't please her because of some defect in me, and then because she hated me I began to hate her back. And it wasn't that at all! I see it all now, why she was lovely to me until

328

I was seven and everything changed after that.'

In her mind her own words echoed back to her, written long ago: 'For a terrible moment of truth, I wished them dead . . .' With hindsight she saw that there must have been other 'Uncles' besides Patrick in her mother's life, just as Erik had no doubt fluttered with Stella Danby, as with others since. She saw in a new light Aimée's absence when she was seven, recalled a look of bitter brooding when she spoke of death-bed promises, 'so sacred they could never be broken'; if she, conceivably, had made such a promise to Grandma, and had then returned, unwillingly, to find him entranced with Stella . . . it would explain so much. Poor Aimée, she thought, she had never been happy. Even in the early days, her songs had all been of sadness and lost love. Who had she loved? Had she even been sure herself – for how could you know who you loved, if you didn't know who you were . . .

If only she had been told all this before! She might have been spared a lifetime of believing herself unworthy, undeserving of affection, when the truth was simply that her mother had been in love with another man!

Louise was watching her, her face pale and concerned under its shimmer of night cream.

She smiled, taking her hands. 'It's all right, honestly. I just wish I'd known this twenty years ago. It could have changed my life.'

She woke to the scent of Gauloise and the rattle of cups.

'Hope you don't mind me smoking in your bedroom, I know it's a disgusting habit. Sugar?'

She shook her head. 'How nice this is. Couldn't you stay a bit longer?'

'Love to, but I've got to get back. It's a bit special, or I'd ring and put it off.'

'Someone interesting?'

'A reunion. An old friend, a colleague, just back after ten years in Argentina.'

Argentina . . . strange how her heart still jumped at the

329

word. But her voice was under control. 'One of the disappeared?'

'No, this was business, a non-political animal. They are beginning to surface, though, in ones and twos. Since the fall of the Galtieri government.'

'Really?' She caught herself holding her breath, expelled it and took a sip of her tea. 'I thought they were all dead.'

'Most are, I suppose, though nobody really knows. Bodies are turning up, buried in pits, no identification. But a few are trickling back as the prisons turn them loose, though they're destitute, of course. The best off are those who managed to go underground.'

'I suppose so . . .' she said with forced casualness. 'What about foreign nationals, are they coming home?'

'Home? I shouldn't think so.'

'Why not?'

'Well, think about it. No money after years in prison, not strong enough to work. And then there's the complication of passports, with their papers lost or destroyed. Any who've survived are likely to be stuck there, I should think. Why, do you know someone?'

'No . . . just interested.'

Why she had lied, why she could not admit to her lapse even now, even to Louise, she did not know. But it seemed that Adam's memory was still shrouded in grief and shame, that her habitual assumption of guilt had not after all been lessened by the truth she had learned last night.

She saw Louise on to her train, driving back from the station with a lump in her throat that surprised her; a lump like the one that had choked her on long-ago stations, saying goodbye to Grandma. For a few hours she had been young again, allowing free rein to emotions she normally kept under tight control; enjoying the nostalgia evoked by their shared memories of childhood, savouring the sense of companionship in the quiet hours of the night, the sweetness of a shared bed. How long was it since she had woken to the sight of another face upon the pillows . . . the sound of a voice . . . the scent of tobacco . . .

Gerald had not smoked. Even George had not smoked in bed. She looked about her at the expensive toys with which she had crammed the little house. Toys, she thought, they're all I have. Toys, and money, and work. I'm hollow inside, all eaten away with loneliness and loss. If I died tomorrow, no one would really miss me. Not even Zoë. I've moved out to the periphery of her life now, we're not closely involved any more. And I don't think Charles ever was, not with me. It's strange, when they're little you can't wait for them to grow up, yet now . . . I love my son and daughter; but I miss my children.

She sighed, went upstairs to her bedroom, glad to find that it had so far escaped the attention of her daily help; she lay down on the circular bed that all but filled the room, and closed her eyes, savouring the ghost of Louise's perfume lingering on the pillow. Trying to recall the scent of another skin.

She lay silent for a long time, listening to the conversation of the birds through the open window, watching the patterns of light and shade sketched on the wall by the wind in the cherry tree; it was true, what Louise had said about the emptiness of her life. She had shied away from looking at it, but she could no longer deny it was there. In excising her unanswerable need, she had tried to plug the wound with artefacts.

Now it seemed there was a possibility, however remote, that Adam was still alive. And there was an added dimension to the speculation: that he, like others, might be trapped in Argentina without papers, without money, destitute, perhaps ill, unable to leave the country . . .

She had money now. It was almost the only thing she did have, that and influence. She sat up, ran a comb through her hair, and went downstairs to the telephone.

CHAPTER THREE

'You're surely not going until after the baby!' wailed Zoë, taking Sally back over the years.

'It's not for another two months, darling. I'll be back long before it's due. I have to take the chance when I can, this is the only time I can get away.'

'But why, why are you going, you've never wanted to go to America before!'

'I've always wanted to go. I want to see where my father's buried, where he lived as a boy. I'll be back in time, I promise.'

She had lied to Zoë, as well as to Louise. But she could not lie to Guy. When she rang him she could barely keep the excitement from her voice.

'Sally . . .' he spoke warily. 'It's been such a long time, a very long time. Don't expect too much.'

'I'm not expecting anything,' she assured him. 'I'd just like to help, if I can. That's all.'

She rang off before he could pour cold water on her hopes. Within the hour she had made all the necessary arrangements; it amused her to note how loudly and clearly money talked in such situations. It was good to know that it would be so on the journey home, and she wondered why Adam's paper had not tried to get him back. Perhaps they had. Perhaps that was what Guy had meant . . . she pushed away the chilling thought.

She sat restlessly in the Jumbo, watching the grey and gold landscape of the cloud layer stretching out to infinity below her. Everything she saw seemed to sparkle, a new brilliance touched the most commonplace of things, almost, she thought, as though she were seeing them for the first time. A new life, she asked herself with amusement; did life really begin at forty? She had left it a little late, but even so . . .

She rejected the earphones and ignored the movie; she had better things to think about. She whiled away the hours ticking off in her mind the things she had had to deal with, matters to provide for in her absence, and felt a small pang of remorse that she would be missing Tiggy's sports day. He had bravely assured her that he didn't mind, but she knew that he did; since neither of his parents was likely to be there, he would shine or fail for an audience of strangers, would have to find answers for other children who would ask where his parents were.

She was sorry for his sake, but from her own point of view it was possibly just as well; in her heightened state she might well have made a fool of herself. The sight of small children, especially Tiggy, shining with baby achievement had the power to threaten her with embarrassing tears. Yet paradoxically, seeing the young allowed to rebuke their parents, lovingly indulged in harmless mischief she would not have dared to contemplate, she was aware that her disapproval went over the edge into resentment, that she had to bite her tongue not to betray a shameful jealousy. That was what Aimée had done to her, whether she meant to or not. She had made the spectacle of happy childhood unendurable.

Or was it what she had done to herself; surely, all children rebelled against their parents, felt hard done by from time to time? They grew up, grew out of it, left it behind. Why, then, had she been overwhelmed by depression that spread like a stain into all aspects of her life? Perhaps her mother had been right to say that she lacked strength of character. One thing was certain, they had never understood one another. The complex personality of Aimée had baffled her as deeply as hers, like Erik's, must have baffled Aimée. Perhaps that had been the problem with the marriage: that her parents, however much in love, had been too widely disparate ever to meet on common ground. She looked forward with interest to meeting her father's widow.

She had decided after all to get in touch with her on this trip; she would need a base, an address where she could be reached in an emergency, and could not in decency use it without spending a little time with her hostess. And on reflection, she had realized that what she'd told Zoë was true. She did want to see Erik's homeland, and she did want to see his grave. It would make his death real to her, rounding off his life, instead of his having vanished into a void.

She tilted her seat and, unconsciously smiling, drifted into sleep.

They sat facing each other on what Donna Braun referred to as the stoop, and what Sally would have called a verandah, a large jug of freshly squeezed orange juice between them, floating with ice against the heat of the day. Across the broad, uncultivated 'yard' where flowers seemingly grew wild between small outcrops of rock, the sun was beginning to dip behind the branches of the apple trees, toasting to gold the broad sweeping landscape of Iowa. The vast geography of America, she thought, that gave all its sons the urgent need to live up to it. How crushing it must have been for an American to be put down as Erik had been . . .

'Is it always this warm here in May?'

It would be hotter still in Buenos Aires. The scent of azaleas had sent her thoughts flying on ahead of her, bringing back irresistibly a day in a park . . .

'Sakes,' laughed Donna. 'If you think this is hot, you should be here August, in good corn weather.'

'I wish I could. But I have to go south tomorrow, as you know.' She smiled absently, her mind still running wild.

Where to go first in Argentina . . . where to go at all? There must be an embassy there by now, perhaps they would help her. Somehow, she would find him. Would they recognize each other? How would Adam look now, after all those years in the kind of prison she had only read about, thin, certainly, no spreading waistline, possibly no hair, teeth rotted with neglect, his brilliant smile ruined . . . would she know him — worse, would he remember her? She had come away on a wild impulse, and knew she should have planned ahead. But she had not, it was as if some instinct had warned her not to look. As if, seeing the difficulties ahead, she might have lost heart, turned back . . . . The same thing that had prompted her to hang up on Guy.

'I planted that tree in memory of Erik.' Donna waved her hand towards a tall specimen standing alone. 'I just wish you could see it in the fall, it turns such fine colours, several at one time.' She paused. 'His ashes are there, I guess he's part of it by now. I like to think of him out there, enjoying the sun.' She smiled. 'I'm sorry there wasn't a grave for you to visit.'

'It's better like this.' Sally squinted into the setting sun. 'What kind of tree is it?'

'A sweet gum, a liquidambar, I guess you'd call it. Do you have them in England?'

'I don't think so. But it's nice to have planted a tree. Something living.'

I might do that when I go home, she thought. When I get the cottage again, and a garden with room for trees. How would Adam fit in there? Well, that was running on too far ahead. But he would need a home, certainly somewhere to lay his head for a time. And why not with her. She was not looking to resume things as they had once been, of course not . . . well, not straight away. But a friendship . . . a helping hand . . . and from such sweet beginnings, something must grow. She would have someone who needed her again, someone to whom she mattered . . . a real home, with room for growth . . . a house needed more than one lifestream running through it to be a home.

Donna was still talking, telling her about the 'yard', about last year's peach crop, the glut of plums that she had bottled and stored away, the crab apples from which she and Erik had made jelly every year until his death, filling shelf after shelf with the glowing claret-coloured jars.

There was room for everything here, she thought, in this comfortable house, large yet unpretentious, in which Erik had spent the last years of his life. There had been room for him, and his hobbies, and his muddle of inventions that never quite worked. She felt a growing warmth towards this woman, large and unpretentious like the house, whom her father had married in his middle age. She wished she could ask the one question she could not ask.

Donna smiled. 'I believe I know what you're thinking, and yes, I guess he was happy. We both were. I always felt that he had his best time in the fall of his life. And me, I only ever had but the one regret.'

'Regret?'

'Uh-huh.' Donna leaned forward to replenish their drinks, the ice clinking musically as it fell into the glass. 'He had such a hankering for children, and I just could not get pregnant. It was the one thing he wanted that I couldn't give him, a real big family.' She sighed. 'I guess it just wasn't to be. But it does seem hard, to have a wife who wouldn't, then get one who couldn't.'

'Wouldn't?'

'Oh . . . well,' Donna looked flustered, tried clumsily to change the subject. 'My, you look so like your father, you know?'

'It's all right,' said Sally. 'I guessed I was a mistake, that they didn't want children. Only I thought it was both of them.'

'Oh, no! Oh, my dear, you mustn't think that of your father, I just know he wanted you. I have all your letters to him, and your photograph, he still had everything when he died. I looked them out when I knew you were coming, I guessed you'd like to have them.'

So, he had cared, after all. Aimée had, as usual, been lying . . . she felt her eyelids prickle. 'Yes. If I may . . .'

Donna leaned forward, laid a gentle hand on her wrist. 'My dear . . . I surely don't want to run down your mother, especially as she's passed away. But I believe there's something you should know. Before they married, he had to promise he would never give her a child. What happened after that I never knew, he didn't care to talk about it. But I know he promised; it was madness, but there . . . he was very young. And very much in love, I guess. He told me your mother was a very beautiful woman.'

'Yes . . .' said Sally absently. 'Yes, she was. When she was young.'

So, that was the answer. After all these years, in this faraway place she had been handed the clue to the puzzle.

She could now see how Louise had gained the impression of her aunt as a loving mother. Aimée had refused to have children at a time when breeding was considered a woman's sacred duty, and characteristically had lacked the courage to stand up and be counted. With motherhood thrust upon her, whether by accident or design, she had put a good face on it according to her lights, a show of loving care to hide a bitter private chagrin, an over-protection which grew to obsession with her dread of discovery as an unwilling mother. 'Take what you're given and pretend it's what you want' — Sally could hear her saying it, and saw now where the dictum had its roots. And Aimée, with her penchant for martyrdom, had let the whole thing fester until the only pleasure she allowed herself was self-pity. Ironically, the knowledge had come too late . . . or had it? She remembered reading somewhere that to understand all was to forgive all. Now, perhaps, her mother's ghost could be laid to rest.

Donna was speaking again, trying to cover an embarrassing silence with light chatter. Talking rapidly about tomorrow's departure plans, pressing on her an invitation to stop by on her return trip. Sally pulled herself back to the moment, remembering that she hoped not to be alone.

'It may not be possible, Donna, much as I'd love to. I may have to go straight back—'

They were interrupted by a caller at the door.

'Excuse me,' murmured Donna, and made her way to

intercept him. She returned looking puzzled. 'It's a cable-gram. For you.'

'Oh, damn,' said Sally, envisaging a peremptory summons from *Gloss*, searching her mind for pretexts for refusal as she ripped it open. She stood rooted, turning cold in the sunlight as she read the words: 'Baby abnormal. Zoë ill. Please return at once. We need you. Mark.'

CHAPTER FOUR

Sally stood outside the door of the side ward where Zoë lay, trying to find the courage to open it and go in.

All the way home she had been dreading this moment, searching the void of her mind for words of comfort, and still she could find nothing fit to say. She felt helpless, inadequate. She counselled readers on the strength of having found her way through the darker forests of life. This was an agony she had not experienced, and she knew no more than Zoë how to get through it.

I'm an imposter, she thought: it's all theory, I don't know how to cope with real life. I'm afraid for Zoë, she doesn't know she's leaning on a hollow branch.

Somewhere along the line she had degenerated to a machine which reasoned but could not feel. Key in a problem and out came an answer. But where was the answer to this . . .

And yet Zoë was there, on the other side of that door, waiting to be told.

She took a deep breath, put her hand on the handle, opened it, and walked in.

Zoë lay motionless on the high bed, frail and trampled, her slight body still distended from the ill-fated pregnancy. Her face turned away towards the rectangle of the window, she did not move as Sally came in, but continued to stare out at the wall of the opposite block.

'Zoë?' Sally spoke softly.

There was no response. Only the hand lying limp on the covers twitched convulsively. So she was not asleep. Sally sat gingerly on the edge of the bed.

'Darling, it's me . . . Sally.'

As she reached for the hand it was withdrawn. Not snatched away . . . not quite. But the message was clear.

Sally was at a loss. She had been prepared for anger, recriminations, tears . . . not the total rejection of silence. She could find no words. She sat helplessly on the immaculate bed, sorrow filling her eyes and spilling down her face.

Long ago, finding the anguish of others unbearable, she had contrived to deal with it only through the safer filter of the magazine. Now it was Zoë's and it felt like her own, came crashing through her armour and found her raw and bleeding. She could not endure Zoë's pain, felt so much compassion that it hurt. And yet Zoë had shut her out, would not look at her, could not even see her tears. She felt impotent, useless, unable to reach her. She could only suffer with her and be powerless to help. It was like watching somebody die.

'Zoë . . .' she whispered, a last appeal that was ignored.

She laid the flowers she had brought upon the foot of the bed. Even to her, they looked funereal. She could do nothing more.

As she closed the door behind her she heard a violent movement in the bed, and glanced back to see the wreck of her flowers cascading to the floor.

Mark was in the passage outside. She flicked tears from her eyes and took a rapid grip on herself.

'I couldn't talk to her, Mark, she's not ready to see me.' She found a tissue and blew her nose.

Mark put his hands on her shoulders, looked at her with all his old perception. 'I'm sorry,' he said gently. 'It's too soon, she's still in a state of shock. She hasn't cried yet, they're worried about her, that's why she's still here.'

'Has she seen the baby?'

He shook his head. 'It was buried straight away, they said it was best. Having seen it, I'm bound to agree.'

'Oh dear . . .' So that was why she hadn't wept. She was frozen, still waiting for the axe to fall. 'She should have seen it, Mark. She really should. She must be able to grieve.'

'You never saw it.' His eyes darkened. 'It was dreadfully deformed.'

'But even so . . .'

He said stiffly. 'Well, it was a pity you weren't here.'

She compressed her lips. 'Yes. Yes, I realize that. Well, please give her my love, tell her how sorry I am, for what it's worth. I can't tell her, she won't speak to me.' Her voice cracked on the last syllable, despite her determination.

Mark increased the pressure of his hands and released her. 'She'll get over it, you'll see. Give it time. I'll keep in touch, let you know how she goes on. You'll be at home?'

She nodded. 'I'll be at home.'

In the taxi she thought, Oh yes, I'll be at home. She had dredged up a smile from somewhere, exchanged a customary kiss, been left alone in the corridor. As Mark disappeared into Zoë's room, the sound of angry, tempestuous sobbing had reached her through the door. That, at least, was some relief.

She could not go flying off again. She must have been crazy to consider it, touched with the madness that had always infected her at the thought of Adam. He had always been an illusion, a recipe for disaster, and what had possessed her to go on a wild goose chase halfway across the world when she was needed at home, she did not know. It was the sort of foolhardy act against which she would have counselled any reader.

Counselled! She laughed bitterly, knowing herself for a fraud. What right had she to call herself a counsellor, how long could she keep up the façade of confidence, knowing what she knew. She had allowed herself to be set up as a fount of wisdom and when faced with real trouble she had failed her own daughter. She could not have saved the baby, of course not . . . but Zoë, in response to some dark intuition, had implored her not to go, and that plea would be with her for the rest of her life.

She was faced with the need to question the whole fabric

of her existence. Readers, over the years, had become mere ciphers, their problems the necessary material for her work. She listened, she pronounced; in justice she did her best. But she did not really care, had quickly learned that she could not afford to, and as a result found praise embarrassing, suspecting that it was not warranted. It was easy enough to sit up there dispensing prescriptions when you didn't have to take them, were not answerable for the consequences; the fact that she never saw the results rendered the advice she gave little better than guesswork.

It was not she who resolved their predicaments, if resolved they were. If they were helped at all, it was because they helped themselves. In this moment of truth she saw sharply that the whole little empire of her career was founded on a sham. Sooner or later, inevitably, she was going to fall down on the job.

'You're out of your mind!' Louise's voice on the line from Brussels sounded shocked. 'You can't just quit like that, they'll tear you to pieces.'

'I can't go on, Louise. It wouldn't be right, I'd feel I was cheating them.'

'Cheating, nothing! Don't be ridiculous. You don't think people really act on what they read in the agony columns, do you? Would you?'

'Not personally, no. But then I don't trust my own judgement, let alone somebody else's. That's not the point.'

'The point is that your judgement is as good as anyone's, and so is your advice. Look, you mustn't go throwing everything to the winds on a moment's impulse. You're all upset and jangled over Zoë, and that's understandable. But for God's sake don't do something you're going to regret. You haven't told anyone, have you, not said anything to the magazine?'

'Not yet. Only to you.'

'Then don't. I've got a couple of days' leave due, I'm coming over to talk some sense into you. Do nothing until then. Promise?'

342

'Promise.' She laughed then, for the first time since her return. 'You sound just like Uncle Charles.'

'He'd have sorted you out,' agreed Louise. 'He used to bully poor Aunt Amy something rotten. He didn't stand for any nonsense, and neither do I. And tell Zoë I'm coming to see her.'

'Oh, but—' She had been about to say that she could not tell Zoë anything, but Louise had rung off. In her mind's eye she could see her, already preparing to leave, and she smiled. If only she had kept in touch with Louise instead of Dotty over the years . . . her life might have run a different course.

She shouldn't be thinking like that, it was an admission of weakness, out of keeping with her public image. She wondered if there were others like herself who had a public face and a private one; a secret face, battered and tear-stained, that no one was allowed to see . . .

'You'd be a fool,' said Louise when she arrived. 'To throw up a good career, one that you've worked on and built up, for a moment's doubt caused by a silly, hysterical girl. She's coming to see you, by the way. I've talked to her.'

'I'm not sure I can face her.'

'Look, Sally, you mustn't let her make you feel guilty. It wasn't your fault.'

'But I should have been here when she needed me.'

'She's got to stop leaning on you and live her own life. You've made a fool of her, I told her so. It's time she grew up.'

But, if Zoë no longer needed her to lean on, she might not need her at all . . . she sighed. 'You see, I always felt they'd been injured by the divorce . . . George and his jealousy, all the upheavals . . . I tried to make it up to them, perhaps I went too far. I could never reach Charles, maybe too much went to Zoë. She seemed so vulnerable.'

'And she's learned to trade on it,' said Louise. 'It's not too late, but you've got to stop somewhere.'

343

Sally smiled. 'You should have been the Agony Aunt, you'd have done a much better job.'

Louise lit a cigarette, leaned back and smiled through the smoke. 'My dear girl, I'm only quoting your own column – oh, yes, I've been reading it. Out of interest. And I can tell you you're an excellent adviser, fair-minded, positive, penetrating. I only wish you'd apply it to yourself.' She treated Sally to a long, speculative look. 'Have you thought what you'd do with all that spare time if you gave up?'

Sally thought. And saw before her a yawning nothingness, a return to dreading Christmas and Bank Holidays, days with no mail and a silent telephone, Tiggy away with Charles and Zoë preoccupied with Mark. To birthdays when she fled straight to the office, averting her eyes from her private mail which she knew contained nothing more personal than circulars or bills. To Sunday mornings when she woke full of tears and reached in desperation for Selina . . . she had left herself with nothing in her life but work. Success had been a jealous mistress, pushing everything else out of its way.

'I'd find something . . .'

'Perhaps you should consider another book.'

'Another? I don't know. I've already said what I had to say.'

'Not about children. Some other aspect of relationships.'

'Marriage – after the hash I made of mine?'

'So much the better. You don't think it's the General planning campaigns from his desk who knows what war's all about? It's the poor bloody infantry slogging it out in the mud who really understand. You think about it.'

The column was fully stocked with material for the next six months, readers with urgent problems already answered by post. 'You reckon?'

'I'm certain. Say nothing to anyone, just get on with it.'

'I'll think about it,' she conceded, tongue in cheek.

She could see the way Louise's mind was working, relying on her having second thoughts by the time the book was finished, taking up work on the column again without anyone being the wiser.

'*Love and Marriage* by Sally Braun,' she mused. 'It would be a laugh for the family, anyway.'

Whatever amusement it might have afforded the family, it had the opposite effect on Sally herself. Searching her memory, her experience, for material in the following weeks reawakened memories she had thought to be safely buried.

Gerald came back to her with all the poignancy of first love, Gerald who had moved on and forgotten her, to whom she was now no more than a youthful mistake. Poor Gerald, he was only human, she had expected too much of him. She had come to the marriage too young, still with the shreds of magic clinging about her, thinking love was the answer to everything . . . Still believing in fairies, as Adam had said. She had grown up looking for the magic, only to find that it didn't exist. It wasn't fair to blame Gerald for that.

With George they had both been on the rebound; if she'd had any sense she would have seen it was a non-starter. George had been looking for a duplicate Diana, and she had been just as unreasonable in expecting his devotion to be transferred to her.

She had never known how much or how little was reasonable to expect. Even with Adam . . .

Her abortive search for him had been a madness, she knew that now, imagining all too vividly her feelings if she had learned so far from home that he was dead. As, of course, he probably was; she had really always known it in her heart. That was what Guy had tried to tell her on the telephone, the bad news she had refused to hear because she wanted to hope. She would ring him some time and apologize; being Guy, he would understand.

She was thankful that she had had to come back, would have been even more thankful if she hadn't gone. She and Zoë were reconciled now, but she sensed that her defection still rankled.

'I'd rather not call you "Ma" any more,' said Zoë. 'I'm too old for that now. Do you mind if I call you Sally as Tiggy does?'

'Whatever you like, as long as you're happy with it. Why the change?'

'Louise thinks it's time I grew up. I gather you agree.'

'Only if you do.' Sally looked at her closely, but Zoë had turned away.

'Why can't you call her Mother, like me?' put in Charles.

'Too cold,' snapped Zoë.

That at least was something, thought Sally. If there was warmth remaining, it could be built on.

The further the book progressed, the more she found herself thinking about Adam. Eventually, she rang Guy.

'Guy, I'm sorry, I realize I was foolish. He's dead, isn't he? I suppose you knew, that was what you tried to tell me.'

Guy seemed to hesitate. 'Not exactly, no. But there's something here for you, to be collected. A message, I imagine. Do you want me to forward it?'

'From Adam?' Her heart threatened to choke her, thudding in her throat.

'I don't know. It has an Argentinian stamp. Do you know anyone else there?'

'No . . . no, I don't. Yes, please send it on – or shall I come and collect it?'

He said hastily, 'Give me your address, I'll put it in the post tonight. It's not worth your coming to fetch it.'

When the envelope came, she held it in her hands, something that Adam had held and touched, and sent to her. He was alive, after all! This was his handwriting, unmistakably . . . it seemed unreal, after so much time and doubt.

She had looked at it and put it aside, savouring the moment when she would open it, had made herself read all her other mail first, saving the best until last, her excitement mounting in spite of herself. Now the moment had come, she could not put it off any longer.

Carefully she took the antique silver paper knife, carefully slit along the upper edge, taking care not to damage the stamp. This was something she was going to want to cherish for years to come, the message from a forgiving world: Come out and play in the sun.

Life was giving her a second chance, and this time she would make it work out. With all she had learnt over the years, and with Adam, she would be able to get it right. Not rush it, not expect too much. Now, at last, when for the first time she was free . . . it was strange, strange and wonderful, how the pattern was emerging . . .

She withdrew from the envelope a single card, a printed card with a picture of the nativity and the words *Feliz Navidad*. She stared at it for a moment of puzzlement, unable to understand why he should be sending her a Christmas card, and so early in the year. Then she opened it out and read inside: 'Greetings, from Adam and Maria.'

CHAPTER FIVE

It hit her like a blow to the solar plexus.

She sank on to a chair arm, stared at it numbly, unable to take it in.

Adam was not dead, no. But 'Adam and Maria . . .'

He was not missing. He had never been missing, had never wanted to be found. He was like Mark, like George, like Gerald – even Erik – happily settled with someone else. And then . . . just to tell her on a Christmas card! Oh, Adam, how could you . . .

God! She shut her eyes, clenched her teeth. She was like a bloody centrifuge, everyone ran away. One look at her and they made for the hills! It was funny. She knew it was funny, why couldn't she laugh . . . she straightened her back.

Tomorrow, she would laugh. Tomorrow, when she and Zoë were alone, she would tell her, and they would laugh together. Only . . . she couldn't tell Zoë, not about Adam, because of the baby, the awful thing that had happened while she was missing, chasing the rainbow . . .

She must sweat it out alone as she always had, be like Charles, play her sorrows close to her chest . . . had he caught that habit from her or from the childhood scarred like her own, the knock-on effect that went on and on through generations, from Aimée right down to Tiggy . . . what the hell was the use of living, she thought bitterly, if you couldn't improve things a bit, if you lived and died and struggled and still nothing changed!

Charles had been the worst casualty of his generation, she had never been able to help him. The things he had really wanted she had been powerless to give, the love and approbation of his father . . . something no woman could supply, not Tina, not Jenny, nor anyone else. Yet still he went on fruitlessly searching, trying and discarding relationships as though they were a box of tissues. Perhaps in that there was an echo of Aimée, an imitation of hopelessness . . . thank God it had not tainted Zoë.

Zoë would be all right. She would be a proper wife, taking marriage in her stride, being an asset to her husband; not like her, limping along like a dog on three legs, trying to be a daughter, trying to be a wife, a career woman, a lover . . .

The agony came flooding back, breaching the wall of irrelevances she had built to keep it at bay, came back so fiercely that she was afraid to be alone with it. She could not think about Adam, not yet, could not stay in the house with that paper weapon, in the room where it had pierced her – needed to escape, to run from it as she had once run from the news of Erik's death . . .

She left the card where it was and drove out into the country, parked on a layby and walked aimlessly, exhaustingly, as if by walking far enough she could leave her pain behind . . . when she found herself choking out her anger, slamming her fists against a tree, she knew it was not enough. She must somehow reconnect herself with the ordinary world, the normal daily routines of working, shopping, cooking, where such things did not happen.

She thought longingly of Tiggy, whose innocent preoccupation with the trivia of daily life might have been her salvation. But today was Saturday, Tiggy away with Charles . . . Mark and Zoë, invited to Sunday lunch, would not be here until tomorrow . . . the twenty-four hours between stretched like a scalding desert before her.

She must do something. Work was useless. With the office closed it would mean going back into the house and staying there. Impossible. There was food to be prepared for tomorrow – her taut stomach rebelled at the thought. She had to get away, right away . . . out of the house . . .

out of the car – even that had suddenly become a cell of isolation, closing her in with the humiliation, the hurt . . . Maybe . . . yes, maybe London . . . tramp blindly through city streets, dress shops, jewellers, surrounded by strangers whose mere presence would help her to sustain her public face . . buy something she did not want and had no room for. The house was full of such consolation prizes she had awarded herself in the past.

She left the car at the station, distractedly boarded the train before realizing that it was the last thing she should have done. She stared fixedly out at the landscape hurtling past the windows, forcing her mind to focus on detail, forbidding it to hark back to the time she had travelled this same route to be with Adam . . . strange, ironic, cruel that he had come back to her so vividly now, that after years of barely thinking of him she should be seeing him everywhere . . . at the bookstall at Charing Cross . . . in Dotty's old flat . . . across the table from her in the cottage, where she had only imagined him . . .

She wrenched her attention back into the compartment. A woman across from her was reading a glossy magazine, its cover flaunting 'teasers' for the articles inside. 'WHAT DO MEN WANT FROM WOMEN? Read our sizzling survey . . .'

Zoë knew, since Mark was clearly devoted to her now, despite the tragic baby, the occasional signs of friction. She seemed to know by instinct what a man wanted from a woman, which Sally had never discovered. Good food, good sex? Perhaps. 'An empty cock and a full belly,' as Geraldine had once remarked, with surprising vulgarity but also with a certain smugness, as if well-satisfied with herself as a good provider of both. 'Sally has a wonderful mind,' she had added with a hint of patronage, causing Sally to retort with unwonted sharpness that she might have done better to have a wonderful body. Yet there must surely be more to it than that, she thought now: some indefinable thing which she herself had failed to give. What had Gerald wanted, what had Dotty offered, apart from mere beauty . . . The answer was charm, a brightness of spirit that sprang from endless self-confidence. Dotty always had what she wanted because she would settle for nothing less, while she had been brainwashed by Aimée and the nuns into believing that even to want it was immoral. Selfish. An eleventh Commandment: Thou shalt not be a nuisance.

Dotty, selfish or not, had never lacked popularity, something she herself had never achieved. She had set her sights, misguidedly, on being 'good'; and so she had been . . . good, kind, dutiful, dull and boring . . .

What had she ever known about love, what had she learned about it, for all her experience? When young, she couldn't understand how those who loved could disagree; later, she had wondered how they could quarrel, come to blows, and still be happy. For her, the first cruel word had always marked the end of being loved. Perhaps others had a strength she lacked, a necessary part she had been born without, like a thalidomide child without a limb . . .

She feared for Tina, seeing in her too much of her early self. Tina too, had been loved and left behind, and nature abhorred a vacuum; a kind and caring female, with her love object removed, was an open invitation to the self-seeking male. The more often Tina was used and discarded, the more abject she was likely to become, the more easily persuaded that her losses were brought upon herself by some deficiency of her own personality. She wished she could have warned her . . . but loyalty to Charles made it impossible . . .

People were standing up, collecting coats and briefcases. The train was coming into a station. Waterloo East . . . dreading the sight of Charing Cross she fled the train, took the Underground to Oxford Street, shrinking from even the solitude of a taxi. She had to stay surrounded by people, kept safe by their presence from the devastation that threatened. Tomorrow, when she felt stronger, she would be able to face it, would be able to turn and fight . . .

She walked swiftly through store after store, barely looking at anything, merely safeguarded from looking within herself; avoiding Harrods where she usually shopped . . . Harrods where they had found the first Selina.

In a boutique stocked with silk dresses in glowing colours she took one from the rack, tried it on. It fitted, suited her; it was kind to the faults, emphasized the few good points . . . but the same old face, now white and strained, looked back at her from the mirror. What was the point, she thought, and put it back on the rack, noting with little interest that her neck was about to betray her age. A few more years and she would look like a tortoise in drag . . . what did it matter.

Wearily, she returned to Waterloo, boarded the train for home. The weather had turned unseasonably hot and she drowsed on and off, drifting in and out of a haunted world.

When she alighted it was still early in the day, too early to go home. Before she did that, she must be too tired for thought, tired enough to sleep when at length she dragged herself to bed. And physical exhaustion had done nothing to still the ragged circus of her mind . . .

She remembered that she had not fed the cat. She called in at the house, opened a can, called to Selina who came chirruping in from the garden, and was on her way again, leaving her still eating, glancing up in puzzlement at being ignored . . .

As she left the house, the woman opposite smiled and nodded, a trifle uneasily as she always did, and disappeared quickly indoors.

These people don't want me here, thought Sally, I make them feel uncomfortable. They think I'm watching to see how they treat their children. They smile and say good morning, almost tug their forelocks, but we can't talk to each other because we've nothing in common. I might have flown in from another planet. And it's not a lot better at *Gloss*. The better my work, the more threatened they feel. Like that deadly game of Trivial Pursuit that you daren't win too easily if you want to be invited again . . .

If that's the price of getting to the top, it's too high. It doesn't matter what you've achieved, if you end up alone and miserable you're a failure. I'm hollow, she thought again; it's all been for nothing. And I've run away as far as I can run. Now I've got to stop, and think it out alone.

She felt numb now, exhausted, mind and body aching like a bruise. She drove her expensive car down to the coast, to the holiday resort where she had once taken the children, laboriously, on the train.

The season was over. In the Indian summer on the empty promenade she sat on the sun-warmed concrete, listening and not listening to the intermittent notes of a guitar being practised by some fellow seeker after solitude, feeling curiously detached now that her panic had burned itself out.

She watched the sea burning sapphire, melting at the horizon as if airbrushed into a paler sapphire sky, its quiet surface flecked with the white breasts of floating gulls, seeing in her mind's eye young Charles, young Zoë, struggling up the beach towards her shining from the sea, their high bright treble punctuated by the mewing of sea birds.

'Mummy, Mummy, look! I've found a starfish.'

'No, it's not, it's a piece of wood—'

'It is, it is!'

'Well, it's dead anyway, it's lost a leg—'

'No, it isn't, it isn't dead! Mummy, tell him . . .'

The beach was empty now. She sat brooding, her arms clasping her knees. A young man ran pelting past her, his feet kicking up the shingle as he made for the water's edge and launched himself for a late swim. Two girls with a carrycot and assorted paraphernalia arranged themselves against a breakwater and stripped off to sunbathe in the summer's parting gift, stretching out on their towels, eyes closed as though in the anticipation of kisses.

I used to be like that, she thought, letting the sun embrace my body, the breeze caress my skin . . . but when I closed my eyes, instead of the lover's kiss it was spattered shingle from the flying feet of children. There was never a time I could call my own, never a time to live my life. I'm still waiting for my turn, even now. There's always someone, somewhere, whose needs are more urgent than mine. Or more important . . .

It is like that for everyone, or was it all my own fault, did I throw myself down before everyone I liked and invite them to walk over me? I always knew I had to try harder than others to be loved. And the harder I tried the faster they ran away . . .

Maybe I did too much grovelling. If you're too scared to voice an opinion you end up not having one, and who wants to live with his own reflection? Giving too much makes people feel guilty, you make a bloody drag of yourself. You have to stand up, fight back, take a chance on their walking out, not forgiving you . . . why didn't I have the courage to do that? If you give in all the time, make no demands of your own, they get bored and leave you anyway!

She sighed. Louise was right, she should have taken her own advice. God knew, she had been dishing it out for long enough. But it wasn't that easy, was it? Learning the cause of your psychological flaw did not effect a cure: she had news for the shrinks, they didn't know the half of it. Knowing your responses were faulty was one thing, getting them right was quite another. You couldn't, after nearly fifty years, grow that missing limb . . .

She sat upright, staring intently out to sea. She could not, never had been able to, hold her own with those she loved, and she saw with sudden insight that she had been saved from making the same mistake again.

The realization had brought her up short: unpredictably, she realized that she was thankful, glad that a door had slammed finally shut between herself and Adam. She had always cherished the thought that, given the right man, she could have got it right. Now for the first time she saw it for the illusion that it was. There was something lacking in her make-up, something that Adam himself had recognized; he had always been wiser than she.

To have tried and failed with him would have been the one truly crushing disaster of her life, the only one she might not have survived, and she was aware of a perverse yet profound relief that it could not after all be put to the test.

With hindsight, she saw that he had never been in love with her, as she with him. He had been charming and sweet and considerate; he had enjoyed her, as she him. 'You are too complicated,' he had warned, and she hadn't understood.

Yet she had, in a sense, been loved; and that knowledge had given her a sense of worth that she had sorely lacked, a core of courage to lift up her head and make something of herself. He had appreciated her, hurried to be with her, made her feel wanted. His memory had sustained her through the ordinary defeats of everyday life.

And now? She sat for a long moment, staring out to sea. Now, she understood the nature of her loss, knew what had brought it about; knowing what had become of him, she would suffer no more moments of futile anguish in the small hours of the night. She had looked upon the face of her grief, could mourn it, lay it to rest and leave it behind.

Adam had found his simple girl, as he had said he would; and whatever he was, whoever he was with, she was reconciled and hoped that he was happy. His memory was still good, still sweet; nothing could spoil it now.

From now on, she would content herself with that, would waste no more effort in trying to win affection from those unwilling to give it, whoever they might be . . .

She relaxed, smiling faintly. Life had after all given her a second chance; it was merely that she hadn't recognized it. Like the Death card in the Tarot, she thought, frightening at first, until you understood that it meant not death but the clearing away of dead wood to make way for new growth.

The smile deepened. She had a large part of her life still before her. She would finish the book she had started with a new, a deeper understanding . . . maybe continue with the magazine as well. On a personal level too, she would make a fresh start, learn how to make the most of it, enjoy her family ties without tearing herself to pieces . . .

It was ironic that so much of your life was taken up just learning how to live. Just as you began to get the hang of it, sure as God made little apples, you were going to hear 'Come in, Number Nine, your time's up . . .'

Well, her time was not up yet. And she wasn't going to waste what remained. She was through with expecting to find happiness in work, through with looking to other people for it. Why, after all, should they be expected to provide it . . . it was up to her to make it for herself.

There was sex, of course; that could be lonely and frustrating to live without . . . when it was good it was sublime, unique, there was nothing to equal it. When it was good. But only too often it was a travesty. And she had lived without it, in the truest sense, for most of her life; she could surely manage what was left.

She wondered, not for the first time, about Aimée's sexual life, if she had ever really had one, whether it had been a joy or a travesty. Had it been sublime with Patrick, a travesty with Erik? Had she really been a virgin until marriage? Perhaps she had never got it right, but remained a scared, disgusted little girl. It was something she had never known about her mother, hadn't felt able to ask her. She would never know now, and perhaps had no right to know. Even the dead were entitled to their privacy.

From somewhere along the beach a man's voice drifted towards her in snatches on the breeze.

'. . . not bad for September, eh?'

She looked idly in his direction. He sprawled alone in a deck chair, surrounded by discarded boots, a battered guitar with a bunch of wild flowers tied to its neck, a plastic carrier overflowing with odds and ends spilling out across the shingle. Some passersby looked uneasy, a few edging away or quickening their pace. He raised a beer can towards the sun and shouted.

'Hallo, universe, how're you doing? Thanks for creating me!'

Sally watched as he drained the can and stowed it in his plastic carrier, smiling about him at the world in general. Someone you could talk to, she thought, without inhibitions or prejudice.

She smiled in his direction, but he took no notice, his attention caught by the girls with the baby in the carrycot. The story of my life, she thought, faintly amused, and turned over, away from them.

She stayed for a while, her mood lulled and deepened by the rocking of the sea, until as the sun dropped and the warmth left the scene she felt the sadness trying to come back. She walked purposefully back to the car and drove home, thinking resolutely of practical matters, preparations for tomorrow. She had salads in the fridge, cream for the trifle – why did it always make her think of Dotty – some more wine would not come amiss. She would make a detour to the supermarket.

It was closed; she should have realized. As she peered in through the glass the blackcurrant cordial winked at her from the shelf . . . she turned her eyes away.

Tomorrow would be better. Tomorrow they would come, she would not be alone. Zoë would be there, dear, lovely Zoë . . .

She leaned her forehead against the cool glass of the car window. The Zoë who was coming tomorrow was not her Zoë, not the little girl who had sought the solace of her arms, but a visitor carrying out a filial duty. Her life revolved around Mark now. And Mark's, as was right and proper, revolved about her.

She started the engine, let in the clutch, and drove on.

CHAPTER SIX

She woke late, having slept heavily, the dreamless, drug-like sleep of nervous exhaustion. She opened dull eyes and looked into the blue ones of Selina, who was lying along her chest, paws neatly tucked into her fur, her small warm body vibrating with her morning purr, a buffer against the awareness that was trying to crash in upon her.

'Don't have to do much to earn your affection, do I?' As she swung her legs over the side of the bed, the cat sprang off, racing ahead of her down the stairs to the kitchen.

Sally smiled. 'All right, I get the message.'

If only people were more like cats, she reflected. They liked you or they didn't, cared nothing for how you looked, what you could or couldn't do, didn't get bored with you and fall in love with someone else . . .

She reminded herself that she was through with fraught relationships. She had done all the grovelling she was going to do, all the slaving for approval, the begging for love, knowing belatedly that both were given unsought or not at all. Let others take chances, scale the heights, hold their breath at the brink of the precipice. She would remain on the ground where she was safe. On the ground, in the quiet garden. That little stray cat had known a thing or two, whatever Mark had thought . . .

When they arrived she greeted them with a brightness bordering on euphoria.

'What's happened to you?' said Zoë. 'You look like the cat that swallowed the canary.'

'Nothing. Just a bit of good news.' Pleased to note the

steadiness of her voice. 'An old friend I thought was dead, is all right after all.'

'That's nice. You know that recipe you gave me last week, I think I must have got it wrong, because it didn't turn out . . .'

Sally smiled, and went to find her the recipe book.

After lunch, Mark announced their intention of going for a walk. 'We'll drive out and park somewhere, then walk from there. Maybe along the bypass, across the fields.' He looked towards Zoë, checking with her before adding, 'Do you want to come, Sally?'

She hesitated. Had his tone lacked enthusiasm, encouragement – had it been her imagination that Zoë had loosed a brief angry dart in his direction . . .

Old habit prompted her to say, 'If you're sure . . .' She bit it back. Perhaps they did want to be alone, to sort something out . . . but they had the rest of the week for that. They had come to spend the day with her, not merely to be fed. And she did not wish to be left alone when she needed their company. Instead, she said, 'Yes, I'm coming,' and saw them exchange a look which she chose to ignore.

They stowed the dishes in the machine and all piled into Mark's little hatchback, since he was the one who knew where they were heading. They parked in a layby off the bypass a few miles out of town where the new dual carriageway ran through farming land, and walked along the grass verge towards where, a couple of hundred yards ahead, a cut-off road led away to a wooded slope.

It was another warm afternoon, scented with bonfire smoke, with birdsong faintly simmering in the hedgerows. In a field on the far side of the motorway a heavy draft horse, enjoying the last of the summer, rolled on his back and kicked his great legs like a kitten in the sun. Sally stood still to watch him, thinking that was the way to live, to savour every moment as it came.

'Look, Zoë, a Shire, you don't often see one . . .'

Zoë didn't turn back. But at the sound of a voice, the

animal rolled on to his feet and started lumbering towards them. She made clicking sounds with her tongue and he quickened his pace.

The others had walked far ahead, forgetting her. Not talking, just watching each other, guardedly.

'Wait,' she called. 'He wants to talk to us.'

They didn't hear, or they didn't want to hear. She shrugged. They had only brought her with them because they didn't like to leave her behind.

But the horse, his grey muzzle stretching forward over the wire, stood waiting. In his dim, innocent way, he wanted her, and she stepped, without looking, on to the motorway . . .

Timing had never been Sally's strongest suit.

CODA

A handful of raindrops spattered the window, tossed aside by a listless breeze.

The cat-flap in the kitchen door slammed noisily as Selina burst in, complaining loudly of the caprices of the weather, indignantly licking water from her coat.

Zoë drew a long, contented breath before opening her eyes, surfacing gently from the first natural sleep she had enjoyed in months. She was not conscious of having slept deeply, only that in a few moments while her eyes were closed the turmoil in her mind had mysteriously resolved itself. Not that the way ahead of her was suddenly cleared, there was no magic signpost saying: This way through the woods. Enough that she now knew there was a way, and was on the brink of discovering where it lay . . .

She ought to ring Mark before he rang her yet again; put his mind at rest and stop him worrying. A cup of coffee first, she thought, to clear her head.

Selina streaked before her into the kitchen, scuffling her empty bowl, leaping up on to worktops, trying to break into the fridge.

'All right, it's coming.' Zoë yawned, opened a can and fed her while she waited for the kettle to boil, her thoughts quietly marshalling themselves as she moved about the kitchen.

She carried the steaming mug back into the living room, picking her way between piles of paper and photographs. All these diaries, letters, poems, the record of Sally's life . . .

It had taken Sally so much of it to get her act together, so long that in the end it had been too late . . . if it could ever really be too late for carrying your tiger to the mountain. The phrase floated into Zoë's mind from years ago, when Mark was studying T'ai Chi. It meant finding your point of balance, he'd said, learning to use your strength instead of wasting it; being still where there was nothing to be done, being active when there was something to accomplish. He'd tried to explain that being self-centred was not the same thing as being selfish . . .

She hadn't understood at the time. Only now, she realized, was she beginning to see, through reading the notes for Sally's unfinished book. What a waste for it not to be published, not to be read! If it helped only one or two others as it had her . . . someone ought to round it off, see it into print. She picked up the heavy file. So much of it, so close to completion. It surely couldn't need much more than editing and typing up, and she knew without doubt who should be the one to do it . . .

There was barely room to work in their tiny flat. Barely room for anything, not even for another baby if she could bring herself to try. She sighed, thinking of Tiggy. How long before Charles tired of him, as he did of everyone? He loved and still needed Sally's home, his refuge in the calm eye of the storm, his familiar bedroom, his cat . . . the one stable point in his turbulent life.

She sat for a while, sipping her coffee and savouring her thoughts; watching and not watching the subtle shifts of colour in Selina's coat as she laundered fastidious whiskers in the glow of the fire. Zoë felt herself smiling as she reached for the telephone.

As she lifted the receiver she heard a car draw up in the road outside, its headlights chasing shadows across the room. Turning to look out she recognized the hatchback and replaced the phone. As she opened the front door, the Siamese slipped out between her ankles to investigate and vanished under the cupressus hedge flanking the drive.

Mark switched off the engine but did not get out. Instead

362

he wound down a window, extended an arm towards her.

'Thought you might need these.'

She walked down the drive to meet him, huddling herself against the wind although the rain had stopped.

'I brought them over for you.' He was holding out the Valium, avoiding her eyes.

'You can throw them away,' she said lightly. 'Aren't you coming in?'

He hesitated. 'Well . . . have you finished?'

'Enough.' She smiled. 'So?'

Still he did not move, staring ahead of him through the windscreen as if he had not seen. She waited.

At last he turned to look at her. 'Forgiven?' he mumbled his face averted.

Did he mean him, or Sally . . . or herself? It hardly mattered.

'All forgiven,' she said softly. He turned to look at her at last, startling her with the expression in his eyes. She had always drawn on Mark for her strength, had looked to him for comfort and reassurance. Now she saw for the first time that he was as vulnerable, as uncertain as herself. She took the bottle from him, squeezed his hand. 'Why don't you put the car up on the drive and come inside.'

As he started to reverse she saw Selina break cover, about to dart crazily towards her under the wheels. She sprang forward to snatch her from his path, holding her tightly, safely as he manoeuvred, unwitting. Murmuring soothingly, aware of the rapid ticking of a small scared heart.

She lingered where she was for a moment, looking up at the night sky. The moon was down, the darkness chilly and intense. But where the wind had cleared a space in the clouds, a few stars were beginning to shine. Behind her she heard Mark go into the house, saw a bar of light fall across the lawn as he turned on the lights. Presently, he called softly.

'Zoë?' She turned to see him framed in the doorway, peering out into the gloom. 'Darling, what are you doing out there in the dark?'

She nuzzled the silky head with her chin, waited for the purr. 'Well, Selina, that was a close shave,' she whispered. 'But we're all right now.'

Settling the cat more comfortably in her arms, she walked up slowly to join Mark.

'Just carrying my tiger to the mountain.' Smiling, she kissed him gently. 'How about you?'

THE END

Riders
by Jilly Cooper

'Sex and horses: who could ask for more?'
Sunday Telegraph

If you thought you knew what to expect of Jilly Cooper —
bursts of restless romance, strings of domestic disasters, flip fun
with the class system — RIDERS will come as a pleasurable
surprise.

A multi-stranded love story, it tells of the lives of a tight circle of
star riders who move from show to show, united by raging
ambition, bitter rivalry and the terror of failure. The
superheroes are Jake Lovell, a half-gipsy orphan who wears
gold earrings, handles a horse — or a woman — with effortless
skill, and is consumed with hatred for the promiscuous upper-
class cad, Rupert Campbell-Black, who has no intention of
being faithful to his wife, Helen, but is outraged when she runs
away with another rider.

Set in the tense, heroic world of show-jumping, Jilly Cooper's
novel moves from home-country gymkhanas through a riot of
horsey events all over the world, culminating in the high drama
of the Los Angeles Olympics.

'Blockbusting fiction at its best'
David Hughes, The Mail On Sunday

'I defy anyone not to enjoy her book. It is a delight from start to
finish'
Auberon Waugh, Daily Mail

0 552 12486 9

A Scattering of Daisies
The Daffodils of Newent
Bluebell Windows
Rosemary for Remembrance
by Susan Sallis

Will Rising had dragged himself from humble beginnings to his own small tailoring business in Gloucester — and on the way he'd fallen violently in love with Florence, refined, delicate, and wanting something better for her children.

March was the eldest girl, the least loved, the plain, unattractive one who, as the family grew, became more and more the household drudge. But March, a strange, intelligent, unhappy child, had inherited some of her mother's dreams. March Rising was determined to break out of the round of poverty and hard work, to find wealth, and love, and happiness.

The story of the Rising girls continues in The Daffodils of Newent and Bluebell Windows, finally reaching it's conclusion in Rosemary for Remembrance.

A Scattering of Daisies	0 552 12375 7
The Daffodils of Newent	0 552 12579 2
Bluebell Windows	0 552 12880 5
Rosemary for Remembrance	0 552 13136 9

Three Women
by Brenda Clarke

'Her work has that rare quality of being difficult to put down'
British Book News

When Joseph Gordon — owner of Gordon's Quality Chocolate factory — married a girl from the factory floor he made it quite plain that her two young nieces were no responsibility of his. Elizabeth and Mary, born to a humbler walk of life, could expect no handouts from their Uncle Joe and their lot was not to be compared with their beautiful pampered cousin, Joe's treasured only daughter, Helen.

But these three girls, Elizabeth and Mary, and the delicate Helen, were to form a bond that all Joe's venom could not break. The passage of two world wars and the years between were to see violent and dramatic changes in their lives and it was Elizabeth, strong, vibrant, working-class and beautiful, who was to be the saviour of the family.

0552 132608

A SELECTED LIST OF FINE NOVELS
AVAILABLE FROM CORGI BOOKS

THE PRICES SHOWN BELOW WERE CORRECT AT THE TIME OF
GOING TO PRESS. HOWEVER TRANSWORLD PUBLISHERS RESERVE
THE RIGHT TO SHOW NEW RETAIL PRICES ON COVERS WHICH MAY
DIFFER FROM THOSE PREVIOUSLY ADVERTISED IN THE TEXT OR
ELSEWHERE.

☐	13260 8	THREE WOMEN	Brenda Clarke	£2.95
☐	13261 6	WINTER LANDSCAPE	Brenda Clarke	£2.95
☐	12486 9	RIDERS	Jilly Cooper	£3.95
☐	12387 0	COPPER KINGDOM	Iris Gower	£2.95
☐	12637 3	PROUD MARY	Iris Gower	£2.95
☐	12638 1	SPINNERS WHARF	Iris Gower	£3.50
☐	13138 5	MORGAN'S WOMAN	Iris Gower	£2.95
☐	11726 9	CHANTAL	Claire Lorrimer	£2.95
☐	11959 8	THE CHATELAINE	Claire Lorrimer	£3.95
☐	13040 0	FROST IN THE SUN	Claire Lorrimer	£3.95
☐	12565 2	LAST YEAR'S NIGHTINGALE	Claire Lorrimer	£3.95
☐	10584 8	MAVREEN	Claire Lorrimer	£3.95
☐	11207 0	TAMARISK	Claire Lorrimer	£2.95
☐	12182 7	THE WILDERLING	Claire Lorrimer	£3.95
☐	10249 0	BRIDE OF TANCRED	Diane Pearson	£1.95
☐	10375 6	CSARDAS	Diane Pearson	£3.95
☐	10271 7	THE MARIGOLD FIELD	Diane Pearson	£2.50
☐	09140 5	SARAH WHITMAN	Diane Pearson	£2.95
☐	12641 1	THE SUMMER OF BARSHINSKEYS	Diane Pearson	£2.95
☐	12607 1	DOCTOR ROSE	Elvi Rhodes	£2.50
☐	13185 7	THE GOLDEN GIRLS	Elvi Rhodes	£3.95
☐	12367 6	OPAL	Elvi Rhodes	£2.50
☐	12803 1	RUTH APPLEBY	Elvi Rhodes	£3.95
☐	12375 7	A SCATTERING OF DAISIES	Susan Sallis	£2.75
☐	12579 2	THE DAFFODILS OF NEWENT	Susan Sallis	£2.50
☐	12880 5	BLUEBELL WINDOWS	Susan Sallis	£2.50
☐	13136 9	ROSEMARY FOR REMEMBRANCE	Susan Sallis	£2.95

*All Corgi/Bantam Books are available at your bookshop or newsagent, or can be ordered from
the following address:*

Corgi/Bantam Books,
Cash Sales Department,
P.O. Box 11, Falmouth, Cornwall TR10 9EN

Please send a cheque or postal order (no currency) and allow 60p for postage and packing for
the first book plus 25p for the second book and 15p for each additional book ordered up to a
maximum charge of £1.90 in UK.

B.F.P.O. customers please allow 60p for the first book, 25p for the second book plus 15p per
copy for the next 7 books, thereafter 9p per book.

Overseas customers, including Eire, please allow £1.25 for postage and packing for the first
book, 75p for the second book, and 28p for each subsequent title ordered.